Love of the Sea

By Lauren A. R. Masterson

Ink Smith Publishing

www.ink-smith.com

Ink Smith Publishing
710 S. Myrtle Ave Suite 209
Monrovia, CA, 91016

To my parents for encouraging my creative spirit. To my little brother for supporting the madness of my imagination. And of course, to all my dear family, friends, and fans who have followed my work at different points on this journey; especially the Chicago writing community, and my mentor Tina Jens.

Most of all, this story is dedicated to my Grandma Bev who never stopped believing in me, who told me I could, in fact, be a unicorn when I grew up. You gave me the strength to keep writing. I would mail you a copy, but I don't know what the postage is for heaven.

Prologue

The candle sputtered as Pamela opened the worn tome. The pages were curling, and the painted illustrations were smudged from curious fingers. She settled into the overstuffed chair next to the fire grate.

"Come on then," Pamela patted her knee, "it's time for a story."

Cormack trotted over and lay on the woven rug. His chubby feet tapped the floor as he swung his legs up and down. "Tell me about the mermaids again, Pamela!"

She chuckled and held up the book. "Already ahead of you, dear."

Long ago, the gods brought life to the world and all the creatures in it. Poseidon wanted to show the gods that he was the best creator, and so he made mer people in his own image. The other gods were so impressed by Poseidon's works that they crowned him king of the gods. One god was jealous and felt that he could form something better, but no matter how hard he tried his creatures all melted back to mud. This god was Kataraménos, the Cursed One. Realizing that he could not beat Poseidon, he chose to steal his creation instead.

Kataraménos dove deep into the realm of the mer people and tricked one of the tribes into coming on land. He coaxed them with the beauty of green trees and plentiful fauna to hunt. He helped mould their bodies so they could stay on the land, producing the first humans. As a last affront to Poseidon, he gave them little seeds from the stars so they would one day pass on from their flesh and be immortal like the gods.

Poseidon was furious when he discovered what Kataraménos had done. Unfortunately, the humans could not go back to the sea after living on land for so long, nor were they willing to give up their new claim to immortality. As punishment, Poseidon cut the humans off from the wellspring, rendering them blind and dumb to magick.

The mer people wept for their lost kin, and soon, the humans forgot about their former lives in the sea. For many years the humans and the mers fought, as the humans were filled with the false superiority that Kataraménos poisoned them with. They believed themselves to be equal to the gods, and that all the world was theirs for the taking—the land, the sea, the air, and all the things in it. The mers would tear down their ships and eat the sailors, warning the humans to stay away from their watery kingdoms. Even Poseidon raised his hand on occasion to beat back the human ego, sending squalls that tore ships asunder and sent wailing sailors to the deep abyss.

After a time, the mer people were defeated, as the humans kept building larger and stronger ships. No longer could they pierce the hulls with their claws and wrent the lumber to splinters. In fact, humans would sometimes catch the mers, forcing them to grant wishes, or worse, curse them to a half-life bound on land.

Eventually, the humans turned away from the Cursed One, as his path only led to destruction and death. Those who find favour with Poseidon are able to wheedle tiny drops of magick from the ancient wellspring. Today, these are the practicers of the White Veil and other shadowy clans who understand the ancient ties we rejected so long ago. Though never will humans again know the true might of the wellspring, as we are all stained with the sins of the Cursed One, and seek the forgiveness of Poseidon and his pure waters of the sea.

It is believed today that there are no mers left in the world, and if there are, that Poseidon has hidden them well. They say that if a human is able to shed his ego, relinquish his immortal soul and enter the watery kingdoms in peace that the curse will be broken, and humans and mers will be one people, at peace once more.

Pamela closed the book, and set it aside. Cormack's eyes were wide as he came out of his childish imaginings. He curled himself into a sitting position and grabbed one of his toy wooden boats.

"I shall find the mer people!" he declared, waving the boat in the air. "I will be a great sailor someday and be the very first to find them!"

Pamela ruffled his hair. "I'm sure you'll find all sorts of kingdoms and peoples when you grow up, lad."

Cormack scowled at her teasing words. She drew him up by the elbow. His body was heavy, and showing the first signs of coltish adolescence.

"To bed with you." She sighed as she steered him to the great four-poster. "You can have more adventures tomorrow."

He clambered up onto the bed, and Pamela pulled up the heavy quilts. Cormack rolled his eyes up to her. "Don't worry, Pamela. I promise I'll visit you and write you letters."

Pamela's eyebrows rose. "What on earth are you talking about?"

"No, under the sea!" Cormack laughed. "When I find the mers, I'll still visit you and write you every day!"

She smiled and kissed his forehead. "Dream of your mers, lad. But be careful they don't gobble you up!"

Cormack nodded, a yawn escaping his lips. "Goodnight, Pamela."

"Goodnight, lad."

Chapter One

Beyond the safe harbour of Paradine, far below the trade routes of ships, lay the ancient kingdoms of mers. The reefs glittered with glimpses of their shimmering scales, teasing sailors and dredging up the old stories. One such mer was the fierce Asrai, cloaked in crimson scales and scarlet hair. She lived in the reef just beyond the safe waters of Paradine's fishing shoals.

Her mentor and only companion, Illyana the sea hag, drilled her above the rainbow of corals. She sought to mould Asrai, the daughter of a great ruler, into the great hag she was destined to be. Their booming water pulses had sent all the fish into hiding and made the waters choppy for sailors above.

"Again!" The sea hag whipped her comb, sending a small water pulse to smack Asrai on the cheek.

Asrai beat her tail hard, her body growing weary. She used the glare of the high afternoon sun to reflect light off her scales and temporarily blind her opponent. When lit, she resembled a burning ember suspended in water. Asrai waited until the sea hag flinched and darted her eyes away before performing the swift dive.

"Not enough power!" Another water pulse smacked Asrai, preventing her from completing the dive bomb. The sea hag shook her head. "Let us break for food. You are clearly growing tired."

The sea hag settled on a brain coral, waiting for crabs to scuttle within reach. Asrai took deep breaths and slid her comb back into her hair. She flicked her tail as she lounged on a large sponge. The sea hag twirled her comb between her fingers.

"There are no second chances in Draum." She pointed the comb at Asrai. "Each move must be performed with precision. Errors on your part can mean death."

Asrai shook her head and snipped some brown seaweed with her claws. "Yes, I know, Illyana. I am all that is left for Sulu, I cannot lose. We train every day. I am more than ready to take what is mine."

"Indeed." The sea hag shifted on the coral and settled her gaze on Asrai. "We cannot wait any longer. The time has come for you to reclaim your title."

"The water is becoming warmer again," Asrai mused, allowing the tide to push her hand in the gentle current.

The sea hag nodded. "Yes, signaling the beginning of a new season—the season you are at last a grown mer. We must find you a mate so you can return to Sulu. There is a small tribe not far from here, only a day's swim."

"I have already found a suitable mate. It is a matter of winning him." Asrai rolled onto her stomach.

The sea hag rubbed her forehead. "Oh, my child, you have never even *met* another mer."

Asrai snared a parrot fish with her claws, ignoring the sea hag's plea. "I am certain. He is the one who will expand my wellspring tenfold. I cannot return to Sulu alone, and I need more than a common mer to unlock my true magick."

"Not this *sailor prince* business again!" The sea hag rolled her eyes. "You must rule with a mer at your side! Or have you forgotten who you are?"

She drew herself up, glaring at the sea hag. "Never."

****

Cormack leaned over the railing, gripping onto the rigging. The afternoon sun warmed his tanned face and the cool salty spray of the sea misted over his skin. A gull screamed overhead. He looked up and grinned. *Anita* was starting to meander toward the fishing buoys. He let go of the manila ropes and jogged back to the helm, turning her with ease. The waves swept the boat further out to sea before Cormack dropped anchor.

King Dominic had scores of complaints from the sailors about Cormack being out at all hours with their fishing ships. As the crown prince, the sailors hardly had the ability to stop him. Nor could they say no to his kind, though cheeky, requests to try his hand at fishing, or find a more advantageous shoal. The single-mast boat *Anita* was then built for his eighteenth birthday.

Cormack clambered onto the railing again and plunged into the sapphire waves. The water was brisk, but it felt good on his sun-kissed skin. Cormack came up for air and slicked his hair out of his face. He dove again, heading toward one of the sandbars to look for seashells and other bits of oceanic treasure.

A large clamshell was his prize this day. Cormack pushed off the ground, sand clouding around him as he surfaced for air. Something slipped from his grip, glittering as it fell toward the ocean floor. He drew long breaths, examining the clamshell. As he did so, he noticed that his finger was bare. His crest ring had slipped off while he was digging in the sand. Cormack slipped the shell into the small rucksack tied to *Anita* for his finds, and dove back down to the sandbar to search for his ring. The water clouded as he flung sand all around him. He was sure the ring could not be far, as it was his first dive of the day.

Love of the Sea

Cormack came up again for air and cursed his fruitless search. He swam back to *Anita* and climbed the rope ladder on the side of the boat. His wet hands mixed with the dried salt on the ropes and made a white paste. He wiped his hands clean on his breeches once aboard. The sun lowered, late afternoon creeping by. He leaned his elbows on the railing, looking into the sparkling waters. Time was slipping through his fingers, as always. Soon it would be time to turn about and head in to the docks.

****

Asrai hid behind the rudder of the boat. She had been holding onto it, allowing it to drag her through the water as Cormack sailed. She crawled along the side of the boat, trying to get a better view. Her needle-like claws dug into the wooden hull.

When Cormack surfaced for air, something glittery fell from his hands. Asrai dove. It tumbled down the sandbar into deeper waters. She plucked the large gold ring and looked up to see Cormack hunting around in the sand. The delight was wiped from his face. His fingers were frantic as he searched.

She clutched the ring to her chest. Excitement surged through her with the thought of revealing herself and presenting this human with his lost treasure. But she could not. It was easy for a human to like a mermaid while in the sea. But eventually, he would leave. Asrai returned to huddle against the rudder, the ring safe in her fist. Finally, she had proof to present to the sea hag.

Through the ripples Asrai could make out his form leaning over the deck. A passion burned in her stomach that made her want to breach like a foolish dolphin. But she steeled herself and held onto the boat, watching him from under the waves. The ring was hard, the gems scratching her palm as her grip tightened. A low thrum escaped her throat, and a nearby school of fish darted away.

Soon, my sailor.

****

Cormack stood at the helm, playing with his instruments. A gold compass, an ornately engraved sextant, the items brought him joy as he embarked on mock adventures in the harbour. Today his mind was stunted with anxiety. His cousin, Peter, had soured his morning with a sly grin, informing him of an evening meeting in the map room. Now with the loss of his ring it was turning out to be an unlucky day indeed.

He turned about, flustered that none of his toys were appealing. Shouts of the sailors and the clank of chains soon became audible. Cormack ran his hand through his hair as *Anita* bumped into place. The sailors waved. Cormack tossed down the dock line, and one of the sailors helped him secure Anita.

"Th' wind be fair today. A fine day t' sail," the sailor chatted as he chewed on the end of a weathered pipe.

Cormack nodded. "Indeed. Yet, the day is not in my favour."

"Just as well, just as well," the sailor muttered, clanking his pipe against his teeth as he chewed. "Lucky ya came in. There's mermaids about t'day."

Cormack jerked his head. "Real mermaids?"

"You bet your sweet soul on Poseidon!" The sailor grinned at Cormack, the pipe clenched in his teeth. He jerked his head at an enormous black galleon. "Th' merchant ship from Denaria said they encountered 'em a-ways out from the harbour."

"Real mermaids," Cormack whispered.

"Aye," the sailor nodded, "real mermaids with all the *real danger*, yer majesty."

Cormack tilted his head. "I have yet to see one. Besides, the tale of Kataraménos states that if you come to them in peace, no harm shall come to you."

The sailor shook his head. "But what man would take such a risk withou' the sweet reward? Ye catch a mermaid, the wishes are yours."

Cormack furrowed his brow. "Wishes? Like a clurichaun?"

"Not the same! Not the same!" He waved his hand. "They be little tricksters, and twist yer wish to dark things. No! Mermaid wishes be fine and true."

"Real mermaids." Cormack looked out into the harbour again.

The sailor chuckled to himself while walking further down the dock. Cormack was torn, the lust for salt and sea igniting once more. His hands fidgeted, his eyes on the tight knot on the dock line. He sighed and ran his hand through his hair.

"Tomorrow, Poseidon grant me sweet winds tomorrow." Cormack headed down the docks toward the grassy shore.

The castle gleamed in the late light of the day. The blue banners of Paradine fluttered high in the turrets. Two guards leaned against the limestone wall, their halberds propped next to them. They chatted, but straightened and grabbed their halberds as Cormack approached. They saluted, their chins parallel with the ground.

"Good evening, your highness!" they barked as Cormack picked his way toward the kitchen garden.

He nodded to them. "At ease, men. Good evening."

The guards loosened their stance, but remained standing. They waited until Cormack had disappeared through the rugged archway of the scullery entrance before picking up the thread of their conversation. The scent of marinade and fresh baked bread hit Cormack's nose as he entered the kitchen. The air was thick and sweltering. His sandy blonde hair became damp and clung to his temples.

"And here comes trouble!" Pamela, the plump head cook, cheered as Cormack scoured the staging table for scraps. She stopped stirring the iron cauldron and turned to him, sauce-stained spoon still in hand.

Cormack sniffed. "What are you making?"

She turned to her cauldron and resumed her ministrations. "The boar that the soldiers caught yesterday." She turned her head to look at him. "The servants have been getting antsy looking for you. Better get to your things."

Cormack bit back a groan. "I suppose, if I must."

"Cheer up, dear." Pamela pointed her spoon at a basket covered with a linen. "I'm sure it's not all that bad."

She winked, and Cormack lifted the linen. Inside the grass-woven basket were fresh baked oat cakes, her specialty.

He grinned at her. "Thanks, Pamela! You're the best!"

"Off with you now!" She shook her head, smiling as Cormack grabbed a handful of cakes and bounded out of the kitchen.

****

The sea hag set down her jeweled comb. The water had changed. Asrai was home.

"Where have you been?" The sea hag's eyes flashed as Asrai peeked from the cave opening. "Don't tell me you were swooning over that stupid sailor again." The sea hag picked up her comb and slid it into her hair. It disappeared. "You're better than that."

Asrai pumped her tail, stirring the sandy floor into little clouds. "But this one is different."

The sea hag laughed. "All sailors are the same. You will realize that in time. For now, we must prepare to journey to the Western Wilds and find you a real mate."

Asrai's hands trembled as she opened her fist, revealing a gold ring encrusted with yellow diamonds and crowned with a lapis lazuli. The center was bare gold, engraved with the runic "P" for Paradine. The sea hag snatched it up, holding it between her claws, her eyes gleaming.

"He dropped it while diving for shells this afternoon." Asrai tried to grab the ring back, but the sea hag turned away.

"A sailor prince! How absurd!" The ring was far too large for her spidery fingers, so she began weaving it into a lock of her hair.

Asrai sighed and settled onto the sandy floor, her tail fins curling and uncurling. "I've been watching him for three moons. He has his own boat that sails around close to the harbour. He wears fine clothes and is not rough like the other sailors."

"That may be so, but he is still a human. You cannot foul your wellspring with blood of the Cursed One." The sea hag settled back onto her stone ledge, her fingers toying with the new bauble in her hair.

"He is not like the other humans." Asrai twirled her comb. "He is of the sea. Never have I seen a human so entranced by the tide and the treasures within. He does not talk as if all were his, the way other humans do. Just the previous day, I watched him free a dolphin from a human fishing net and lose the entire catch. But he cared not once he knew the dolphin was free and safe."

The sea hag sniffed. "Do not forget all I have taught you; all that you have worked toward. You will need a strong mer at your side to create the new tide."

"That is why I need *more* than just a mer at my side." Asrai swished her tail. "I need a champion who can crack open my wellspring tenfold! Like that of Fredsmegler."

The sea hag whirled about. "Do not speak that name!"

Asrai stuck out her chin. "If I am to take my place in Sulu, I must have the Peacemaker spoken of in those ancient tales."

"And you believe this *sailor-prince* is he?" The sea hag examined the ring once more.

"Don't worry," Asrai's eyes flashed, "he will be."

****

Cormack slowed his gait as he neared the top of the stairs. The oat cakes were warm in his hands, but the expectations of his father blew out the fire in his heart. The orange light of a day's end blazed through the arrowslit windows. He could hear the faint roll of the waves breaking as a warm breeze filtered through the hall, taunting him.

The doors to the map room were heavy mahogany wood, carved with the talents of war—the archer, the swordsman, the gunner, and the horseman. Cormack rested his hand on the cold, black iron handle. His jaw tightened as he pushed open one of the heavy doors. King Dominic, his faithful general Weston, and Cormack's cousin Peter gathered around the large map table in the center of the room. Cormack swallowed the rising tension in his gut. He made a smart bow.

"Good evening, Father." He kept his gaze on the king's chest.

King Dominic nodded. "And good evening to you, my son. Come, sit here at the peninsula of Umber."

Cormack did as he was bid. The table was an oblong round, the surface concave. It scooped down to reveal a map of the world with sculpted forests, mountains, and the sea. The map was littered with figurines of soldiers and horses. Cormack slid into the chair closest to the district King Dominic had indicated.

"To what do I owe the pleasure of an invitation to your map room today, Father?" Cormack's hands fidgeted on the lip of the table.

The king's eyes were drawn to the bare tan line on Cormack's hand. He scowled. "Where is your crest?"

Cormack froze. He slid his hands into his lap. "Oh, I must have forgotten it."

"*Forgotten your crest?*" King Dominic's face reddened. His face crinkled further. "How can you possibly forget that which is all you are?!"

Peter smirked at Cormack. He twirled his plain gold ring around his finger on the lip of the table. Weston's eyes darted between the boys, but said nothing.

"What am I to do with you?" The rage seeped from King Dominic. He blew the air from his pursed lips and rubbed his face, making a strange whistling sound. "What am I to do with you?"

Cormack kept his gaze on the table, his eyes flitting among the figurines. He knew there was no suitable excuse, much less a lie. He waited for the subject to change.

"We'll have the jeweler cast another." King Dominic shook his head, his eyebrows knitted together. He slapped his hands on the lip of the table, making Cormack jump. Peter snickered. The king sent a scowl his way. "Quiet, boy!"

Peter bit back a scowl. "Yes, Uncle."

King Dominic picked up a figurine of a carriage. He placed it at the border of Paradine. "Yes, well, we have great matters to attend to. Great matters."

"Father, if it is another one, please—"

"I said quiet!" the king roared. He picked up another figurine, painted black with a gold crown. He placed it in Umber and did not look up from the map. "That dog Richard is skulking about our borders once more. Umber is currently under siege. We are able to send in supplies through the forests here…"

Cormack stared at the map without seeing while his father chattered, moving figurines about on the board. His hands fidgeted in his lap as his thoughts returned to that afternoon. The memory of the sailor speaking of Denarians and mermaids made his chest tighten with excitement. A smile curled his lips.

"…and so, I have arranged for a most special guest. She is due to arrive tomorrow."

"Wh-what?" Cormack blinked, his senses returning to the map room, away from the sea.

Peter rolled his eyes. King Dominic shook his finger at Cormack. "The Princess of Caraway is arriving tomorrow. We have planned a welcome feast in her honour. *You* will be there to greet her *personally*."

Cormack bit back a groan. "*Another* of your princesses, Father? How many has it been? A dozen? Ten dozen?"

"Now you listen here!" King Dominic's face began to turn red once more. "You are my son, the crown prince of the most powerful kingdom in all the world! And as my son, you shall be wed and continue the proud lineage of Paradine, *and that is that!*"

Peter toyed with a figurine of a horse near Altruse. "Yes, dear Cousin. After all, we are running out of princesses to woo."

Cormack rolled his eyes. The king slapped the table again.

"Enough!" he bellowed, his face fully red now. "You will be there tomorrow night, and so help me if you are *not*, I will have every last guard, woman, and child seeking you so I can tear you limb from limb! Understood?"

"Yes, Father," Cormack whispered. He kept his gaze on the table. His heart clenched. "I will be there, Father."

King Dominic leaned back in his chair, his face returning to normal. "Good. See that you are."

Peter toyed with the carriage. "Rest assured, Uncle, I will ensure our guest experiences all the glory Paradine has to offer."

"Yes, yes," the king waved his hand, "pomp and all that, all taken care of." He ensnared Cormack's gaze. "Tread careful with this one, boy. The Princess of Caraway is a proud creature. We cannot afford to insult her, or her people."

Cormack's eyebrows rose. "I will be sure to take care, Father."

King Dominic deflated. "Good. Good."

Weston nodded to Cormack, then to Peter. They were dismissed. Cormack lagged behind, but Peter waited for him in the hall. His eyes glinted.

"Dear Cousin, I do hope you will not be meeting our esteemed guest in such a fashion." He raked his eyes over Cormack's sailing tunic and stained breeches.

"If she is to be my betrothed, then she should know me as I am." Cormack edged past him.

"Yes," Peter's voice was acid, burning into Cormack's back as he strode off, "if only you were all that you are, *your highness.*"

Chapter Two

Asrai darted about the reef, ensnaring a fish between her claws. She bit off the head, but her stomach felt shriveled, full of anxiety. Her body quivered as the tide grew warmer.

The sea hag sat upon a large sea sponge, spearing small crabs onto her claws and crunching them whole. "You are sure of your choice? To snare a human, it has never been done."

"Yes." Asrai offered the uneaten fish to the sea hag. "He is different."

"Should you fail," the sea hag's eyes flashed, "you shall be no more. Sulu shall be no more."

This is for Sulu, all is for Sulu. Asrai's gaze hardened. "He is the life mate I have been seeking. With him I shall bring about the new tide."

The sea hag pulled out her comb. "Then you must be prepared. Humans are too fond of their precious souls, given to them by the Cursed One. But, if he is to be your mate, he must relinquish his soul to become a true mer and fulfill the prophesy of Fredsmegler. Such greatness would restore Sulu and its reefs."

"I am certain I can convince him, one way or another." Asrai fidgeted with her comb.

"No, you must not use magick." The sea hag wagged her finger. "In order to ensnare the soul and follow the prophesy, he must choose you of his own accord. You cannot force his love with magick. Only *true* love magick is strong enough for this kind of bond."

Asrai pouted, her scales flashing. "I understand that I am an attractive creature. Selecting me as a mate would be to his benefit."

The sea hag straightened her back, leaning forward to lock her gaze with Asrai. "That may be so, but humans are capricious and selfish creatures. Many mers have fallen for their charms and sacrificed their lives for legs on land. But never has a human been willing to lose their soul to the sea."

"I shall convince him to love me on his land," Asrai mused, "and then once he cannot live without me, he will willingly follow me to the sea."

"That is dangerous!" The sea hag's eyes flashed and her face became pinched. "Once you set such a plan, there is no going back. Much like Draum, there are no second chances. You will either die a slow death, drying to the bone, or you will die of heartache and become nothing but seafoam. And then where will Sulu be?"

Asrai waved her hand. "I understand the risk. I am risking just as much challenging Draum as I am sneaking onto land. I must do this. If I cannot win this mate, then there is little chance I can win at Draum."

The sea hag sighed, knowing that Asrai had made up her mind. "You are certain of the challenges that lie ahead? There will be much pain and many dangers, even if you do succeed."

"Yes, I understand." Asrai squared her chin. "I will settle for no less than the Peacemaker as my mate, and I will fight to the last drop of my wellspring in order to win his love."

The sea hag touched her fingers to her lips. "Go."

****

Cormack held his boots in his hand, walking in his bare feet past Peter's bedroom. Waking him would result in Peter stalling him until King Dominic came and steered Cormack toward the map room, to be harangued about campaigns in Umber and trade relations in Denaria until the Princess of Wherever arrived. He could at least escape for a few hours before meeting his fate.

A cool morning breeze filled the hall with the scent of brine. A tapestry fluttered. He groped his way down the cold stairs. The sky was still grey, and only the faintest glimmer of sunlight filtered through the arrowslits. Cormack sat down on the bottom step and began pulling on his boots. From the window, a lonely seagull called. Another answered; their cries echoed through the stone hall.

The kitchen was hot as ever. Pots and pans banged and clanked, preparing for the feast to come. A basket covered with a white linen napkin sat on the table, waiting for him.

"Up early I see," Pamela called to Cormack over her shoulder. "I supposed you would be sneaking off before the feast. A nice hearty breakfast and lunch for you, dear. And of course, a couple of goodies too."

Cormack grinned. "Thank you, Pamela!"

Pamela clucked her tongue as she chopped vegetables. "You know I'm not going to let you starve out there on that silly boat of yours."

"The Denarians said they encountered mermaids on their journey here. Think, Pamela, *real mermaids!*"

She turned to look at him. "Don't you be swimming with any of those mermaids now. You spend enough time out there as it is!" Pamela waggled her knife at him for emphasis.

Cormack laughed. "Don't worry. I'll be back in time for the banquet."

Pamela handed him the basket, and patted him on the shoulder. "Now then, get to your things."

Love of the Sea

The Denarian galleon was still at the docks when Cormack trotted up to *Anita*. He set the basket down near the dock line and wove his way through the bustling crew. He found one of the Denarian sailors sitting with a handful of Paradine sailors, playing Kings and Wogs with old, stained cards.

"Good morrow!" Cormack chirped.

The Paradine sailors looked up and gave Cormack a hearty greeting. One even slapped him on the back. "Good morrow, yer majesty!"

The Denarian sailor eyed Cormack, confused by the mix of formality and familiarity. Cormack extended his hand. "I am Cormack, Prince of Paradine. It's a pleasure to meet one of our close allies." He tipped his head. "Your trade is the bloodline that flows through Paradine."

"Aye." The sailor took Cormack's hand and shook it, his grip rough and firm. His wary gaze scanned Cormack.

"No need to worry!" One of the Paradine sailors clapped his hand on the Denarian's shoulder. "Our prince is right up! A friendly sor' o' fellow!"

Murmurs of agreement rose from the other sailors. Cormack broadened his smile. The Denarian relaxed. "T'is a pleasure to meet ye, yer majesty." He dipped his head. "An' what brings ye to th' docks?"

Cormack turned and waved his hand at *Anita*. "A fine day of sailing awaits me! But, I heard tell you encountered mermaids?"

The Denarian broke into a grin. "Aye, we did! Bright glitterin' things! Flittin' about in th' reef."

"So, it's true!" Cormack felt his heart quiver. "They *are* real!"

"Real as c'n be!" The Denarian's face hardened. "I warn ye, mess not with the likes o' them! Mermaids be dangerous as th' sharks. Fit to sing ye a pretty song, then slit yer throat fer supper! Save yer wishes fer the stars, yer highness. T'is safer."

One of the Paradine sailors punched the Denarian in the arm. "Aw, come off it! Let's play! I got a hot hand, I do!"

The sailors cheered and went back to their game. The Denarian gave Cormack a curt nod before examining his cards again. Cormack turned and walked back to *Anita*, his packed lunch waiting.

Real mermaids.

Cormack scanned the water and filled his nose with the salty air. He was uncertain that he should go for a swim after what the sailor had said. Once or twice, he could have sworn that a large fish sometimes swam near him when he did go diving for shells.

Could it have really been a mermaid?

He dropped anchor and looked over the railing. The sapphire waves beckoned. The king's words echoed through his mind, seizing his heart.

We cannot afford to insult her, or her people.

Cormack sighed and ran his hand through his hair. His father often chastised him for "stinking of the sea." He would have to hunt for shells and things another day. Cormack settled for playing with his compass, charting an imaginary course on his map, an old worn scrap of parchment that one of the sailors had given him. The sun charted its own course across the sky, a burning reminder that his time was not his own that day.

When Cormack's shadow grew long, he rolled up his map and packed it away. The basket of food was long since empty. He turned his gaze to the castle, bathed in golden light once more. He would have just enough time to dress and drink a flagon or two of ale before the feast. Cormack raised anchor and turned *Anita* about.

****

Asrai swam toward the harbour. She dodged past the large trade ships coming and going, keeping a wide berth from the fishing vessels and their nets. The water was cooler in the harbour. It sharpened her mind, the nervous energy dissolving. Asrai pumped her tail hard against the boat's current and sunk her claws into the rudder. She climbed her way to the hull, allowing the vessel to tow her through the water.

She looked up, but Cormack was not leaning over the railing. The boat turned; he was at the helm steering. Asrai waited as he took the familiar course to the sandbars, out past the fishing fields. Ripples boiled as the anchor fell from the side of the boat. She peeked up again, but Cormack did not appear. She curled up against the rudder, scanning the water. There was nothing of interest, as the fish were avoiding the vessels. Soon, she felt herself nodding off as boredom clung to her.

The day slipped by until Asrai felt the boat shudder as the anchor slinked up from the sea floor. Cormack had not left the boat all day. Panic filled her mind as she felt the boat lurch forward. *Illyana will not give me a second chance! I must reveal myself now!*

She beat her tail hard against the current, getting out in front of the boat. Asrai dove down into the sand. She dug deep into her wellspring and pulled her golden comb from her hair. She whirled it about in the sand, stirring up a riptide. *Anita* spun and floundered in the rogue current. Asrai whipped her tail hard for the grassy shore. She broke the surface, and looked back at the struggling boat, then flung herself from the surf and dragged her body up onto shore.

For Sulu! Her heart thundered as the air cut through her. *For me!*

The sun was much brighter on the surface, and she held up her hand to shield her eyes. The sand was scorching, not cool and silky like on the ocean floor. Asrai looked out onto the water, and saw the boat halt its progress. The anchor slid down once more. Asrai bit back her pain as she pulled bits of hot seaweed to cover herself. It did little to shield her.

How can humans stand the naked sun? I never knew the light was so hot, and so dry!

The burning sands scorched Asrai's scales and skin. She could feel her strength ebbing away. She dared not waste a spell on her comfort, knowing she would need the power of suggestion once Cormack found her. If he found her.

Oh, my sailor! Don't leave me here to dry out!

****

Cormack flinched as *Anita* floundered against a strong riptide. It pushed the boat away from the docks, and he was forced to head toward the small sandbars that blocked an old grotto. He did his best to steer *Anita* in the shallow waters. He managed to dodge the sandbars, but ran aground at the shoreline. He dropped anchor and tossed the dock line, unsure of what else to do. Cormack climbed down from the craft, his boots sinking into the wet sand. As he walked around the prow, dragging the dock line with him, he tripped over a clump of seaweed.

"That's odd. I haven't seen this type of seaweed wash up on shore before."

He picked some up to examine the strange hair-like substance. He pushed aside the familiar green seaweed. This revealed more of the fine, hair-like fronds. Startled, Cormack brushed aside more of the green seaweed, and exposed smooth flesh. Cormack's hands were shaking as he dug through the seaweed. It was a beautiful face, and the fine fronds were actual hair. He froze.

"By the wave of Poseidon!" Cormack exclaimed.

The face stirred, and more seaweed fell, revealing her body. It was a beached mermaid. Her scales were rough and dry, and her body radiated heat. Cormack stroked her cheek; it was soft like human skin. His fingers traced down to her neck where red slits appeared like gashes— her gills.

"It is true," Cormack whispered, "a real mermaid."

The mermaid groaned and her tail flopped.

"Are you hurt?" Cormack slapped his forehead. "What am I saying? You're a fish on a beach, of course you're in pain!"

The mermaid's eyes snapped open, startling Cormack. They were a deep blue, like the depths of the sea. They brightened until they appeared clear.

A jolt went through him and he jerked his head. A team of fishing boats were trawling their net toward the east side of the harbour, right under the rock shelf grotto that held the castle cellars. Soon, *Anita* would be in their sights. The riptide boiled, sending small waves crashing into

Lauren A. R. Masterson

Anita's hull, preventing him from climbing aboard. He looked down at the mermaid again.

"What am I to do?" He recalled the sailor's warning. "They will surely capture you if I leave you. Perhaps I can drag you back into the water."

He noticed how dry and brittle her scales were, baking in the hot sun. Images flooded his mind of the young mermaid floundering in the water, confused and exhausted, being swept into the nets. His panic rose.

"I suppose I could take you in until you recover. How would I sneak you into the castle? Sneak in a mermaid! This is madness!"

The fishing vessels appeared to be closing in. Cormack made up his mind and lifted the mermaid. He stumbled, his muscles straining to compensate. Her blush-coloured tail drooped at his side. Unlike a human maiden, both her upper body and lower body were equally weighted, her thick tail contributing twice as much weight as a maiden's slender legs and dainty feet. The tail slapped his thigh as he trudged through the sand up to the rocky grotto.

The mermaid drew closer to his chest. She wrapped her arms around his neck, much like a maiden would. Cormack blushed. He tipped his head down to smell her hair. It was briny, like the sea, but there was also something else he could not place. His limbs ached as he carried her up the sandy hill onto more dense sands. They were far enough from the docks that they would not be seen. Cormack plodded along the crest toward the grotto. The ground became rocky and proved difficult footing. His legs screamed as he bore the mermaid's weight, the vision of sailors stealing wishes from her spurring him on.

Cormack leaned against the inner wall of the grotto as he laid her down so he could rest. The cave was a cool respite from the sun. The cellars were a labyrinth of small stone-carved rooms filled with foodstuffs. It led up to the stone-cut stairs, and the archway into the servants' halls. They were empty, as all were preparing the feast in the Great Hall. Cormack hoped no one, most of all not Peter, would notice as he trudged up the worn servant staircase. Lucky for Cormack, no calls had yet been made, and no servants were scurrying up or down the cramped space.

When he reached the landing, Cormack peered around the corner to see if any servants were about. Peter was typically in the map room this time of day, but Cormack struggled to keep his footsteps quiet in case his cousin decided to duck out and grab him from out of the hall. His arms shook as the muscles strained under the dead-weight of the mermaid. She was quiet, but Cormack could feel her breath on his neck. He struggled to juggle her and fumble with the door latch. Once inside, he dropped the mermaid onto his bed. She sank into the cool linen sheets.

The old sailor's words echoed in his mind. *Some men take the risk for th' sweet reward. Ye catch a mermaid, th' wishes are yours.* He brushed the thought away as she stirred, her face puckered with pain.

"Lady mermaid, are you all right?"

Cormack stroked the pale scales on her arm. Small flecks flaked off onto his fingers. She had passed out, and Cormack's eyes darted about the room. Her scales had scratched his skin. Bits of red scales sat on his arms like little petals. She was drying out.

"Oh gods!" he hissed. "Water! Water!"

Cormack charged into the bathroom. A chambermaid had always drawn Cormack's baths for him, and sure enough, he flung the door open to discover the tub already filled. Cormack returned to the bedroom and heaved the mermaid up from the bed. His muscles screamed as he tromped toward the tub. She slid from his arms with a small splash. Her tail stuck out of the water and the fins draped over the edge of the tub. The colour began to seep back into her scales. There was no way for him to pilfer salt from the larder without being questioned, so he had to hope plain water was enough. Cormack grabbed the wooden washing stool and sat down next to her. He stared at Asrai, hoping that she was not already dead.

Her eyes fluttered open, and Cormack sucked in his breath. She straightened her back against the end of the tub. Asrai touched her cheek. She noticed Cormack watching her, then lowered her hand back into the water and smiled.

"How are you feeling?" His eyes flitted from her face to her tail. Cormack stifled the urge to barrage her with questions, and settled for staring into her jewel-like eyes.

"I'm much better, thank you." The mermaid's voice was deeper than that of the breathy princesses he had previously entertained. It was soft and rich, making Cormack's blood run hot.

He wrung his hands. "I hope the water is okay."

She giggled and a hot blush erupted in Cormack's cheeks. The water had soaked into her body and restored it like a wilted flower in a vase. Her scarlet hair flowed to her midsection, and her scales were deepening into a spectacular shade of crimson. Cormack's eyes traced down her body to her arms where the red and gold scales spiraled upward into a thick armour at her shoulders. The scales whorled her naked bust and dotted her stomach. They became thickest below her navel where they blended into the solid shingling of her long muscular tail. Her body seemed to Cormack a gorgeous ember.

"What's your name?" The mermaid flicked her tail, sending water droplets all over the floor. Her scales shimmered as she moved.

"Cormack. What's yours?"

Lauren A. R. Masterson

She cupped water in her hands and poured it over her tail. She then looked up directly into Cormack's eyes. Her own eyes flashed ice blue for an instant and then darkened back to their blue-green colouring.

"Asrai."

Chapter Three

"As-ray." Cormack whispered each syllable, his eyes glazed over. He felt a strange warmth spreading through his body. His pulse quickened. She lifted her hand to touch his face, but a dull thudding startled them.

"I'll be right back." He scampered off the washing stool and closed the bathroom door. His father burst into the bedroom just as Cormack was about to get the door.

"Cormack! Couldn't you hear me knocking? You aren't even dressed and the Princess of Caraway will be attending!" King Dominic looked Cormack's sailing rags up and down in disgust. "And you stink of the sea."

"Father, please, enough of this already."

King Dominic rounded on him. "Do you think this is a game? Do you think I like sending away every suitable bride that passes through our doors? The other kingdoms are beginning to doubt the might and virility of the future king of Paradine!"

Cormack's voice filled the room. "Well, I, um, that is—"

"Bah!" The king shook his head. He opened his palm, revealing the replacement crest. "Put this on and make yourself respectable! Caraway is a wealthy kingdom. Cannot have you looking like a dockhand."

Cormack took the ring and placed it on his finger. The familiar weight felt good on his hand. The lapis lazuli sparkled, clear as ever.

King Dominic sighed. "Just get yourself cleaned up. I'll call the maid to run you a bath."

"No!" Cormack racked his brain for a proper excuse. "I mean, no, it has already been drawn. Besides, I'm sure they're busy with the preparations."

King Dominic squinted and cleared his throat. "Have it your way." He shook his finger in Cormack's face. "But no more shenanigans!" He turned and slammed the bedroom door shut.

Air rushed from Cormack's lips, but a new problem presented itself. How was he going to bathe with a mermaid in his tub? "Asrai?" Cormack whispered as he opened the bathroom door.

She was brushing her hair with a golden comb. It gleamed as she flicked it through her crimson locks. "Hello, sailor."

Cormack scratched the back of his neck. "I need to somehow bathe."

Asrai stared at him, the comb still in her thin fingers.

"Uh, I'll just go get a bucket then." Cormack closed the door and leaned his back against it. *Idiot!* He shook his head and headed to the scullery.

Pamela's thick arms jiggled as she hacked the roasted boar carcass. Blood and juice spattered onto her face and apron. Cormack slipped past the flurry of plates and knives, hoping Pamela was too busy with her work to notice him. The scullery maids and lesser cooks ignored him as they sautéed vegetables, painted marchpane dolphins, and built a cookie castle. He approached a scullery maid that was filling buckets with boiling water to wash dishes.

"May I please have a bucket of water?"

The maid jumped. "Oh yer 'ighness!" She bobbed a curtsy.

Cormack smiled. "I'm sorry, I just need—"

"Does yer 'ighness need a maid to draw yer bath? I c'n call 'er straight quick!"

He shook his head and waved his hand. "No, no. I just need a quick scrub. A bucket will suffice."

The prospect of the crown prince washing in a scrub bucket horrified her. She handed him a bucket of fresh steaming soapy water. Her hands trembled, sloshing water onto herself. "'ere yer 'ighness." The poor perplexed maid stared after Cormack as he trotted off with his bucket.

Pamela guffawed. "Don't worry, my dear, you'll get used to him."

Careful not to spill, Cormack rushed up the stairs and back up to his room. He stopped short before the bathroom door, unsure of what exactly he was going to do with his little bucket. He turned the knob and saw Asrai grooming her scales. She looked up and smiled.

"Oh my, I hope you don't think you're going to fit in there." Asrai giggled, pointing to the bucket.

Cormack grabbed a bar of lye soap from the cupboard. "I should think not."

He stripped off his sailing tunic and glanced at Asrai. Her eyes shimmered as she watched him scrub his chest and back. Cormack glanced at her again, his body tense. He always made the maids leave the fleece towels, rather than have them handed to him in the bath. The thought of a lady, or a lady mermaid, watching him made his mind whirr.

"Um..." He fumbled with the ties on his breeches. "Could you look away?"

Asrai twisted a lock of hair between her fingers as she glanced at her tail. "I apologise, how rude of me."

Cormack's face burned as he peeled the rough breeches off and began to scrub. Once finished, he picked up the bucket and poured the last of the water over himself.

****

Love of the Sea

Suitable brides? Coming here? The older human's words had struck her heart. Asrai pulled out her gold comb to soothe herself. Her sailor seemed to be such a bouncing, anxious creature. Quite unlike the peaceful and wistful sailor she had spent the season following.

He seemed nervous to shed his vestments in front of her. She fidgeted with her comb, finding it odd for a creature who dove in the sea with ease to be so uncomfortable with his own body. Asrai took a deep breath, pushing down the gnawing doubt. The sea hag had warned her that man was capricious and that patience was paramount.

Once he had begun the task of washing, she dared to peek. Flicking her eyes over Cormack's naked body, she was pleased to see he was as strong and virile as she remembered. Clinging to rigging and playing in mock-battles had chiseled the prince's body. His tanned skin gleamed, clean and bare. Asrai made sure to look away and occupy herself with her comb as Cormack dried himself.

"I'm afraid I must prepare for the party now," Cormack muttered. "Is there anything you need before I go?"

Asrai took in his frame, now swathed in a towel. She shrugged. "No, my sailor. Thank you."

Cormack grinned. He stood between the tub and the door. The air was thick, and his chest shuddered as he took a deep breath. He fidgeted his hands. Asrai cocked her head at him. Cormack flinched.

"Well! Good evening!" he blurted, fumbling for the door.

****

Cormack took another stuttering breath once the door closed. The lock clicked on its own, further startling him. His hands shook as he ran one through his hair.

There is a mermaid in my bath. There is a mermaid in my bath and I feel torn leaving her there. What is the matter with me? Doing such dangerous things? Am I mad?

He regarded the clothes the king had sent, lying on the bed. Cormack shook his head and got to work dressing for the feast. A blue-and-gold doublet and grey tunic sat with matching blue breeches made of soft, dyed kid-skin. The buttons were tricky, as he had no groom to assist him. Cormack's willful nature to do everything himself left the servants idle, and further confused his poor father. Heavy gold chains and large jeweled rings sat on the wooden jewel tray on his nightstand. Cormack settled for the simpler rings in his own jewel box. Grey leather boots he easily laced with his boot hook, a trick he had mastered from watching Pamela. The embroidered tunic itched, but Cormack knew better than to scratch. Making the shirt threadbare would only give his father an excuse to buy new, more fashionable, ones. While the Paradine court was simple, diplomatic appearances were everything.

He took a deep breath and strode into the hall. Music floated up as the minstrel sang a jaunty tune. The combined melody of a mandolin and a flute created a lively atmosphere. This was overlapped with the low chatter of conversation, as the people of Caraway were already seated with the Paradine court. The princess's procession would not begin until he was seated, but he knew her entourage was enjoying ale and the dancing girls.

The guests in the Great Hall greeted Cormack as he entered, bowing their heads, raising cups to him. He lifted his hand and smiled in response. A valet pulled back a chair and Cormack was seated, his father not far away at the head of the table.

"You certainly took your time. You're missing all the fun!" King Dominic raised his cup.

Peter leaned over the table. "Lost track of time on that boat of yours, dear Cousin?"

Cormack ignored the comment. A serving girl filled his flagon. Her hands were shaking, and she spilled some ale on the table. Cormack put a hand under hers to steady her.

"Careful now. No need to be nervous." He smiled at her. She nodded, bobbing a curtsy. Her nose and cheeks flared pink. She giggled as she trotted off to serve the officers.

Cormack raised his cup. "To your happiness, Father."

King Dominic laughed. "I would rather toast to your happiness! Perhaps you will find it tonight." He drank deep.

Thoughts of Asrai tumbled into his mind. Cormack tipped his head as his pulse quickened and his face grew warm. *Oh, but Father, I believe I have already found that happiness.*

He wet his lips with a sip of ale, and took in his surroundings. The people of Caraway were a bawdy group. He sighed as he set down the cup. It was going to be a long evening.

A horn trumpeted, and everyone turned toward the entrance. A troop of ladies dressed in crimson entered first, their eyes downcast. Their black hair was pulled back and plaited into circlets atop their heads. A red ribbon was tied around each of their necks, the ribbons streaming down their backs. Their gossamer dresses seemed to float over the stone floor. Their satin shoes darted beneath the hems.

Two men dressed in yellow followed the ladies. Each man held a yellow satin pillow bearing a small fluffy dog. They had leashes tied to the pillows, preventing them from jumping down. Their gold fur shone bright against their inky black eyes and noses. Their excited panting revealed tongues the shocking colour of blueberries.

Many grand processions such as this had graced the Great Hall. Each revealed a corner of the world to Cormack and Paradine. He had seen princesses with silver trays stacked high with treasure, princesses with elabourate masquerade costumes and headdresses, princesses with endless troupes of armoured warriors, princesses bearing chains leading large exotic beasts. The wonder if it all quickly became tiresome for Cormack. All were decadent, but none seemed true to the personage of the lady.

The princess was not carried in a litter, as some were. This princess walked on foot. Her black hair flowed down her back, the curls bouncing free. Red ribbons had been tied loosely around the crown of her head. She resembled a bleeding sacrifice of sorts. Her dress was red, like that of her ladies. The outer layer was delicate as a dragonfly wing, revealing the deep red skirt beneath. The dark fabric clung to her body. Cormack could see the shape of her legs as she walked.

A wide yellow brocade sash was embroidered with gold and red thread. This was tied about her waist tight like a corset. A red cord was tied around the sash, the tassels in a square knot to the left. They bounced on her hip as she walked. The gossamer sleeves were great bells that hung down to her knees. As she passed, Cormack could see the back of the dress dipped low to expose her spine and shoulder blades. The officers seated at the table elbowed one another.

Two ladies walked three paces behind the princess. They were dressed in long red robes with no sleeves, their muscular arms laid bare. Red hoods with gold hems hid their hair and masked their faces. Each had a small dagger strapped to their left forearm. Behind the hooded ladies were two more yellow-clad men. They each led a large greyhound on a yellow brocade leash, the same fabric as the princess' sash. They were followed by a man dressed all in gold, who bore a large wooden box with elabourate carvings.

Peter ran his middle finger around the rim of his cup as he watched the procession. His leg bounced under the table. Cormack was surprised to see his cousin so fidgety. Typically, the processions bored him, save for the greedy gleam that would rise in his eyes when piles of sparkling treasure were sometimes carried in as potential dowry. Cormack frowned, then returned his gaze to the princess and her entourage.

Two ladies dressed in yellow robes followed two paces behind the man in gold. They too had red cords tied about their waists with the tassels to the left. They carried large gold cymbals with long red tassels on the handles. After them came a group of ladies and young men all dressed in yellow. Each had their head covered with a yellow scarf.

The tail end of the procession was a yellow-clad man pulling a large wooden cart bearing a heavy bronze cage. Inside was a bird with striking green and red plumage. A tall red crest crowned the bird's head. It squawked and pecked at a bronze bowl of bleeding meat.

The procession circled the head table until the princess came to her designated seat. Cormack could see that she had large brown eyes.

They struck through him as she met his gaze, like a cold shock of ice. He swallowed and let his gaze wander. A large ruby sparkled in the centre of her forehead, held in place with a gold setting braided into her hair. Red garnets sparkled across her collar bones and chest like fresh droplets of blood. Delicate filigree gold wire held each jewel. She swept a stray lock of hair behind her ear, revealing her red painted nails. The lacquer shone like polished glass.

King Dominic stood, and everyone followed suit. "Please grace our table, princess." He lifted his cup in salute.

The men raised their cups as well. The red-clad ladies pulled back the princess' chair. She seated herself and locked eyes with Cormack again. The man in gold brought the box to the princess. The yellow-clad ladies took their place on either side of the princess. They clanged their cymbals once and announced. "The Princess Nephara of Caraway! Keeper of the Silver Key, and Tamer of the Red-crested Panya!"

The gold-clad man stood at attention as one of the red-clad ladies opened the box, revealing a heavy gold crown set with fiery rubies and amber. She lifted the crown high, then lowered it so it touched the princess' head.

The cymbals crashed again. "Look well upon the beauty of Caraway!"

The people of Caraway applauded. King Dominic followed suit, and soon everyone in the room was clapping. The cymbals crashed again, and the crown was placed back into the box and taken away. King Dominic seated himself, and everyone found their chairs. The yellow-clad servants brought stacks of red and yellow cushions and arranged them on the floor behind the princess. The ladies in red gowns sat upon the cushions, all facing the princess' back. The two hooded ladies flanked either side of the group of cushions. They remained standing.

****

Asrai dipped her comb in the water of the bathtub and swirled it, summoning a water mirror. In it was a perfect vision of the procession entering the Great Hall. Her eyes darted about, trying to decipher which was the 'suitable bride' the father human had spoken of.

One of the ladies stood out, her elaborate costume designating her the leader of the group. Asrai nodded, sizing up her competition. Though it was clear this "Princess of Caraway" was indeed beautiful, her vestments and jewels were no match for the splendor of Asrai's scales and tail. Asrai's eyes brightened, crackling with magick as she pointed her comb at the Princess Nephara.

Make this princess fine, rich, and gaudy, not at all fun, playful, or bawdy. May her words sting and annoy, so my sailor will see her only as an overwrought toy.

24

Love of the Sea

The water mirror shimmered as her spell was cast. Though the sea hag had warned Asrai that she was not to use magick on Cormack, that wasn't to say she was barred from using magick on everyone around him. Asrai smiled, her fangs gleaming.

The princess sat down at the table. Asrai scanned the scene, seeing that all the men stared at her in wonder, especially one young human in particular. He sat next to her sailor, and though they looked of the same family, their faces and demeanor differed. Asrai twirled her comb. Her thoughts were broken as she watched a large gold crown placed on the princess' head. Greed snared her heart, but Asrai tamped down the heated desire.

We are here for the real treasure. Focus!

Food was brought to the table, and the humans began to chatter to one another. Asrai frowned as she heard Cormack talking to Princess Nephara. She looked down the table again, and saw the other human enthralled with the princess' words. His eyes were glazed over, resembling a mer during the warm tides of mating season. Asrai thrummed, pleased at her luck. She pointed her comb again.

The heart grows fond over things we cannot have, so it seems these two cannot cross paths. May we change the stars, and in turn their lives. Give them love that is otherwise deprived!

Asrai squeezed her comb between her hands, watching the scene unfold. Her excitement was distracting her from the deep ache in her bones, and the weariness of magick sapping at her resolve. The humans chattered on, eating food and darting their gazes about. Cormack was speaking less, his gaze far off as the princess and the other human became more confident in speaking to one another.

"Cormack, my boy! Head in the clouds again?"

The heavy voice of the father human crashed through the water mirror, startling both Cormack and Asrai. She growled, flicking her comb. The magick was becoming more difficult to summon, and Asrai dug deep into her wellspring as she fought to maintain the water mirror and cast one last spell of suggestion.

Though this princess be bright, beautiful, and benign, see her through a different lens, full of worry for a mate in decline. Doubt her charms and see how she might undermine, so I might step in and see my sailor's love at last align.

Asrai held her comb tight, her hand shaking as she pressed the powerful suggestion into the older human's mind. Try as she might, the magick fell away in useless ribbons. Asrai pressed harder, but the magick snapped back, shattering the water mirror with it. She sat in the bath, panting, her exhaustion settling in at last.

****

King Dominic looked around to make sure the ceremony was indeed over, and then lifted his cup. "Let us fill our bellies and revel in the delights of Paradine!"

The crowd cheered and all drank to the toast. The procession melted away, and chatter returned; pitchers of ale, wine, and water circulated about. The serving men came out and placed the heavy crockery and platters upon the tables. The first course was a Caraway specialty, whole roasted toucans. The bills were filled with spiced sauce, and then poured over the poultry in front of the guests. The bills were then set upright in the centre of the dish.

King Dominic speared a leg off one of the tiny birds, leaned over to his general and whispered. "They say this is the food of kings. Give me a proud boar and see a real king eat!" He popped the leg in his mouth and pulled out the bone. His general laughed.

Cormack picked at the toucan; he knew the spice would not sit well in his stomach. The princess ate her bird in tiny portions and slipped each bite between her blood red lips with grace. Cormack realized she had been painted with cosmetics. She was probably not as pale as she appeared.

Peter toyed with his goblet and addressed the princess. "What exactly was that bird you presented? I have never seen such a creature."

Her eyes darted from Peter to Cormack. She then lowered her eyes, and darted them up again from under her lashes at Peter. "It is the dreaded red-crested panya from my homeland. They are known to slaughter livestock and in rare cases carry off small children."

"And how does one tame such a dangerous creature?" Peter's words petted the air.

Nephara hid her smile with a red fan she had slipped from her sleeve. Her eyes flicked again to Peter. Cormack fidgeted. While he had every intention of rejecting the princess at the end of her visit, he was surprised at Peter's boldness. He took a gulp of ale and watched as the princess fluttered her fan, her eyes shining.

"As a child, I was skilled with falconry, but the small prey grew tiresome. The panya is a marvel, and I won Quinquetta in body first with a wooden trap, then won her heart with careful tidings and exercises. Now she adores me and takes down the mighty antelope as tribute."

King Dominic perked up at the mention of the hunt. He grinned when the princess punctuated her speech with a sip of wine. "A lady that hunts! If I were years younger!" He turned to his general. "A fine lady!"

Nephara turned her gaze to Cormack. "And do you hunt as well, my prince?"

"No." Cormack could feel Peter's gaze burning into him. "I prefer to sail at sea."

Love of the Sea

She lifted her eyebrows, but said nothing. Nephara returned to her food. Cormack felt his unease tie into a knot. He drained his cup of ale.

Chapter Four

The second course sounded, and Cormack was dragged away from his strange thoughts. Alarm rang in his mind. *Asrai has not eaten! How long was she stranded on shore? She must be starving!* He began to wonder what mermaids eat.

The plates of toucan were removed, and seared sea turtle steak was set before the party. Rubbed with simple black pepper and drizzled with olive oil, they were garnished with marigold petals. It was one of Cormack's favourite dishes. His stomach growled as he cut into the familiar food. It was a treat only available during the summer. He wondered if Asrai had ever dined upon sea turtle, and if she too would enjoy it. The princess took an experimental bite. Her eyes widened, and she hid a smile with her fingertips. He watched as her hands shook. She cut only small bites and ate slowly, though her eyes devoured the plate.

"Please enjoy, princess. There is nothing wrong with eating delicious food with vigour." Cormack smiled and nodded to her plate. He took a large bite of his own food to reassure her.

Nephara dipped her head. "Thank you, my prince."

Cormack could feel Peter's hot glare on him. He chose to ignore his cousin. Her eyes darted about as she cut a large piece. She stretched her mouth open and chewed the bite, again, hiding her mouth behind her fingers.

Peter smoothed his glare and smiled at the princess. "Our dear king loves the hunt. Have you ever hunted wild boar, princess?"

Nephara dabbed her lips with her napkin. She lowered her eyes, a blush creeping into her cheeks. "I have not. It would be a thrill for me, and a joy for Quinquetta."

"Uncle!" Peter called to the king. "What say you? Shall we arrange a hunt for our esteemed guest?"

King Dominic was caught off guard, his mouth full of food. He swallowed and drained his ale. "Why yes, my boy! That sounds marvelous!"

Peter ensnared her gaze once more. "What is the kingdom of Caraway like, princess?"

Nephara paused between bites and smiled at Peter. "Much different than your kingdom. Our mines are filled with bronze for our warriors' axes and swords. We have jungles filled with large beasts to hunt.

Love of the Sea

Our land is flanked by a sea of golden grass rather than water. We harvest the grass for our bread."

"You mentioned the antelope, your highness. What other beasts do you take as your prize in the hunt?" Peter's voice softened.

King Dominic had been preoccupied with eating, but upon hearing Peter's voice dominating the conversation he looked up from his plate. Cormack's gaze was far away, as if deep in thought. Peter was leaning over his plate, his eyes burning into the princess. Worst of all, the princess giggled and simpered with coquettish charm. Her eyes locked with Peter's gaze.

"Cormack, my boy!" His growl jolted Cormack from his thoughts. "Head in the clouds again?"

His gaze was glazed over. "No, Father. In the sea."

The king spluttered. Peter smirked as the princess giggled and batted her eyelashes. King Dominic balled his hand into a fist, but his attempt to regain control was thwarted by the third course being served. Platters of sliced fruit were set before the party. The rind was bright yellow, but the pulpy flesh was blue.

Cormack looked up at Nephara. "Princess, is this from your kingdom?"

She nodded, cutting a section of fruit from the rind. "Yes, my prince. It is the jubjaleb. They grow in the jungle where we go to hunt for toucan. They are most refreshing."

The fruit had a citrus bite, but the flesh was cool and a welcome change from the heavy meat courses. It had a hint of sweetness that made Cormack's mouth water.

Peter turned a section of fruit on his fork this way and that. The light shone through the translucent flesh. "This would be an incredible import."

"A fine idea!" King Dominic attempted to redirect the conversation again. "Cormack, my boy, what say you?"

Cormack shrugged and cut another section of fruit. "Yes, Father. I think the people of Paradine would enjoy this fruit. Especially after a long, hot day of work."

Peter elbowed Cormack. "Ah yes, our man of the people!"

Nephara's eyebrows lifted. "You often go out amongst your people?"

"Oh, yes, princess." Cormack smiled, remembering the Denarian sailor from the docks that morning. "A prince must learn about his people and love them in order to serve them one day as king."

King Dominic smiled while Peter stewed, glaring at his plate. Cormack fidgeted with his fork. Dinner was taking too long. When one of the serving girls leaned over to fill his cup, Cormack tapped her arm.

She leaned forward. "Yes, your highness?"

Cormack whispered in her ear. "Please have Pamela send up another plate of the second course to my chambers"

The serving girl nodded. "Right away, your highness." She secured her pitcher, and scurried off.

****

The kitchen was hot, and Pamela was waving her great wooden spoon and barking orders. The serving girl entered and handed her nearly empty pitcher to a waiting girl. She approached Pamela, unsure of the request she carried.

She bobbed a shallow curtsy. "Miss Pamela, the prince has requested another plate of the second course be brought to his chambers."

Pamela stared at the girl, then nodded. She pushed her aside and tapped two assistants. "I'll be back in a moment. Man the fort!"

They nodded, and Pamela sheathed her spoon in a tin cup. She wiped her hands on her apron and examined the pile of uneaten sea turtle steaks. She hefted three onto a wooden platter and climbed the servant staircase. She knew Cormack must be worried about being hungry after the party, as he usually was. The exotic foods tended to upset his stomach. She set the platter down on the small table in his bedroom.

Something splashed in the bathroom, and Pamela jumped. Her ears strained, and she heard moving water. She approached the bathroom door. When her hand rested on the doorknob, something jolted her mind. "The party!" She fled the room and ran down the stairs back to the kitchens.

Pamela grabbed her spoon from the tin cup. Her assistants had sent out the final course before the dessert presentation. New barrels of ale and wine were opened. She scanned the organised chaos.

"All right, we're on the dessert now?"

"Yes, mum!" A serving girl chirped.

Pamela stabbed her spoon in the air. "Perfect! We're almost there!"

****

Two serving men carried out the final platter, a replica of Paradine castle made of butter cookie and fresh cream. The crumbled cookie beach sported marchpane dolphins. King Dominic, now quite red in the face from ale, cheered. Everyone clapped as the castle was set on the head table. The flag tower was cut from the top of the castle, placed on a plate with a marchpane dolphin, and served to the king. Pieces of castle were cut and served to the rest of the guests. Cormack fiddled with his fork. The sooner he ate his piece, the sooner he could leave

The princess fluttered her fan. "My prince, you seen unmoved by the night's festivities. Are there such lavish parties often?"

He straightened and put his fork down. "I just prefer simpler things, princess."

She cocked her head and then laughed behind her fan. She snapped her fan closed and playfully smacked Cormack's hand. "Oh my, you are funny!"

"Thank you." Cormack forced a smile. He imagined her horrified reaction over their regular fare of boar and potatoes.

Peter shook his head. "You will have to forgive my cousin, he is not the sort to keep up with the finer aspects of court life."

Nephara lowered her eyes to her plate, then looked back up at Cormack. Her eyes darted to Peter once more. "I would love to hear more about Paradine and its people. I have heard such outlandish tales during my journey here. The true face of this country would be refreshing to my sensibilities."

The servers set down plates of candy castle before them, cutting off conversation. King Dominic raised his cup and stood. His other beefy hand clutched the arm of his oak chair. "My friends, thank you for sharing this delicious evening. All who wish to retire, we bid you goodnight. All who wish to continue with the late revels and dancing, we bid you a very good night!" He winked before drinking more ale and seating himself.

The crowd cheered and drank. Cormack shoveled a bite of sugary fluff into his mouth and drained his ale. Nephara picked at the castle, her eyes darting about the table as others held out their plates for another helping. Cormack rose, and the princess offered him her hand. He took it, bowed and kissed her hand, then looked into her eyes.

"Thank you, princess, for a lovely evening. I fear I must retire. Early to bed, early to rise. As a future ruler, I have much to do. I bid you goodnight." A speech long since rehearsed and repeated, Cormack now said it to every princess he entertained at these grueling parties.

"Ah, but my prince, the night is young." Her fingers gripped his hand. "Come, dance with me."

Cormack stuttered as she stood and led him toward the open floor. The musicians had struck up a lively tune, and the officers were dancing with the Caraway court ladies. Cormack fell into the rhythm and began dancing with Nephara, his mind busy with worry for Asrai.

King Dominic smiled when he saw Cormack and the princess begin to dance. He nodded to his general. "Ah, it seems this one might stick." He watched as Nephara twirled.

His general nodded. "I certainly hope so, sire."

Nephara tried to capture Cormack's gaze once more. She twirled and jumped. Her dance master had spent weeks teaching her the dances of Paradine. But Cormack's movements seemed automatic, and his eyes went right through her, as if she weren't even there.

Peter tapped Cormack on the shoulder. "Pardon me, Cousin, do you mind if I cut in?"

Cormack bowed to the princess and allowed Peter to take her hand. "As you wish, Cousin." The princess looked from Cormack to Peter. Cormack bowed to her again. "Do not fret. Peter is a far more spirited dancer than I. Goodnight, princess."

Her face darkened at the veiled rejection. Her smile slipped back into place. "Goodnight, my prince."

Cormack turned and exited the Great Hall. King Dominic was too far-gone with ale to notice, and the party was becoming boisterous. He kept his gate slow and even until he reached the stairs. Once out of sight, Cormack rushed up them, his mind frantic that Asrai had fainted, or worse, been discovered. He burst into the bedroom and saw the neat platter of cold sea turtle steaks, sitting untouched. The candles had been lit. His ears pricked at water sloshing in the bathroom. He knocked on the door.

"Asrai, it's me! I'm here!" His voice rushed out with unabashed excitement.

The lock clicked. He opened the door and saw the gleam of Asrai's comb in the darkness. "You have returned!" She clutched her comb to her chest. Her face broke out in a smile.

Cormack fumbled with the cupboard door and found the tinder box. Igniting the quick twigs, he lit the large candles around the room. The light flickered and reflected off Asrai's eyes. "Yes! I'm sorry for taking so long." He put the quick twigs away in the cupboard. "I didn't want to arouse suspicion. You must be starving!"

Asrai tilted her head. She gripped her comb to calm her excited breath. "You are here now. That is all that matters."

Cormack grabbed the platter from the table and brought it to her. He settled onto the washing stool again, quite close to the tub. He held the food out to her. "It's sea turtle steak from the banquet."

Asrai stabbed one of the steaks with claws from under her nails, rendered a piece and tasted it. Her face lit up. "This is delicious!"

"Here," he handed her the fork on the plate, "this should make things easier."

Asrai took the fork, stared at it, and then poked the steak with it. "Amazing!"

"You don't have utensils?" Cormack watched her eat, fascinated by her excitement.

She shook her head, her mouth full of food. She wrestled another bite from the steak. Cormack smiled. "I'm glad you're enjoying it. I was worried. I have no idea what mermaids eat."

"Mostly seaweed." Asrai cut another hunk of meat. "Small fish and crabs. Sometimes larger game for special occasions."

Love of the Sea

After consuming two turtle steaks, Asrai set the fork down and slumped in the tub.

"That was wonderful." She looked up at him. "Thank you."

Cormack walked back into the bedroom to set the plate down on the table. When he returned to Asrai's side, her eyes were heavy, her body satiated by the meal. "To be you and know the hidden wonders of the sea," Cormack whispered as Asrai's breathing slowed, her limbs relaxing. "How I wish for such a life."

Asrai kept her eyes closed, but muttered at him. "The sea is vast, my sailor. Much has gone unseen."

He felt the excitement bubbling up, despite Asrai's despondent lounging. "To explore the far corners of the sea has always been a fancy of mine."

Asrai nodded, her lashes curled on her cheeks as she struggled to stay awake. "Yes, it has been foretold, my sailor. Though you and I are mer and man, at one time our people were one and the same, swimming together in tide."

"I have heard that somewhere before," Cormack ran his hand through his hair, his brow furrowed. "Asrai, what do you mean 'one people swimming together'?"

The slow rise and fall of her chest made her scales shimmer. Cormack sighed when he realized she was asleep. Asrai nestled her head on the side of the tub. Cormack stood, stretching his back. He stepped on the toes of his boots to prevent them from clicking on the floor.

"Goodnight, my lady." He blew out the candles, save one, and closed the door.

The room seemed large and empty. He sat down in one of the wooden chairs, the quiet calm unwinding him for the first time that evening. The stone walls blocked the music and sounds of revelry from the banquet. The silence was soothing. He could hear the rhythmic beating of the surf from his window.

Chapter Five

The polite, but sturdy rapping on his door jolted Cormack from his dreams. They had been strange: a desert creeping over the ocean, and hundreds of carts bearing gold heading toward the castle. He rubbed his eyes and ran a hand through his hair, willing the dream to leave him.

"Enn-ter." Cormack yawned.

The door creaked open, and a maid appeared, bearing a tray of bread, cold cuts of boar, and an apple. She left him a flagon of ale and a linen cloth bundle tied with twine.

"What's all this?" Cormack stretched and slipped out of bed. His bare feet met the rug, chilled from the stone floor. He shivered.

She bobbed a smooth curtsy, unlike the jerking bob the kitchen maids would do as they scurried about. "Pardon, your highness, the princess wishes you to break your fast early this morning. She has an agenda for the day. Your presence is requested in the receiving room once you have eaten and dressed."

She curtsied again. Cormack looked from her to the food. "Will your highness be needing anything else?" Her polite gaze maintained contact with his chest, rather than his face.

He shook his head. "No. Thank you. That is all."

The maid curtsied a third time and closed the door behind her. Cormack untied the twine, and the linen cloth fell open, revealing a small jar of honey, a wooden honey spoon, and Pamela's oat cakes. He smiled and gathered up the tray and flagon. He struggled to knock on the bathroom door.

"Good morning, Lady Asrai." His grin widened when he heard water sloshing.

****

The candle from the night before had burned down to a melted stub. Asrai's eyes were bright. "Good morning, my sailor." Her eyes darted over the tray.

Cormack pulled up the washing stool and settled the tray on his lap.

"I know you have probably never seen one before," he held up the apple, "but how would you like this?"

Asrai stared at the red fruit. "What is it?"

Cormack took the small dagger from his hip and cut a slice for her. "It's called an 'apple.' They grow on trees."

She plucked the moist wedge of fruit and crunched it. Her eyes flashed and a smile spread across her lips. A strange warmth spread through her. She felt as if Poseidon had reached down and spilled a drop into her wellspring of magick. Cormack handed her another slice, which she snatched. The feeling intensified as she ate more. "I shall miss apple when I return," Asrai whispered.

Cormack's hand froze. He looked up at Asrai and licked his lips. He weighed each word, both spoken and not. "You are returning?"

Asrai jolted. *Humans are capricious things.* She turned her eyes downcast. "Everything returns from whence it came eventually, my sailor."

He handed her the last of the apple slices. "Here. I'll bring you more later." She ate these slowly, savouring the tender fruit. The warmth became a strange fire in her chest.

Cormack spread honey over one of the oat cakes and bit into the chewy pastry. He took a swig of ale and spread honey on a second oat cake. He held it out to Asrai. She watched as the excitement was extinguished from Cormack's eyes. She felt a pain in her chest.

Careless! You cannot throw about your words with a human! Take them back! Reassure his heart!

The unspoken words crackled between them. She accepted the oat cake, hardly tasting the sweet honey. They finished their meal in silence. Cormack drained the rest of the ale. He cleared up the mess onto the tray. He looked down at his hands. "The Princess of Caraway is expecting me. Excuse me."

He stood, and Asrai's heart quailed to see him go. "Will you return this evening, my sailor?"

Cormack turned and smiled at her. "Yes, Lady Asrai."

****

The bathroom door clicked. Asrai had set the lock. Cormack gathered his thoughts. He wiped his face with his hand. He recalled her words about returning to the sea. The delicate fantasy that had sprouted in his mind during the banquet withered. *What? Did you really think a mermaid would deign to marry you and live in a bathtub?*

He was unable to linger on these painful thoughts, as the princess was waiting for him to indulge her in some obstinate activity, which he would have to pretend to enjoy. The groom had laid out another outfit on the bed. Cormack dressed, once again rejecting the heavy jewelry for his own simpler selections. He trod down the stone steps toward the receiving hall.

The Princess of Caraway was attended by the two hooded ladies in red. They stood on either side of her chair. Her head was bent over a book. At the sound of Cormack's boots clicking on the stone floor, she looked up and saved her place with a bit of ribbon. "Good morning, my prince." Her voice was wry. "I hope I am not intruding on your duties."

Cormack tilted his head. "Not at all, my lady. It is a pleasure."

He kissed her hand. She stood, her hand atop his. The hooded ladies walked three steps behind them. Cormack's neck prickled. "And what does the princess have planned for today?"

She cocked her head. "Your cousin was most generous to organize a hunt for us. I am certain Quinquetta will enjoy stretching her wings as well."

Cormack suppressed the urge to shudder. The thought of that giant beast running loose made his blood run cold. He plastered on his smile and squeezed the princess' hand. "Shall we head to the stables, then, princess?"

She nodded. "Yes. I expect your cousin has already had the horses tacked for us."

"Peter will be joining us?" He flinched.

Nephara allowed a small smile to curl her lips. "Peter informed me that he knows the best tracks for finding these boars Paradine prizes."

Cormack ignored Nephara's familiarity. "Peter is a skilled huntsman. I am sure you will find your prize today, princess."

They made their way toward the stables. Nephara had them take the long way through the grand halls, rather than through the night run. Cormack felt a knot form in his stomach, tightening as they neared the horses. He took a deep breath to stave off his discomfiture.

"Good morrow!" The stable boy waved. "The mounts are readied, your majesties!"

"Thank you." Cormack took the bridle of his steed, Brontlé. He rarely rode the gelding. The tack was lightweight for hunting, but embellished with gold accents, and the royal crest was pressed into the leather bridle and saddle.

Princess Nephara alighted her horse. It was a slender creature, and appeared fleet of foot. "Are you ready, Raquisa?" She stroked the mane and the horse nickered.

"Good morrow!" Peter approached from the night run. The stable boy held the bridle of Demos, Peter's burly war horse.

Cormack nodded at his cousin, but Nephara greeted him with a cheery lilt in her voice. "Good morrow, Prince Peter! We are eager to begin."

Peter alighted his horse. "We shall ride East toward the forest. From there I know a dell that is excellent for the ambush."

Two more stable boys appeared, leading mounts that were similar to Nephara's horse. Cormack shivered as the hooded ladies mounted their steeds. Large swords were sheathed at their hips. One of the stable boys strapped the hunting spears to the saddles. They pointed skyward, their iron tips gleaming in the early morning light.

The stable boy shook as he led the panya out toward them. It had a gold muzzle ring strapped over its gruesome beak, but the sharp eyes bore into the boy, sizing him up. Nephara whistled, and the stable boy let go of the thin gold chain as the mighty bird spread its wings and alighted onto the back of the princess' horse. She threaded the chain through a gold hoop on the left side of her saddle. Two guards on horseback emerged from where the soldiers' steeds were kept. They bowed their heads and waited for orders.

"E-yah!" Peter bellowed, signaling the horses.

Nephara crooned to her horse, and soon they were cantering toward the trees. Cormack could feel the distance between him and the sea widening. He pushed aside the gnawing annoyance and focused on Peter's horse. The beast was a white Andalusian, tall and fierce, trained to rear and smash shields. Cormack's horse was a gentle Bay, the rust-coloured coat gleaming against the crow's wing mane and tail.

Though Nephara's horse was wearing tack that included gold embellishments and red ribbons, it did not lack speed. Cormack found the princess quite close, the nose of her horse just behind the shoulder of his. He could feel the awful bird staring at him. The two hooded ladies rode their grey mounts off to the side. The two guards flanked wide, allowing the party ample room while keeping watch.

Peter held up his fist, signaling for them to slow their horses. The forest was thinning out, allowing the sunlight to filter in. The deer track opened into a shallow basin of grassy scrub. They reined up their horses as Peter pulled out his spyglass. Unlike Cormack's gold spyglass for charting the stars at sea, Peter's was bound in leather so it would not reflect light and give away his position during the hunt.

He put it away and motioned three fingers for them to follow him round the south bend. The horses' ears swiveled as the sounds of the forest came into focus: birds calling, frogs chirping, and boars snuffling. The forest shaded them from the climbing sun, keeping them cool in the early afternoon light, but Cormack was growing restless. He fidgeted in his saddle. The leather creaked as he did so. It sounded like a cacophony in the crackling silence. Peter bristled at the noise.

A breeze ruffled the tree canopy, sending the smell of the sea rushing into the forest. Cormack stifled a sigh as Asrai bubbled into his thoughts. The pleasant warmth was ripped away as he remembered their morning tat. His morose brooding sank deeper as irritation buzzed in his mind. Peter raised his hand again, this time the fingers up. Cormack grabbed his spear, as did Peter. Nephara hooked her finger into the muzzle ring and slipped it off. Peter swung his arm perpendicular, eliciting the charge.

"Hah!" Peter bellowed, signaling the horses.

Squeals erupted from the brush as the horses closed in on the boars. Quinquetta sprung from the back of the saddle, her great wings flaring. Nephara whooped as a spray of blood exploded from one of the downed boars. Quinquetta snapped its neck with her powerful talons, ending the burbling screams. The hooded ladies had not pursued the boar, keeping close to Nephara instead.

Demos galloped alongside a group of fleeing boars until she had wheedled one into the open. It had large, cracked tusks. The boar tried to swipe at Demos' legs, but the horse knew their tricks and danced about, allowing Peter striking range.

"Hee-yah!" Peter screamed as he thrust the spear clean through the boar's skull. The spear remained upright in the dead creature as Peter turned Demos about to slow down.

Cormack had followed the charge toward the boars, his hand ready on the spear. As Brontlé brought him into striking range, Cormack saw the little piglets rushing at the boar's side. His hand wavered, and he missed his shot. He circled about with Peter, the horses chuffing as they slowed.

They said nothing; Peter simply smirked at him. Princess Nephara reigned up next to them. Quinquetta squawked and flapped her wings, standing over her bloody prize. The hooded ladies kept their distance. Their horses flicked their ears and snorted. The guards reigned up, close to the party. They kept their gaze off in the distance, not wanting to cause further offense to their crown prince.

"We have plenty to present this evening." Peter's smile widened.

Cormack nodded, refusing to meet his cousin's gaze. The boys hopped down from their horses. Nephara's boar was a youth, only half grown, but Peter's was a bull in its prime, easily four hundred pounds. They unpacked the leather sleigh from Peter's saddlebags, strapping it to the back of Demos. Peter wrenched the spear from the boar. It made a great sucking noise as blood burbled from the wound. They dragged the bleeding corpse onto the sleigh, tying down the neck and forelimbs with the cords attached to the main sling. Their clothes were soiled with earth and blood. Cormack did his best to wipe his hands clean on his breeches.

Nephara trilled, the whistle warbling, and silenced Quinquetta. The great bird alighted onto her saddle, and Nephara replaced the gold ring and chain muzzle. Her kill was trussed up the same way. The sleigh was strapped to Brontlé as Nephara's horse was already overburdened.

"Shall we?" Peter grinned as he wiped his brow with the back of his hand, smearing blood across his face.

Love of the Sea

Cormack fought the urge to sneer back. They both led their horses on foot, the boars dragging behind. Nephara rode between them. The hooded ladies rode at the sides, the guards at the rear.

"It is a joy to supply our feasts with such honourable game," Peter chatted.

Nephara kept her gaze on the trail, but her clear voice rang true. "You feed your court often?"

Peter kicked aside a rogue stone in the path. "Yes, princess. Such a kill as this will feed the feast, the servants, and even the guards. Though, the soldiers must fend for themselves. Training and such."

"The servants typically take part in the hunt in Caraway." Nephara bowed her head as they passed a low branch. "The hunt is enjoyed by all."

"The servants do not join us in the hunt, as they have their tasks to fulfill," Peter chatted. "However, the soldiers are free to hunt on the royal grounds any time they wish. It is their privilege as they are the strength of Paradine."

Nephara nodded. "Yes, our soldiers also receive privileges in Caraway. It is an honour for our men and women to fight for their homeland."

Cormack glared at their backs. He shuddered as Quinquetta swiveled her head. The bright yellow eyes stabbed through him.

A group of kitchen hands were waiting when the trio arrived. Strong hands dragged away the boars for dressing. The stable boys led the horses away for a good wet down and brushing. The dim, hapless boy of the bunch was stuck with corralling Quinquetta back into the stall that housed her cage. Nephara frowned as the panya threw a tantrum.

"It is only for a little while," she crooned to the squawking bird. "Please do be good, for me?" A final squawk and flap of the wings was Quinquetta's last protest. The stable boy let the air rush out of his lungs as he led the soothed beast away.

Cormack tore his gaze away from the scene and laid his eyes upon Nephara. "I was informed that your highness has a full itinerary for the day. What else do you have planned for us, princess?"

He was hoping that the hunt would tire her, but it had invigourated her. Her eyes sparkled as she rolled them up at him. "A bit of refreshment is in order." Nephara flashed a coy smile. "It would not do for a princess to smell of the stables all day."

Peter shook his head. "Ah! But it is the musk of the hunt! I wear it proudly, princess."

Cormack rolled his eyes at his cousin. "Yes, well I could use a bit of refreshment myself." His thoughts returned to Asrai. He fidgeted his hands as his stomach prickled. His tat with Asrai was fresh in his mind once more, and it stung.

Nephara patted Cormack's hands to still them. "I believe our next activity will be more suited to you, my prince. I will meet you by the grand staircase." She softened her eyes with a gentle smile. "Do not delay."

****

The water mirror shimmered as Asrai's hands tightened on her comb. The glow crackled. Her glare bore into the reflection of the hunt. She watched as Cormack dawdled and spoke to the princess. She did not dare allow her magick to reveal their words. Even without sound, the scene unfolding before her was unbearable.

How can this be? I was so careful to entice him with the sea, and yet this trollop is making him nothing but tide betwixt my fingers!

Asrai dashed the water mirror, not wanting to see anymore. She combed her hair, soothing her frantic thoughts. The sea hag had warned her that man was an elusive creature to snare. The magick pulsed through her veins, overflowing from the apples Cormack had fed her. Asrai's grip on her comb tightened.

Magick would make my sailor see that I am the mate his heart needs. Perhaps Illyana is mistaken.

She summoned the water mirror again, this time revealing the reef where the sea hag was lounging. The sea hag flinched when she noticed the water mirror, a small crab slipping from her claws.

"What is it, my child?" Her eyes were bright with worry. "Are you all right? Did the humans capture you?"

Asrai shook her head. "I am fine, Illyana. My sailor prince brought me to his castle, and I am still undiscovered. He is enamoured with me, but there is another mate presented before him."

The sea hag shook her head. "I warned you there would be many trials. A human is not easily won."

"Yes, I remember." Asrai fiddled with her comb. "Being near him has made my wellspring grow even stronger. Perhaps it is strong enough to *push* my sailor in the right direction—"

"No!" The sea hag's eyes flashed as she bared her fangs. "You *must not* use magick! His love must be true to you alone. If you push his heart, the spell will not work!"

Asrai glared at the sea hag. "What difference does it make? He *will* grow to love me! I simply *must* prevent this other mate from getting in the way!"

The sea hag pulled out her comb, a spell of calm pushing through water mirror, blanketing Asrai in soothing magick. Her impatience dulled to a low buzz at the back of her mind. She sighed, allowing her arm to drop, splashing water onto the floor.

"I warned you, this *will* be difficult." The sea hag held the spell of calm. "Remember, you are the daughter of the great Tuande and

Love of the Sea

Seelacante. You have more beauty and charm than any silly human to attract this *sailor prince* of yours. You shouldn't need the crutch of magick to win his heart."

Asrai nodded, her tantrum cooled. "Yes, Illyana. I understand."

"Good." The sea hag allowed the spell to dissipate. "Do not waste your magick on such trivial nonsense again."

The water mirror disappeared back to clear water. Asrai ran her comb through her hair, her thoughts swirling.

I must make myself more pleasing than this silly princess. I will show my sailor how 'suitable' I can be.

Asrai swirled her comb in the water again, the water mirror shimmering at its surface. Her eyes drank in Princess Nephara as she walked beside Cormack, studying her gestures and her etiquette. She tamped down the hot jealousy as Nephara touched Cormack's shoulder, her eyes glittering.

He is my sailor prince. You shall not have him.

Her body thrummed, almost a growl as she continued to watch, her eyes sharp as she learned what it was to be a human princess, a suitable bride.

****

Cormack ran through the night run toward the stairs. His steps were heavy as his mind whirred to find a suitable apology. He had been so rude to Asrai, he wondered if she would even deign to unlock the door.

How does one apologize to an offended lady, and truly mean it? He shook his head. *I have offended a mermaid of all ladies! What am I going to do?*

A second set of footsteps startled him. Cormack whirled about, coming face to face with Peter. He relaxed his arm, dropping his hand from the hilt of his dagger at his hip.

"So tense in your own home?" Peter raised an eyebrow.

"You of all people should understand the feeling of *unease* in your own home," Cormack snapped.

Peter balked at the cutting remark. "What on earth is bothering you, Cousin?"

Cormack ran his hand through his hair, his agitation growing. "I'm simply in a hurry. You startled me."

"In a hurry? *You?*" Peter snorted. "It's not like you to be so accommodating to our *special* guests."

"Yes, well, it will keep Father happy." Cormack shrugged. He edged up another one of the stairs. The air crackled between them. Peter joined Cormack on the lower stairs. He was a head taller than Cormack, which made them at eye level now.

"Come now, Cousin. You seem just as bored with this one as you do with all the others. And yet, you refuse to send her packing. Are you finally falling in love?" Peter's glare had a hardness that cut into Cormack. A challenge.

Cormack went up another step. "Don't be ridiculous. I'm merely being polite. Just as always."

Peter twisted his face into a scowl. "Polite? You didn't seem the least bit worried about being *polite* when the Princess of Denaria was here dancing with her maids, waiting for you all night while you played on that revolting boat!"

"And what of you?" Cormack took a step back down toward Peter. "*You* never cared for these princesses. You were equally pleased to torment them with empty promises of my imminent return. *You* who has always been content to play in the servants' 'gardens' as you fancied! What interests you now?"

The hall echoed with their bickering. Someone cleared their throat, startling the two. They flinched, turning to see the princess in a fresh gown, the two hooded ladies behind her. Peter was quick to bow.

"Apologies, princess!" Peter fidgeted. "We were, that is—"

Cormack bowed, his hands shaking. "Yes, my apologies, princess."

Nephara smiled up at them, tickled by their discomfiture. She held out her hand.

"I was hoping to visit the gardens next. That is, if you are ready, my prince."

Peter glared at Cormack, then hurried down the stairs. He snuck another glance at Nephara, locking his gaze with hers, before bowing again and striding toward the main hall.

"Yes, though I did not have time for much refreshment, I am afraid." Cormack descended the stairs and nodded to her. He offered his hand, which she then placed hers upon. Cormack let her lead him down the hallway toward the gardens. His stomach churned as he thought of Asrai, still alone and bearing his cold departure.

"We do not have such elabourate gardens in Caraway. I was hoping my prince would show me the flowers of your kingdom."

Cormack hid his annoyance. He plastered a smile on his face. "My lady, I am also lacking in knowledge of our flowers and trees. Perhaps I can entreat our head gardener to give us a tour, and he can educate the both of us."

Chapter Six

They wandered into the apple orchard and found the head gardener grafting tiny seedlings onto larger saplings. He jumped when Cormack cleared his throat. Upon seeing the royal pair, he bowed his head, then returned to his work.

"Good morrow to your highnesses. What can I assist you with this fine morning?"

Cormack cringed. He hated taking servants away from their work for trifling things. He swallowed his irritation and tilted his head at the princess. "Her highness, Princess Nephara, and I, would like to see what projects you have been working on."

The old gardener's face lit up. He turned and waved them over. "Please, come closer so you can see."

The three of them were quite close. The princess fought not to wrinkle her nose at the smell of sweat and earth. He pointed a rough knobby finger at the place where he was grafting the plants together.

"You see, we have four different varieties of apples in our orchard: snow apples from Altruse, blush apples from Denaria, hardy green apples from Teem, and our very own ruby apples. But, I wanted to see if I could use grafting to grow an apple tree that would yield fruit with the sweetness of ruby apples with the strength of snow apples. If it is successful, we will be able to have sweet summer apples even in winter!"

Nephara regarded the tiny plants sitting in earthenware pots. "How long will they take to bear fruit?"

The gardener swept his hand over the row of trees that stood next to them. "If the grafting is successful, it would take anywhere from five to six years, possibly eight if they favour the snow apple."

The princess tilted her head toward the canopy of pale apple blossoms. "That is a long time to see if your project is successful." She looked back to the gardener. "You must be blessed with an abundance of patience."

The gardener laughed. "Aye, your highness. A garden such as this does not flourish in a day. It takes years, even decades, of careful planting and experimenting. And even then, there are always improvements to be made."

He led them to a row of trees that appeared stunted compared to the rest. Their dark green leaves did not yet bear flowers. "These were an experiment of mine. They did not yield the desired results, but they are useful all the same. The horses especially seem to like them."

Nephara raked her gaze over the tiny trees. "What is the matter with them?"

"They bear fruit that is too hard and knobby for humans, your highness. But horses have good strong teeth."

She nodded. Cormack listened with one ear as the gardener led them through the orchard, talking about the differences in the apple trees. Cormack's thoughts drifted back to Asrai. She had been enchanted by the apple he had given her. He swallowed the chuckle in his throat at the idea of her excitement hearing the doddering old gardener go on about his trees. He looked down at Nephara. Her bright eyes seemed glazed over. She gave polite nods and smiles when prompted, but her face did not glow as Asrai's had.

The gardener plucked an apple from one of the ruby trees. He wiped it clean with a handkerchief. He offered it to the princess. "They say if two lovers share an apple, their hearts will be bonded in this life and the next." He smiled at them. "At the very least, I think your highness will enjoy the sweet flavour."

Nephara handed the apple to Cormack. He took out his small dagger, as he had earlier that morning. He cut a slice and offered it to her. "Here you are, princess." She accepted it. Her red nails shone in the afternoon sun. It reminded Cormack of Asrai's scales. He cut a slice for himself.

Nephara smiled as she chewed the apple. "Thank you, my prince. That was refreshing." When Cormack offered her a second slice, she declined. He fought to keep his smile in place, eating the apple on his own.

"I have a new planting of blue ranunculus if your highnesses are interested."

Cormack noticed how the gardener's body was stiff. Before he could respond, Nephara rolled her pretty eyes to meet his. "I think that would be lovely. Don't you think so, my prince?"

He wiped his dagger before replacing it on his hip. He offered the princess his hand once more. "Yes, princess."

She placed her hand atop his, and they followed the gardener through the orchard toward a maze of green hedges. A servant prised the blooms from their pots with a trowel and buried the soil and roots in the rows of holes waiting for flowers. The gardener picked one of the potted plants up and touched his fingertip to the bright blue petals.

"This is a rare blue ranunculus all the way from Kern. It's said that the Faerie Queen Deirdre grew them herself, and that a human stole them from the Faerie Realm."

The rich colour reminded Cormack of a beautiful afternoon at sea, the water deep and blue as sapphires. He turned to Nephara, wishing she was Asrai on his arm instead. His smile was genuine. "Do you like them?"

Her polite smile widened. "Yes, my prince. I have never seen such flowers before."

Cormack regarded the flower again, the desire gnawing his heart. He touched the velvet petals. "Would there be an extra bloom I could keep in my room?"

The gardener narrowed his eyes at the strange request, then smiled. "Of course, your highness. There are always extra. I'll have one sent up for you."

"Thank you." Cormack removed his hand. He looked down at the princess again. "What would you like to see next?"

Nephara looked at the sun. "The morning has left us." She looked back at the men. "I would much enjoy a light meal, if my prince would indulge me."

Cormack bobbed his head. "Of course, princess." He gave a warm smile to the gardener. "Thank you, sir, for sharing your treasures with us."

The gardener bowed, relief evident in his wide smile. "It was a pleasure and an honour, your highnesses. Please enjoy your day."

****

Cormack led them back toward the castle. He could hear the soldiers running their drills in the courtyard. A seagull's cry warbled on the wind. Their shoes clicked on the stone floor as the entered the receiving hall again. Cormack was startled when he heard footsteps behind them, then remembered the hooded ladies. He fought the urge to shudder.

"I was not expecting Paradine to have such leisure." Nephara did not look at Cormack as she spoke. "With your armies busy at war it's hard to imagine your kingdom has the time to cultivate such incredible gardens."

"My father believes that, while war is crucial to keeping a kingdom strong, appearances are equally important to maintain diplomacy and trade relations." Cormack allowed his gaze to wander as they walked toward the smaller dining hall, opposite the Great Hall. There was no need to sup in such a yawning expanse by themselves.

The princess noted the smaller room, a hint of disappointment in her eyes at the simple wooden tables and benches. Apart from the banquets, most of the common meals were had in the dining hall. The benches were worn smooth and the tables pock-marked from forks and knives.

Quick as a whisper, the maidens in the gossamer red gowns seated themselves at the table behind them. The hooded ladies joined them, allowing Nephara and Cormack the opportunity to sit together, alone. The maids and servers appeared from the kitchens, bearing wooden platters and pitchers of wine. A flagon of ale was set at Cormack's elbow. There were slices of herb-crusted toast, bowls of mussels in a red soup, and cutlets of squab. The rich smell of rosemary and roasted tomatoes filled the air as portions were served.

Cormack waited for the princess to eat her first bite. He himself was a bit peckish, as breakfast had been hours ago. He wondered at her manners. She had to be ravenous, and yet she did not hurry in her reach for platters and bowls. Her hands did not shake, nor did her eyes betray excitement.

"I was curious to see what the people of Paradine sup on." She sipped the thick red soup. "Such a lavish meal. But then, shellfish is a rarity for me."

He dipped a slice of toast into his soup, enjoying the sharp rosemary and rich butter against the acidic tomatoes. "What do the people of Caraway sup on, princess?"

She swallowed and dabbed her ruby red lips with a linen. "We make a bread that is flat, roasted in a bed of coals. We often use this as a vehicle to eat grains and meats. It is common fare, but it fills the belly and warms the soul."

Cormack nodded. He was not expecting the princess to be so knowledgeable of peasant life. He scooped another mouthful of bread and soup. "I enjoy the common sailors here in Paradine." Cormack kept his gaze on the food. "They have taught me much."

A few more bites were shared in silence. Then Nephara took a sip of wine and looked at Cormack. "I am uncertain of the practices of other kingdoms, but in Caraway it is of the utmost for a ruler and his people to be of the same heart. One must learn what is in the hearts of the people to rule them."

Cormack took a few more careful bites. This princess was surprising. Even so, his thoughts still carried him to his chambers with Asrai. He speared a mussel and chewed it, contemplating his next move. An icy thought stabbed his heart. He remembered Asrai's words about returning to the sea. He looked up at Nephara.

"Won't you miss your people, princess?"

Her eyes widened as her fork clanked against her bowl. Her ladies whipped their heads to face her. "My prince, whatever do you mean?" Her voice shook as she fought to regain her composure.

Cormack stabbed another mussel. "Forgive me, princess. I only meant, one day when you marry, would you not miss your people and the traditions of your kingdom?"

Love of the Sea

Nephara looked down at her food. Cormack balked when he saw her lip quiver. She bit it, then looked at him again. Her eyes blazed, her anger from embarrassment palpable. It sent shivers down Cormack's spine. "Forgive me, my prince." Her voice was taut. "I suddenly feel unwell."

Nephara stood, and Cormack stood as well. He froze, bewildered as the ladies made a train behind the princess. She strode off, her pace quick. The food sat, forgotten. When the last red gown swished out of the room, Cormack slumped onto the bench. His hunger had fled. One of the maids took a tentative step toward the table.

Cormack nodded. She approached and began clearing the platters. "Please take the food to my chambers. I will sup there."

The maid bobbed a curtsy. "Of course, your highness."

His body was heavy with dread. King Dominic would upbraid him with the ferocity of a foxhound if he did not make amends. Cormack followed the hall back toward the gardens. He was unsure of where else the princess might have gone. The hall was empty, save for a few servants scurrying about. He was about to turn toward the gate when he heard soft murmuring. Cormack turned the opposite way, toward the East staircase that led to the observatory tower. He kept his step light, putting weight on the toes of his boots to avoid clicking. The voices became clearer. He looked up and saw the ladies sitting on the staircase. They flinched when they spotted him. One of the hooded ladies rushed to her feet.

Cormack was startled by how fleet she was, and without a sound. His eyes narrowed. "What's the matter?"

The hooded lady kept her gaze on his chest. "My lady, she is unwell, please—"

Cormack pushed past her. "If the princess is unwell, then I should think a staircase is hardly the place for her to rest." Rage coursed through his mind when he saw Nephara wrapped in Peter's arms, her head resting on his shoulder. He felt his anger drain into the floor when he heard Nephara crying.

"It...is...cus-cus-customary!" She hiccupped into his shoulder. "In-n-sulting a marriage proposal! Di-disgrace! I shall...shall...loo-lose my h-head!"

Peter's arms tightened, causing Nephara to gasp. His eyes were closed tight, his face pained. "I will not allow it to happen," he whispered in her ear.

Cormack was frozen to the spot. Cold horror clenched his heart as the words echoed in his mind. *I shall lose my head!* Such a punishment had never occurred to Cormack. He found he could not swallow, his throat dry. *She would die if she were to choose Peter over me?* He recalled the princess of Teem who was said to be in love with one of her royal guards.

He wondered if she had met a similar fate. Peter opened his eyes, and spotted Cormack. He flinched. The princess bristled at his presence, then jumped, her eyes wide in terror.

"My prince!" Her eyes darted about, her mouth working to form a response. "I-I did not...I was heading to my chambers and—"

Cormack looked from her to Peter. His mind freed his body. He took a deep breath through his nose, and took Nephara's hand, making her freeze and Peter stiffen. "Princess, you do not have to explain to me." He kissed her hand, and then released her. "I left you dancing with my cousin at the banquet. I am not entirely surprised."

She gaped at him. Her mouth fought to splutter another excuse, but her body sent her into a fit of shivering. Peter tightened his embrace. Cormack nodded to her. "Do not worry, princess. I understand."

"My dear princess, please do not tremble." Peter's voice was silk. It made Cormack sick. "No harm shall come to you."

Cormack turned heel as Peter placed a kiss just above the ruby set at Nephara's hairline. He did not want to see anymore. A strange relief washed over him. *Well, at least that is one princess I will not have to send away in tears.*

"My prince! Please!" she called after him.

Cormack quickened his pace, ignoring her. Then he heard Peter's voice. It cut through him like a dagger to the back. "Leave him to his little boat. I am your prince now."

Chapter Seven

Cormack stormed up the stairs, startling a maid carrying water. He wrinkled his nose when he arrived in his room and saw the dishes covered with linens. He flopped into one of the chairs and put his fingers to his forehead, his mind spinning.

Peter is up to something. He never gives one wit for the silly princesses Father parades about. What is it? What is he plotting?

Nephara's words rang through his mind again. *I shall lose my head!* He pushed them away, shaking his head. *Even so, Peter never moved to protect one of them before. Why now?*

A splash jerked Cormack back from his thoughts. He regarded the food again. "Asrai!" He jumped from his chair and knocked on the door, his fist colliding with the wood harder than he intended. The lock clicked and the door flew open, shocking him into stilling his hand midair.

****

Asrai drew herself up in the tub and began running her comb through her hair. "My sailor, there is no need to rush. I'm right where you left me."

Cormack's face scrunched in confusion. "What? Oh, I was not in a hurry. I just—"

"Come now, my sailor." Asrai tilted her head to the washing stool. "You seem exhausted."

He nodded, his motions stiff as he sat down. Asrai leaned toward him, lowering her lashes as she had seen Nephara perform. "It has been a long and dreary afternoon without you. Won't you tell me of your adventures today?"

Cormack wrinkled his nose. "Asrai, what is wrong with you? Why are you talking like that?"

Asrai flinched, then flicked her tail and giggled. "I'm certain I don't understand, my sailor. I simply wish to listen and learn of your cares."

"Asrai, you sound *odd*." Cormack scanned her face, his eyes narrowing.

Annoyance churned in Asrai's chest as her mind flipped through all the vapid nonsense Nephara oft employed to keep the humans around her smiling. She flicked her wrist the way Nephara did while arching her neck. A graceful, simpering gesture. Her eyes locked onto Cormack, her gaze soft and half-lidded. "I simply wish to hear more about you, my sailor."

Cormack edged away from her. "What are you talking about?"

Asrai felt her nervous energy building as Cormack continued to pull away. She could feel his uncertainty growing, walling off his heart. She took a deep breath. *What does he love talking about? To speak of the sea now would alarm him.* Her heart leapt as a thought struck her, the smile slipping back into place.

She touched her fingers to the back of his hand, the featherlight stroke the same Nephara employed while whispering to Peter. "I know you go out among your people and enjoy their company. Perhaps if—"

"Stop it!" Cormack snapped and wrenched his hand away. His body shivered, his face puckered with disgust. He gathered his wits and rubbed his face with his hand. "I'm sorry, my lady. I'm just out of sorts."

Asrai watched as his shoulders slumped. His forlorn gaze dulled her anger, replacing it with desire. She held her comb tight, her body in agony as she fought not to reach out and touch him.

You must take care. Humans are fragile, their empathy confuses their true feelings and weakens their resolve. It was like netting a delicate jellyfish. She needed to be firm, but keep the net slack so as not to crush her prey. Asrai twirled her comb, unsure of what to say.

"I feel as if the world has been turned upside down." Cormack shook his head.

Asrai leaned closer to him, her body pressed against the side of the tub. "I'm sure things are not as strange as they may seem. Fate unfolds as it will."

He looked up at her. His eyes were dark and tired. "I am sorry for today. You must think poorly of me."

"My sailor, whatever is the matter?" Asrai pushed down the panic bubbling up her throat. "What is there to apologise for?"

Cormack sighed. "Asrai, please stop pretending. I know that I offended you by leaving abruptly, and leaving you on your own for the better part of the day. Hiding your feelings only makes it worse."

She fidgeted with her comb, her mind screaming as she fought to maintain her composure. Her scales glimmered.

"I despise the flattery and false words of the princesses Father sends me." Cormack looked away toward the floor. "Please do not suppose yourself to be one of them. I'm fond of your honesty."

Asrai flinched. All her plans of being "suitable" flew to the wind. The fear of uncertainty strangled her senses, and the words tumbled from her lips. "You say that, and yet you continue to seek the company of another!"

Cormack snapped his head up, his eyes wide. "Only because I must, my lady. I don't enjoy it."

"But you do it all the same!" Asrai glared at him, her scales flashing.

Cormack took a deep breath and stood. "I'm certain your dinner has grown cold. I shall fetch you something suitable."

Asrai balked. She longed to stuff her angry words back down her throat. "My sailor, that is not necessary, please—"

He took her hand and kissed it, his lips warm on her cold skin. "Please don't fret. I'll be back in a moment. I promise."

She stared after him as he hurried off again. Doubt crept over her shivering skin as she flicked her comb, setting the lock.

****

Rumours were rampant amoung the servants from his frantic running about, raising concern that the Princess of Caraway had done something to agitate him. Cormack did not have to go far to find one of the servants. He accosted a maid leaving the king's chambers. Her eyes were wide when Cormack bounced on his heels as he called out to her.

"Miss! My apologies, miss!"

She whirled around and bobbed a quick curtsy. "Your highness! You gave me a fright!"

He shook his head. "My apologies, would you be able to bring me some supper? Two portions worth, if you please?"

"Y-yes, your highness." She gave him a puzzled look, but curtsied again and headed to fulfill his request.

Cormack put his hand on his door and found that all the excited energy had deserted him. He took a deep breath and quieted his whirring mind. As he stepped into his bedroom, a booming voice scared him nearly out of his skin.

"Cormack! What on earth is the matter with you?" King Dominic shouted.

He jerked his head and saw his father standing in the hallway. "Father! I thought you were out hunting!"

"Bah!" King Dominic waved his hand, his eyes locked on Cormack. "What are you doing running all about? The princess had an agenda for the day! What have you done to spoil it?"

Cormack groaned and ran his hand through his hair. "Father, please! Not this again."

The king followed Cormack into the bedroom. King Dominic sank onto the bed and wrung a hand over his face, a mirror gesture of his son. "My boy, Cormack, how you exhaust me." He placed his hands on his thighs and leaned heavily on them. "We're running out of options. How could you turn your back on this one? She is of good breeding, a wonderful family line. Her country is a mighty warrior people, and she even loves the hunt! What more do you need in a woman?"

"That is the sort of woman *you* would like, Father." Cormack shook his head.

King Dominic looked up at his son in disgust. "The only woman I have ever seen you take interest in is the head cook!" He groaned.

"Father, enough!" Cormack grimaced at the thought.

"Fortunately, I do know Denaria has captured an Eastern duchy, and is offering the prettiest of the lasses as tribute to us." The king lifted his chin. Cormack laughed. King Dominic looked sharply at him. Cormack retreated to the wall, leaning against it for support.

"Boy, have you finally gone mad?" King Dominic gaped at his son. "Raving mad!"

"No! No, Father!" He took deep breaths to calm himself. He shook his head. The thought of seeing another princess filled him with such desperation he felt as if he were drowning. "But any more of your princesses Father and I might."

The king shifted and stared at his son. "Tell me, what is it that's wrong with this one?"

Cormack shrugged, pressing down the strange anger that was coiling up again. "She is already spoken for."

"What?" King Dominic spluttered. "Some tryst at home? Well! We'll straighten that out and—"

"Peter." Cormack locked eyes with his father.

King Dominic fell silent. "Peter? *Peter?*"

Cormack nodded. "Yes, Father."

The silence crackled between them. King Dominic stood, shaking his head. "Oh no, no. No!"

"Please, Father." Cormack put his hand on the king's shoulder. "It's my fault. I let her dance with him last night."

"No, this will never do," the king muttered under his breath. "We shall send her away! Send her away in disgrace!"

"Father!"

Cormack's sharp voice snapped King Dominic back to attention. The horror bubbled again as Cormack remembered how Nephara had trembled like a leaf in autumn, proud face shining with tears. His mind whirred. He knew he could not reveal what Nephara had said; such a thing would put a strain on their alliance with Caraway. King Dominic was known to crush kingdoms with policies that he saw as barbaric and unjust. That would only seal Nephara's fate.

"And what good would that do? Sending our princess ally home in disgrace?" Cormack shook his head. "It chills me to wonder at what exactly Peter is plotting, but the princess seems endeared to him."

He winced at the mental image of Nephara in Peter's arms again. He pushed down his annoyance. "You have always given me the right to choose. Now, I want to give her that right, Father."

King Dominic opened his mouth, then closed it again, his eyes wide. He sighed and shook his head. "Your heart is too big, my boy. Far, far too big."

A knock sounded, startling them both. Cormack opened the door, allowing the maid to come in. She curtsied deep to the king, holding the tray. She unpacked it, linens covering platters of prawns, a wooden board of bread and a wedge of fresh ewe's milk cheese. There was a wooden bowl full of apples, and a fresh flagon of ale and a pitcher of water. She cleared away the old dishes and linens, then bowed to Cormack.

"Will you be needing anything else, your highness?"

He shook his head. "No. Thank you, that is all."

She curtsied deep to the king again, then a shallow curtsy to Cormack, before leaving the room. King Dominic looked from the food to Cormack. The lines on his face seemed deeper than before. Cormack had never thought of his father as old, but now the king certainly looked it.

"Son, please," the king put his hand on Cormack's shoulder, "please just try."

Cormack patted his father on the shoulder again. "I will, Father."

The king followed the maid, his mind heavy with worry. His shuffling slow steps echoed off the stone floor and walls. Cormack closed the door and leaned against it.

****

Asrai fidgeted in the tub. Her stomach rumbled. She did her best to ignore it. Cormack would be back soon; he had promised. Her mind drifted over the past two days she had spent in this strange stone palace. Her heart clenched remembering her confidence against the sea hag. What had seemed like a careful plan was now clearly a fool's errand.

What have I done? The sea hag had warned me, but I listened not! And now here I am, drying out in a pathetic excuse for a tidepool!

She ran her comb through her hair, the gold glowing with magick as she soothed herself. The idea of her sailor prince attending some human princess made her blood boil. The possibility of him becoming enchanted by some 'Princess of Caraway' made her mind frantic.

I have been patient for long enough! The magick may be stronger when the heart is won fair and true, but time is running out and I may not have a choice.

The door opened again. Cormack was bearing a new tray of food. She bolted upright at the smell, the water sloshing onto the floor. Cormack sat with all his weight onto the washing stool. "Forgive me, my lady mermaid. It has been a long day."

She regained her composure. She knew his heart lay on a spider's silk, what with this 'Princess of Caraway' mucking things up. She toyed with her comb; the gold had a faint glow. "Yes, it has been rather long. But all that has drifted away now, my sailor."

Cormack brightened. He held up the bowl of plush apples. Asrai's eyes sparkled. "The kitchen must have seen what was in our hearts." He chuckled. "There are plenty here for you."

Asrai accepted one slice after another, her hands eager. She crunched the first three quick, but savoured the rest with more care. The strange warmth built in her again with each slice. After eating two whole apples she could feel magick crackling through her.

"My sailor," she licked the apple juice from her fingers, "are these *apples* considered sacred by your people?"

His eyebrows raised. "Sacred? I don't know about that. Some believe that apples were the original fruit of the gods, stolen from their golden orchards by a traveling hero. Others believe that if you share an apple with," his face grew warm, "with someone you have feelings for, that your love will last forever."

Asrai felt a thrill rush through her as Cormack darted his eyes away. He busied himself with peeling the shells on the prawns. She grinned at him, revealing her fangs.

"And we are sharing apples together, aren't we?" she teased.

Cormack nodded, his face reddening as he handed Asrai a large piece of prawn. "Yes, I suppose."

Her eyes flashed as she gobbled up the meaty treats. Her stomach seemed pleased with the familiar food. She licked the butter from her fingers. "I do love prawns." She accepted another piece. "But they are too much trouble to catch."

Cormack felt the thought from the afternoon well up. He tilted his head. "Asrai, will you tell me about your homeland?"

She flinched at the question. Her comment from the morning haunted her. She dropped her gaze to her tail. "Well, my sailor, my memory of it is quite beautiful." She ran her hand over the water. The ripples shimmered and glowed until a tiny vision appeared in place of her reflection. Cormack flinched, startled by the magick.

"My home is the Southwest kingdom known as Sulu. The castle spires are decorated with the most beautiful abalone shells. The sands are smooth and cool. The waters are warm and bless us with favourable migrations of our staples. Though there are storms from time to time our castle is a fortress against the rage of Poseidon."

Cormack watched as the vision shifted from the outer castle to a small room. Inside was another mermaid, her hair and scales a deep purple.

Love of the Sea

"But there was a plot against my family. My father was slain. A pretender sits on the throne." Her voice grew soft and quiet. "The sea hag took me far away to the outer reefs where I would be safe until the day I could take my kingdom back." She wiped away the vision. The ripples obscured the magick until only clear water remained.

Cormack stared at her. "Then, you are a princess?"

Asrai nodded. Her eyes flashed. The comb began to glow. "Yes, my sailor. I am a truly suitable princess. Am I not?"

"I suppose, Asrai." Cormack shifted his gaze. "I'm not entirely certain of what Father means when he blathers on about 'suitable' princesses."

She burned the magick further, deeper into his heart. The comb grew warm in her hands. Cormack's forehead furrowed as he looked at her. "Asrai, what is the matter with your eyes? Are you unwell?"

The magick snapped, and her eyes darkened once more. Her comb dulled in her hands. She flinched, then touched her fingers to her forehead. "I'm not sure what I am feeling, my sailor," she whispered, her eyes darting up to him again.

Cormack began eating again. He spread a thick layer of the soft ewe's cheese onto a hunk of bread and bit into the coarse grain. He chewed the seeds that had been baked in, and his mouth watered at the creamy mellowness of the cheese.

Asrai tried again. Her comb glowed and her eyes turned to ice. *I am sorry my sailor prince! But I must!* Her magick wrapped tendrils around his heart. She clenched the magick, but it fell away in useless ribbons. Her magick faded, and her eyes darkened once more. Cormack looked up and offered Asrai a slice of bread and cheese.

"Please try some, I think it might help you feel better." He sighed and looked away after she had plucked it from his hand. "I know your feelings are most likely caused by my selfish actions."

She hid the shake in her hands by eating the bread. The bite of salt in the cheese made her hungry for more. She focused on chewing the grainy bread as her mind screamed. *How was my magick undone so easily? How did his heart escape?* Her mind jolted at the realization. *Unless—*

Asrai looked into Cormack's eyes again, this time without magick. He locked his gaze on hers and smiled. A warmth spread through her body. Her heart leapt.

Unless he already loves me!

Cormack set aside the tray, the food reduced to scraps. He reached out and took Asrai's hand in his. The warmth of his skin enveloped hers. His touch was electric. She felt a yearning in her bones deeper even than the call of the sea. She squeezed her comb.

He darted his gaze away, but kept holding her hand. "Asrai, I must apologise to you. I am not sure what exactly I thought I was accomplishing by bringing you here. I should have put you back in the waters, back to your home. I thought I was saving you from those sailors, worried they would take you away and force you to grant wishes, but here I am doing the very same."

Asrai was unable to speak as the excitement strangled her throat. She gazed at him in earnest, willing him to look at her again. Cormack shook his head, his face pinched.

"I want so much for these princesses to stop coming here. I have no desire to join my life with someone who is merely designated to me. I want nothing to do with Father's war games—marrying for strategy and positioning as if we are all just pieces on a map to be won. I pity them. I pity those princesses and their station. Forced to join with men most likely twice my age. But if I do not love them, then I would be forsaking myself to the same fate I am trying to save them from. I do not want to live my life joined with someone I do not love. That would be a lie."

Cormack looked at her again. A thrill ran through her body as she met his gaze. She felt the magick surging through her, but with no purpose it simply throbbed and flashed in her eyes.

"And therefore, I cannot ask you to do the same." He squeezed her hand, his face pained. "I cannot force you to love me. I cannot steal a wish from you to make you love me."

All at once the magick burst. It fizzed about the small bathroom, bouncing off the stone walls. They glowed and hummed. Sparks of magick fell from the ceiling where it had struck, and rained down on them. Cormack stared, his mouth agape. Asrai startled him as she leapt up, her arms thrown about his neck. Her heart was singing. She was singing. Her strange wailing voice echoed and called to tell the sea her triumph.

"You do not need to wish it!" She squeezed him in an embrace, the scales on her chest cutting into his doublet. "You do not need to wish it, my dear sailor prince!"

Cormack was frightened at first, thinking Asrai had turned into a deadly siren, like in the sailors' tales. Instead, a rush went through him as sparkling light flew from nowhere and was suddenly everywhere. She embraced him, her joy palpable. He felt a rush like none other that steed nor sword, boat or wave had ever stirred in him before. Cormack wrapped his arms around the stiffness of her scales and held her tight. The water from her skin dampening his clothes, but he cared not.

Chapter Eight

Cormack held Asrai's hands in his, his eyes locked on hers. He found he could not stop grinning. She was smiling as well, her teeth large and pointed. They were beautiful, like glistening daggers for life in the cruel sea. "Lady Asrai, is it true? Do you—"

Her eyes flashed, her smile growing wider. "Please, my sailor, please say it first. Say it for me."

He squeezed her hands. "I love you, Asrai."

The fire in the lit candles burst, the flames growing into fireballs. Asrai's scales shimmered, appearing as flames themselves. Her eyes were bright, like frost in the sun. A great wailing escaped her throat. The song made Cormack's hair stand on end.

> *Here we are in this tiny room*
> *Watched by now this blessed moon*
> *Two worlds, one heart be joined how soon*
>
> *The sea is calling out to bring us home*
> *That you my sailor, no longer roam*
> *May your heart be filled with ocean blue*
> *Now carved upon with ancient runes*
> *The path of love, the way of Truth*
> *Shall e'er be the path we choose!*

The candles returned to their tiny lights, but Asrai's scales continued to shimmer, as if they were made of quicksilver, or the shifting ocean itself. Her eyes met his, and her lips parted.

"I have always loved you, Cormack. My dear beloved sailor."

The sparkling in the air shattered when a frantic banging sounded on the bedroom door. Startled, Cormack released Asrai's hands and jumped up. He tripped over the washing stool as he scrambled for the bathroom door.

"...your highness! Are you all right? Your highness!"

Cormack threw open the bedroom door. A servant and a pair of guards stood at attention. He blanched. "What's all this?" His gaze bobbed from one to the next.

"Your highness," the servant bowed, keeping his eyes on Cormack's chest, "we heard a great wailing from this wing of the castle!

The guards are searching in the gardens below! We fear a banshee may have entered the kingdom!"

Cormack swallowed the urge to laugh. He set his face into one of concern. "A banshee? Aren't they only found in the deserts to the West?"

The servant bowed again. "We fear it may have followed the caravan from Caraway. Please, we ask your highness to remain in your room until it is determined the grounds are safe."

"Oh, er—yes!" Cormack nodded. "I will do so. Thank you. I'll call for the guards if anything is amiss."

The servant nodded, the fear plain on his face. "May Poseidon keep you, your highness!"

Cormack tilted his head. "By the wave of Poseidon."

The guards bowed to him, and stood at attention outside his door. The servant turned heel and strode down the hall. Cormack shut the door and bolted it. The grin returned to his face. He knocked on the bathroom door, hoping the guards would not hear. "Asrai!" he whispered. The lock clicked. He opened the door and shut it behind him.

****

"My sailor! What has happened?" She clutched her comb.

Cormack waved his hand. "No, no. Everything is all right." He laughed. "They heard you singing. They think there is a banshee about!"

At first, Asrai was offended to have her beautiful voice compared to such a dastardly creature. But Cormack's laughter was infectious, and soon she too was laughing at the silly thought. Cormack righted the stool and sat again. He shook his head and swallowed his laughter.

"Yes, well, we will just have to be quiet for now." He took her hand in his.

Asrai nodded. She squeezed his hand. The excitement still pulsed through her heart and veins. She flicked her eyes up at him. Cormack frowned and met Asrai's gaze. "My cousin, Peter, seeks the hand of the Princess of Caraway."

All at once the excitement was extinguished from Asrai's heart. Her voice was low. "Why should such trifles plague you, my sailor?"

Cormack shook his head. "He must be plotting something. Many princesses have visited our kingdom, and never before has he taken such an interest."

Asrai bristled. The fact that this princess filled any corner of Cormack's mind set her heart alight with hot anger. "Is it so terribly hard to believe he has fallen in love, as we have?"

Cormack wrinkled his nose. "Peter does not love."

Asrai made a rude noise and crossed her arms, glaring at Cormack. "I grow weary. Goodnight."

He started, taken aback by the swift change in mood. His eyes scanned Asrai's face, pleading, but she would not budge. Cormack sighed and stood. "As you wish, my lady." The door clicked shut and Asrai whipped her comb, setting the lock. Alone, her anger dissolved, leaving her empty.

****

Cormack leaned his back against the bathroom door. He slumped when he heard the lock click. *I suppose it's possible for a mermaid to feel a lady's jealousy.*

He peeled himself off the door and regarded the empty room. The soft summer wind wafted through the arrowslit. In the quiet, he could hear the soldiers still trying to find the "banshee." Further still, he could hear the rhythmic waves of the sea. They did not soothe him, not this night. The yawning emptiness of the darkness pressed on him from all sides. Cormack slumped onto the bed, then flopped backward, letting his limbs sprawl. When he was certain Asrai would not call him back, he let sleep take him into its dark tendrils.

Breakfast was a sordid affair. The bathroom door remained barred. He ate alone in silence. What had once been a typical morning routine was now painful. He headed toward the kitchen, hoping for some distraction, when he crossed paths with Peter, Nephara on his arm. They looked at him from the landing, Cormack frozen on the stone stairs. Peter smirked, then gave Nephara a warm smile. They continued, as if he weren't even there. The anger welled up again, but was promptly extinguished when he remembered Asrai. His body felt heavy. He managed to stumble to the kitchens without further delay.

Pamela was first to notice Cormack's sour mood. It was one even oat cakes could not fix, and she knew it. "A storm is heading in from the North," Pamela said to no one in particular. She stretched and rolled her great, broad shoulders. "I can feel it in my bones."

Cormack sneered at the floor. The weather would not afford him solace. Even the sea knew of Asrai's jealous rage. He sighed and shuffled out of the kitchen. He wove his way through the castle without cause. His feet led him to the outer gates. Sheets of rain fell upon the garden beyond. Cormack resigned himself and headed back up to his bedroom.

The candles had been lit due to the dark stormy sky, though the day was not yet half over. There upon his small table was a simple vase bearing a spray of blue ranunculus. He traced his finger over a velvety petal. He plucked a blossom from the vase and took a deep breath.

Cormack stood before the door. His body leaned until his forehead rested against it. He pushed away again and lifted his fist to knock. The image of Asrai's furious face flashed through his mind again. His heart clenched. He let his arm drop. "Asrai, I am sorry. I am so sorry. Please forgive me."

****

Asrai swirled her comb in the tepid water. Watching Cormack wander through the castle had broken the last of her anger. At last, when she heard his pleading apology, she flicked her comb and allowed the door to swing open a crack.

Cormack stumbled into the bathroom as the door gave way. He locked eyes with her, looked about him, then closed the bathroom door. He stood, staring at the floor, at the foot of the tub where little puddles had formed. He twisted the ranunculus between his fingers. Asrai turned her comb around and around in her hands, wondering which of them was to speak first. The air between them crackled.

"I-I'm sorry." Cormack repeated, daring to raise his eyes to her tail.

She nodded, bringing her gaze up to his chest. "It seems so."

Cormack flinched and dropped his gaze. He shook his head and caught Asrai's gaze once more. He knelt before the tub, the puddles soaking the knees of his breeches. "My dear lady." He took one of her hands, halting the worrying of her comb. "My Asrai. I am sorry."

He presented the blue ranunculus to her. The stem was bruised from his fidgeting, but the petals were bright. Asrai took the flower, the soft scent whispering as the blossom rustled from her movements.

She squeezed his hand and smiled. "I did not mean to become so angry—" She shifted her gaze, her cheeks darkening. "These feelings are strange and take hold without my will."

Cormack chuckled. "From what I have heard, that is what love does — it does as it wills and we are left dancing in the wind."

Asrai nodded. She slipped her comb back into her hair and arranged the flower behind her ear, a vivid pendant of sapphire against her fiery hair. Cormack took both her hands in his, his eyes darting about her face.

"The thought of another ruling your heart made me want to beat my tail against the reefs and scream. I have never felt such a strange rage ensnare me."

"The skies and the sea certainly heard you." He laughed. "A squall has taken over the day. I was left quite lonely with no distraction. My penance for offending you." Asrai grinned, revealing her small fangs.

Cormack cupped his hands in the bathwater and poured it over her tail. "Shall I fetch you fresh water, my lady?"

She shook her head. "No, my sailor. Please stay a while." Cormack seated himself at her side. He squeezed Asrai's hand.

****

Love of the Sea

"I recall you had said you have always loved me." Cormack took a deep breath. "Have we met before?"

Asrai's cheeks flushed. She lowered her eyelashes, then swirled her comb in the water, creating a vision once more. "Yes, my sailor. Though you were unaware."

The sky was bright upon the blue marble sea. Calm waters enveloped Cormack's boat. The sun blazed, almost noon, as Cormack pulled the ropes of the main sail, catching the wind. He was unaware of the jeweled eyes watching him below. A mermaid with flowing scarlet hair was attached to *Anita's* rudder. She allowed the boat to drag her further out into the harbour. Moments later, *Anita* halted near a sandbar where conches were plentiful. The vision in the bathwater rippled from the dull vibration of the anchor hitting the sea floor. Then Cormack dove. His shaggy hair floated about his face, tied back with a scrap of linen.

He scanned the sea floor around the shallow waters of the sandbar. The mermaid used the rigging to crawl across the side of the boat, then a slow pump of her crimson tail sent her a stone's throw from Cormack. Her body bristled as she watched him surface for air, and dive back down. His calloused fingers sifting through the sand to find shells he liked. Cormack turned to search for shells in another area of the sandbar. The glittering mermaid darted behind the rudder once more. The comb plunged into the vision, dissolving it into ripples. Cormack looked at Asrai. Her wistful eyes glistened.

"You were that fish," he murmured, epiphany rolling over him. "You were the presence I always felt when I was out with my boat."

Asrai nodded. She slipped her comb back into her hair. "Yes. It was I."

Cormack ran his hand through his hair, then looked at her again. "But why? Why not approach me? Make yourself known?"

She wrapped her arms around herself and shook her head, looking down at the water. "It is easy for a sailor to love a mermaid in the sea. It is easy to pledge to a mermaid when all is fun and games. But then the land calls them home, and all the sailors eventually leave."

Cormack felt a rush well up in his throat. He desperately wanted to argue with her and declare that he was different, that he would have stayed. But as he thought about it, if Asrai had revealed herself on one of those afternoons, he knew that would never have happened. He sighed.

"Yes, it is as you said—all things must return from whence they came." He took her hand again and looked up at her. "The sea calls strongly to me, even now. And yet, I am always called away back home."

Asrai nodded, still not meeting his gaze. "So, you understand."

The silence flowed between them, growing private thoughts of sorrow. Cormack allowed his thoughts to wander into curiosity to escape the circular despair. His gaze scanned Asrai's shimmering scales. "Have you ever left the sea before?"

She started, absorbed in her own thoughts. Asrai shook her head. "No, my sailor. This is my first time on land."

"I have heard stories of mermaids coming and living new lives on the land. Are they true?" Cormack tilted his head.

Asrai nodded. "Yes. A mermaid may make a wish for legs and live on the land. Love bonds the mermaid and allows the legs to be permanent. However, without the sea she will dry out, and eventually die."

Cormack felt the happy thought snuffed out. "A mermaid would agree to such a painful death?"

"Yes. They do it for love." Asrai took Cormack's hand. "Though I think it is an incredibly selfish and despairing sort of love."

Cormack stroked her hand with his fingers as he held it. "What if a mermaid stayed to her true form, and only used temporary legs. But lived as you are now?"

Asrai wrinkled her nose. "Live in a tiny pool such as this? No wide ocean to frolic and twist? No reefs to explore and no life to play with?" He winced, knowing how selfish his thoughts were.

"Even so, this is not the sea," Asrai swirled the bathwater with her free hand, "and I would still dry out."

Cormack nodded. The selfish thoughts multiplied in his heart. The idea of putting Asrai back in the sea filled him with a horrifying panic that took his breath away. He squeezed Asrai's hand. "I would never want you to suffer such a fate."

Asrai's face softened. "Thank you, my sailor. It would break my heart for you to ask such a selfish wish of me. I would be forced to grant it, but inside I would be broken—"

"That is not real love." Cormack stroked Asrai's face, running his fingers through her hair. "Forcing the one you love to wither away is not real love."

"Thank you," Asrai whispered. "You are not like other humans, and I am glad for it."

Cormack gave a shallow laugh. "Yes, well, that seems to be the trouble with me. I am not at all like what Father wishes me to be. At times, I feel I have no purpose here—"

Asrai shook her head and took Cormack's hand in both of hers. "I believe you are destined for great things, my sailor. They simply have yet to be revealed."

Chapter Nine

A lonely seagull called. Another answered. Cormack stretched and threw off the bed covers. The sky was still grey, with only the first glimmer of morning peeking out. He crossed to the bathroom when a voice startled him.

"His majesty has requested your presence in the map room." Cormack whirled. A maid stood near his small table. A spread of cold squab, dark bread, honey, and oat cakes sat upon the table with a flagon of ale.

She curtsied, keeping her gaze level with his chest. "My apologies your highness. I was instructed to wait with your breakfast, lest you find other items on your morning agenda." He could see the maid struggling not to smile at the last order. His body burned with heated electricity. He fidgeted his fingers, his eyes darting to the bathroom door again.

"Now that you are awake, I will wait outside your chambers." She curtsied again. "His majesty urges you to make haste." Cormack watched as the maid exited the room. The latch clicked. Once the room was clear, he threw open the bathroom door.

Asrai started, sloshing water onto the floor. "My sailor! What in Poseidon's blue sea is the matter?" She had her comb crossed over her chest. It glowed. Her scales bristled.

Cormack reeled, embarrassment creeping up his neck. "My apologies, my lady. The maid startled me and I was delayed in seeing you."

Asrai laughed. Her mirth tinkled and bounced off the stone room. She slid her comb back into her hair. The scales on her chest lifted as she took a breath. "Here we are now, my dear sailor."

He stood near the tub, knowing that if he gathered up the washing stool he would never leave. "My dear Asrai, I only have a moment with you this morning. Father has called upon me. Even now the maid stands guard outside my door."

Asrai flinched. She looked at her tail. "And where are you off to?"

He shook his head. "A council in the map room, nothing more, but knowing Father it could take the better part of the day."

"Then we shall make our moment last, my sailor." Asrai smiled and reached for his hand.

He gathered her hands in his. "My lady, every moment my heart burns for you, as though I am alight with fire."

Asrai rested her forehead against their hands. "I have never touched flame, but I do think that which I feel is the same."

They stayed that way for a moment, willing time to halt. The dull thud of their hearts slowed and quickened together. The warmth from Cormack's hands permeated Asrai's cool skin, until it reached her chest where that warmth blossomed in her heart. She gasped at the beautiful pain. Cormack at last pulled himself away. "I'll bring you breakfast. Then I must be off, I'm afraid."

She nodded. He trotted out of the room, then returned with a tray of food. They broke bread and Cormack drank deeply. When the last of the oat cakes were shared, Cormack sighed and captured Asrai's gaze.

"It is not forever," she assured him. "I shall be fine."

He nodded, his body unwilling to move. "And as always, I shall return."

Cormack closed the door, hearing the familiar click. His hands shook as he dressed. The maid curtsied when Cormack emerged from his room. He strode down the hall, his heart screaming with every step. Only King Dominic and his faithful general were present. Cormack swallowed the rising tension in his gut. He made a smart bow.

"Good morning, Father." He kept his gaze on the king's chest.

King Dominic nodded. "And good morning to you, my son. Come, sit. We have much to discuss."

Cormack sat near the edges of the known world, near San Bai. He leaned his elbows on the lip of the table.

"They have been a faithful ally to us, my poor sister's lands. Poseidon keep her." King Dominic moved one of the ships to the crescent moon harbour. "Richard's siege on Umber holds strong. And with the changing trade routes it is difficult to get supplies through. Once again, their future is uncertain."

Cormack sighed. "Father, I am certain you did not call me here to discuss Umber."

King Dominic straightened in his chair. "Quite right. Quite right, my boy." He moved more catapult miniatures onto the table at Umber's border. "I fear history is repeating itself. Should Umber fall, I worry your cousin will slip into madness." He moved a horse toward the flat, brown expanse that was Caraway. "Peter has made his intentions with the Princess of Caraway clear. I have decided to allow them to marry. The wedding should distract him, should his homeland be stolen once more. Do I have your blessing, son? She was promised to you after all."

"I have no ill thoughts against their union, Father." He toyed with a soldier on the edge of the map. "Perhaps the princess will do Peter some good."

The king tilted his head. "Yes, perhaps. I cannot disagree with you. Peter is a troubled lad. Richard took his family and birthright from him, and now his heart is empty. Hopefully, she can change that."

The image was burned forever in Cormack's mind: Peter as a child, dressed in tattered clothes, delivered to their doorstep by Denarian guards paid with Paradine gold. Cormack pushed the dark memory away. He scooted the ship from Umber to Denaria. "Caraway is a powerful kingdom. A great ally. Their soldiers would be enough to crush that old dog once and for all."

King Dominic leaned over the map table. He took one of the soldiers and planted it on Teem. "Weston! What are our current relations with Dere?"

The general leaned over the map as well and placed a ship in Teem's harbour. "We trade our excess fish and limestone for their lumber and pitch."

"I cannot keep all of them straight. Have we entertained any of Dere's daughters? Does Dere even have lasses?"

"The Princess Ianthe was rejected several moons ago. She has been married off to the eldest prince of Altruse."

"And of Relk?" King Dominic moved the soldier from Teem to an inland space on the map.

Weston sighed. "They are one of our best inland military allies. They keep the Foiters from entering our territories. King Francis has married off his two eldest daughters Bridgette and Lyonette. His third daughter, Princess Nann, is but a child."

Cormack felt the tension in his stomach tie itself into a sturdy knot. His excitement from his morning with Asrai turned into hot anxiety. He fidgeted his leg as the conversation swirled around him.

"What of Bekhalm? Surely they have suitable—"

"Enough!" Cormack's hands were planted firmly on the lip of the map. The chair screeched as Cormack flew to his feet. "I have had enough, Father." His voice was low.

King Dominic's face reddened and he shook a finger at Cormack. "Oh no! You have not had enough until you finally choose a bride! You have sent away every lass on this earth and *I* have had enough!"

A jolt went through Cormack's heart. Words spilled from his lips before he could think. "I already have, Father. Send them away, for I already have my bride!"

"I told you—you what?" King Dominic's finger hung in the air, his mouth agape.

The madness pushed Cormack further, his grin widening. "I have found my bride." Cormack gripped his father's shoulder. "I have fallen in love, Father."

Rage and confusion melted into joy. King Dominic stood and embraced Cormack, thick arms like tree trunks encircling his midsection. "My boy! My boy!" the king shouted. "My boy has a bride!"

The general laughed with them. His eyes glistened. "Well done, lad," he whispered.

King Dominic broke out into a deep guffaw and released Cormack. His meaty palm smacked his son on the back, knocking the wind out of him. "How did you manage to meet a lass under my nose? Well, it doesn't matter. When can I meet her?"

Cormack froze, his smile melting. "Uh, well, um, it's far for her to travel you see."

King Dominic nodded. "Good, good, plenty of time to prepare a proper welcome." He gave Cormack a side glance. "And for you to make yourself presentable."

The madness ran screaming from Cormack's mind, leaving him with the acrid lies upon his tongue. His insides withered as he watched his father punch his general in the shoulder, their jubilant faces wide and shining. Cormack stood frozen, his hands on the lip of the table, his body shaking.

****

Asrai stirred the water with her glowing comb. She fidgeted, worrying over the possibility of the older human father bringing more 'suitable' brides to the kingdom. She watched as Cormack entered a large room lined with wood rather than stone. Upon the walls hung various maps of places she did not know, and weapons that would frighten even a shark.

Cormack sat. The men spoke to one another, pointing to areas and moving about baubles. Cormack seemed more and more agitated. The vision rippled as he stood in a rush, slamming his hands on the table. "I have had enough, Father."

Asrai watched as the old human scolded Cormack, his finger jabbing and shaking. Cormack seemed further angered by the offending appendage. "I already have, Father. Send them away, for I already have my bride!"

Asrai dropped her comb. It lay at the bottom of the tub, nestled at her side, still glowing. Her hands flew up to her mouth. *He couldn't mean me, could he? The way he had looked into my eyes, there had been love there.*

The king was as confused and hopeful as Asrai. His face in the vision mirrored hers. "I have fallen in love, Father."

The water rippled until the vision melted away. Asrai's scales glistened, gold sparks rippled through the bright crimson. She threw her head back, her arms outstretched on either side of the tub. Her voice vibrated over the water.

A vow is forever!
A vow is true!
My heart bursts forth
and sings this song just for you!
My dear one, my only one, the pearl of my eye
Come away with me on waters sweet as a lullaby
Behold my love, strong and true
Old tales that shine forth renewed
Bold is my tongue, all thoughts askew
Untold was this destiny of mine, I must see it through!

A Southern seat upon Poseidon's wave
Shall bear us upon the golden mer enclave
Stories shall be told of a risk taken and depraved
Ne'er again shall our hearts part ways!

Tears stung Asrai's eyes. She surprised herself; mermaids cannot cry. She caught one on her finger; it crystallized and fell. The tub glittered with them. Asrai jumped, the jewels falling from her fingers and plinking into the bathwater.

****

Cormack opened the bathroom door, and his heart fell at the sight of Asrai's tear stained cheeks and red eyes. "Asrai, I—"

"Did you speak the truth, my sailor?" Her eyes cut through him. "Am I the bride of which you speak?"

She had looked at me with love, hadn't she? Can mermaids truly love? Or are they only bound by the wishes of others?

He kneeled on the floor again, at her side. He took her hands in his. "Only if you wish it, Lady Asrai."

Asrai's eyes widened and a smile peeled across her face. She glowed as she embraced him. "Oh, my sailor! Yes!"

"Please," Cormack whispered, "no more crying." He brushed a tear off her cheek. It crystallized and plinked into the water. He gasped and drew back. "What is that?"

"My tears." Asrai scooped a small handful of the jewels from the tub and brought them above water. They shone like stars. "Mermaid tears."

Cormack closed her hand over the gems. "Then I shall see about having the jeweler make them into a fine necklace for you."

Asrai's eyes glittered. "Cormack—" She leaned toward him.

Their lips met, hers cool and vibrant like the sea, his warm and comforting. Cormack wove his fingers into her hair. He could feel her heartbeat in the back of her neck. It thundered like the beating surf against the reef. She could feel his heartbeat as she laid her hands over his chest, her needle-like claws digging into his grey tunic. Her fangs scraped his bottom lip, but did not cut. His fingers dug into her cold flesh, making it warm and flushed with blood. Her scales glowed, as if alight with fire. A dull thumping separated them, their chests heaving as they touched foreheads.

"You were singing again, weren't you?" Cormack laughed.

Asrai grinned, her fangs exposed. "Perhaps."

Cormack groaned as he got up, stretching his left leg and turning away. He looked over his shoulder. "I shall return."

She giggled as he shut the door. Cormack's face crumpled into annoyance as he strode toward the bedroom door, his excitement fading away. A startled guard was received as Cormack glowered into the hallway. "Your highness, we have reason to believe the banshee still stalks the castle!"

Cormack shifted his feet. "Yes, so I heard."

The guard darted his eyes, perplexed at the prince's bored demeanour. "Please, stay in your chambers until we have determined the castle safe once more."

"Of course. We thank you for your concern." Cormack nodded to the guard. He fidgeted his hand.

"Yes, at your service, your highness." He bowed and strode off down the hall.

Cormack sighed and closed the door again. As he returned to the bathroom he could hear the guards calling to one another in the courtyard. He almost felt sorry for them on their fool's errand. He smiled as he opened the door.

Her scales radiated golden light. It shimmered through them, like mother-of-pearl. Asrai appeared to be a pure white maiden set ablaze her hair a crown of flames. His breath caught as her luminous eyes rolled up to meet his. "Hello, my sailor."

He gathered up the washing stool again, grinning at her. "They're looking for the 'banshee' again."

Asrai pouted. "A banshee calls to the dead, and its voice in itself is dying."

Cormack put his fingertips under her chin. "These walls must distort everything with the echoes. Your voice is beautiful. Please, sing for me so I may hear your song for myself, my dear lady."

"Won't that attract the humans outside?" Her glance was coy, making Cormack shudder.

"Perhaps." He took his fingers away and stared at her. "Perhaps not."

Love of the Sea

"Not this day." Asrai dragged a lazy finger through the water. "The song has already been sung."

Chapter Ten

The room brightened with the high afternoon sun. The soldiers ran a drill in the courtyard, their shouts melding with the confused guards. It dragged Cormack's mind back to the map room. His face fell.

Asrai shivered at the change in mood. "What troubles you?"

Cormack shook his head. "I have made a promise to Father I cannot keep." His eyes scanned her scales down to her tail. "Not when I already promised not to make you an unwilling bride."

She took out her comb again. She twirled it between her fingers. "I am not unwilling, my dear sailor. There is another way." Cormack's head snapped up.

Asrai swirled her comb in the water again. The vision of her ocean castle came into view. "I could give you the sea," she whispered as she traced the highest tower, her fingers rippling the water.

"How do you mean?" Cormack watched as the vision shifted to a small caricature of himself.

Asrai's voice was low. She spoke slowly to prevent it from shaking. "You say the sea calls out to you, even now." She looked up at him. "I could make it so you ne'er return to land again."

The vision sparkled, and his caricature rippled. When it stilled again, he was a mer. Cormack's jaw lay slack. His mind whirred. Asrai continued. "But at a price. As I'm sure you have heard from your human tales, we do not have souls."

"I would lose my soul?" He looked at her again and closed his mouth.

"No desire is won without sacrifice." Asrai ran her hand over the vision, distorting it. "In exchange for the life your heart craves, you would lose the opportunity to experience whatever afterlife you humans seem so bent on believing in."

Cormack swallowed. His throat had gone dry. Asrai continued, her heart racing. "You will also lose some of your human emotions. Certain things that make you human will slip away."

His eyes darted over the floor, trying to process what he was hearing. "Will losing my soul be painful?"

Asrai turned to him. "Only as painful as it is to forget anything."

Cormack withdrew even further into himself. His body felt strange, as if he were in a dream.

Love of the Sea

"Cormack?" Her whisper shook him. Cormack's eyes jumped to meet her gaze. His heart leapt. His breath caught.

I love her. And I love the sea. But can I leave all I know behind?

"I'm sorry, Asrai." He shook his head and dropped his gaze. "I must think on this."

Asrai put her hand over his. He turned his hand and grasped hers. He smiled at the softness of her skin. He had failed to notice before the delicate translucent webbing at the base of her wrists. It looked like the edging of fine gloves. "In any case, I cannot present a mermaid bride to Father."

Asrai looked away. "I understand."

Cormack squeezed her hand. "But I want him to meet you. To know you."

She looked at her scales. The golden glow was gone. "I would need to visit the sea to be granted a temporary human form."

"And the guards currently make that impossible." An idea struck Cormack. A grin broke out on his face. "But if we were to disguise you—"

Asrai tilted her head. "Dress me like a human?"

Cormack nodded. "I know nothing of a lady's dressing, but I know someone who does!" He jumped up, upsetting the washing stool. Asrai stared after him as he bounded out of the bathroom. She could hear him galloping down the hall. She sighed and locked the door again.

****

Asrai dipped her comb into the water and swirled it. Her eyes glowed ice blue. The small room came into focus, but this time it was alive, not simply a memory. The sea hag started, then swam toward the water mirror.

"My child! I have waited in earnest for your news!"

"I have much news, but I cannot impart now! Please, I need to meet you when the moon is brightest over the sea."

The sea hag bristled. "Ask."

Asrai tilted her head. "I need to move about on land as a human."

The sea hag's eyes widened and her mouth twisted in disgust. "What have I told you of pining after sailors?"

Asrai shook her head. "No! No! Illyana, please! Listen! It is my sailor prince. He has declared his love for me!"

"Sailor prince! Indeed." The sea hag's eyes flashed. "Have you forgotten your destiny?"

"Never." Asrai's voice hardened. "I shall kill him by my own jaws."

The sea hag flicked her tail. "Then why under Poseidon's blue sea would you need to take human form?"

Asrai darted her eyes at the door. "The humans need to be appeased first, and my dear sailor prince needs reassurance before giving himself to the sea."

The sea hag scoffed. "A human surrender to the sea? And I suppose he is willing to lose his precious soul?"

"Yes." Asrai's eyes flashed.

The sea hag froze. Then her gaze softened. "If you are sure. Magickal heartbreak is not something a mer can survive."

Asrai clenched her comb. "I am sure."

"Then I shall meet you. You will have three moons to settle your human affairs until your scales return."

"Thank you!" Relief washed over Asrai. "Thank you, Illyana!" The sea hag nodded and touched her fingertips to her forehead. Asrai did the same. She dissolved the window with her comb.

****

Cormack stole out of his room, careful to avoid Peter. He dashed down the hall and almost bowled over a maid carrying a pitcher of water. "My apologies!" he spluttered.

The maid bobbed a frantic curtsy. "Pardon me, your highness!"

Cormack nodded, allowing the maid to continue on her way. He gathered his wits and slowed his step. He dodged a group of guards hunting through the storerooms. Despite the possible "danger" of a banshee being on the loose, the kitchen was still at full tilt. Pamela was turning a whole boar on the roasting spit, meant for entertaining the Caraway visitors.

"They say a banshee is about the castle grounds," Pamela muttered. "What are you doing out of your room?"

Cormack touched her shoulder. "Pamela, it's urgent. I need your help."

She sighed and sheathed her spoon. "All right. What is it?"

Cormack shook his head. "Not here." He led her into the hall, where the sound of cutlery and cooking implements dimmed. "I have a dinner guest tonight, and I need you to help me dress her."

Pamela was aghast and stopped herself from outright slapping Cormack. "How dare you sneak around so and not make an honest woman out of her! Asking me for help? The very idea! I expect this nonsense from Peter, but you?"

"It is not what you think. Please come!" Cormack stood his ground, his eyes pleading.

Pamela crossed her arms. "I hope you know what you're doing."

Cormack grinned as she returned and barked curt orders to her kitchen hands. She reemerged to find Cormack beside himself with anticipation. "If you weren't your mother's son," Pamela muttered, a smile turning her lips.

They skirted the guards. The maids gave the pair strange looks, no doubt wondering what the head cook was doing outside the kitchen so close to supper. Cormack paused before the bathroom door. He darted his eyes to Pamela, then knocked. When the lock clicked, Pamela gasped. He opened the door, and gestured for her to enter.

Pamela held her hand over her heart, her fingers crossed in a ward. "Oh, Cormack! What have you done?"

He entered the room and took Asrai's hand. "Asrai, this is the head cook, Pamela. She is my dearest friend."

Asrai furled and unfurled her tail. "Hello."

Cormack and Asrai joined their gaze. Pamela felt her breath catch when she saw the fierce devotion in their eyes. Her hand flew to her mouth.

"I need Asrai disguised as a fine lady in time for the banquet tonight." Cormack's words broke through Pamela's shock, making cold sense take over.

She nodded and looked from Asrai to Cormack. "What do you expect me to do? A simpler lady I could have dressed up, but laddie, she has no legs!"

Cormack swallowed; this complication had not occurred to him. Asrai dramatized a swoon. "I could be carried in, feigning fragile health. But I'm not sure how desirable a bride that would make me."

Cormack shook his head. "That won't do."

"Princesses in the East are carried in litters," Pamela said. "It's customary. She doesn't have to be ill." She shook her head. "Oh, what am I saying? This is ridiculous!"

Asrai and Cormack stared at Pamela. She threw her arms in the air. "All right! I know where some old things are stored that shan't be missed." She trudged out of the room.

****

The late queen's clothing was locked in the West tower. Pamela was the only person who carried keys to the door and the many chests inside, aside from the king himself. The skin on her neck prickled and her palms began to sweat as she climbed the forgotten stairs. She bowed her head. "Forgive me."

The key crunched in the old lock and the door squeaked open. Inside, the floor was covered in thick gray dust. The candles were all buried or eaten by rats. She groped her way in the darkness until she reached the chest at the foot of the great, now dilapidated, bed.

Another key was selected and the lock stuck at first. A cloud of dust swept up as she threw the lid back. Pamela coughed and wiped her face with her apron. She pulled back the plain linen, revealing beautiful clothes. The scent of lavender filled the air, wrenching forth the memory of the day Cormack's mother had died.

The birth had been difficult and bloody. The boy was born breech and the midwife had cut the queen to make more room for the babe to slide out. Pamela's fine court gown was covered with an apron, stained in blood. She had stood by the queen's side that long day, sponging sweat and tears from the queen's face, offering what little comfort she could.

"Ella." The queen's voice was thin and tired.

Pamela took the queen's hand, and she could feel the queen weakening. Pamela's strong Altrusean frame had always been a funny pairing with the dainty queen. Their opposite silhouettes belied their matching souls and strength of heart. "Yes, Ammi?"

"Please, care for my boy. Give him all the love I wanted to give." Her voice trembled, and her chest shuddered from the effort of speaking. Her eyes were bloodshot, and veins in her face had burst from her efforts in labor.

Pamela kissed the queen's fingers. "Don't say such things. You will love your little boy! See how he wriggles for you now."

The midwife placed the infant in the queen's arms as the assistants tried to stem the flow of blood. "Help me, Ella." Her arms trembled, unable to support the baby. Pamela held the queen's arms with her own. "You are my dear heart. I know I can trust you to love him, as I cannot. Please promise me."

Pamela nodded, tears streaming down her face. "Yes." She swallowed a sob. "Yes, Ammi."

The queen leaned her head against Pamela. "Oh, my boy. My boy. You shall be Cormack." She kissed his forehead. "I love you."

Pamela scrubbed a tear from her cheek as she fingered the fine lace and gold threads. She took a deep, shuddering breath and gathered up as much of the clothing as she could carry, then locked the chest again. She stood and scanned the room once more before bowing her head. "Forgive me, Ammi."

****

Cormack was giddy when Pamela returned with an armload of fabric and small contraptions. Asrai snaked her arms around his neck as Cormack lifted her from the tub and set her on the bed. He began to dry her off with clean linen. Asrai clenched her teeth as the moisture was wiped from her skin. The fabric of the linen felt rough, like dead coral, scraping against her scales. She took a deep breath, pushing past her discomfort.

Pamela began piling on underclothes and finery. She dragged the simple chemise over Asrai's head. Asrai picked at the light cloth, but Pamela batted her hands away and pulled the corset around Asrai's body.

She laced up the eyelets in the front with difficulty as Asrai tipped her head down to watch. Pamela climbed onto the bed and tossed Asrai's hair over a shoulder. She threaded the back lacing of the corset and tightened it until Asrai's scales began cutting into her flesh.

She hissed. "Must it be so tight?"

The petticoats were pulled over her head, enveloping her in fluff. "I'm afraid so, my dear. We don't need anyone getting suspicious."

Cormack did as he was bid, Pamela pointing to wads of fabric that needed to be pulled into place. A lady would have been waited on by her maids, not the head cook, and Cormack would never have been allowed in the room. They were an odd party, and Cormack's heart thundered as he waited for a maid or a groom to discover them.

Pamela sewed the sleeves into place. The heavy dress came to the hollow of the neck. A well-placed choker hid her gills. The sleeves fell past the fingers in points, covering the fringe of fins around her wrists. Asrai appeared a fine lady, so long as she stayed sitting.

Pamela patted Asrai's hand. "I will ensure they serve you plenty of water, love, just don't overdo it. If you need to return here, simply swoon something awful and we'll fetch you right away."

Asrai nodded. Cormack helped her sort out the velvet pouch of jewelry that Pamela had brought. Pamela groaned as she lowered herself onto the floor and began stitching the hem of the dress into a sort of pocket to hold Asrai's tail.

"All right, I'm sure the herald will need some sort of official statement for the lady's arrival." Pamela rolled her eyes.

Cormack dug a bit of parchment from his cabinet and scribbled a few lines on it. Pamela looked Asrai over again, ensuring none of her scales were showing. "By Poseidon's wave, I hope the two of you know what you're doing!" She shook her head and exited the bedroom. The door thudded behind her.

Asrai stilled her shaking hands. The clothing was incredibly painful. "How are we to properly present me? I know nothing of these human things, my sailor."

Cormack tucked the parchment into his belt. "I have an idea." He cracked open the bedroom door and checked the hall, then turned to Asrai. "I will return."

****

He trotted through the castle, avoiding the servants, until he was able to dash through the night run. It led to the stables, allowing Cormack to pass unhindered. He found one of the younger stable boys and pressed a silver coin into his hand.

"Your highness!" the boy squeaked. He was gangly, his body just leaving boyhood. He stared at the prince.

"Fetch me Nonna, saddled with the finest tack for a lady. Then wait for me here."

The boy scampered off. Cormack ran back through the run and dodged through the servant access hallway. He came upon a group of maids sorting the cutlery for the banquet, and the footmen lazing about.

"Men, I have a task for you this evening!" Cormack felt a bit silly as they snapped to attention. "Is the palanquin from Denaria in the storeroom?"

The most senior footman nodded. "Aye, your highness."

Cormack smiled. "Please bring it round to the front entrance of the Great Hall, and wait for me there."

All the servants bowed, and a chorus of "Yes, your highness!" echoed in the narrow hallway. Cormack jogged back to the bedroom, his mind whirring.

Chapter Eleven

Asrai started as the door opened, but relaxed when she saw Cormack. He was panting. "Are you ready...my lady?" He gulped his breath.

She nodded, and fluttered a delicate lace fan. "Yes, my sailor."

Her appearance was odd, different now that she was clothed to appear as a lady. Her eyes seemed to hold the same shimmer that her scales often did. Cormack nodded and gathered up the last of his strength. "Please trust me."

Asrai wound her arms around his neck as he gathered her up off the bed. His muscles screamed with her weight. "I trust you, my sailor," Asrai whispered as his efforts jostled her in his arms.

He checked the hall again, then hurried down the stairs, back to the night run. The stable boy was floored when Cormack returned. He gaped at Asrai. "Boy! The horse!"

The stable boy snapped back to attention and tapped Nonna's shoulder. The obedient old mare dropped to her front knees, allowing Cormack to slide Asrai into the side-saddle. The stable boy tapped the mare again, and Nonna rose as if she were carrying but a sack of grain. Asrai's eyes were wide as she gripped the great beast's mane.

Cormack gave the boy another silver coin. "Not a word to anyone. Ever."

He nodded; confusion and fear had stolen his voice. He pocketed the coins and watched as Cormack took the bridle and led Nonna round to the servants' entrance. The guards had slackened their search for the "banshee," but snapped to attention when they saw Cormack leading Asrai toward them.

"Highness!" The most senior guard gaped at the procession. "We were not informed of any other visitors this day."

Cormack's patience was wearing thin. "This is my guest of honour. She will be treated as such."

The guards scrambled to bow as Cormack walked past, Nonna clopping behind him. Asrai kept her gaze forward. Her anxiety balled tight in her chest. The servants' hallway was narrow, but allowed them safe passage to the Great Hall. The footmen were as shocked as the guards when they saw Cormack leading the mount and fine lady.

"Awaiting orders, your highness!" The senior footman bowed low, not daring to sneak a glance at Asrai.

Cormack nodded. He snatched the parchment from his belt and held it out. One of the footmen rushed to receive it. "Take this to the herald. I want my lady properly announced."

The young footman bowed low. "At once, your highness!"

"Her feet must never touch the ground. Is that understood?" Cormack stood aside, allowing the footmen to finally assist.

"My lady, your hand please." The senior footman extended his hand.

Asrai took it. She was shunted into the old palanquin, left by a princess of Denaria who had insisted the muggy summer sea air had ruined it. It had been two years since her visit. Cormack hoped his father would not recognise it. The footmen did not comment on Asrai's unusual weight. They hefted the poles onto their shoulders, and waited for the horn to sound.

****

King Dominic shifted in his chair, the scents from the kitchen thinning his patience even further. Peter glanced at the old king and smirked. Nephara scanned the table, her eyes bobbing over her retinue. Peter gulped the last of his ale and set the mug at the edge of the table. A young serving girl bent to fill his flagon. Peter tilted his head and whispered into Nephara's ear. The serving girl had been close enough to hear, and her face blossomed with a fierce blush before escaping back to the kitchens. The king was too preoccupied with his annoyance to notice.

When footsteps echoed off the stone floor, King Dominic rose, ready to unleash his fury upon Cormack. But it was only a footman hurrying on some errand. King Dominic sat back down, muttering to himself.

Peter turned to the king. "Don't worry, uncle. I'm sure he's just playing with that boat of his."

King Dominic grumbled something, but did not look at Peter. Again, footsteps could be heard. He furrowed his brow when he saw it was the herald. "What game is that boy playing?"

The herald brought forth the ceremonial horn to his lips, the blue pennant of Paradine fluttering on the thin stem. The horn echoed through the Great Hall, silencing the guests. King Dominic's face reddened.

"Announcing her royal highness, Princess Asrai, the royal guest of honour to his highness Prince Cormack!" The herald stepped his left foot forward, then clicked his right heel to the left foot, and spun.

Cormack led the short procession. Behind him the footman carried the golden palanquin into the hall. The curtains were drawn back with gold ropes, and a beautiful lady sat inside. Peter's mouth gaped. Nephara's eyes narrowed. The red hooded ladies straightened and rolled their shoulders. Neither the king, nor Peter, recognised the Eastern style litter.

Asrai's eyes flashed. She played with the fan and kept her gaze forward. Her red locks were a shock against the pale sage coloured dress. The gold embroidery sparkled as she breathed. King Dominic stood to receive them. Peter closed his mouth, his face reddening. The king stared at the delicate fan for a moment, unable to place the familiarity, but when he looked up into Asrai's shimmering eyes, he felt the nagging thought melt away as it was replaced with joy that Cormack had found a lady at last.

****

The footmen came to a halt before the head table. Cormack lifted Asrai from the litter himself. Two of the footmen pulled out their chairs. Once everyone was seated, King Dominic was beaming. He raised his flagon in toast. "We are blessed with the jubilant company of Caraway, and now this fine lady has joined us to sup this evening. What wonders for Paradine!"

The party raised their goblets, cheered, and drank. The serving girls hurried to fill cups. The wine passed over Asrai's cup, and instead was filled with water. King Dominic raised an eyebrow. "No wine?"

Asrai's eyes flashed as she inclined her head and lifted the water glass to her lips. "Thank you, majesty, but too much drink is unseemly for a lady." Nephara rolled her eyes as she drank from her cup, but was careful that only Asrai saw. Asrai ignored her.

The king blinked and turned to his son. "Indeed. Cormack, will you introduce me to your guest? I'm afraid I do not know her."

Cormack nodded. "This is Lady Asrai, Father. She comes from several provinces away."

King Dominic glowered. "Speak up, boy! None of that dog, Richard's provinces! That's not why you've been sneaking about!"

Cormack shook his head. "No! None such provinces, Father! My lady comes from an Eastern duchy, farther even than San Bai."

Asrai nodded, her eyes bright and sparkling as she batted her lashes at the king. "I come from Sulu." She could not think of a better name than the true underwater kingdom of her birth.

King Dominic nodded, glancing at Asrai's smooth, white hands folded in her lap. "I see. What is the trade in your province?"

Peter scoffed. "Our dear lady cannot boast of warriors like those of Caraway. Of that I am sure."

King Dominic waved his hand at Peter, but his words had the desired effect. The king glowered at Asrai. She fanned herself, trying to think. "Your town seems to be one of hard working people as well, your majesty." Asrai tilted her head, and lowered her dark lashes in a pleasing way. Her eyes flashed. She used her magick to hold the king, moulding his mind. Her tongue dropped the words she knew he wanted to hear. "While my family's duties are not as grand as yours, we take the same pride in justly governing our subjects. After all, collecting precious jewels can be grueling work."

King Dominic's eyes widened, and his mouth dropped open in a hearty laugh. "Oh, my dear, such wit!" He cleared his throat, but the smile stayed on his lips. "I see why you desired her, my boy. But why keep her stashed away for so long?"

Peter gritted his teeth. "Uncle, there is plenty of *wit* in the kitchens as well. That doesn't mean Cormack should marry a scullery maid!" Princess Nephara's eyes widened. She flicked a heated glare at Peter. He withered under her gaze, something Cormack had never seen before.

King Dominic turned his head. "And why would a groomed boy such as yourself know of 'wit' in the kitchen?"

Peter turned a dark red. "No reason, majesty. Just making a point." He avoided the king's gaze.

Cormack cleared his throat, recapturing King Dominic's attention. "I was worried for your disapproval, Father." He placed his hand over Asrai's and met her gaze. "Her household is not the grand ally you seek in your battles. But she is certainly the ally of my heart."

King Dominic nodded. "Yes, that is true, but plenty of allies can be had without the pomp and delight of marriage. Paper works just as well. Besides, gold works well in war, better than any man!" He laughed.

Asrai hid a blush with her fan, and Cormack snuck a grin. The king watched this and could not be more pleased. The first course, blackened prawns, was served. Asrai was starving, but she resisted the urge to gorge, and picked at her food bite by bite, mirroring Nephara's measured habits. The men enjoyed the prawns, and even sucked on the heads. Cormack invited Asrai to do so as well, and she relished the barbaric moment. She darted her eyes to Nephara, who sent her a disgusted glare.

The next course came and went — stuffed partridge crusted with rosemary — but when the boar came, Asrai went to pick up her goblet of water and tipped it over by accident. Servants rushed to mop up the mess.

"Are you unwell?" Cormack's eyes darted over her.

Asrai snapped open her fan. "I'm all right." She looked up again and smiled. "I think I'm just getting tired."

Before Cormack could call a valet, King Dominic stood, holding the carving knife aloft as the great boar was hefted onto the table. "Nothing excites me more than a well killed boar!" He stabbed the roasted corpse, sawed off a mighty hunk, and slapped it onto his plate. The servers cut proper portions and passed them out to the guests.

Love of the Sea

King Dominic brought the fork to his lips. "Any man is welcome to his fancy pheasant and swan, but I prefer the simple boar."

The others at the table murmured in approval. Nephara's face was sweet and placid, save for the glint of disdain in her eyes. Peter was too busy shoveling meat into his mouth to notice. Asrai consumed her portion with measured forkfuls, taking care to drink between every bite. Cormack ate his cut of boar with more care than he typically would, keeping an eye on Asrai. King Dominic began telling a story of his younger days, and his pursuit of wild boar.

Cormack whispered to Asrai. "Do your people not partake flesh?"

Asrai shook her head. "Flesh does not bother me, my dear sailor, but the flesh of land creatures is far less delicate than fish and crab."

Peter leaned toward them, his wine glass paused midway to his lips. "Does boar not please you as it pleases our dear king, my *lady?*" Peter's poignant emphasis made Cormack flinch.

Asrai took another sip of water. "No, my lord, this boar is excellent to sup on. My prince and I were merely discussing what a rarity it is for me."

Peter scoffed, raising his voice in hopes the king would overhear. "If it is such a treat for you, then why do you take such particular amounts rather than consuming with zest?"

Asrai smiled, setting her water glass down and staring into Peter's eyes. The magick crackled. "It would not do for a lady to eat hastily, now would it?"

Peter glowered, embarrassed. He turned and saw that Nephara too was taking particular bites of her boar. He grumbled into his food. King Dominic let out a roaring laugh. "Oh, my dear! You are quite the diplomat! Maybe I should have your quick wits on my council!" He laughed again, his men joining him.

Peter snorted. "A lady on the council, indeed, Uncle."

King Dominic turned his head, his hand on his flagon of ale. "What was that boy?"

Peter spread a forced smile and picked up his own flagon. "Nothing, your highness. I was merely contemplating your rouse."

The king nodded and drowned his flagon, Peter muttering into his own cup. Cormack smiled at Asrai, her clever eyes flashing as she cut another tidbit of meat. She fought her shaking body, holding the magick to keep the king feeling delighted. Her face was growing pale, and Cormack flagged down one of the servers.

"M'lord." The maid bobbed a curtsy and drew close to hear Cormack's whispering.

"Please send for some charges to bear Lady Asrai up to her room. Tonight's festivities seem to be draining her."

The maid nodded and hurried back to the kitchen. Cormack touched Asrai's hand, and she looked from her water glass to Cormack. He waved for someone to refill her cup for the third time. "Thank you." Asrai said as the servant poured the water, but her words were intended for Cormack instead.

****

Cormack watched as Asrai began to deteriorate. She hid her shaking hands by keeping them in her lap, her head tilted, as if listening to the king. Relief washed over him when he spotted the two valets bearing the palanquin. King Dominic set down his knife. "I have but begun to sup!"

The company gave a tight, nervous laugh. Cormack cleared his throat. "It is for Lady Asrai, Father. She is feeling out of sorts from her travels."

"She will have to gather up her strength for the wedding night, eh m'boy?" He winked at Cormack, throwing the men into raucous laughter. Princess Nephara flinched at such distasteful conversation.

The king spoke again. "Travel always tires out the women. Good night, m'lady." The men murmured to Asrai as Cormack lifted her into the palanquin. She waved goodbye as they bore her away. Cormack sat back down at the table, Peter's eyes boring into him.

"My boy!" Cormack snapped his attention back to the king. King Dominic waved his knife. "All that talk of travel, and yet here she is! A most amusing jest. What a lady! I see your little sea adventures brought you a bounty."

Peter rolled his eyes as he carved a hunk of boar. "It all seems too good to be true, Uncle." He tilted his head to Nephara, giving her a lavish grin. "And her entrance was rather lacklustre."

King Dominic plunked the meat onto his plate. He lifted his fork. "Nonsense. She seems a fine lady."

Cormack searched for words. "I understand that Lady Asrai is a bit different, but our customs must seem strange to her as well."

King Dominic nodded, his mouth stuffed with boar. The three men sat, chewing in silence for a moment as the guests of Caraway chattered around them. Nephara's eyes glittered as she listened to the talk. Peter cut more from the boar's haunch.

"Where were her attendants? I noticed it was men of our household who brought her in." Peter gestured with his fork.

Cormack's fork froze halfway to his mouth. He thought for a moment, then remembered his father's talk of trade and alliances. "She is a tribute prize. Sulu wishes to extend their generosity in return for our good favour."

Love of the Sea

King Dominic sat back in his chair, stroked his beard, and belched. "Seems everyone is throwing tribute brides at us, eh my boy?" He sat forward again and cut more meat. "I bet Ol' Richard is hot under the collar just thinking of all the lovelies you could have!" He winked.

Cormack blushed. "Father!"

"Oh, don't act like such a ninny!" Peter rolled his eyes. "Are you a man, or a fragile-eared maid?"

The king paid Peter no heed; he was busy laughing at his own joke. Cormack cleared his throat. "I don't think anyone wants to imagine Richard with a lady."

At this, the king roared with laughter, slapping his broad hand on the table. "Oh, Peter! He has bested you!"

Peter clenched his teeth and shot Cormack a fiery glare. Nephara was seething from hearing such crass conversation. Her face was smooth, and gentle, but eyes radiated her disgust. Cormack did not flinch as he normally would; something about Asrai had emboldened him.

"A round of ale! A round of ale!" King Dominic bellowed.

Several serving girls made their rounds about the table, flitting from cup to cup like frightened deer. Cups overflowed and the king cheered. "Such fine lasses, ale for all!"

The girls giggled and retreated to a respectable distance from the table. Everyone raised their cups to the king. They drank deep and banged their cups down on the table. "A fine end to a fine meal," King Dominic announced.

Cormack nodded. He pushed his cup away. "I think I too shall retire, Father."

"Don't be dipping into the honey jar early." The king's face hardened. "A tribute bride is nothing to sneeze at. Who knows what Eastern allies they might have?" He looked into his cup. "It is best to wait and see things through." He shot a glare at Peter. "That goes for you as well! Your wedding will come soon enough!"

Princess Nephara glared at her plate as Peter smirked at the king. He put his arm around Nephara's shoulders. She allowed a smile to turn the corners of her lips, though her eyes still revealed her annoyance.

Cormack nodded, his eyes glued to the table, his face red and hot. "Yes, Father."

King Dominic lowered his voice, his smile tired, but joyful. "Goodnight, my son."

Chapter Twelve

Cormack scampered up the stairs, unsure of what apartments Asrai had been assigned to. Finally, he spotted a maid leaving a room. She walked down the opposite end of the hall, toward the servants' staircase. Cormack hurried and found the door unlocked. Asrai was seated on the bed. When she saw that it was him, her placid mask dropped.

"Please hurry!" Asrai's voice sounded raspy and the rims of her eyes were red. "These clothes are strangling me!"

Cormack nodded and helped her struggle out of the dress and underpinnings. The corset proved to be a challenge. When Cormack finally pulled the stiff fabric away he saw that some of Asrai's scales were stuck in the folds. He plucked one and stared at it.

"Asrai! Why did you stay at dinner so long?" Horror crept up his throat.

She shook her head. Cormack gathered her in his strong arms. He bore her to the bathroom, grateful the maids had already filled the tub with clean water. He slid her in, sloshing water all over himself. Asrai gasped as if taking her first breath. Cormack watched as her scales bloomed, filling them back to their fierce crimson blaze. Her skin brightened and returned to its dewy moonlit sheen. Asrai sighed and flexed the fins on her tail, the thin membranes coming back to life.

Cormack looked around and then stared at his feet. "Is there anything I can do for you?"

Asrai closed her eyes and her scales popped as she flexed her tail. "Just leave me to soak, my dear sailor. I am so tired."

Cormack nodded. He scanned her body. A few loose scales had fallen onto the floor. The candles in the room flickered, and all was quiet. Asrai's chest rose and fell, her scales opening and closing around the delicate skin. Cormack felt the buzz of excitement draining from his body. For the first time that day, he realized how truly exhausted he was, and reached for the door. "Goodnight, Lady Asrai."

The castle was in an uproar when Cormack rose that morning. The halls buzzed with servants rushing here and there. A maid had burst into his bedroom, leaving him a meager breakfast of bread and cheese on the table before bobbing an apology and rushing off to some other task.

Cormack gathered the tray and snuck into the hall. The frenzied servants remained oblivious of him as they rushed to their tasks. He found

Love of the Sea

the door to Asrai's new apartments unlocked. An identical tray sat on the small table. Cormack knocked on the bathroom door. "My lady?"

The lock clicked, and Cormack pushed the door open. Asrai was glowing, her pale skin luminous in the dying candlelight and the blossoming dawn. The light was as soft as a dove's wing, and played upon her scales, sending gold sparkles and miniature rainbows about the room.

"Good morning, Asrai." Cormack set the tray on his lap as he made himself comfortable on the worn wooden stool.

Asrai ran her fingers through her damp hair. "Good morning, my sailor."

"Our announcement has everyone running mad." Cormack grinned. "The servants seem beside themselves."

Asrai giggled, her eyes flashing. Her lips were red as blood on snow. The evening soak had done her good. "As a princess of my standing would expect."

Cormack laughed and handed her a wedge of soft yellow cheese and a hunk of coarse bread. "Though I'm not sure how long we can continue this masque."

Asrai nodded. She brushed crumbs off her fingers. "That is why we must visit the sea tonight. Then all will be well."

Fear gripped Cormack's heart. "We are to leave tonight?"

She shook her head. "Tonight, the sea hag will grant me legs."

Cormack's eyebrows shot up. "You intend to stay here on land?"

"No!" Asrai snapped.

Cormack stared at Asrai, his mind turning over what they had talked of before. *I will lose my soul if I lose my legs to the sea.* "Why is my love for you not enough? In all those tales I read as a child, they spoke of the old binding magick that love can bring. Could it be powerful enough to grant you legs and stay here forever with me?"

Asrai gave Cormack a cold look. "You yearn for the sea, and here I am to give it and all its wonders to you, and yet, you shrink from it." She chewed the bread. "Even with the binding magick that love fuels, I would still dry out. It would be a slow painful death over the course of a short human lifetime."

"You would still dry out, even with magick?" Cormack rubbed the back of his neck.

She lowered her hand, the crust of bread soggy in her hand. "I tire of this endless circle of questions. I cannot live on land, my sailor. Please do not ask such a cruel thing of me."

Cormack balked. "You ask the same of me! To leave all I know behind and join you in the sea, is that not the same?"

Asrai flinched at his impassioned words. She lowered her gaze. "You seem unhappy here in your kingdom, seeking comfort in the sea with your little boat. I know you feel the call. It is part of your true nature. Why deny who you are?"

He wrinkled his nose. "My true nature?"

"Long ago, humans were once mers, but then they left the sea and forgot the pull of the tide." Asrai set the bread back onto the tray and wiped the crumbs from her hands. "You are one of the few who feels that tug to return. To deny it would be to deny your true purpose."

...the humans could not go back to the sea after living on land for so long...we are all stained with the sins of the Cursed One, and seek the forgiveness of Poseidon and his pure waters of the sea.

His heart trembled. He ran his hand through his hair. "I am sorry Asrai, this is just so difficult for me."

"I know." She put her hand on top of his. "Don't fret, my sailor. I will be with you through all of this. You have nothing to fear."

Cormack brushed the crumbs off his lap and kissed the crown of Asrai's hair. "I will see if Pamela can steal away and aid us tonight. I have to think on things."

Asrai lowered her head, twisting her comb in her hands. "I understand, my sailor. I shall wait for you."

He kissed Asrai's forehead again, wanting to dispel her grim frown. "I will come for you as soon as I can."

Cormack flinched when he exited Asrai's apartments. Peter was standing there, waiting for him. "Dear Cousin, where are you off to in such a hurry this afternoon? Off to see your *princess?*" He sneered the last word. His rich cobalt-blue jacket and breeches contrasted starkly with Cormack's typical sailing tunic and worn breeches.

Cormack danced on his toes, trying to see a way around Peter. "Asrai was not well last night. I wanted to check on her. She has asked me to fetch her something from the kitchens—"

Peter laughed and clapped a hand on Cormack's back. He steered him down another hall toward the map room. "That's what maids are for. Come, the king is waiting." He looked down at Cormack's hand. "Why are you carrying around your shoes? I swear Cousin, the sea is turning you into an animal."

Cormack looked back down the hall, craning his neck, and saw a maid heading for Asrai's room. Peter shut the doors behind them before he could break loose from Peter's grip and stop her. King Dominic sat at the round map table, surrounded by his advisors.

The king cleared his throat. "Please excuse my son's odd habits. He is a bit eccentric." He turned to Cormack. "It's good to see you here, my boy! Come join us, we were just discussing our plans to advance on that dog Richard's new hold on the western line of Umber."

Love of the Sea

Cormack nodded, defeated. He took the chair at his father's right. Peter sat in a chair a few seats to the left. Peter raised his eyebrows, and a smile crept across his face. He watched Cormack pull on his boots.

"Majesty, the people of Umber are already in a state of turmoil since Richard's invasion. I am certain another battle would only frenzy the peasants, and pose a threat of immediate rebellion against us, should we succeed against Richard's men." The head advisor pointed, careful not to knock the markers. "I suggest we send emissaries to Gables to extend our leadership. I'm sure with Richard at their doors they will welcome the security of our support."

King Dominic nodded. "Yes, I see, Ruben. But how would that return Umber to us?"

Cormack twirled a quill, staring at the tiny horses and men on the map. He had often played with them as a child, making his father exclaim that he was a natural born strategist. King Dominic was too engrossed to notice Cormack's boredom, but Peter narrowed his eyes.

"Umber is the crown jewel of our lands." Peter lifted his glare from the map to Cormack. "Cousin, what strategy would *you* employ to protect Umber's borders?"

Cormack dropped the quill and scanned the board, then looked up at King Dominic. "Well," he looked up to Ruben, "I think we should heed Ruben's plan. He is, after all, the man who conquered the wilds of San Bai with a broken retinue of barely ten and one-hundred men. I'm sure he has thought up something that is far more efficient than I."

King Dominic smiled, nodding. "Very diplomatic, son, well said. I trust the skill of my advisors just as much as I trust myself. No king stands alone."

Peter scowled as Cormack leaned back in his chair. He turned his gaze to the king. "Uncle, strategy is only part of the art of war. Might I suggest allowing me to head the main retinue? Seeing our royal colours would strike fear in even the bravest of Richard's lap dogs!"

King Dominic shook his head. "That is unwise." He traced his finger over the narrow forest pass. "These are not the grand hills that kings battle upon for glory. This is a tight, winding patch of land that is choked by ancient trees and rough bluffs. We must employ our most cunning men for a surprise attack if we are to throw off Richard's hold."

Peter gripped the edge of the map table, his knuckles turning white. "Yes, Uncle."

The king and the advisors continued moving the pieces about the board, talking about taxes and revolts. Cormack tried to listen to footsteps outside in the hall, but it was impossible over the chatter of tactics. While Cormack was thinking of an excuse, his stomach gave a loud, embarrassing, rumble.

King Dominic looked up. "Cormack, have you eaten?"

Cormack shook his head. The bread and cheese had hardly been a meal, and he feared Asrai was just as hungry. "I was on my way to the kitchens when Peter brought me here. He said that your plans today were vital for my ears."

The king waved his hand. "A ruler cannot battle on an empty stomach! Go and see if Pamela will give you some of those oat cakes that she's famous for. We have only just begun the plans. Go now, my boy."

"Thank you, Father." Cormack bowed and exited the map room, Peter's eyes burning into the back of his skull.

Cormack ran for Asrai's apartments. He opened the door and found the bedroom empty. He tried to open the bathroom door, but it was locked. He knocked. "Asrai? I haven't much time!"

There was a click and the door unlatched. Cormack let himself in. The second tray of bread and cheese was still on the table as he had left it. Cormack plucked it up, and brought it with him into the bathroom. He saw Asrai lounging in the bathtub; he worried that the water had grown cold.

"Hello, my sailor. Have you spoken with Pamela?" Asrai curled the fins on her tail.

Cormack set the tray on the washing stool and edged it next to the tub. He fidgeted his hands. "I apologise, Peter diverted me. Has anyone disturbed you?"

Asrai shook her head. "I sent them away."

"I will be back as soon as I can. I must return to the map room, but I will speak with Pamela first." Cormack took her hand and kissed it.

"I will be fine. I can look after myself." Asrai smiled as he kissed her hand. "Just take care, and return quickly, my sailor."

"I shall always return to you." Cormack gave her a quick peck on the lips, and dashed back out into the hall. His determined stride led him to the muggy kitchens.

"You had me worrying all morning." Pamela waved her wooden spoon at Cormack, her voice hushed. "What have you been up to?"

"I'm sorry, Peter delayed me. Asrai is doing much better. The water did her good."

She sheathed her spoon and eyed Cormack. "Well I'm glad to hear it. I'll have her down and dressed in time for supper."

He nodded. "Yes, and after supper we need your assistance for an errand."

Pamela's eyes darted about the kitchen. "Tell me later." She slipped him an oat cake and gave him a wink over her shoulder.

Cormack smiled as he devoured the oat cake. He grabbed a warm loaf of bread out of the basket, and made his way back to the map room.

Peter's annoyed face met his as Cormack sat next to his father, tearing off chunks of wheat bread with his teeth.

"Good to see you are ready for the afternoon plans, my boy!" King Dominic clapped Cormack on the back, causing him to choke.

Cormack coughed and swallowed hard, gulping ale from the flagon a maid had set out for him. "Yes Father. I'm always happy to hear of your campaigns." Peter rolled his eyes at Cormack.

"We will strike here, holding back, behind this copse of trees." King Dominic pointed to some green blobs that were near tiny horses and soldiers. "Once our archers have lost range, we will flood the hill here..."

His initial hunger satiated, Cormack picked at the coarse bread, watching his father move things around on the table. His war plans became muffled as Cormack's mind drifted to Asrai. He wondered what Pamela would dress her in for dinner that evening. He leaned his elbow a little farther, tipping his ale.

"Woah there, son!" King Dominic righted the cup before it could spill. He let out a hearty laugh. "Get your head out of the clouds, or rather, out of your lady's skirts!"

The council laughed and clapped in approval. Cormack shook his head, a blush rising in his cheeks. One of the council men leaned over the table to address the king.

"When is the wedding feast, sire?"

Cormack froze and turned to his father. He could see Peter scowling. King Dominic stroked his beard and puffed out his chest. "This will be a grand feast, gentlemen. My son has been slow to choose a hand, but now that he has, I am prepared to table twelve strong boar and a flock of fowl. Dress richly, men, for it will be such an occasion as you have never seen!"

Shouts for ale were answered with more clapping. Cormack breathed out a sigh as the men pounded the table and cheered. King Dominic turned to Cormack and gave him a brisk slap on the shoulder. "My bones can finally rest easy, my boy, knowing that you're safely wedded off."

Cormack jumped, ice pumping through his veins and turned to the king. "What kind of talk is that, Father?"

King Dominic took advantage of the ruckus and discussion of the wedding feast. He slumped in his chair and folded his hands on the table. For the first time, Cormack noticed how wrinkled and veined they were. "I'm an old man, son. Nothing makes an old man happier than knowing his line is safe."

Cormack swallowed hard as King Dominic smiled, the wrinkles deepening in his cheeks. Before Cormack could catch his father's attention, the king clapped his hand on the table. "Supper is going to be set. What do you say to a leg of boar, men?"

The council cheered and King Dominic hefted his wide girth from the chair. Cormack found that he could not stand, his eyes fixed on his father. Only Peter stayed behind.

****

Pamela pressed the bedroom door open and locked it behind her, slipping the copper key into her apron. Splashing sounds could be heard behind the bathroom door, and upon opening it, she found Asrai combing her hair.

"Doing better I see?" Pamela fetched linen from one of the shelves.

Asrai nodded and the comb seemed to disappear back into her hair. She pulled herself out of the tub, dripping water onto the stone floor. Pamela draped the linen around her, drying her.

"Poor dear," she said as Asrai winced. "Your love is bold, but it might do you in."

"Wouldn't you do the same?" Asrai lifted herself onto dry linen, and let Pamela drag her into the bedroom. "Wouldn't you suffer for your mate?"

"Poseidon bless his soul, I did many things for him, dear." Pamela brought Asrai against the bed, which she hoisted herself onto. "But what use is it to throw your life away and leave that lover?"

Asrai bowed her head. "I am sorry for your loss."

Pamela clucked her tongue and pulled a chemise over Asrai's head. "No need for tears, it's gone and done with. Right now, we need to get you to supper."

Asrai clenched the bedsheets as Pamela tightened the corset, the whalebone squeezing her scales against her body. She did not complain. A pale blue gown slipped over her head, and Pamela began the arduous task of sewing Asrai's tail into the dress.

Asrai played with the lacey cuff of her sleeve. "I heard Cormack's father say that many brides were brought here. Why has he taken so long to choose a mate?"

"Poseidon only knows, dear." Pamela sighed. Her knees popped as she stood. "Cormack has always had trouble with his place in the world."

Pamela clapped her hands and rubbed them together. "Back to the kitchens! I'll be sure a fish course is set for supper." She pecked Asrai on the cheek and strode out into the hall.

****

Cormack broke from his reverie and rose to head out of the map room. Peter followed close behind. His grin revealed his teeth, and Cormack focused his attention on the hall, rather than his smirking cousin.

"Further than even San Bai?" Peter goaded, matching Cormack's stride. "How incredible that her journey was so quick, and her arrival so timely to your rejection of the princess."

Cormack continued to stomp down the hall, his anger boiling, fear curling at the corners of his mind. Peter's voice lifted. He was a purring cat toying with a doomed mouse. "And yet, she is a tribute bride? Rushed here for you? With no message to the king?"

Cormack began to clench his teeth. The holes in his story glared at him. Fear ignited into a small flame in his chest. "Your declaration of love was quite charming." Peter had followed Cormack to the main hall where his apartments were. "And yet, it implies you met the lady previously. How is it possible that you met a lady from a kingdom that lies so far from our borders?"

Cormack stopped before the door. He ground his teeth as Peter hovered behind him. "The lady especially power hungry? Is that why she has enchanted you, dear Cousin?" Peter's words were barbs wrapped in his silky voice. "Seeking an alliance for her insignificant little province?"

Cormack snorted and continued staring straight ahead. Peter choked back a laugh. "Do not think I'm fooled. You are a poor liar." Peter's voice was cold, and Cormack did his best to suppress a shiver.

Chapter Thirteen

A polite knock sounded on Asrai's door. The footmen entered, revealing Asrai seated on the bed in a powder blue dress. A choker with rows of pearls was wound round her neck, hiding her gills. The petal pink cuffs swallowed her hands. A motif of roses and bees was embroidered on the dress, showing small pops of colour here and there.

The head footman bowed. "Good evening, princess. The feast is about to begin. Are you ready to depart?"

Asrai nodded. The pearls slid against her throat as she swallowed. Her scales strained against the corset. The head footman carried Asrai to the waiting palanquin in the hall. He made sure Asrai was comfortable. They hoisted the poles, and made their way to the dining hall.

****

King Dominic was onto his second flagon when the party arrived. His face lit up, and he raised his flagon as Asrai came into view. "A pleasure to see you, my lady!"

Cormack stood and helped slide Asrai onto the wooden bench. She smiled and bowed her head. "A pleasure to be at your table again, Majesty."

The king grinned and took a swig of ale. "Now if that cousin of yours can find his way to my table, we may sup!"

Asrai took a sip of water. Cormack seated himself next to her, his eyes darting over her blue gown. The way the air shifted around her was odd, like sunlight on the waves. He pushed down the feeling of unease and looked up and down the table. Peter and Princess Nephara were indeed absent. Two maids hurried about pouring ale. A third maid stood a few paces back from Asrai, holding a pitcher of what must have been water. The gesture was most certainly from Pamela. He would need to thank her later. Hurried footsteps sounded, and Peter and the princess appeared soon after. King Dominic frowned.

"Our apologies, Uncle." Peter bowed. "Please excuse us."

King Dominic muttered something as they were seated. Princess Nephara kept her eyes lowered. The king banged the butt of his fork on the table. "Let us feast!"

The servants flooded the room, bearing large wooden platters. The table was soon covered with sections of boar, delicate cold cuts of squab, and flaky white fish, just as Pamela had promised. Bowls of roasted potatoes and root vegetables were butted up against boards of bread and cheese. The party began filling their plates once King Dominic had sawed off his first bite of boar. There was no pomp at the main tables, as there was in the Great Hall. The guests had already been impressed. Now they would learn daily life in Paradine.

One of the servants set a bowl of honeyed figs before Princess Nephara. She turned to Peter, her eyes sparkling. "You remembered?"

He grinned at her and nodded. "Of course, princess. How could I forget that your favourite dish is as sweet and colourful as you?"

Cormack looked away as Peter fed one of the figs to Nephara. He turned to Asrai, who was busy with her plate of fish.

"Are you enjoying yourself, my lady?" Cormack grinned at her. She seemed normal again, the odd shimmering about her gone. Asrai nodded, her mouth full. "Then I am pleased." He reached to fill his own plate.

The Caraway guests were enjoying the sumptuous spread. The king was already on his second helping of boar. Asrai was eating in small bites, but Cormack could see the speed in which she made the food on her plate disappear.

King Dominic banged his flagon onto the table for silence. "Tonight, my friends, we share with you the story of Paradine. All that once was and now is."

A group of musicians and a minstrel entered the hall and took their seats on the small platform across from the great table. The herald took up position just to their left, and extended his arm in grand presentation.

"My lords and ladies, tonight our royal musicians of the court will play for you while our wonderful minstrel, Daniel Ratherford, will take us back in time to the birth of our dear Paradine."

The herald bowed, and a smattering of claps rounded the table as he exited into the hallway. The musicians struck up a soft tune as Daniel cleared his throat and bowed.

"'tis always an honour to perform for my lords and ladies. I am especially delighted to enchant your majesties all the way from Caraway, and our dear princess from Sulu. Now, let us begin.

In wondrous days of olden yore
A set of brothers three did explore
The world was light, the world was young
Their epic battles and earnest quests not yet been sung
These brothers three, alighted upon the sea.

The map yet drawn, the dawn in mystery
Such boldness in the face of Poseidon

Lauren A. R. Masterson

Once challenged, no one may deny him
These brothers three, wrapped in a storm upon the sea!

With waves as tall as apple trees
and winds that howled a thousand banshees!
Their mighty boat splintered and plundered
By Poseidon's booming thunder
Their limbs flailed as mouths filled with sea foam
Calling their mother's name and wishing for home
These brothers three, drowning in the sea

Upon a strange shore they settled on
Their souls baptized for this new age, new dawn
The eldest brother was first to wake
First to be born, and the first to break
He cursed the land, the sea, the sand
And headed West to seek remand

The youngest brother was next to wake
Last to be born, and first to claim his stake
He was on to greater things
And wandered East for battles with kings

The middle brother was last to wake
The forgotten child, and the first to feel heartache
He found his brothers gone
And headed North to find where he belonged

This brother was our first brave king
None other than the bold and wistful Great Aries
He found a tribe and ruled them right
He showed them tools and made them bright

The kingdom of Paradine was so aptly named
For no place so close to paradise was ever made
We love our land, and we love the sea
For it delivered unto us the wisest of the brothers three."

The minstrel bowed, and King Dominic started a hearty clap. The rest of the guests followed suit, offering thunderous applause. The minstrel bowed again, a grin on his face. The musicians struck up again, and the minstrel began singing a simple ditty, encouraging the guests to move from their food induced stupor to dance.

Love of the Sea

Peter stood and offered his hand to Princess Nephara. She smiled and accepted. The two hooded ladies followed, keeping a safe distance to allow for twirling, but always watching. Cormack put his arm around Asrai's shoulders.

"Do you grow weary, my lady?" he whispered in her ear.

Asrai shook her head. "Not quite yet. I am enjoying your music. It is very different from ours."

He nodded and squeezed her shoulder before withdrawing. King Dominic watched the exchange, but said nothing. A few of the Caraway guests paired up, and even the maids joined in. The king leaned his elbows on the table and smiled at the dancers, his mind far away to the days when he himself was a young man twirling his beloved lady.

Cormack watched as Peter grinned at Princess Nephara. She threw her head back as Peter spun her, the raven locks bouncing and her face glowing with joy. A maid jumped out of the dance and refilled Cormack's cup, and Asrai's water. He took a deep draught from his flagon.

Can the princess of Caraway truly change him enough to become king? Can I entrust Paradine to Peter, or will I doom my kingdom for my own selfish desires?

****

Asrai bristled at Cormack's change in mood. She sighed and took a delicate sip of water. Her scales were cutting into her body. Her skin was on fire. The dryness was settling deep into her bones, making her body ache. Her eyes flashed as Princess Nephara laughed and twirled.

Perhaps I can give him the chance that was robbed of me and assuage his fears by strengthening his kingdom before his departure.

"My dear sailor, would you please inform the head cook that tonight's banquet was splendid?" Asrai put her hand over Cormack's and kept her smile small, so as to hide her fangs.

He flinched, dragged from his thoughts. "Of course, Sweetheart."

Cormack pecked her on the cheek before rising. He strode toward the kitchens to find Pamela.

Asrai waited until he had gone. She knew he would detect the magick, and did not want him to know. Asrai focused again on Princess Nephara as she laughed and pranced about with Peter. The music was gay and bright, the dancers a jumble of arms and legs. Her eyes brightened to icy blue. The tendrils of magick snaked around the princess and sunk deep into her heart. Nephara flinched, but did not stop dancing. Asrai held her, as if cupping flowing water in her hands.

Become the queen this kingdom needs. Be the mother these people crave once Cormack leaves. Your destiny is bright and true. Believe in it, and be exactly you.

The magick squeezed Nephara's heart. She shivered, and gasped. Peter drew closer to her, dancing a bit slower and watching her upturned face. The princess was the perfect picture of a tidy fruit, ripe for plucking. Asrai held the magick a moment longer, then let it recede until her eyes darkened, and Nephara none the wiser.

Asrai leaned back into the table behind her. The fabric of the dress scraped the delicate fins of her tail as she moved. The corset made it difficult to breathe. Asrai dug deep into her wellspring and bathed her body in glamour, ensuring that no one noticed the shake in her limbs or how her skin was losing its luminous sheen.

****

Cormack entered the sweltering kitchen. The scullery scrubbed the soiled plates, pots, and pans from the feast. He found Pamela cooking a simple stew to feed the kitchen hands once the cleaning was finished.

"Excuse me." Cormack hovered near her. "Asrai wanted me to thank you, for everything."

Pamela nodded, her great wooden spoon stirring in a handful of sage. "It was the least I could do. The kitchen is busy as a hive, best be off now."

Cormack nodded and left Pamela to her things. He was careful not to slip on the soapy water. He returned to find Asrai staring at the dancers. Nephara and Peter twirled about as if they were the only creatures in the room. Cormack shook his head and sat beside Asrai. He took her hand and squeezed it. Her fingers were limp, her hand warm. Cormack leaned closer and noticed that Asrai's breathing was becoming laboured.

"Shall I call for the footmen?"

Asrai nodded. "Yes, my sailor. Be sure to have Pamela attend me."

****

A maid entered the kitchen. The staff gathered about the worn table, eating their own dinner at last. She nodded to Pamela. "The Lady Asrai wishes for your attendance."

The kitchen hands glanced about the table, but said nothing. Pamela nodded and heaved herself up, exhausted. She bypassed the drunk guests by mounting the servant service stairs. They led closer to Asrai's apartments than the main staircase, which made her job easier. Cormack had already settled Asrai into the bedroom. He had hurried off on an errand that left the footmen scratching their heads.

"My lady!" Pamela called as she knocked.

"Enter!" Asrai's voice was muffled by the door.

Pamela sighed as she approached the bed. "The scullery will be thinking I have an itch to return to court life at this rate."

Asrai bowed her head. "I am sorry to cause you distress."

Love of the Sea

Pamela smoothed Asrai's red locks and smiled. "Not to worry. It's lovely to see him so happy with a lady."

Asrai stiffened, her eyes wide. Pamela shook her head. "Whatever is the matter, dear?"

The door creaked. Pamela's smile dropped as she whipped around, cursing herself for forgetting to set the lock. She blanched when Peter stepped into the room. "You are dismissed." His voice boomed in the small space. He spoke to Pamela while staring straight at Asrai.

Pamela drew herself up and stuck out her heavy bosom. "You cannot dismiss me. Not while I'm attending a lady!"

Peter snorted. "Out, you old wench, before I break one of your precious wooden spoons or whatnot."

Pamela put her arms around Asrai, who was trembling. "You have no right to be left alone in a room with a lady, sir! Especially not this one."

Peter drew his dagger, and Pamela screamed, pushing Asrai behind her. "You dog! Drawing a knife in a lady's room!" He held the dagger high and bashed the hilt against Pamela's head. She dropped to the rug, her flabby limbs quivering. She groaned as her head throbbed.

****

Peter advanced on Asrai, who was scooting away from him on the bed. His voice was low and anger shone in his eyes. "Never before has my cousin shown such interest in a lady. It is rather *peculiar* that you just so happened to show up with such perfect timing. Our men are blocked from fighting a glorious battle on the plains of Gables because Richard's men changed strategy, laying siege to the western cities so the only route to head them off is the choked forest pass. Such *perfect timing* indeed."

Asrai's heart thundered as her lungs strained against the corset. Her wellspring was low, and she didn't have the strength to summon her magick. "I don't know these places you speak of!" Her throat was dry, her voice hoarse as she pleaded.

"Oh, forgive me!" Peter took a few slow steps toward the bed. "How could I forget that you come from *further than San Bai.* Of course you don't know what I'm talking about. But somehow you know the prince of the most powerful kingdom in all the world!"

Asrai flinched as Peter bellowed. She was near the edge of the bed, her body straining not to fall off. Pamela was lying still on the floor, the rise and fall of her back revealing that she still lived.

"You may have enchanted my cousin, and fooled the king, but your little tricks shan't work on me." Peter walked to the foot of the bed, and grabbed Asrai's arm, dragging her toward him.

"You're hurting me!" Asrai clenched her teeth, careful not to show her fangs. Her tail ignited with raw pain as it hit the wooden chest at the foot of the bed.

"I know what you are. You have no title, no land. You're a common whore carrying Richard's gold." He thrust the dagger in her face. "Well, I'll show you your place!"

Asrai screamed as Peter stuck the knife downward into the blue stays of her dress front and yanked. The silk ribbon cut like a whisper and he pried the stiff fabric open like flaps. He found the shoddy stitching Pamela had done and stuck the blade into the loose fabric of the dress. He drew the knife down, slicing through the dress and the bed sheets. Asrai was frozen, fearing the bite of metal in her flesh. As Peter pulled on the fabric, he pulled on the front stays of her corset, pulling it taut and sealing her ribs. Asrai's eyes widened as she felt the sharp tug squeezing the air from her lungs.

When Peter threw the dress open, his lewd smile disappeared and he jumped back. The knife dropped to the floor. Under the froth of petticoats, Asrai's scarlet tail gleamed in the candlelight, the scales shimmering. Her fins furled and unfurled, the thin membranes almost transparent.

Chapter Fourteen

Cormack stood in the doorway, frozen. His father had kept him at the feast with endless questions about his new engagement to the Lady Asrai. Cormack did not realize Peter had left the feast until he saw Nephara lounging with her retinue at the table. Her strange glances his way had unnerved him, and now he knew why.

Cormack lunged, knocking Peter to the floor. Their flailing bodies shook the furniture. Asrai's chest heaved as she struggled to breathe, the corset strangling her. Cormack's face was a deep crimson, his jaw tight with rage, his fist red with blood. Peter sprawled on the floor. He pushed himself to a standing position and touched his upper lip, his tongue tasting the blood.

"Get out!" Cormack roared, and Peter jumped. He stumbled from the room, his boots echoing down the hall.

Asrai waved her hand, begging for release as her lungs screamed. Cormack flew to her side, examining her face. "What's happened? Are you hurt?"

She tried to wrench the top of the corset, her throat burning as her lungs and gills floundered for any sort of oxygen. Cormack grabbed his own dagger from his hip and sliced the front stays of the corset. Asrai's scrambling hands wrenched the garment apart, her gold claws scrabbling against the fabric. Her chest rattled as she drew breath, filling her starved lungs. Cormack gripped Asrai's arms and shook her.

"Are you all right?" His eyes darted back and forth over her face. "Did he hurt you? Are you all right?"

Asrai nodded. She panted, the air clearing her head. "Yes. I am unharmed." Her voice was a strained whisper. She swallowed, trying to loosen the tightness in her throat.

Cormack swallowed hard and whispered in a husky voice. "I'm sorry. I was scared for you."

"Pamela is hurt!" Asrai's eyes darted to the head cook.

He followed Asrai's gaze and stepped around to the side of the bed. There he found Pamela face down on the rug. His mind screamed as he scanned her motionless limbs. He turned her over. Pamela was still unconscious, her chestnut hair splayed out on the ornate rug. Cormack knelt and pressed his fingers to her neck. Her pulse was sluggish, but apparent. Relief washed over Cormack as he watched her chest rise and fall. A dark bruise was beginning to form on her forehead.

Asrai leaned over the side of the bed. "Peter struck her because she was protecting me."

Cormack nodded. He dragged Pamela out from between the wall and the bed, onto the center rug of the room. He snatched a pillow from the bed, and placed it under her head. "I will fetch the doctor." Cormack looked up at Asrai. His heartbeat roared in his ears. "But first, we must hide you."

His fingers drew the ruined dress away and his arms enveloped Asrai in the warmth of his body. She pressed herself tighter against him. Cormack heaved her from the bed, her tail slapping his thigh as he carried Asrai to the bathroom. The water had already been drawn and gone cold. Asrai shivered, but was glad for it. The clean water seeped into her scales and skin.

Cormack squeezed Asrai's hand. "Keep quiet for now."

He hid the ruined dress in the chest at the foot of the bed, his hands shaking as he imagined the blade slicing the fabric. Cormack kneeled beside Pamela, checking again that she was still breathing. "Hold on, Pamela," he whispered, then pecked her on the cheek.

He jogged out of the bedroom and down the hall. His ears strained for the sound of footsteps. He managed to flag a maid down without startling her. "Please attend to the head cook. She has fallen in Lady Asrai's room, and injured her head." Cormack pointed back down the hall. The maid nodded, and trotted toward Asrai's apartments. Cormack ran to the southern hall to alert the doctor.

****

Asrai traced the deep lines the corset had left in her flesh. She had not expected Peter to be so volatile. Yes, he was suspicious of her, and Asrai wondered if he was capable of seeing through her glamour, but she had never imagined he would dissolve into violence at only their second meeting. Perhaps she had underestimated how much she was risking. Perhaps she was unprepared for the trials of Sulu. Her heart withered at the thought.

There are no second chances at Draum. I cannot treat this endeavour any different.

She lifted her hands, watching them tremble as the water soaked into her bones. She had been defenseless, her wellspring used up keeping the king pliant and holding her glamour for so long. Garradi would have ripped her to shreds. Asrai shuddered, horror creeping into her heart at the prospect of losing at Draum.

For too long I have been confident in my destiny as queen. I was ensnared by a human. Garradi is a cunning warrior who uses his wellspring for greed and terror. My efforts thus far have been those of a spoiled child.

Love of the Sea

Asrai leaned her head against the lip of the bathtub, listening to Pamela's groans on the other side of the door. A female voice was whispering to Pamela, and Asrai kept still, not wanting to slosh the water and alarm the maid. Her head ached as the thoughts barraged her, visions of Peter standing over her, laying her bare. Asrai shuddered.

****

Pamela sat up and gripped the maid's arm, causing her to drop the wet cloth she had been sponging Pamela's sweating brow with. "Where is Lady Asrai?"

The maid pushed Pamela back down and picked up the cloth. She dipped it back into the pitcher of cool water and wrung it out. "That is not your concern. You had quite a fall."

Pamela clenched her fists on the rug. "Fall nothing! That scoundrel Peter did this to me!"

The maid sat back on her heels, her hand over her mouth. "He did this to you?"

Before Pamela could answer, Cormack returned with the doctor, a coat thrown over his nightshirt, his satchel in hand. The maid stepped aside, allowing the doctor to pull out instruments from his case and examine the bruise, which now spanned back into Pamela's hairline.

He tested Pamela's reflexes and sighed. "There is no immediate danger, just a nasty knock to the head." He pulled out a silver knife and a small basin. "We will bleed the bruise to avoid swelling against the skull."

Cormack nodded and held Pamela's hand, the maid holding the other, as the doctor went about the gruesome task. A quick intake of breath and a hissing between her teeth was the only sound Pamela made as the doctor coaxed the blood out by pinching her skin.

"Will she need bedrest?" Cormack looked from Pamela's closed eyes to the doctor's downcast face.

"She should not be moved tonight. Make up a sleeping pallet for her here. Then tomorrow, she will need to rest. Pamela is a tough woman, but knocking about in the scullery would certainly risk a swoon." The doctor cleaned up the cut, stemming the flow of blood.

Cormack darted his eyes over Pamela's face. "But she will be all right?"

The doctor nodded. "Yes. She will have a splitting headache to say the least. But a blow like this is not enough to take her out of commission." Pamela opened her eyes again and saw Cormack's smiling face, the bleeding over. The doctor applied a wrapping, careful to place the linen under her hairline.

Pamela squeezed Cormack's hand. "I will attend to Asrai tomorrow. It will be less stressful than the kitchen." She managed a weak laugh. "Those fools might do without me for a day or two, but they'll certainly be needing some sense knocked into them when I'm back in action!"

Cormack patted Pamela's hand and kissed her forehead. "Thank you."

The maid helped Cormack and the doctor get Pamela to her feet. The doctor and maid supported her as Pamela was shuffled to a servant's pallet near the window. Cormack piled blankets over Pamela. Her eyes closed again. The maid and the doctor exited, allowing Cormack a moment of peace.

****

"I am so sorry, Pamela." Cormack took her hand and squeezed it. She did not respond. The gentle rise and fall of her chest showed she had fallen unconscious. Cormack gave her hand another squeeze, then closed the bedroom door. He crossed the room and knocked on the bathroom door.

"Asrai, they are gone." The click sounded, and the door swung open. Cormack walked in and shut the door.

"Is Pamela hurt?" Asrai was worrying her gold comb between her hands. Her skin had taken on a bluish tint and looked strange with her fiery scales and hair.

"Yes, but the doctor assured me she will attend you tomorrow. We are lucky Peter merely disarmed her, though it is poor form to strike a woman." Cormack kneeled next to the tub, lacing his fingers between Asrai's; they were ice cold.

"You are freezing!" He stood. "I will fetch you—"

"No!" Asrai ensnared his hand. "We must go, tonight! You must help me reach the sea hag. Now that Peter has seen me, we must finish the spell."

Cormack sat again and nodded. "All right. If you are sure."

He pulled linens from the cupboard and dried Asrai off. Asrai winced, as her body was still dry. The water had only teased her scales and skin. Cormack pulled a sage dress from the chest, ensuring that the ruined one was still hidden on the bottom. He pulled it over Asrai's head and laced up the front as best he could. His hands shook as his mind went over the path they would need to take to dodge the servants.

Asrai placed her hands over his. "Be still, my sailor. Soon all will be well."

Cormack nodded, taking a deep breath to calm his nerves. He drew Asrai into his arms, his muscles aching from the weight. Asrai pulled out her comb, helping to open the door and Cormack darted his head back and forth in the hall. Most of the servants were busy cleaning up the last of the feast. He trotted off toward the servants' staircase, and Asrai flicked her comb to the shut and lock the door.

Love of the Sea

Footsteps echoed at the base of the stairs. Fear spiked Cormack's brain, and he threw himself against an alcove. He could feel Asrai's heart racing against his chest. A maid trotted past, busy carrying a tray of sweets. She was unaware of their presence. Cormack strained his ears. The staircase was silent, and he galloped down them as quick as his legs would carry them.

Cormack thanked Poseidon when he found Nonna dressed in her tack and left tied to a post. Pamela had already given the stable boy the instructions and a coin from Cormack that afternoon. Now he was busy swapping stories with the sailors for a few hours. Cormack hoisted Asrai onto the horse. She was careful to swing her tail over the beast the way a human lady would ride sidesaddle. He helped arrange the skirts to hide Asrai's tail.

Cormack patted the mare's neck. "Ready old girl?" Nonna snorted, and Cormack untied the lead rope and looked at Asrai.

Asrai nodded and turned to Cormack. "Do not fear, my sailor. The dark will hide us as its own tonight."

Cormack lifted the lantern in his other hand. He gripped the mare's bridle, even though the gentle old nag hardly needed directing. Asrai clung to the coarse black mane and balanced her torso against the horse's neck.

****

She stiffened as the musky smell of the horse was overpowered by the fishy salt of the sea. She tilted her head back and let her lips part, running her tongue back and forth along the roof of her mouth, tasting the air.

When they reached the shoreline, Cormack patted Nonna's neck and the heavy clop of her hooves fell silent. Asrai wrapped her arms around Cormack's neck, and he compensated the weight by leaning against Nonna. Asrai let her body slide to the ground, using the heavy gown for leverage. Cormack undid the loose stays, and slipped the gown over Asrai's head. There were no underclothes, so she was freed at once. A few dull scales slipped out of Asrai's tail like loose teeth, but she was still holding her colour. She scooted toward the water, her arms pulling her forward as her tail thrashed back and forth, sending a spray of sand. Asrai sang to the ocean, the notes clear and haunting.

A wave crested, and out of the foam appeared a mermaid with violet hair. Her purple tail had an emerald sheen when the moonlight reflected off the scales. Asrai's tail became more vibrant. The mermaids embraced in the sandy water, only a few feet deep. The sea hag cupped Asrai's face in her hands and smiled. "My child, it is good to lay eyes upon you again."

The sea hag pulled out her comb— a gold one encrusted with shells resembling garnets —and began combing Asrai's hair. "This will be a trial. One that cannot be softened by magick. Do you understand?"

Asrai pulled out her own gold comb. She held it out to the sea hag. "Yes. I must accept the spell. There is another human, and he knows of my true form. I must take the guise of a human to protect both my mate and myself."

The sea hag stroked Asrai's comb, making it glow. "My heart trembles for you. May Poseidon protect you." The sea hag stroked the comb again, and it glowed brighter. She then touched her own comb to the crown of Asrai's head. "My heart shall rejoice at your return."

Both combs glowed bright. Asrai clenched her teeth. The dryness was nothing compared to this heat that set her flesh ablaze. Asrai threw her head back, strangling the scream in her throat as her body felt as if she were caught in a squall and dashed against the rocks over and over. Her skin felt tender and raw as her scales sucked into her skin until all her body was vulnerable white flesh. Asrai's large writhing tail split down the middle, as if with an invisible knife. Her lower lip bled from her teeth clenching. Darkness crept into the corners of her mind as the pain overwhelmed her senses.

"It will be over soon." The sea hag sang a low soft note as the legs formed.

The bones in her new toes popped, and with a deep sigh, Asrai's body was complete. Her hands shook as she stretched them out to the sea hag. She pulled Asrai close and they embraced. "The night you say your vows your true self will return and the sea will call the names of you and your mate."

Asrai let the sea hag kiss her cheeks and her eyes. When she opened them, she watched the violet tail disappear under the indigo crest of a wave. Cormack offered Asrai his hand, which she took. Her new legs trembled beneath her weight, and Cormack caught her.

"Easy now, that's it." Cormack hugged Asrai's shivering body. "Let's get you dressed before you freeze."

"Does walking always hurt?" Asrai grimaced as she sat again, allowing Cormack to slide the dress over her head.

"No." Cormack carried Asrai to the waiting horse. "You're just not used to it yet."

Asrai gripped the saddle horn with both hands. Once seated, Asrai wove her hands into Nonna's mane and leaned into the horse's neck. "I am weary, my sailor." Asrai whispered as Cormack took up the lead.

"You'll sleep in a bed tonight. I think you'll enjoy it." Cormack patted the horse's neck.

****

Love of the Sea

The stable was empty when they approached. Cormack pulled Asrai from the saddle, her body light now without her tail. He found that he missed the weight as he took her into his arms. Nonna remained steady and placid as ever. The stable boy returned, and when he saw the small party, he bowed his head and held out his hand. "Shall I wet down your horse, m'lord?"

Cormack nodded and pulled Asrai deeper into his embrace. The stable boy removed Nonna's gear and gave her a solid pat on the rump. She moved to the back of the stable as Cormack mounted the stairs at the end of the night run. His arms bore Asrai's weight easily.

The halls were quiet as Cormack headed toward Asrai's apartments. The guests of Caraway were already asleep in their own. Pamela was propped on the servant's pallet, just as they had left her. Cormack laid Asrai onto the bed as gentle and quiet as a whisper. She had fallen asleep in his arms. Cormack covered her sleeping form. The sage dress peeked out from the blue covers. Her fiery hair spilled over the pillows.

"Goodnight, my lady." Cormack kissed her forehead. Asrai sighed in her sleep. His heart burned as he drew away, taking one last look over his shoulder before he closed the door behind him.

Chapter Fifteen

His own apartments felt empty without Asrai. He opened the door to the washroom, the water in the tub cold and empty. Cormack left the door open, allowing the maids to finally have access in the morning. He crossed to his cabinet and pulled out the top drawer. A riot of sparkling rainbows caught the light of the candles. He reached his hand in and swallowed up a fistful of mermaid's tears.

To lose my soul and live my life in the sea...to leave my life behind and give Peter Paradine.

He rolled them around in his hand, then let them fall, save one.

What if I could find a way to make her spell permanent? What if she could live on land and learn life as a human? Then I would be king of Paradine... he shuddered, *and forced to become my father at last.*

The jewel was warm in his hand. It sparkled the way Asrai's scales would at times. His heart warmed at the thought. He missed the way her scales shimmered, now that she had the silky legs of a woman. Cormack's heart gnawed at an odd thought.

Or what if I did make my life in the sea? What if I did give all this up...maybe Peter could finally find peace.

Cormack placed the jewel on his wooden tray of rings and clasps. He fished the remaining jewels from the tub and hid them at the bottom of his dressing chest. His mind was made up, and the bed felt as soft as a cloud when his head finally sunk into his pillow and pulled him into a deep sleep.

The morning air was brisk. Cormack shivered as he forced himself to wake. The sun was barely risen, tucked behind a blanket of grey clouds. He stretched and shook off the tendrils of slumber. After dressing, he bounded toward the South end of the castle, his treasure tucked in his pocket. He pounded on the door, his excitement getting the better of him. Cormack fidgeted his hands as the startled jeweler opened the door.

"Y-y-your h-hi highness!" he stuttered. "G-good-d mmm-mor-nning!"

Cormack bowed his head. "My apologies for startling you, sir. I simply cannot wait a moment longer."

The jeweler nodded and opened the door. "Y-yes, yes. C-come in-n."

He followed into the dark room. The jeweler lit a few candles. He had an overcoat thrown over his nightshirt, his greying blonde hair in disheveled disarray. "W-what c-can I d-d-do for you, majesty?"

Cormack dug the jewel from his pocket and set it upon the smooth worktable. The jeweler gasped as he picked it up. It sent a flurry of sparkles and rainbows twirling about the room. "B-b-buh-by P-P-Poseidon's wave!" He snatched his eyeglass magnifier. "Is this t-truly-?"

"Yes. That is a mermaid's tear." Cormack shuffled his feet.

The jeweler nodded. He set the magnifier down and placed the jewel on a velvet square. "Wh-what does y-your hi-highness re-require?"

Cormack fidgeted his hands, his face reddening as he stared at his feet. "I require a ring. Quickly. For a fair maiden of the sea."

"Ah." The jeweler smiled. "At o-once, yo-your hi-highness."

"Thank you." Cormack looked up and shook hands with the jeweler. His grin grew wider. "Make it grand!"

The jeweler chuckled. "N-noth-ing-thing less, m-majesty."

Cormack bounded toward the kitchens to pilfer breakfast. His stomach complained, making him gallop. His boots echoed on the stone floor. He was shocked when he saw Pamela was waiting for him, sitting on a worn wooden stool. "Good morning, lad." She pressed a warm basket covered with linen into his hands, and leaned on his shoulder as she stood.

"Pamela, what are you doing up? The doctor said you needed your rest." He helped her shuffle toward the servants' service stairs.

"I had a maid bake them for me, don't fret." Her breathing was laboured, but her face did not show it.

A beleaguered maid rushed to help Cormack aid Pamela up the stairs. "Thank you, your highness." The maid bowed and then turned to Pamela. "You shouldn't be out of bed! The doctor said you could fall and injure yourself."

Cormack ushered them into the servants' quarters so Pamela could rest. She sank into the straw mattress with a groan. Pamela smiled and let the maid fetch her a mug of tea. She turned to Cormack. "Look after her for me, dear. I will see to her as soon as they let me leave this room."

Cormack nodded. "First you must recover. Your health is paramount." He squeezed Pamela's hand.

She squeezed his hand and then batted him away. "No need to dawdle with me. Go and see your princess!" Cormack grinned as he trotted down the hall to Asrai's apartments. At first, the fear of discovery prickled his chest, but strange relief spread as he remembered that she was no longer a mer.

"Hello my dear sailor." Asrai lounged on the bed. "How is Pamela?"

Cormack took her hand in both of his, stroking the supple white skin. "She is doing better. She snuck down to the kitchen and baked us these." Cormack lifted the linen from the basket, the thick scent of wheat bread and oat cakes filling the room. He handed Asrai a cake, dripping in honey.

She bit into it, honey trailing from the corner of her mouth. She licked it off and ate the rest of the cake. Cormack bit into a soft loaf of bread, his teeth crunching the flax seeds, which Pamela knew he enjoyed.

"How very kind of her." Asrai reached for another cake and Cormack handed it to her. "Such a generous human, putting others before herself."

Cormack nodded, his mouth full of bread. He swallowed and set the loaf down. "Yes, she has been like a mother to me."

Asrai rubbed the crumbs from her fingers. "Your mother is gone?"

"Yes. She died when she bore me. I never knew her." Cormack stared at the floor.

"I am sorry." Asrai reached out and stroked Cormack's hair. "My mother also died when I was young."

Cormack looked up, letting Asrai trace his face with her fingers. "What happened to her?"

Asrai sighed. Her dress ruffled as she shifted her weight, exposing her bare feet and ankles. "She was out collecting seahorses for market when a pack of sharks caught her off guard. They devoured her before help could arrive."

Cormack put his hand over Asrai's. "I have found it makes things easier if you find family in others you care for."

"As I have found kinship with the great hag Illyana," Asrai mused.

He tilted his head. "Is that the mer who granted you legs?"

"Yes. The sea hag was the royal advisor of Sulu, and was the one who took me into hiding to train. I am well versed in magickal and physical combat. Even so, one does not expect victory against a shark."

Cormack leaned back, allowing Asrai to slip her hand from his grasp. "As crown prince, training in combat is a part of my duties. Though, I doubt I will ever see true battle."

Asrai raised an eyebrow. "You train without purpose?"

"No," he mused. "I must prove to the soldiers of Paradine that I am just as worthy of sword and shield. They cannot be expected to respect a king who is without knowledge of a soldier's work. Though, I prefer bow and arrow. I find peace in competing with the target."

She shook her head. "What is this 'bow and arrow'?"

Cormack mimed loosing an arrow with his arms drawn up as if holding an invisible bow. "It is a long piece of wood fitted with a string.

Love of the Sea

We set smaller pieces of wood that are fitted with metal heads that pierce. In battle, they are to disarm or kill at a distance. In competition, it is to showcase accuracy."

Asrai murmured, wondering at such a thing. "This sounds similar to throwing a spear."

His face brightened. "Yes! Exactly like that, but smaller!"

"Perhaps your world is not so strange after all, my sailor." Asrai shot him a playful grin.

He tweaked a fold of her dress. "Sometimes my home is strange even to me. Seeing my kingdom through your eyes makes me further question my place here."

"Perhaps that is the tide calling out to you, my sailor," Asrai mused. "Otherwise you would find your place quite natural here."

Cormack tilted his head. "I suppose. Though I am certain life on land is far less strange to me than it is for you."

"This form *is* certainly strange to me. It is vulnerable and awkward." She took out her comb and ran it through her curls. "I hope that Pamela is well enough to assist me this evening."

Cormack lifted the basket so that Asrai could select an oat cake. "I know this must be difficult for you."

Asrai ran her fingers along her upper arm where the scales and fins used to be. "Last night was painful. I have never known such agony."

Cormack leaned against one of the bed posters. "Being out of the water seems to hurt you immensely. How did you manage to get yourself up on that beach?"

Asrai blushed. Her eyes flashed again, but this time Cormack's eyes did not glaze over. "A riptide caught me. The surf near the shore was too strong. I was pushed far up on the beach."

Cormack nodded. "My boat got caught in that same riptide. I'm only glad that you made it to shore before I did. *Anita* may not be a warship, but she is still large."

Asrai sat up and leaned against the headboard. She inspected one of her feet. Cormack watched her.

"My sailor prince, is it true that you wish to be bonded to me? Or was that an explanation for your father?" Asrai fixed her eyes on him.

Cormack shot up. "I meant what I said. I do love you, Asrai. But how can I leave my kingdom behind? Is there no magick that can grant you a life with me?"

Asrai's eyes darkened. "I thought you had ceased these selfish questions. As a mer, I still can never be 'human' as I do not have a soul. Only the Cursed One may grant souls, and Poseidon destroyed him long before the glory of Sulu."

"Are *you* not also selfish in asking *me* to give up *my* soul?" Cormack felt his body stiffen as fear pounded in his racing heart.

Asrai shook her head. "My sailor, don't you love the sea? Even now, I know your heart cries out for the abyss! Is this soul worth living a lie?"

"I don't even *know* if I am living a lie!" Cormack's voice raised. "My love for the sea may be just that – simple enjoyment, an escape from my duties, and nothing more!"

Asrai bristled at his aggressive tone. "One *enjoys* a good meal, or *escapes* for the day for simple enjoyment. One does not go out to the sea nearly every day and look so longingly at the glittering waters for *simple enjoyment!*"

Cormack clenched his fists. "That may be so. Perhaps it is more than *simple enjoyment*. But how could that possibly mean I should run away from all I know and am responsible for?"

"Is that deep love so unimportant to you?" Asrai narrowed her eyes. "Are you truly ready to throw away your love for the sea and your love for me?"

He ran his hand through his hair. "My love for you and the sea has driven me to madness."

Asrai shook her comb at him. "Is our love for one another truly *madness*?"

Cormack shook his head. He had read many tales of lovers being driven to madness in an attempt to reconcile their differences in station or eligibility, and these stories tended to end in disaster. He fidgeted his hands as the thoughts swirled in his mind, pain raking through his chest.

I love her! I can feel it burning, day and night. Even before I knew her, I loved the sea and still do. Though my heart cries out to have this crown taken from me, how can I abandon Father and my people? Peter would scorn me to the ends of the earth for my frivolity, and my people shame our family for bringing the kingdom to ruin.

Asrai leaned toward Cormack again, her eyes darting about his face, searching. "My sailor, you *do* love me, don't you?"

He winced at her words as the truth fluttered through his heart. *That I should given in to this madness and follow my heart. But why me? Why would such a beautiful and powerful creature love a human like me? What have I to offer but a ridiculous obsession with diving into the depths and exploring the sapphire waters? Surely, those are not suitable reasons. There must be something else.*

Cormack sighed, meeting her gaze at last. "I just do not understand. I am sure you could have any mer you choose. Why choose me?"

Love of the Sea

She flinched at his words. "I have told you, my dear sailor, I fell in love while watching you dive and play in the sea."

"I don't understand it. But then, I also fell in love with you when I carried you from the beach." Cormack sighed and shook his head. *Love is so strange.*

"Would you curse me to a half-life here on land?" Asrai fiddled with her comb.

Cormack darted his eyes away. "There is something I need to attend to first."

Her heart jolted. "What do you mean? I have gone through agony for you."

Cormack took her hand and stroked it. It was warm. "It is a human thing. But it will take some time."

He stood up to leave but Asrai grabbed his wrist. "Please don't go."

Cormack sat back down. "Is something the matter?"

"Well no," she twisted the comb between her hands, "but yes. Yes, there is something the matter." Asrai darted her eyes away. "I-I cannot lose you, my sailor. I need you."

Cormack leaned toward her. "Are the tales true? That mermaids cannot truly love humans the way other humans do?" Cormack thought to himself about the tales he had heard from the sailors.

Asrai looked away. "It is true that many of our kind simply like to play with humans." She looked at Cormack. "But I would not have beached myself for something so petty."

Cormack frowned. "But didn't you know that this would happen to you? Didn't you know the air would hurt you?"

Asrai nodded, looking down at the comb in her hands. "Yes. I knew."

"And you came anyway?" Cormack's face reddened and he began to whisper.

"Lady Asrai!" A woman's voice came through the door. "Lady Asrai, I'm here to assist you for the day!"

Cormack froze, holding his breath, hoping the maid had not heard them speaking. The doorknob jiggled. "Lady Asrai, please, the king has an agenda for the day!"

Asrai shook her head, and Cormack sighed. He slid off the bed and unlocked the door. Asrai slid down the headboard, pouting, as the maid entered. The maid flinched when she saw Cormack, then bowed low.

"Apologies, your highness! I did not realize you were with the lady." She straightened, but kept her gaze on his chest. "I was set to fetch you next. His majesty, the king, has requested your presence in the map room. There is urgent news."

Cormack turned to Asrai, his shoulders slumped. He took her hand and kissed it. "I'll have to leave you, my lady. Hopefully, not for long."

Asrai fidgeted, annoyed at the maid's presence. "I will be waiting, my sailor." He released her hand and nodded to the maid. His boots echoed off the stone hall.

****

The maid closed the door and clucked her tongue as she began pulling back the covers. "My lady, sleeping in your dress cannot be comfortable. Here, let's get you in fresh clothes."

Asrai straightened, curling her legs under her. She watched as the maid fussed with the chest at the foot of the bed. "Where is Pamela? She is to attend me."

The maid shook her head. "The head cook is in the kitchen, attending to her duties. Not to worry, I will see to it that you are off to enjoy the day."

Asrai pulled out her comb. It glowed betwixt her fingers. Her eyes brightened. "I'm afraid I need Pamela to attend me."

The magick seeped into the maid's mind, pressing the urgency of the request. She closed the wooden chest and nodded to Asrai. "Of course, my lady. I will fetch her straight away." She bobbed a curtsy and exited the room.

Asrai leaned against the headboard, waiting for Pamela to arrive. She grumbled at having been interrupted once again by foolish human matters. Cormack was still teetering on the edge of his decision. She only had three moons to seal the bond before the sea called her back and broke her heartbroken body into seafoam.

A heavy knock sounded on the door. "My lady, it's Pamela." Her voice was strained and tired. Asrai flicked her comb, unlocking the door. She slipped the comb back into her hair as Pamela and a pair of maids entered. "There are maids with me, dear."

Asrai flinched. "Must they?"

The maids scowled. The old woman sighed. "Yes, dear. My apologies."

Asrai bristled as Pamela allowed the maids to enter. "My lady," they whispered.

Asrai nodded. Pamela came 'round the bed and held out her hand. "There we are, dear. Nice and easy."

Poseidon help me! Asrai's legs quivered as they took her full weight. She clung to Pamela's arm like a babe just learning to walk. The maids flicked their eyes at one another. Pamela kept her gaze steady on Asrai.

"This is why the lady wanted to be left alone. The ladies of Sulu do not walk, they are carried. The poor dear was embarrassed." The maids flushed, their eyes dropping. They murmured apologies. Asrai smiled to Pamela.

"Yes, well, hurry up!" Pamela snapped at the maids. "The poor thing can't stand here all day!"

"Yes, mum!" The maids scrambled to pull garments from the dressing trunk.

Pamela pushed aside the painful thoughts as she recognized each article of clothing, each beautiful piece of jewelry. The maids buzzed about Asrai, dressing her quickly while Pamela held her steady.

One of the maids dug around in the trunk as Pamela helped Asrai sit. "My lady...where are your shoes?"

Asrai stared at her. "My what?"

The maids froze. Pamela rolled her eyes. "The princess is carried everywhere. What does she need shoes for?" She smoothed Asrai's skirts.

"Shall we call the footmen?" The maids huddled by the bed, unsure of what to do.

Pamela shook her head. "Let's be off then. Off! Off! I expect the lady will be seeing her prince before dinner."

Asrai crawled back onto the bed, leaning against the headboard for support. The way her hips and legs bent was strange to her. She sighed once the door was closed, grateful the dressing ordeal was over.

****

Hushed whispers and a wall of tension hit Cormack upon entering the map room. The council looked at him as he took his seat to the right of King Dominic. The lines in his father's face were deep, his eyes dark. The general nodded.

"Now that we are all assembled—" Weston nodded to the king.

King Dominic took a deep breath. "Quite right. Gentleman, our siege on Richard's men has gone on for eight moons. The men have grown tired, and supply routes are choked with bandits and sabotage from the opposing forces. A broken retinue came into the outskirts of Paradine last night. They bring grave news."

His gaze passed over Peter. "It seems that history is repeating itself. Umber has fallen."

All eyes shifted to Peter. He gripped the map until his knuckles were white. He locked eyes with the king. "No! You promised on my mother's grave that Umber would never again feel the wrath of Richard! You cannot tell me that every man has fallen? That there are no more soldiers with breath in their lungs and swords in their hands? This war has just begun!"

The king shook his head. "I am sorry, my boy. The army on the western border was crushed. Richard has taken many good men captive. Umber is a good three days march from Paradine. There is nothing to do but to tend our losses and regroup."

Peter flew to his feet, the chair rocking behind him. "Is Paradine not the most powerful kingdom in the world? The people of *Umber* are bleeding and that blood is on your hands, *Uncle!*"

The men stiffened as he bellowed, slamming his fists onto the rim of the map. King Dominic nodded to the general. Weston sighed and grabbed Peter by the shoulders. Peter roared, flailing as he tried to escape. Weston wrenched his arms behind his back, pressing his chest against the map. Peter screamed and raged, his eyes wide and wild. Tears streamed down his red face. He flailed as Weston struggled to contain him. His agony was palpable as Peter was dragged away. Cormack shivered as he caught his cousin's gaze. The animalistic hurt in his eyes shot straight to Cormack's heart. The door slammed shut, muffling Peter's hysterics.

King Dominic shook his head and righted the figurines on the map. His voice was low. "There are fifty odd men being held for ransom by that old dog. As much as it pains me to have Paradine lose such good men, we cannot afford to give Richard a single stone of Paradine gold. That will only seal Umber's fate…and possibly even our own."

The men muttered in agreement. Their shoulders slumped, the weight of the moment pressing down as if Richard himself were pressing each of them into the mud of their failed venture. King Dominic began rearranging some of the figurines. "I will send word that we are not to comply. Bran, we'll need you to draw up the pittance for each family—"

"Father, how can you send these men to slaughter?" Cormack's voice warbled. "These are good men! They can live to fight another day!"

King Dominic dropped the horseman figurine. "My boy, these men knew they might be sacrificing their lives for Paradine when they went to arms. It is their way. They would first die before giving Richard the upper hand with such a greedy sum."

Cormack stood, his chair scraping the floor. "Father, these men are dying needlessly! Richard is a crooked leader, and we are Paradine! Our military makes the world tremble! Can we not send—?"

"Enough." King Dominic raised his hand, his voice quiet. "My decision is final."

The door opened again, revealing Weston. His arms burned with red scratches. He whispered into the king's ear, then sat down. He nodded to Cormack, and Weston sat down again. "Due to the gravity of this news, my nephew shall be barred in his chambers. However, the wedding feast preparations are not to be delayed. He, and Paradine, need the distraction."

Weston toyed with one of the soldier figurines. "My lord, perhaps we should honour our brave men. A tournament would give their families the honour they deserve and help lift their spirits."

King Dominic nodded. "A fine idea. Ruben, see to it that the tournament is organized as quickly as possible."

Cormack was frozen inside his body as the men discussed what knights remained in Paradine to compete, and what soldiers were to be knighted. Their voices moved around him, muffled as if he were underwater. Then all at once, he found the room was too stuffy and small. He stood up, startling the men. "Excuse me, Father." King Dominic and his men stared, wide-eyed, as Cormack bowed, then left the map room. The door creaked shut behind him.

Chapter Sixteen

The sun hung lower than Asrai had expected. She slid off the bed, the weight of the gown cushioning her fall. She grunted as she pulled the weight of her legs and the thick layers of fabric across the rug. Her chest heaved as it strained against the corset. At last, she reached the washing stool next to the tub.

Her comb glowed as she summoned the water mirror. She found Cormack walking through the hallway, his face pinched with worry. Asrai searched for clues in his brisk walk as to the nature of his discomfiture. Her concern died a swift death as Cormack approached Princess Nephara. Her head was held high, her gaze poisonous as she argued with one of the guards that stood at attention before a door. Asrai flicked her comb, enabling her to hear.

"...Peter is my betrothed! Surely I can bring him comfort!"

The guard shook his head, his mouth tight. "Apologies, m'lady. King's orders."

"And *I* am the Princess of Caraway, soon to be Princess of Paradine." Her voice raised several octaves. "You *will* stand aside!"

"King's orders. There's nothin' we can do, m'lady." The guard kept his gaze forward.

Nephara tried to push past and grabbed at the door, but the guards stopped her. "How dare you lay hands on me!" she screeched. "I am Princess Nephara of Caraway! The mighty warrior and tamer of the wild Panya! Let me in this instant!"

The hooded ladies bristled, their hands ready at the hilts of their swords. Cormack waved his hand, stopping the guards. He placed his hand on Nephara's shoulder. His gentle touch startled her. "Princess." His voice was low and pained. "Princess, I am sorry."

Nephara's eyes shook as she met his gaze. She took a deep breath, then straightened her back. The placid mask slipping back over her features. The tremble in her lip gave away her distress. Asrai's heart erupted with hot anger as Cormack placed his arms about Nephara, comforting her.

"How *dare* you!" Asrai growled. She bared her fangs at the water mirror.

Cormack whispered something into Nephara's ear, further inciting Asrai. She flicked her comb at the water mirror, causing Nephara to flinch, and push away from Cormack's embrace. He took her hand in both of his, and squeezed it.

Asrai felt her heart wrench watching his tender smile. She swiped the water mirror with her comb, destroying the vision. Her head ached as she clenched her teeth. The gown was suffocating her, the stiff fabric sealing in her growing fury. Asrai tore at the dress, her screaming echoing in the small bathing chamber.

Fabric hung in ribbons from her limbs once her rage subsided. Her body shook as her mind righted. Asrai hoisted herself into the cold bathwater. She gasped and shivered, but the water was a balm on her nerves. She wrapped her arms around herself. The soggy fabric felt like odd seaweed fronds clinging to her. Asrai huddled against the side of the tub, her mind whirring as she tried to make sense of the scene.

I was so careful. And yet, he still clings to that human! How can I hope to reclaim Sulu when I cannot even claim the one I love? Her throat burned as her chest shuddered. *Has all my training been for naught?*

****

Cormack released Nephara. "Princess, as you know, my cousin is a difficult man. Give him time to sort things out. He will seek your company when he is ready."

Her anguish melted into annoyance. She glared at him. "He is my betrothed. It is my duty to bring him comfort."

"Yes, I am aware, princess." Cormack tamped down the old heat of jealousy. "However, it is in your best interest to leave him for now. It is not safe."

Before Nephara could argue, Peter's fit picked up from screaming to sharp thudding. Then there was a smash. The guards unbolted the door. Nephara ran after them, but stopped in the doorway.

The wall tapestry was torn down from the hangings, piled on the floor. A splintered chair was scattered about the floor, as if it had been thrown against the wall. The table was upturned, and foodstuffs were trampled into the rug. The guards held Peter down, pressing his body into the floor. One of them reached for a small vial in his belt. Cormack pulled Nephara back into the hallway. Her face was pale, her eyes wide.

"They are giving him an extract to soothe him. It's an old remedy we used when he was a child," Cormack whispered. "The White Veil makes it. Father must have found some in the storerooms when he first heard the news."

Nephara waved her hand. "And what is this *news* that has the world upturned?"

He shook his head. "Umber has fallen. It is Peter's homeland."

Her brow wrinkled. "But Peter is of Paradine. What is this 'Umber'?"

"Umber is a neighbouring territory of Paradine. My aunt was queen when Umber first fell to our great enemy, Lord Richard. Peter was a hostage, and we paid a hefty ransom for his safe return. Now Richard has taken those lands again."

Nephara's face fell, the haughty annoyance wiped clean. "And his family?"

Cormack shook his head. "We are his family now."

"I see…" Nephara whispered. She dropped her gaze, then turned and nodded to her hooded ladies. The trio took their leave, their shoes echoing as Nephara sped toward her chambers. Cormack bristled, realizing his cousin had fallen quiet. The guards bolted the door shut and resumed their vigil.

"Our apologies, yer highness." One of the guards nodded.

Cormack held up his hand. "Do as you must."

Old memories of young Peter's fits of hysteria assaulted Cormack's mind. He felt his insides turn cold and quivered recalling the day Peter was relocated further from Cormack's apartments, as Peter's night terrors were beginning to send Cormack into hysterics. Peter had screamed for hours as the servants moved the furniture, and finally Peter himself. He was convinced they were sending him back to Richard, to whatever nightmares he had lived through while imprisoned. Cormack fought to keep his breathing even, pushing the dark thoughts aside. His step quickened, his heart crying out for Asrai.

****

Cormack sailed round the harbour in lazy circles. For three days Asrai had barred her doors. He suspected she somehow knew about the incident with Nephara; he wondered at her jealousy. Even the sea afforded him no solace. The clouds threatened rain, and the water was too choppy to dive for shells. He turned about and headed back toward the docks. The tournament was set to begin, and he was in poor condition to compete.

News of Umber spread through the village like wildfire when the injured soldiers returned home. The unease was softened by the tournament, though rumours grew rampant over the fields. The armoury buzzed with squires and servants. Cormack squeezed toward his cubicle. His squire jumped to attention, and two of the servants abandoned their posts, bowing.

"Your highness! His majesty, the king, has enlisted you for the hand to hand combat, sword fighting, and the archery events!"

Cormack nodded and began stripping off his sailing tunic and pulling on the underclothes the squire presented. "No joust?"

The squire flinched. "His majesty felt that such an event would be ill-advised due to the coming wedding celebrations."

Love of the Sea

Chainmail was thrust over Cormack's head, leaving little room for argument. The servants began buckling on the plate armour and tying back Cormack's hair. He played with a bent ring in his chainmail shirt.

"Is Peter competing as well?" Cormack fidgeted his hands.

Peter had recovered from his hysterics after the second day, but his mood was foul and he snapped at all the servants, and even the king. At first, he sent Nephara away when she came to his chambers, but her persistence wore him down. She hovered over him, snapping just as much at the servants.

"Yes." The squire hesitated. "His highness insisted."

Cormack nodded. He held his helmet against his hip while the servants tied his banner shirt over his armour. Some of the knights began heading out into the tourney arena. He wondered if any of them had been at the battle of Umber. Cormack took a deep breath and followed them, the squire on his heels. The clouds refused to dissipate, making for a dreary and ominous day. The stands were packed, and many of the farmers and fishermen were crowded around the fence. They cheered as they saw the knights enter the arena. Cormack recognized Peter's black-and-red banner shirt; the colours for Umber. He took his place near the registry.

King Dominic sat in the king's box, the blue pennants of Paradine flying high. Asrai and Nephara sat on his left, and Weston at his right. Nephara was surrounded by three of her red-robed ladies, and two of her yellow-robed servants. The two hooded ladies loomed behind her. Pamela sat on a stool at Asrai's side. A little bench with a pitcher and a spread of foodstuffs sat before them. Asrai caught his gaze. Her eyes tore through him, sending a chill down his spine. He fidgeted his hands, looking at his father.

The crowd fell silent as the king stood. He raised his hand and bellowed into the speaking horn. "My people! We bring you this tournament to celebrate the brave men who fought for our dear sister lands of Umber, and to honour those who gave the ultimate sacrifice for Paradine. Please enjoy!"

The crowd cheered as the king sat. Cormack peered at the other knights. Many were advanced in years and experience. He straightened his shoulders, and looked again at Asrai.

Her gaze had softened, but her mouth was pinched in a frown. She looked away and spoke to Pamela. Cormack sighed and shifted his feet. The armour was stuffy, and his sword heavy at his hip. He plunked on his helmet, and fell in line for the swordsman event. They were broken into pairs, to fight simultaneously on the large open field. Cormack was paired against a large knight who wore green; a newly knighted soldier. He bowed to Cormack.

"Your highness, please do not take offense to my blows this day. May Poseidon grant you victory."

Cormack nodded. "May Poseidon grant honest victory. Do not withhold."

****

The horn blew, signaling the event. Asrai pouted. She had cajoled the head cook into attending the tourney, as Nephara had plenty of servants to entertain her, and would hardly have made good company. Pamela provided her with a small feast of snacks and gave instructions to the kitchen hands. The sky threatened rain and Asrai drew the Altrusean shawl closer about her shoulders.

"Don't fret, dear. I believe you've punished the lad enough." Pamela nodded as Cormack appeared from the armoury. "See how he moons over you?"

She stared him down. He looked silly in his armour, like a hermit crab with too large a shell. "And yet, how easy it was for him to fall into another's arms."

Pamela patted Asrai's leg. "Now, now, he's a kind soul. Always looking to help others where he can. I'm sure he meant nothing by it."

Asrai slid in her chair, pouting. She reached for another slice of apple. The anger had washed away after she had destroyed her gown. However, the yawning emptiness and the fear of failure strangled her body and mind. She looked out at Cormack again, her heart pleading.

Why must you be so capricious? You keep sliding from me, and returning once more, like a frightened eel in its cave. Let me hold you in my arms! Ne'er to leave again!

The herald blew the horn. Asrai flinched at the noise, but her body grew stiff when she saw Cormack square up to another human in armour. They drew their swords, and sparks flew as the metal clashed in a symphony of staged war. Asrai felt the magick crackling, her eyes catching on every flinch and stumble.

"Cormack is a skilled fighter." Pamela broke through her thoughts. "These tourneys are meant to show skills, not become a blood bath. The men yield. Not to worry."

Asrai wondered at the strange battle. Their weapons seemed to all be dead items; not a shred of magick. Their blows were heavy, and sparks flew as swords met armour. Without the cradle of water, the men were stuck battling on the dirt. There was no dive bombing their opponent as mers would perform in the sea. The sky was grey, affording no light for them to flash off their armour and blind their opponent, as mers would do with their scales.

Some men fell to their knees, surrendering their blade. None of the warriors were slain. The losers walked off the field, some with minor injuries. It reminded Asrai of the peacocking that would occur when mers would fight over a mate. Neither individual sought to maim their opponent, only beat them in the name of pride and virility. Asrai shivered. In Draum there would be no such niceties. She would have to fight fang and claw, and dig into the depths of her wellspring for her most powerful magick. There were no second chances in Draum.

Cormack moved up through the ranks until a large, burly knight caught him across the chest with the broadside of his sword. The blow knocked the wind out of him, and sent him sprawling on the field. Asrai jumped to her feet. Pamela grabbed her arm, coaxing her to sit back down.

Cormack held up his hand, yielding. The knight fell to one knee, bowing as the prince pulled himself upright. Cormack gestured for the knight to rise, and they clasped hands. Cormack walked toward the king's box. He removed his helmet, revealing his red face and his sweaty hair plastered to his skull. His chest heaved as he took heavy gulps of fresh air.

"My lady, Asrai!" he called. "I did not win you a trophy. However, if you would be inclined to give me your favour I might find fortune to win the next event."

Asrai stood again, leaning over the railing. She stared down at him, her eyes brightened with magick. "And what is this favour you ask?"

Cormack faltered. "N-no, not a service, a token of your love for me."

Pamela tapped Asrai on the arm. She spun around and saw her holding a blue ribbon frothy with lace. "He means this, dear."

"Oh." Asrai took the ribbon, confused as to how a scrap of fabric would help him in battle. She leaned over the railing and handed it to him.

Cormack grinned. He caught the ribbon and tied it to his belt. "Thank you, my lady!"

He waved, then trotted back to the armoury. Asrai stared after him, confused by the exchange. She sat down again and nibbled another apple slice. Her gaze wandered over the arena. She saw Peter fighting with an opponent, his sword slashing and hacking the air. At his belt was a bright red ribbon, sparkling with gold lace.

Asrai turned to Pamela. "How do these *favours* grant them strength in battle?"

Pamela laughed. "No, dear. The ribbons don't actually do anything. You would be surprised how much stronger a man feels when he knows his sweetie is cheering for him."

The human sentiment confused Asrai. She could see the other defeated knights chatting up ladies in the stands or over the fence. Many of the girls were waving ribbons, hoping to catch their attention. Asrai wrinkled her nose and turned back to the field. A knight in black-and-white colours was named the victor. King Dominic stood to present the trophy, a gold dagger with a ruby set in the hilt. The knight held his treasure aloft, and the crowd cheered.

Chapter Seventeen

A team of servants raked the field, then the herald announced the next event. The knights filed out, their armour removed. Each was paired off for the hand-to-hand combat. Asrai saw that the ribbon was still tied to Cormack's belt. The blare of the horn sent the men into action, grappling against one another. Nephara was enjoying herself, a bowl of honeyed figs held by one of her servants while another massaged her feet. She grinned as Peter bested the first two competitors, his energy working into a frenzy. The crowd buzzed as the next round of competitors were paired off, and Peter was faced with Cormack.

Asrai flinched when the horn blew, signaling the men to fight. She turned and caught Nephara's gaze. The two women stared each other down, as if they too were on the field, squaring off. Asrai raised her eyebrows in challenge, then swiveled her gaze to the field.

I will not allow this dangerous human to harm what I have worked so hard to win. Her eyes began to brighten until they were clear ice blue. The magick flew up before Cormack, acting as an invisible wall.

****

Peter and Cormack danced about in a circle, daring the other to make the first move. Cormack felt an odd tingling sensation, almost like the feeling of putting one's hands before a fire. Peter lunged when he saw Cormack pause. His right arm swung, but failed to connect. Cormack leapt back, feeling the moving air as Peter's arm was deflected. The strange feeling lingered, as if a presence coated Cormack's body. The crowd buzzed as the two princes fought, though Peter could not seem to lay a hand on the crown prince. Cormack landed blow after blow, which seemed to enrage Peter further, his throws becoming wild.

"You are cheating!" Peter hissed as he dodged one of Cormack's punches. "Your damned sorceress has cursed me!"

Cormack flinched at Peter's words. Peter tried to grab at Cormack's arm, but it slid out of his grasp. "I know not what you speak of, Cousin." He panted, squaring off to land another blow. "Asrai is no sorceress. She is a princess."

Peter flung himself at Cormack, which he easily dodged. Peter's foot slid as he tried to catch himself. Cormack pulled back as his cousin bellowed in frustration. "You are a poor liar!"

The tingling sensation intensified. Cormack felt as if invisible forces were guiding his body. He recalled how Asrai had spoken of mer magick, and the strange visions she had created while in the tub. *Is this Asrai's doing? Is she ensuring Peter loses?* He flexed his hands, trying to shake off the feeling. *I have to be sure.*

Cormack took position, as if he were to throw another blow, but stayed still, waiting for Peter to strike. Peter flew at him but his hands could not connect, as if an invisible wall kept him at bay. Peter was beginning to spiral, and shivers went down Cormack's spine as he recognized the signs of madness. He laced his fingers together, and held them over his head, sinking to his knees.

"I yield!" he called out.

The sensation was gone, making Cormack unsure if he had just been imaging it. Peter leaned down, and snarled in Cormack's ear. "Get up and fight me like a man! Fight me without help from your foul sorceress!"

Cormack shook his head. "I yield, Cousin. The match is yours."

Peter straightened, disgust radiating from his body. "Coward!"

****

The crowd jumped to their feet, screaming in protest. Their crown prince had been winning, landing solid blows while Peter had been floundering like a wounded ox. Fury cascaded through the stands when Cormack forfeited the match. Asrai added her voice to the uproar, her eyes bright with fury.

"Fight him! Show your people your strength!" Asrai screamed.

Pamela pushed on Asrai's shoulders, forcing her to sit down. "Now, now, dear. I'm sure he has his reasons."

"Kings do not yield to their lessers! This fight should have been easily won!" Asrai hissed.

Nephara's glare burned into Asrai. Her servants petted her and crooned, trying to placate their princess with her lover's victory, hollow as it was. Cormack approached the railing, earning him a poisonous look from Nephara. Asrai stood and leaned over the railing.

"Lady Asrai," he tried to keep his voice down, "the match is to be fought on the field, not by those in the stands."

She tilted her head. "I do not understand, my sailor prince."

Cormack shook his head. "I only need your *favour* to help me win. Nothing more."

It was Asrai's turn to glare at him. "*And let harm come to you? I think not!*" she hissed.

"They are just games." Cormack sighed. "Competitors are to yield before true harm is done. Please Asrai, just watch the match." He went to rest near the fences, his head bowed.

Asrai sat back down, bristling with wounded pride. Pamela distracted her with bits of cold prawn, though her mood was still sour. The horn sounded, calling for the next round of competitors. The crowd did not shout and cheer. Chatter and whispers buzzed through the stands as Peter was matched against a young man, a new knight from Umber. They squared up, then the horn blared again. The man threw the first punch, a wide shot that Peter dodged. He countered, and swung a throw, catching the man's tunic, and flung him to the dirt. The knight scrambled to his feet, bouncing, waiting for the next move. Peter's rage from his strange battle with Cormack had not subsided. Instead, it twisted as he watched the Umber soldier's inferior sparring moves. The madness began to glaze his eyes.

The knight attempted a throw, bringing him against Peter's shoulder. His miss threw him off balance, and Peter swung his body away. The knight recovered, spinning back around to face him. Peter charged, bellowing with his arms raised. The knight tried to dodge Peter's attack, which left him open for Peter to bring down his fists into the knight's back. He went down, hard. The wind was knocked out of him, and his movements were jerky as he swayed on his feet. He was unable to yield, but it was clear that the match was over. The thin cheers from the crowd died as Peter swung his foot into the knight's side, rolling him over. The knight drew himself into a ball, unable to escape Peter's barrage.

****

"Stop the match!" King Dominic bellowed. "Guards! Stop the match!"

Five armoured guards rushed the field, separating Peter from the wounded knight. The squires ran out with the doctor. A horse with a small cart was led out, and the man was carried onto the cart, blood oozing from his face. Peter shouted and kicked his legs as the guards led him away into the castle. The blood drained from Nephara's face. The silence broke and the crowd began hissing and booing at the poor display.

Asrai stared as Peter was dragged away. Her insides shook as she repeated the match over and over in her mind. *That would have been my dear sailor. That poor, bloodied creature would have been my sailor prince had I left the match to them.*

"It's such a shame," King Dominic muttered as the event continued. Cheers swelled again in the stands as the remaining knights fought hard for the trophy.

Nephara shooed her servants and approached the king's chair. "Majesty, is my prince to return?"

He shook his head, his face pained. "No, my dear. I'm sorry, but Peter is unwell."

Her frown hardened. "I request to compete in his stead."

King Dominic flinched. "My lady, the tourney is no place for a princess—"

"I am a mighty warrior of Caraway. I am not barred from competition there." She tilted her chin a fraction.

The king sighed. "And what would you be competing in?"

Nephara's eyes gleamed. "I am talented with the bow, and skilled in the hunt. Let me take over his spot in the archery event. Then, I can show the people of Paradine the might of the great Panya."

He shook his head. "My dear, I worry that the crowd might be frightened by such a spectacle as that beast of yours. Perhaps just the archery?"

"I am Quinquetta's keeper. She obeys my every whim. You have nothing to fear." Her defiant gaze held firm.

King Dominic cast his gaze over the crowd. They were twisting in their seats, fidgeting and whispering to one another. A distraction was required, though the joust was not set to begin for some time. He sighed and turned back to Nephara.

"I trust you will have full control. We do not need another outburst, lest the peasants start a mob." King Dominic thumped Weston's shoulder. "See to it, would you?"

"Of course, majesty." The general stepped down from his seat and escorted Nephara to the armoury, her retinue of servants following close behind.

King Dominic shifted his gaze to Asrai. "I don't suppose you feel the need to compete, my dear?"

Asrai started. She shook her head, recalling her human guise. "These are games I am unfamiliar with, your majesty. I am content to simply watch my prince compete."

The king smiled. "Of course, of course." He waved his hand, and a serving girl refilled his flagon.

Another knight was named victor, wearing red-and-yellow colours. He received a gold plaque bearing the Paradine crest. The crowd clapped and cheered. The field was raked again, and servants brought out wood and straw targets. The crowds moved away from the fence to protect against stray arrows. The knights came out again, bows and quivers slung over their shoulders. Cormack waved at Asrai, though his grin was replaced with a stony gaze. She found herself waving back.

Asrai's cheer was snuffed out when she saw Nephara dressed in a modified archer's uniform, all in red and gold. Her bow was tied with red ribbons and her gloves sparkled with gold embroidery. Together, they marched onto the field and took their place at the targets.

Cormack loosed his arrows with ease, all but one finding their mark. The targets were removed, and the losing knights left the field. New targets were set up, and Cormack loosed his arrows again. This time all made their mark.

Love of the Sea

Asrai was enthralled by the sharp whistling before the sharp thunk of the arrows into the targets. Cormack's face was calm, almost serene as he brought the arrow to his lips before setting it free. Nephara's face was stony with concentration. Her red-shafted arrows whizzed to their targets, hitting their mark in tight clusters. Asrai felt the magick coursing through her body, longing to help her mate win, but winning by cloaked scale would make her no better than the usurper. She watched as the targets were removed, and only Cormack, Nephara, and one knight were left standing.

A troupe of servants came out, holding small targets. Then, when the horn blew, the servants tossed them in the air and fled. Asrai was captivated as she watched the targets tumble back to earth. The arrows raced through the air. She would not have had the time to blink the magick into her eyes before the arrows went their course.

The knight's arrow missed completely, whizzing over the fence as his target fell into the dirt. Nephara's arrow found the target, but hit near the outer ring. Cormack's target landed with the arrow vibrating in the dead center. The crowd screamed with delight when one of the servants held the winning target aloft. Cormack grinned at Asrai. She felt her heart melt as his adoration washed over her. King Dominic prodded Asrai, handing her a solid gold arrow.

"Go on, my dear." He smiled.

Asrai smiled back, taking the trophy. She leaned over the railing as Cormack beamed. "Hello, my sailor." Her smile grew wider. "It seems you are victorious."

He tweaked the ribbon at his waist. "It is all thanks to you."

She handed him the prize, their fingers brushing. Asrai was warmed as he kept her gaze for a moment longer before holding the arrow aloft for the crowd to see. She sat back down, her heart fit to burst.

****

The king stood while the servants scurried to reset the field. He used the speaking horn to announce the next event. "Our dear Princess of Caraway would like to present skills from her homeland. Please enjoy while our knights take a moment to rest before the joust!"

Nephara reentered the field, the panya following closely. A gold chain threaded the beast's neck, hanging and dragging the ground. The gold muzzle ring was secured over its beak. The crowd gasped and whispered as they watched the beast enter the field. Nephara glared up into the stands. She tossed her hair and took her place in the center of the field.

Nephara had a large quiver attached to her back, a strange looking bow in her free hand. It was thicker than a typical bow, and the center was warped, allowing for a larger projectile. She removed the muzzle ring and clipped it to her leather belt. The panya squawked. It flapped its wings and took flight. The crowd gasped, and a few screams cut through the buzzing whispers.

Cold dread trickled down Asrai's spine as she watched the predator take to the air. Nephara jogged a few paces, then grabbed one of the items from the quiver, notching it in her bow. The arrowhead was a rounded, harmless ball. The end was fletched with a furry tail. She loosed the arrow. The panya dove. It caught the arrow with its powerful talons in midair. Nephara clicked her tongue, and the panya flew over her, dropping the arrow at her feet. It circled overhead and the crowd clapped, but gave half-hearted cheers.

Asrai fidgeted as the panya chased arrows about the field, catching them in its talons and cruel beak. She could feel a low pulse of magick from the creature, like that of a hippocampus from her watery kingdom. Such creatures could be won as companions, but such a thing was rare and did not erase the potential danger of owning a wild beast.

Nephara gathered herself for the grand finale. She loosed one last arrow that flew high toward the king's box. Asrai froze as she saw the great beast flying toward her. The arrow landed on the canopy, but the panya did not change course, its eyes locked on her. Pamela was frozen with fear, but Asrai sent a blast of magick at the bird, sending it sprawling toward the field. The panya screamed and stopped itself midair, then came back at her, talons flared. The crowd began to scream, and spectators fled the stands.

"Quinquetta! Stop! Stop this instant!" Nephara grabbed the long gold chain that hung from the bird's neck. Asrai pushed the magick again, hitting the panya in the chest as Nephara yanked on the chain. The bird fell onto the field, squawking with rage. She managed to clamp the gold muzzle over the bird's beak. King Dominic jumped to his feet, his face reddening.

"Get that infernal thing out of here!" he bellowed.

The guards charged the field, but Nephara's servants surrounded her, helping to contain her panya. Nephara fell to her knees before the king. "Your majesty! I did not mean for this to happen! I have never seen Quinquetta behave this way!"

King Dominic approached the railing. "See to it that the princess is dismissed to her chambers, and that beast locked up!" The guard nodded, relaying the message to Nephara's servants. They scurried off the field with the armed escort.

The king rushed to Asrai. "My dear! Are you hurt?" His eyes scanned her face and body.

Asrai shook her head, her heart fluttering as the magick receded. "N-no, your majesty! I'm quite unhurt."

King Dominic patted her hand. "By the wave of Poseidon." He took a deep breath to steady himself. "Poseidon keep you, my lady."

He climbed back into his chair. The crowd returned to the stands, though the damage had been done and many gave dark looks to the Caraway spectators. Cormack rushed out of the armoury, dressed in his sailing tunic and breeches once more. He climbed over the railing and threw his arms about Asrai. "By Poseidon, you are safe!"

Asrai could feel Cormack's heart racing against her. She threw her arms about him, all fear and anger forgotten. Her fingers dug into the fabric of his shirt. Cormack leaned back, and Asrai loosened her grip. He kissed her on the mouth, the intensity making her heart leap. He broke away and laid a gentle kiss on her forehead, then his lips brushed her ear with a whisper.

"I have missed you, Asrai. Please bid me to see you tonight, my lady. There is much to be discussed."

Asrai's breath tickled his cheek. "As you wish, my sailor."

The tournament resumed with the joust. Cormack seated himself beside Asrai, so she was nestled between him and Pamela. Asrai flinched as she watched the knights break lances. One knight was unseated and thrown from his horse. The squires dragged him away before his startled horse could trample him. She found the whole affair confusing and disagreeable.

"Why would the warriors risk their lives in such a way? Surely there are threats to Paradine that would be better served?" Asrai whispered to Pamela.

Pamela laughed. "Of course, dear. That's why the king's holding the tourney. The soldiers that fought in the war need their spirits lifted with a little sport."

A young knight in green-and-white colours took the trophy for the joust. His hand was injured from a lance spearing his shield, but he held his prize aloft with his good hand to the cheers of the crowd.

Chapter Eighteen

The footmen were called, and Asrai was lifted into her litter to float above the crowd surging into the castle. The farmers and fishermen went home to their own suppers. Cormack fought his way through the crowd and walked beside the litter, glancing at Asrai every now and again.

The crowd surged into the Great Hall. Asrai and Cormack took their places at the head table, while the knights and soldiers of high rank took the lower tables. Pamela rushed to the kitchens, taking her place as head of her own army. Nephara and Peter were absent, their seats empty. Nephara's servants were tucked away in her chambers, leaving the plush cushions behind her chair vacant as well, though the Caraway court enjoyed the feast with the honoured knights.

Cormack felt unease creeping into his chest. He had not seen the panya attack Asrai. One of the squires had come running into the armoury, screaming that Nephara was attacking the royal box with her beast. Cormack had rushed out onto the field, his heart in his throat. The bird was falling out of the air, screaming as it hit the dirt. The air around Asrai had seemed to ripple in a strange way for the smallest moment. The guards had stopped Cormack from reaching Asrai as another group escorted Nephara and the panya off the field. That moment had been agonizing. Gathering her up in his arms and feeling that she was unhurt had flooded his heart with relief and the strong realization that his life would have stopped had the panya slain her. He had wanted to press her against his chest and never let go.

There was no way for Cormack to be sure if the panya attack was an accident or if it had been calculated by Nephara. He feared that her pride and hot temper combined with Peter's reawakened madness put Asrai at risk. Though the fear of discovery was gone, Asrai was limited in her human guise. She was easy prey without Cormack to protect her. He shivered at the thought.

Cheers erupted at the head table as the victors took their seats. They had changed into simple soldiers' uniforms of Paradine blue, though they wore gold crests denoting their status as knights. They gazed about the table wide-eyed, excited to wonder at the royal family up close.

The red-and-yellow knight gave Asrai a warm smile as he lifted his flagon of ale. "It does us good to see a lady on our prince's arm at last."

The other knights followed suit and saluted Asrai with their flagons. She raised her goblet of water and drank with them. "And it pleases me that my prince has such strong and valiant warriors to protect this kingdom."

Her words were met with hearty cheers. Cormack grinned as the knights complimented him on his victory in archery. Asrai turned her gaze to the king. Despite the celebratory mood, his shoulders were slumped and his eyes appeared tired. He talked with his general as the knights made boisterous conversation with Cormack. When he noticed Asrai, he gave her a worn smile, then drank deep from his flagon. She turned her attention back to the conversation.

"…just glad to be back with friendly faces. I'll see my bonny lass soon! But not before the wenches take pity on me!" The knight in black-and-white colours laughed as he showed off a jagged wound on his arm, healing from his battle in Umber.

Cormack took another swig of ale. "I only wish we could have done more for the soldiers. It's hard to imagine the battlefield when you're here in the castle."

The knights nodded. The knight in green colours gripped Cormack's shoulder. "It is our duty, your highness! We all have our place in the world."

The knights cheered and raised their flagons again. The feast was a simple affair with boar, potatoes, and root vegetables. King Dominic wanted to give the knights and soldiers a taste of home before they went back to their families. Simple fruit tartes were passed out for the final course. Pamela saw to it that fish was sent to Asrai in addition to the boar. The knights raised the eyebrows, but said nothing.

Daniel Ratherford entered the hall with his musicians, and the knights cheered. He struck up a song for the battle of Umber, then allowed the music to swell into a charming ditty, inviting the guests to dance.

The knight in green colours stood and bowed to Asrai. She stared at him, perplexed. "My lady, may I have the honour of stealing you away for a dance?" He grinned.

Asrai fidgeted her hands. Cormack cleared his throat. "My lady would be honoured, however, the ladies of Sulu do not walk."

The knight flinched as Asrai lowered her gaze. He lowered his voice. "A thousand pardons, my lady. I did not know. How terribly rude of me to embarrass you."

Asrai lifted her gaze again. "Thank you, dear knight. You are most kind."

He winked at her, then bowed his head to Cormack before finding one of the Caraway ladies as a dance partner. Soon the hall was filled with whirling colours and laughter.

Cormack took Asrai's hand. "Shall we retire for the evening, Lady Asrai?"

She nodded. Cormack startled her by taking her into his arms and heading toward the entrance. The knights cheered. He laughed and hurried up the stairs toward Asrai's bedchambers. The maids had left a pitcher of water, a goblet, and a neatly wrapped oat cake on her table. Cormack settled Asrai onto the bed, then poured her some water.

"Shall I help you out of this?" Cormack toyed with the ribbon stays of her dress.

Asrai nodded and handed him back the water goblet. He helped her peel off the gown and petticoats. The corset proved to be a challenge, but Asrai was able to help with a bit of her magick. He lounged on the bed next to Asrai as she snuggled into the Altrusean shawl and buried her legs under the covers.

She turned to Cormack. "I fear that Paradine is becoming more of a danger."

He flinched. "We will always be safe in Paradine. It is my home."

"But it's not my home." Asrai's voice was firm. "Soon, Sulu shall be our home."

Cormack turned away. "Asrai, how am I to leave Paradine in the hands of Peter? He has become volatile since the fall of Umber. I know that if Father does not recover Umber, once Peter becomes king, he will sacrifice every man of Paradine and every gold coin to win Umber back. He will ruin this land."

"We are left with little choice." Asrai held her gaze, forcing Cormack to look at her. "Your cousin will be consumed with madness if left unchecked. He will forever be a danger to you and your title...and I am sure that if I stay on land he will kill me long before I dry out."

Cormack balked at the thought. "You talk of your training in combat...could you not-?"

"My training is in the sea. The land is strange to me. There are no currents to call upon, no water to aid my attacks. My magick can only sway and suggest with no elements to call upon." She took Cormack's hand in hers. "But, my dear sailor, there is another way."

Cormack sighed and looked back at Asrai. "What other way were you speaking of?"

Asrai squeezed his hand, then released it and pulled her comb from her hair. "If you were to bond with me, you would lose your soul." She began running the gold comb through her fiery locks. "You would also lose some of your human qualities, such as empathy. Merfolk do care for one another, just not in the same way you humans do."

Cormack nodded. "What else will I lose?"

"Your throne will be at risk with Peter in his current state." Asrai ran the comb through her hair faster. "Though there is a way to ensure he would be a kind and just leader."

Love of the Sea

"I never cared for my title." Cormack looked out the arrowslit window. "But I have always cared deeply for my people. They need a leader that puts the needs of the people first."

Asrai stopped combing her hair. "Your soul will help us achieve that." She flicked her eyes at Cormack.

He avoided her gaze. "What will happen to my soul once it's gone?"

"That will be our key." Asrai's eyes darted about and she twirled her comb. "In my studies, the sea hag told me stories of ancient merfolk that would capture human souls for dark spells."

A chill raced through Cormack's body. He wondered just how far off the sailors' stories of mer cruelty truly were. She tapped her comb in her palm. "The other way I speak of is, if we were to capture your soul before the transformation is complete, we could have the sea hag create a spell to transfer it into Peter's body." She began spinning her comb again. "I would have to cast it, but—"

Cormack felt a hopeful, foolish feeling take hold. "You mean, give Peter my soul? And make him kind? Like me?"

Asrai nodded, musing over her comb. It began to glow. "Yes, it might work. But I don't think such a spell has ever been cast. But there is the legend of a human who gives up his soul for life in the sea. I think it could work."

"I know you can make it work." Cormack took Asrai's hand. "I have to trust you. I cannot bear to separate from you, nor watch you dry out and die."

Asrai slipped her comb back into her hair and leaned her head against his shoulder. "I trust you, my sailor."

He kissed her forehead, then stood. "It is late. Please get some rest, Lady Asrai." He leaned over the bed and whispered in her ear. "I love you."

Cormack could feel Asrai's eyes burning into him as he shut the door. The hall was buzzing with servants running to and fro. Their voices and shoes echoed off the stone walls. The chants of the soldiers drilling in the courtyard spilled in from the windows. Cormack pressed his fingers to his forehead. He could almost hear the roll of the waves and the call of the sailors at the docks. His heart burned. How many days had it been?

The sun at his back, the smell of salt rooted in his nose. Cormack closed his eyes and leaned his back against the door. He longed for the hollow thud of his boots on *Anita's* decks. His skin craved the cool embrace of the sea—a sapphire world full of beautiful shells and magnificent creatures. His heart jolted.

And Asrai, she was always there.

He remembered flashes of something bright darting away behind *Anita*. Shimmers in the shadows. A change in the feel of the water. A wisp of a wave. It had all been her. "Is this what I've been feeling? Have I been answering not the call of the sea, but her?" Cormack ran his hand through his hair and straightened. The servants ignored him and went about their errands. He went to his bedchambers and slipped into dreams of the sea.

****

Cormack woke early the following morning. A gull cried outside his window, a siren's call for the docks. He threw off the covers, but when his feet hit the floor, the previous day welled in his mind. He dropped his head into his hand, his elbow on his knee.

I cannot deny that things are becoming more dangerous. Though Nephara dislikes Asrai, as to be expected from my rejection, it is uncertain if she is acting on those feelings. His thoughts circled back to the tournament. *And Peter has seen Asrai's true form, and suspects that she is using magick. Surely Peter has told Nephara of his discovery, which puts Asrai at risk. But how can I leave my kingdom to a mad king?*

Suppositions floated through his mind until a thought struck him—the jeweler was still crafting the ring. He had heard tales of noblemen finding peace with their decision to wed once the ring was in hand. He pressed his palms on his thighs and stood, stretching his back.

The maids scurried about as he strode to the jeweler's apartments. As he reached the old door, Cormack felt his shoulders press back, and a smile curl his lips. "Mm-ma-a-jes-jest-y," the jeweler was startled when he saw Cormack, "I-I-I have oh-only j-just b-begun."

Cormack's face fell, his glimmer of confidence snuffed out. "Oh, my apologies."

The jeweler opened the door and gestured for Cormack to enter. "P-please, yo-your h-highn-ness. C-come in."

A small fire crackled in the grate. The jeweler stoked it. The small room was dark, the furniture old and worn, but comfortable. Cormack followed the jeweler as he returned to his work table. Small sparkling shavings littered the surface, along with various tools. "I-I j-just f-finished p-po-polishing the b-band." He held out the small silver ring.

Cormack took it. It was delicate, fit for a fine lady. He traced the intricate seashell designs. "How did you know?"

The jeweler laughed as Cormack handed him the band. "H-how c-could I n-not?"

"I guess my particulars are rather obvious, aren't they?" Cormack grinned. "I hope she likes it."

"I-I have n-not made a ring this f-fine since your F-father and h-her m-majesty. P-Poseidon p-protect her ss-s-soul."

Cormack shrugged. "What about Peter's ring for the Princess of Caraway?"

The jeweler shook his head. "A-already f-finish-shed th-that one. N-not w-well b-ba-balanced. B-but it's wh-what the p-prin-cess wanted. H-her hap-hap-pi-ness is what c-counts."

"I suppose." Cormack watched as the jeweler cut little shreds off the mermaid's tear. "All I want is her happiness."

"Mmm." The jeweler was absorbed with his work. Cormack fidgeted.

"Suppose her happiness is the same as your happiness," Cormack mused, "but that's not everyone else's happiness?"

The jeweler had his top lip curled up, exposing his teeth. His fingers clenched his tools as he worked the tiny jewel. Cormack sat down in the moth-eaten chair next to the fireplace. "I feel as if I bear an impossible decision. I don't know what to think anymore."

"L-love is the gr-greatest p-power anyone c-can p-possess." The jeweler paused in his work to select a new tool. "S-s-some use it as a weap-p-pon. S-some use it to u-unite a pe-ople. And others...others oh-only see it as the s-smallest twi-twinkle in-in their l-lover's eye-eyes...m-majesty."

Cormack shifted in the chair. The jeweler was absorbed in his work. Little speckles of light flashed about the room as he mounted the mermaid's tear into the band. "N-no o-other j-je-jewels, yo-your high-ness?"

"No." Cormack shook his head. "Just that one."

The jeweler worked in silence, save for the grinding and scraping of his tools. Cormack stoked the fire again. He began to wonder how impatient Peter was for his ring. Cormack poked the fire with an iron, watching the coals split.

"It i-is done."

Cormack jumped. He scrambled out of the chair and leaned over the work table. In the old man's hands was a beautiful little ring with a radiant jewel for its crown. Cormack gasped, his heart thundering.

The jeweler smiled, his eyes fixed on the ring. "P-please m-majesty...if-f y-you ever f-find another of these..."

"Done." Cormack grinned at the jeweler. "I have more..." he paused remembering how overcome Asrai was when she cried. "But they are not exactly mine to give."

"O-of course." The jeweler looked at Cormack. "I sh-shall m-make a f-fine p-piece for the l-lady. If-f only I-I can k-keep one f-for m-myself..." He bowed his head. "F-forgi-give m-my im-imp-pert-tinence. M-majesty."

Cormack shook his head. "I understand. I was just as thrilled when I saw them. There are many. She won't mind a few."

"Th-thank you, high-highness." The jeweler set the ring in Cormack's palm, then curled his fingers over it. "G-give the l-lady m-my best."

Cormack turned the ring this way and that between his fingers. "You already have. Thank you."

Cormack paced his room. He twirled the tiny metal band around and around in his trouser pocket. *Lose my soul forever to the sea. Forever in the sea.* Cormack shook his head. *What of Pamela and Father? Can I truly trust the spell, and leave the kingdom in Peter's hands?*

Chapter Nineteen

A maid startled Cormack, replacing the smooth white pitcher at his washstand with one full of fresh clean water. She bobbed a curtsy. "Excuse me, my lord."

Cormack wiped his face with his hand and stared at the maid. He put his hands on her shoulders and a flicker of fear went across her eyes. "What would you do if you had to choose between everything you know and someone you love?"

The maid's fingers tightened around the empty pitcher. "M'lord, I don't quite understand."

Cormack let his arms fall to his sides, but kept his gaze on her. "I am to wed Lady Asrai, but I-I am afraid."

The maid's face softened and a smile spread across her lips. "My dear lord, it is natural to have misgivings before your wedding day." A sigh escaped her lips. "Trust in your feelings, m'lord, they won't steer you wrong."

Cormack nodded and smiled. "Thank you."

The maid bobbed a curtsy and closed the door. Cormack pulled the ring out of his pocket and examined it: a silver band engraved with seashells, the mermaid's tear in the centre. He sucked in his breath and placed his hand on the doorknob. With a heavy exhale, he opened it and made his way down the hall to Asrai's apartments.

A disgruntled maid exited the bedroom, carrying a full pitcher of wine. She bobbed her head in respect to Cormack as she hurried past. He went inside and, before he could rap his fingers on the door, the latch clicked from the inside and swung open.

"Good morrow, my sailor." Asrai was pulling at a curl, her comb draped in her languid hand.

Cormack closed the door behind him. The ring burned in his hand. *Trust in my feelings.* "Good morrow, Lady Asrai."

She tilted her head. "What are you hiding?"

He flinched, squeezing the ring in his palm. "There is something I wanted to give you."

Asrai straightened as Cormack knelt before her, his hands clasped. He kept his eyes on his hands. His body trembled as the words tumbled out. "I have thought on our decision. I trust in my feelings for you."

Lauren A. R. Masterson

Asrai leaned forward and pushed herself straight. Her curious green-grey eyes studied his face and his hand. "And what are your feelings, my dear prince?"

Cormack lifted his face to her and took her left hand in his. "I want to take you as my wife, Lady Asrai." He lifted his clenched hands and opened them.

"A gift?" Asrai stared at the ring, her eyes soaking up the glittering jewel.

"It is a token we humans give to express that we are bonded. Should you accept." Cormack moved his hand closer to Asrai.

She stroked her curls with her right hand and stared at the ring. Her eyes glinted, the magick flashing through them. "We will be bonded?" she whispered.

Cormack placed the ring on her finger, kissing the tear before pulling his right hand away, embracing her left hand with his left hand. "Not yet. That is what the ceremony is for. But this is a physical showing of it."

Asrai looked at Cormack. He pressed his forehead against hers, the skin cool against his heated brow. She opened her eyes again. "We will be home in the sea soon, my sailor." Asrai held out the back of her hand, examining her tear. It shone bright like a star captured from the night sky. "Soon we shall be home."

****

The hall echoed with the chatter and footfalls of servants. The footmen were silent as they carried the gold palanquin toward the Great Hall. Dinner had been prepared as a banquet for the double announcement. Cormack's hands were sweating as he strode before the palanquin. He wiped them on his breeches once they had stopped before the entrance.

Peter was already seated, but Nephara was nowhere to be found. Cormack helped Asrai into her chair and seated himself. Pamela had ensured a goblet full of water was waiting at Asrai's place setting, along with a servant girl standing at attention with a full pitcher.

Asrai took a delicate sip from her water as ale was poured for Cormack. She could still feel a faint dryness in her body, though the thirst was not as desperate as before. A few more sips of water proved this feeling was easily quieted.

One of the men dressed all in yellow pounded a decorative wooden staff upon the stone floor. The Great Hall fell into a hush. He drew his shoulders up and stilled. "People of Paradine! We, the people of Caraway, are pleased to announce that our two countries shall be united in the beauty of marriage. Rejoice at such a happy peace!"

138

Love of the Sea

A wave of clapping went 'round the table. The man held up his hand for quiet again. He then moved his arm in a fluid arc, poised toward the entrance. "Presenting the fire of Caraway, Princess Nephara!"

A procession entered the hall, much livelier than the introduction procession. Three dancers dressed in yellow and three in red spilled into the room. Swirling scarves attached to fans created clouds of bright colour. Following them was Nephara and her troupe of ladies. The two hooded ladies carried large gold ceremonial scythes.

Nephara was dressed all in gold. This time the large crown was settled into her curls, not simply lifted from a box. Tiny rubies set in gold filigree had been braided into her hair. They glittered like a bonfire against the night sky. Her long gossamer gown swished. Six red cords were tied about her waist. The princess stood before the table. She held up her arms in salute. The dancers froze, and all her ladies bowed their heads.

"I, Princess Nephara Tasinim, promise on this day to join my dear heart, Peter of Paradine, in marriage of both diplomacy and love! Celebrate with me!"

A thunderous applause followed. The people of Caraway banged their fists on the table. Asrai was overwhelmed by the display. She flicked her eyes to Cormack, but he was absorbed in the presentation. Her nerves coiled into a ball of anxiety as the manservant in gold lifted the crown from Nephara's head, allowing her to take her seat beside Peter.

King Dominic stood, raising his flagon. "To my dear nephew and his bride to be, I bless this union in the name of our two united kingdoms! May we prosper together!"

Shouts of agreement echoed in the great stone hall. Cormack clapped with them. He froze when King Dominic turned and saluted him with his flagon. "I believe we have a double announcement this fine evening!"

Cormack swallowed and nodded. He stood. The table became quiet again. Asrai stared at him. "Today, we are all one people," Cormack gestured to Nephara, "united by the wonderful discovery of love."

He put his hand on Asrai's shoulder. "As many of you know, I have sent away every lady that has walked through these doors. None had shown me such wonder as the sea. None had made me feel as wondrously alive and free as the sea."

Cormack looked at Asrai. She smiled and placed her hand over his. "None such, until my Princess Asrai."

He pushed his chair aside and kneeled before Asrai, still holding her hand. "My heart is yours, my lady. I shall love no other. At last, I am complete." He kissed her hand. King Dominic bellowed in approval, and everyone clapped. Asrai blushed. Cormack took his seat. He took her hand again and squeezed it.

"To see the two finest men in Paradine finally settling down does an old man good." King Dominic raised his flagon again. "To a bright future for us all!"

Cheers erupted and fists banged the table. Cormack grinned. Asrai found herself smiling too. She flicked her eyes at Cormack, the magick crackling with her excitement.

Dinner was a feast with coconut-breaded whelk, sweet and sticky grilled fruits, poached grouper, and boar. Asrai found that the foods were easier on her body, though she kept more of the fish on her plate than anything else. Nephara's face lit up when figs were brought out for dessert, accompanied by a cream pudding.

Princess Nephara waved and swished her hand in gesture as she chatted during dinner, making the spectacular ring on her finger flash and glimmer. It was a thick gold band encrusted with rubies. Cormack recalled the jeweler's comment and chuckled. Nephara's face glowed with excitement. Even Peter seemed at ease.

Asrai focused more on her dinner and observing the people around her. Whenever her ring caught the light, it sent sparkles and rainbows showering the table. After the third time, King Dominic paused in his revelry and shouted across the table.

"Cormack!" The king banged his flagon on the table. "What on earth did you strap to your lady's finger to make such a display?"

Asrai lifted her hand for the king to see. Cormack leaned over the table and shouted back. "A mermaid's tear, father!"

Conversations lowered. Peter's head snapped up, his eyes darted from the ring to Asrai's face. His eyes narrowed, and he whispered to Nephara.

King Dominic froze. "A what?"

Cormack turned to Asrai. "May I, my lady?"

Asrai bit her lip as jealous possession of the item gripped her heart. After a moment, she slipped the ring from her finger, and surrendered it to Cormack. He stood, strode to the head of the table, and presented the ring to his father.

"A mermaid's tear," Cormack repeated. "It belongs to Lady Asrai."

King Dominic muttered as he took the ring and turned it this way and that. The jewel flashed and sparkled. He handed it back to Cormack, his brow furrowed. "A real one?" he whispered.

Cormack nodded. "Yes, Father."

The king turned his gaze to Asrai. Her eyes flashed for a moment, the odd shimmering making her eyes bright blue. Cormack looked from Asrai, to the king's puzzled face. He frowned.

King Dominic shook his head, and then grinned. "A fine gem! Of course! Only the best for my new daughter!" He laughed and raised his flagon. "Another round! Another round!"

Cormack hurried back to Asrai and slipped the ring on her finger. She sighed, happy to feel the warm band of metal against her skin again. She fidgeted with it, then placed her hands in her lap. "Are you enjoying the evening, my lady?" Cormack whispered.

She nodded. "Yes, my sailor. Thank you."

Once the feast was cleared away, the musicians struck up a lively tune. Peter and Nephara rose to dance. One of Paradine's generals elbowed Cormack. "Too bashful to ask your lady to dance?"

Cormack shook his head. He lowered his voice. "My lady is unable. It's customary for princesses of Sulu to never walk."

The general's eyebrows flew into his hairline. "Never walk?"

"Yes. Their feet are to never touch the ground." Cormack glanced at Asrai. She was absorbed with watching the dancers.

The general glanced at Asrai. "So strange. But what about the wedding march?"

Fear jolted through Cormack. He swallowed and fidgeted his hands. "It did not occur to me."

"Well, I'm sure you will think of something, majesty."

Cormack turned again to Asrai. A tide of thoughts washed over him. There were many things that required mobility for the wedding; the march down the aisle, turning about the altar times thrice, the dance of the heart, all of it rushed past in his mind's eye. Asrai noticed his change in mood. She slipped her hand over his.

"Do not fret, my sailor," she whispered. "All is temporary."

He nodded, but the knot in his stomach tightened. All of it *would* be temporary. And then they would be in the sea. And then, what then? His heart trembled at the unknown. Cormack kissed her hand, pushing away the frantic thoughts.

****

That evening, Asrai requested the maid bring her a pail of clear water. The maid lifted her eyebrows, but said nothing. The servants were growing accustomed to her strangeness. Once the door was closed, Asrai pulled out her comb and flicked it. The lock clicked, protecting her from interruption. She dipped her glowing comb into the water, causing it to turn cloudy, and then colours and shapes surfaced. Once again, the sea hag appeared before her.

"Hello, Illyana," Asrai called out.

The sea hag started, but when saw Asrai in the water mirror she smiled. "My child, how goes your bond? Is it strengthening?"

"Yes." She lifted her hand, revealing the silver band. "Humans give these to show they are bonded."

The sea hag moved closer. Her pupils contracted, and then widened when she looked back at Asrai. "Few are able to achieve such a feat! You have done well."

Asrai withdrew her hand and stared at the ring. "Yes. I am truly happy."

The sea hag flicked her tail. "What other news?"

"My human guise pains me." Asrai sighed. "I am weak, and the humans are whispering about it."

"Is that all?" The sea hag rolled her eyes. "You are the daughter of Tuande, the glorious warrior king! The pain in your body is nothing compared to the pain of your lost legacy!"

Asrai shook her head. "Illyana, what can I do? This form, how can I go through the ritual like this?"

The sea hag's eyes flashed. "You must. I told you, magick cannot help you. This is the trial of a true bond. You must bear it."

Asrai nodded, the painful realization welling in her heart. *This is why mers do not fall in love. This is why humans are oft nothing more than playthings. This is simply too much.*

She looked at her ring again. Cormack's promise at dinner had flooded her with emotions she had never known. No surf had been that exciting, no school of fish had been that enticing, and no treasure had been that precious. Her longing went beyond the quickening she had felt at mating season. Much more than that.

"The pain is only temporary. Soon I shall deliver us home. Then all will be well."

The sea hag nodded, a smile creeping onto her lips. "Until we meet again." Asrai nodded. She swirled the comb, breaking the spell.

Chapter Twenty

The grey morning revealed sparkling dew drops on the long grass. The town crier startled peasants in the fields, shouting as he rode his lathered horse. They dropped their plows and crushed their straw hats against their heads as they followed.

"T'is a wedding!" he bawled, the horse's drumming hooves kicking up dirt clods. "T'is a wedding!" Flocks of peasants surged along the dirt road until they came to the market. Merchants shouted their wares, but fell silent when the crier galloped into the square.

"T'is the wedding o' th' prince!" He waved his hat and the crowd stared at him until he dismounted. A stable boy from the inn led the tired horse away.

The crier waited until the people shifted, staring him down for details, then cleared his throat. "His majesty, the king has declared the crown prince is to be wed!"

Cheers erupted, but the crier held up his hands, and the air grew tense and quiet. "His highness, Prince Cormack, has taken the hand of the fair Lady Asrai to be his betrothed! His majesty the kindred prince, Peter, shall also be wed!" He licked his dry lips and continued. "Our lands shall know great strength and wealth with the new alliance with the Princess of Caraway, the bride of Prince Peter!"

The crier let his hands fall, indicating that they could yell and stamp their feet while he pressed through the masses. He was followed by a few into the inn, where he ordered a goblet of weak wine to soothe his throat.

A farmer with large chapped hands sat down at the crier's table. "T'is true? Th' prince finally found a wife?"

The crier nodded, gulping the wine and motioning for the wench to bring more. The farmer whistled and nodded. "We was certain he would show up with th' monks this spring."

The crier gave a raspy laugh and the farmer ordered mead for the both of them. The crier nodded and smiled. "Never thought I would see the day."

The knight guards in each town had been instructed by King Dominic to allow his people the exciting day of rest. The fields lay untended, but he smiled knowing his people were rejoicing with him.

****

Cormack was trapped in the map room yet again. This time the strategy was of auspicious dates and lists of guests. They were seated at the low table, next to the map table. The king was beside himself, and babbled to the royal staff as their quills raced over sheaves of parchment.

"All are welcome!" King Dominic slapped the table. "All shall make merry on this joyous day, nobles and peasants alike!"

The staff nodded, copying the king's instructions. The head servant of each sector was at the table, including Pamela. Cormack leaned his elbow against the table, his shoulders slumped. He found no comfort in this, as only tedious details of the feast were discussed. It seemed thoughts of Umber had been wiped from the king's mind.

King Dominic clapped Cormack on the shoulder. "My boy, so quiet! What say you for this wondrous day?"

"It is more your day than mine, Father." He shrugged. "Whatever you like." The staff looked between the two men, their quills hovering.

"Nonsense!" King Dominic shook his head. "Come now, speak for your lady and yourself."

"Father, this wedding seems at odds with the current state of our vassals in Umber. Wouldn't our resources be better served tending to the soldiers and their families?" Cormack leaned back in his chair. His eyes darted to the map table.

King Dominic shook his head. "My boy, we have already made arrangements for care and stipends. As for Umber, it will take months for us to rebuild our army large enough to squash that old dog for good. Now is the time to give the people hope, and what better way than with a secure future?"

Cormack straightened his back. "This all just seems so *frivolous*."

"T'is a wedding, my boy!" King Dominic cheered, trying to raise Cormack's spirit. "This is the biggest event of your life! Of course it's supposed to be flashy and frivolous!"

The royal staff nodded, coaxing their prince. Pamela tilted her head. "If I may, your highness, we all need a bit of happiness right now. This wedding will do you good if only you let it."

Cormack sighed. He locked eyes with Pamela. "Lady Asrai would like fish and prawns at the banquet."

Pamela nodded. She scribbled a note to herself. "Does the lady have a preference for their preparation?"

"I don't know." He shrugged. "Whatever goes best."

The head gardener cleared his throat. "Does his majesty know the favourite flower of the lady?"

Cormack tilted his head. *I don't even know if Asrai knows what flowers are.* "I'll ask her."

The head musician and minstrel glanced at one another. The minstrel spoke. "My lord, are there any particular works you would like to include for the festivities? I personally have been working on a special piece to honour you and the Lady Asrai."

The head musician nodded. "Yes, a beautiful and triumphant ballad!"

Cormack fidgeted his hands. "That is very kind of you, thank you. My lady did enjoy your saga of Paradine. Perhaps another tale would interest her."

The minstrel was taken aback. "The lady has a taste for adventurous tales?"

"Oh yes!" Cormack grinned. "Asrai loves the thrill of the sea! Exploring and finding treasure—" The men smiled at Cormack, pleased their prince had found an interest in the planning.

King Dominic nodded as Cormack chattered. "It's a mystery to me how this will work, but I trust you. You are all the best of my household. I know you will do our family proud."

Cormack flinched. "What do you mean, Father?"

"Don't you remember, boy? It's to be a double wedding."

"Oh. Yes." Cormack dropped his gaze to the table, his excitement snuffed out. "I'm sure Peter and the Princess Nephara have all sorts of plans."

****

Asrai cried out as her ankles buckled. A warm, strong arm curled around her before her knees hit the floor. Cormack grunted with the effort to lift Asrai's dead weight into a standing position. Her legs trembled. Sweat rolled down the back of her neck. She cringed at the tickling perspiration.

"Please, you need to rest." Cormack tried to steer her toward the bed.

"No!" Asrai pushed against him, her body swaying. "This body will obey me!"

Cormack sighed and readjusted his arm. Her fingers dug into his bicep again, her other arm to the side for balance. When Cormack had returned from the initial planning meeting with his father and the staff, Asrai had demanded she practice walking. What had started as an endearing struggle quickly became a tiresome argument as Asrai refused to rest.

"You'll hurt yourself if you keep this up." Cormack helped her take another step. "The wedding is still two moons away."

Asrai gritted her teeth. Every step raked pain up her legs and into her heart. Her body was warm and she was uncomfortable in her damp, sweaty shift. They had removed her gown to prevent her from tripping over the long hem.

"I yield." Asrai panted, allowing Cormack to take her full weight. "I yield."

Cormack turned and helped shuffle her onto the bed. Asrai collapsed onto the quilt, her body shaking. He sat beside her and stroked her back. "I'll send for a maid. Some water and a bath will do you good."

Asrai curled into a ball, bringing her knees to her chest, lying on her side. Her hands tried to knead the soft flesh. Cormack flagged down a maid, and soon she was tutting her tongue while sponging Asrai's forehead with a cool, wet linen.

"My lady, you over-exert yourself," she whispered as she dunked the linen into the bucket of water and wrung it out. "You must be careful, what with the wedding to come."

"Why do you think I'm doing this?" Asrai snapped. "I cannot appear before my dear sailor's kingdom an unsuitable mate! I must show my virility and my strength!"

The maid flinched. "My lady, I am certain all the kingdoms will see what a magnificent princess you are."

Asrai grumbled and allowed the maid to continue. Cormack sat in one of the overstuffed chairs, watching. He found he liked the way Asrai's crimson hair sprawled over the bed, her curls like flames consuming the quilt. Her body had stopped quivering, and the colour was returning to her face.

"She is right, Lady Asrai." Cormack leaned back in the chair, propping his feet. "I will make certain all our guests know of your splendour."

The maid helped Asrai sit up and poured her a cup of water. Asrai struggled to hide her smile, as she was still annoyed. Cormack's words warmed her, and the water eased the pain in her bones. "I'll draw your bath, my lady." The maid left the pitcher of water on the nightstand and curtsied.

Asrai's arm shook as she tried to pour herself another cup. Cormack eased himself out of the chair and helped steady her hand. Asrai glowered at him. "You're just worn out." Cormack replaced the pitcher. "You made a great effort today."

The maid reentered the bedroom and curtsied. "The bath is ready, my lady."

Cormack nodded. He scooped up Asrai and walked into the bathroom. His arms trembled, exhausted from holding her up for hours, but his will won out as he slid her onto the washing stool.

"M-my lord, I-I don't think this is proper!" The maid stammered as Cormack walked past her.

Love of the Sea

Asrai's eyes brightened, the strange shimmering making them appear like dappled sunlight on the water's surface. The maid curtsied, and left on another errand. Cormack frowned as the door latched shut. He fumbled with the lacing on Asrai's shift.

"A bath should restore me. Then I can begin again." Asrai fidgeted.

Cormack loosed the last of the stays. "Arms up."

She obeyed and Cormack slid the shift over her head. He helped her slip into the bath. Her muscles relaxed as the steaming water swallowed her body. Asrai sighed, her eyes rolling into the back of her head.

"Asrai, why did the maid leave?" Cormack sat on the washing stool, his eyes darting over her face. Her eyes were back to their usual green-grey.

"I'm sure she had other things to attend to." Asrai shrugged. "Why do you ask, my sailor?"

Cormack leaned forward against the tub. "You made her leave, didn't you?"

Asrai darted her eyes down to her feet. "I don't see why it matters. We are able to talk freely now."

"You can't just make people do whatever you like!" Cormack narrowed his eyes. "Asrai, you cannot use magick to force people to do your bidding, just like you cannot use magick to force Father to like you."

Asrai pouted, refusing to meet Cormack's gaze. "I am only protecting myself, my dear sailor. I am not *forcing* anyone to do anything. I am merely using *suggestion* to sway them to *want* to do or think something else."

Cormack rolled his eyes. "That's hardly different. Think how you would feel if this usurper you have talked about was to use *suggestion* on you."

"That is hardly the same!" Asrai spat, her fiery gaze reaching his at last. "Garradi is a monster! A tyrant!"

"And you will be the same if you keep using magick instead of your words and actions," Cormack whispered. "I know in your heart that you want to be a good queen to your people, but you must act on that."

Asrai's shoulders slumped as she dropped her gaze. "I am not a tyrant."

Cormack took her hand in his. "No. You are not a tyrant. But you must learn to win people's trust, and eventually, their love on your own. Magick makes for a false bond."

"A false bond." Asrai echoed, lost in her thoughts. "Perhaps you are right, my dear sailor."

He squeezed her hand. "I know all this is strange to you. But your people should love you for your actions, not *suggestion*."

Asrai nodded, her eyes closing as the water seeped into her bones, rejuvenating her weary body. "Yes. Love forges a true bond."

Cormack allowed his gaze to slip over her body. Her skin was the same, pale and luminous, but without her shimmering scales, Cormack felt she was more of a porcelain doll than a living being. He missed the way her scales spiraled up her arms and into the translucent frills on her wrists. She was now small enough in the tub for her legs to lie flat, rather than her great strong tail hanging out over the edge.

"You are staring," Asrai muttered. "I can feel your eyes."

He leaned his arms on the lip of the tub and kissed her forehead. "My apologies, my lady. I'm simply remembering."

Asrai opened her eyes. "And what are you remembering, my dear sailor?"

Cormack smiled and traced his finger where her scale plating used to be. "Your true form."

She stared at her legs and frowned. "Yes. I miss it as well."

"A wise lady once told me all is temporary." Cormack put his fingers under her chin, forcing her to look at him. He smiled.

Asrai could not help herself and smiled as well. Cormack kissed her. She still tasted of the sea and wild things. He kissed her harder. Asrai wove her arms around his neck. Cormack broke off the kiss, his heart thundering. He rested his forehead against Asrai's, the heat rolling off his body.

"Not like this." His voice was low and thick. "I want to know you as you, only as you."

Asrai nodded, her chest fluttering as she regained her senses. "This form confuses me. I would not know where to begin."

Cormack kissed her forehead and sat upright again. "I cannot wait for you to show me."

She leaned back into the water once more. Her eyes closed, and a smile spread on her lips. "I will have *much* to show you once we are home."

"I dream of it." Cormack leaned against the side of the tub, a yawn escaping his lips. "I dream of all the incredible things in the sea you will teach me."

Asrai stroked Cormack's hair, her fingers soft and wet. "There are also many dangers in the sea."

Cormack nodded, his eyes closed as Asrai's fingers continued their soothing methodic movements. "Yes, but you shall be there with me."

Asrai kissed Cormack's forehead. She shifted her weight so that she was lying against the wall of the bathtub. She pulled Cormack's head onto her chest and continued to pet his hair. "Yes. I will be there with you to see every reef and fend off every shark, my darling sailor."

****

"My lady! My lady!" A high-pitched voice and a dull thudding startled them awake. Cormack groaned as he sat up, his back popping. Asrai's eyes flew open as the maid disregarded protocol and rushed into the room.

"Are you all right?" The poor flustered maid took in the strange sight. Cormack was perched on the washing stool. Asrai's hair floated in the water like living flames. Only her nose was above the now-frigid bathwater.

Asrai sat up, her teeth chattering. "Y-yes. I'm-m all r-right."

The maid threw open the cabinet and fetched a towel. "You'll catch your death, sitting in a cold bath!"

Cormack helped Asrai slip out of the bathtub and stand up. The maid swathed Asrai in the towel and helped Cormack walk her to the bed.

"Forgive my impertinence, your highness," she shot Cormack an icy glare, "but such negligence is dangerous! Falling asleep while your lady nearly drowned herself!"

"Yes, my apologies," Cormack muttered, thoroughly chastised. He helped slide Asrai onto the bed while the maid rifled through the trunk for warm clothes.

Asrai shivered in the wet towel. Cormack retrieved another from the cupboard and began drying Asrai's hair. The maid pushed him aside and peeled the towel from Asrai's body. "Here, my lady." She pulled a chemise over Asrai's head. "Let's get you dressed."

The maid worked quickly, dressing Asrai into a night-shift and the wool shawl from Altruse. Cormack helped Asrai burrow under the covers and smoothed the quilt. "I'll fetch you something warm to drink from the kitchens, and have someone light the fire."

Cormack sat on the bed as the maid rushed off. He stroked the crown of Asrai's hair. "Feeling better?"

She nodded. "You humans are ill-equipped. You are harmed by such insignificant things."

"Yes. But there is something to be said about our strength on a battlefield. My father swears by it."

Asrai took his hand. "Such nonsensical creatures."

Cormack's chest fluttered when Asrai smiled. He squeezed her hand. Before he could kiss her again, the door flew open, startling them both. Two maids curtsied and rushed in. One carried a large pitcher and two goblets to Asrai, while the other busied herself with igniting the tinder in the grate.

"Here you are, my lady." Steam curled up from the goblet as she poured an amber liquid from the pitcher. "Spiced punch. The head cook made it herself."

The cup brought tingling feeling back into Asrai's chilled hands. Warmth swirled in her mouth as she took a sip. Cinnamon, clove, and ginger flooded her blood with comfort as she drank the spiced apple juice. Crackles of fiery magick raced through her veins.

"This is amazing!" Asrai held out her cup for more.

The maid refilled it, and poured Cormack a cup as well. "She will be pleased to hear that."

"How did she make this so quickly?" Cormack sipped his punch, grateful to feel his stiff muscles relaxing.

"Practicing for the wedding." The maid bounced her gaze between them. "The wee hours are upon us, your highness. Best be getting some rest."

Cormack nodded, and handed the cup back to the maid. "Thank you. Goodnight, ladies."

He kissed Asrai on the forehead before sliding off the bed. Her eyes were becoming heavy again. "Goodnight, my sailor prince."

Chapter Twenty-One

Cormack awoke the next morning stiff and cold. His bed had done little good. His limbs popped as he stretched and swung his legs over the bedside. The grey light of dawn shone through the arrow slits. The weak light did nothing to warm his body. He slipped his nightshirt off and pulled on his tunic and breeches. Cormack yawned as he inspected his face in the mirror above the washstand. The water was cold, but it banished the sleep from his mind as he washed his face.

The sound of voices floated into his bedroom. Cormack looked out the window and saw soldiers walking in formation. Beyond were the gardens. They sparkled with dew in the early morning light. A sea breeze tickled his hair, tempting him with salt and spray. Cormack breathed deep through his nose and smiled.

Soon we shall be home.

He headed into the hall, his boots clicking on the stone floor. Servants scurried by on their errands. Cormack found his way down to the kitchens. The kitchen staff were bleary-eyed from lack of sleep. Pamela yawned as she stirred a cauldron of marinade.

"Good morrow," Cormack chirped as he scavenged for breakfast.

The kitchen staff were startled, but murmured a greeting and went back to their tasks. Pamela stretched and nodded to him. "You're up early, even for you."

Cormack nodded, pilfering a grainy loaf of bread from the pantry. "Yes. I could not sleep."

Pamela handed off the marinade to a kitchen hand and began pulling ingredients from the pantry. Two scullery maids rushed in with baskets of food from the larder. "Wedding jitters," Pamela muttered as she began arranging the food stuffs on a broad table and delegated instructions.

One of the kitchen hands cut a hunk of soft ewe's cheese and handed it to Cormack. "Thank you." He accepted the cheese. The mellow bite was good against the dark, coarse bread. "Asrai is still asleep, I expect. I wanted to pay *Anita* a visit this morning."

Pamela nodded, helping the staff chop root vegetables. "You shan't be missed. I'll see the lady is informed."

Cormack swallowed the last of his breakfast. "Thank you, Pamela!"

She chuckled as Cormack trotted out the side door. The cool morning sent a chill through Cormack. He ran faster to the docks, his heart thundering in his chest. Gangs of sailors were packing their ships for a full day of fishing. They cheered when Cormack approached.

"Congratulations, highness!"

"A lady at last! Well done, my lord!"

"Poseidon smiles upon us! A wedding! A wedding!"

Cormack was overwhelmed as the sailors clapped him on the back and shook his hand. "Thank you! Thank you all!" Cormack laughed, his heart fit to burst. "Poseidon bless my princess of the sea!"

The sailors clapped and cheered. Cormack grinned so hard it hurt.

"What a fine sight, I bet she is!" one of the sailors teased.

Cormack shook his head. "You will see her splendour and her strength! All are welcome at my table for this blessed day."

A hush fell over the sailors. One of the younger men spoke. "*All* are invited, your highness?"

"Yes!" Cormack threw out his arms. "Father has said all will revel at the wedding."

Murmurs rippled through the crowd. One of the older sailors stepped forward and bowed. "We simple men would be honoured, majesty. Thank-e."

Cormack smiled and waved to the sailors, heading toward *Anita* once more. "May Poseidon's breath fill your sails and his bounty fill your nets!"

Cheers followed him. Cormack felt his breath catch when he hoisted himself up *Anita's* rigging. The blue expanse of the harbour was laid before him. The first golden rays of sunlight shimmered on the water. Cormack whooped as he took the helm.

****

Asrai rubbed the sleep from her eyes. Her body was heavy and sluggish. She cursed her newfound weakness and forced her limbs to cooperate. Bright cheery sunlight filtered through the arrowslit windows. Asrai grumbled. She had overslept.

Bread, cheese, and water had been left for her on the small table. Asrai slid her legs over the side of the bed. Her ankles gave way, and her body crumpled, the dull thud muffled by the thick rug. Asrai gripped the bed poster and pulled herself up again. Her legs trembled as her feet took the weight. The few paces to the table seemed a great chasm with no furniture in-between for her to hold onto.

Asrai strode toward the table, her right hand still gripping the poster. Pain shot up her legs and into her chest. She took a shuddering breath and forged ahead, her hand releasing the bed. Her body wobbled as she lurched forward. Each step was knives shooting up from the floor and into her feet. At last she gripped the chair, sweat rolling down her back.

Love of the Sea

The water eased her burning throat. The dry ache in her bones subsided. Asrai poured herself more water and downed it, calming her heaving chest. She slammed the cup on the table and gasped for breath, her mind focusing again.

A polite knock sounded. The door opened. Asrai straightened and willed her body to stillness as a maid entered and curtsied. "Hello, your highness. I'm here to assist you. The head cook is busy with the wedding preparations."

Asrai glowered. She bristled at the idea of her vulnerability being on full display. "I am quite well, thank you."

The maid ignored Asrai's quip and strode into the room. She busied herself with making the bed. Asrai tore off a hunk of bread and chewed the coarse grainy texture. Her body was starving, and yet she had to put on a pretty show for the humans, lest Cormack lose his nerve.

Asrai sighed, slowing her pounding heart. *All is temporary.*

The maid began pulling a new set of clothes from the trunk. Cormack had ordered the chief seamstress and head tailor to begin creating new garments for Asrai after their evening excursion to the sea. A soft butter yellow gown had been made with patterns of apple blossoms. A human princess would have been thrilled by the beautiful craftsmanship, but Asrai was uninterested in the strange fabrics. Her heart *did* flutter at the strands of pearls and hair bands crusted in gems.

Asrai used the back of the chair for support while the maid dressed her. A warm breeze found its way through the arrowslit windows and ruffled Asrai's hair. "All right, sit for me and I'll have your hair dressed." The maid toyed with a crimson curl.

The gentle tugs of braiding struck Asrai with a strange yearning for the sea hag. When she was young, the sea hag used to enjoy braiding seashells and small trinkets into Asrai's hair. Now, that memory seemed warmer and had a strange quality to it that made her feel fond, but also lonely.

"Illyana," Asrai whispered.

The maid halted. "Did you say something, princess?"

Asrai caught herself and straightened. "No. I just remembered something."

"I'm not sure what Sulu is like, your highness, but here in Paradine we're friendly folk. You don't have to worry about being guarded about everything."

Asrai ran her hand over the embroidery on her bodice. "I suppose. Your people have been quite hospitable to me."

The maid slid her hands so that she embraced Asrai for a moment. "My dear lady, we understand that it is hard to adjust to a strange new country. Please know that we are here to guide you, and assure your happiness in all things. Do not fret, princess."

Asrai fought to keep her head still when the maid retreated, and the braiding continued. Perhaps we have misunderstood humans...perhaps they are more like Fredsmegler than I had previously imagined. After all, it was The Cursed One who divided us.

She fidgeted her hands in her lap. The jewelry sparkled on the table. Asrai plucked the ring Cormack had given her. She slid it onto her finger. Tiny rainbows danced over her skirts.

"That truly is a beauty," the maid chatted. "I've never seen anything like it."

Asrai played with the light reflecting off her ring. "My dear sailor prince has a kind soul."

"Indeed, he does, my lady." The maid lifted the jeweled headband from the table and tucked it into Asrai's hair. The braids were left half done, as the weight of her hair was too much. Her curls clustered about her shoulders, while the coils of braids held the headband in place. The maid helped latch the string of pearls around Asrai's neck.

"Shall I send for the footmen?" The maid stepped aside and admired her handiwork.

Asrai nodded. "Yes. I would like to see my prince."

The maid looked at the floor. "My apologies, my lady, his highness is out with his boat."

"What?" Asrai snapped up her gaze. "Why has he gone off?"

"Don't fret, princess, he will return soon. He always does."

Asrai glowered at the floor as the maid curtsied and left to find the footmen. The call of a seagull taunted her. She balled her hands and clenched them until she could feel the prick of her nails. *Even now the sea calls out to me. My bones ache for the strong waves and the mysterious deep. How dare he leave me a prisoner on land while he frolics in the sea!*

The sound of footsteps startled Asrai. The maid curtsied as the footmen hurried to her side. "Where would my lady like to go today?" The maid stood before Asrai, smiling.

"I know little of this castle." Asrai kept her voice measured, masking her frustration.

The maid nodded. "The gardens are quite beautiful. Would your highness like a tour from the head gardener?"

Asrai pushed aside her dark thoughts. She remembered Cormack speaking about flowers. She nodded. "Yes. That would be suitable."

The maid relaxed. The footmen loaded Asrai into the palanquin and bore her out to the grounds proper. The sun was bright, but Asrai found that it did not hurt her as it had before. The breeze was sweet and bore whispers of the sea. She drank it all in as they approached the gardens.

Love of the Sea

"A fine day, princess!" The head gardener waved at the procession. In his other hand he held Nonna's bridle. The stable boys had been alerted, dressed her in fine tack, and braided flowers into her mane and tail.

"Hello, gardener." Asrai waved.

The footmen lowered the palanquin. The gardener halted Nonna and held her steady as one of the footmen carried Asrai. Once she was astride the gentle mare, the footmen disappeared back into the castle.

"I'm pleased to have the honour of showing you my work," the gardener chatted. "This garden was planted by the first queen of Paradine."

He led them to a small grove of weeping willows engulfing a bench. A pond sprawled before it for a perfect view of water lilies and turtles. "This was the original garden." The gardener swept his hand over the serene scene. "It has grown considerably since."

Asrai nodded. She spotted a small obelisk next to the bench. The peak was flat and bore a plaque. "What does that inscription say?" She pointed.

The gardener halted Nonna and approached the obelisk. "This is the dedication to the first queen from the royal gardener. It was put here many years after the queen's passing. It reads:

A healthy plaine where good things grow,
Delicate flowers to seed and sow,
Beauty carefully tended as only gardeners know,
Blessed are we that our fair queen loved the willow,
And the sword traded for the peaceful hoe."

Asrai smiled, enjoying the charming ditty. The gardener began leading Nonna again. "Each royal family has left their mark on the garden, some beautiful, and some not."

He led Asrai to a gnarled hawthorn tree. Most of the great trunk was black with char, but branches of green hung low on the tree's south facing side. A plaque was affixed to the wide trunk. "This tree survived the burning that started the Antioch War." The gardener's voice grew quiet. "An army came from over the sea and pillaged Paradine. Their ships were carved like sea monsters. They wore paint on their faces and bodies. Their attack was swift in the wee hours of the morning. Many were taken as slaves, and many more lives were lost."

Asrai nodded. *That is the way of things— those who seek to take, those who delight in shattering a way of life.*

"Our King Lionade and fierce warrior Queen Mariana of Altruse began amassing allies and vassals through diplomacy and war. Twenty long years they built Paradine into a sprawling empire. Their son Damien finished their work and led our armies to the barbarians' homeland. They took back our enslaved people and decimated their warriors."

"What of the innocents?" Asrai kept her gaze on the tree.

"That is not our way." The gardener shook his head and touched the plaque with his fingertips.

It seemed each corner of the garden held a fragment of lore and history. Asrai especially enjoyed the marble founts that were at the centre of the garden to honour Poseidon, his great form characterized in marble with fanciful beasts and fish surrounding him. The gardener at last led them to a small cluster of tiny white flowers huddled under a stand of white birch. There was a low stone platform, and upon it was an offering of mead and fruits.

"The passing of our dear Queen Amaris was tragic." He gestured to the offering. "Our king mourns her to this day."

Asrai shifted. "Would you tell me about her?"

The gardener nodded. "Let's sit down, shall we?"

He led Nonna to the wooden bench near the queen's flowers. He tied her bridle to the bench, then lifted Asrai as if she were nothing but sea foam. He set her on the bench with care. Asrai smiled as he sat beside her.

"Her majesty, Queen Amaris, was the jewel of Paradine. Some say that the king wooed her from the Unseelie Court. Others say she was a selkie that had washed ashore, so great was her beauty. The king loved her with all his heart, and showered her with poetry and little trinkets every day." Asrai twisted her ring. Before she had found such frivolity foolish, but now her heart ached for it.

"The queen loved her people, and they loved her. She would oft go out for rides into the villages and farms to speak with them first hand. Her gentle words would always reach the king's ear, and the people prospered."

A butterfly landed on the bowl of fruits. Asrai watched its yellow wings flutter. She smiled. The gardener pointed to the insect. "Seems we have a visitor."

"Enjoying your tale, I'm sure." Asrai followed the butterfly's flirting with her eyes.

"I suppose." The gardener turned to look at Asrai. "Long have we waited for a new queen to brighten our halls and make Paradine merry once more. I am overjoyed that his majesty has chosen a lady at last."

Asrai kept her gaze on the butterfly. Her mind whirred for a proper response. At last she rolled her eyes up to the gardener. "I am utterly undeserving of your kind words. Thank you."

The gardener looked at the sun and cleared his throat. "The table should be set soon. Let's get you back inside. I'm sure everyone is waiting."

Love of the Sea

The yellow butterfly landed on Asrai's skirts. She smiled and coaxed the insect onto her finger. It was pleased with its perch for a moment, then fluttered away deeper into the garden.

Chapter Twenty-Two

The people of Paradine were buzzing with anticipation. Their joy shifted to anxiety as the day for the wedding drew ever closer. Their crown prince had rejected so many ladies before; now there were rumours that he may reject this lady and call off the nuptials. Such ominous whispers were dispelled when a small retinue stopped in the village pub. Their banners were white and gold, drawing the attention of the villagers and farmers, soon packing the pub with noisy banter.

One such farmer wandered into the dark, cozy building and sat down at one of the less crowded tables. At a table on the far side of the pub sat a small group of soldiers and a holy man in splendid gold silk robes.

The farmer pointed in their direction. "Who is that who would have so many men at his disposal?"

A villager at the table gestured with his flagon. "T'is the Archdruid of Umber. He must be presidein' over his majesty's weddin'."

The farmer nodded. A wench brought him a flagon of ale, which he pulled closer. The archdruid looked their way and made the gesture of peace, his fingers pressed against his lips. The men returned it before going back to their drinks.

The archdruid turned back to the soldiers. "I think it is time we resumed our journey. What say you, men?"

The soldiers raised their empty flagons in response. The archdruid rose, the soldiers with him, and exited out into the bright sunshine.

****

Archdruid Cian let his eyes wander toward the castle. He had been told Paradine was home to the warlord King Dominic. Upon seeing the limestone castle gleaming next to the ocean, he wondered why the king had followed the temptation of conquest.

"We are nearly there, your holiness," the guardsman to his left announced. "His majesty will give you a formal reception and your horse will be cared for."

The archdruid nodded, patting his mare on the neck. She was an old grey horse, her mane lacking the sheen it had possessed in earlier years, but she was the most reliable steed in the temple's stables. He had purchased her himself from Eastern traders; they assured him that her training was sound and that even bats at night did not spook her. Archdruid Cian did not know if this claim was true, but Phillipina had never thrown him from the saddle. He watched as the brown gelding a few yards in front danced around a rogue rock. The archdruid reined Phillipina to the side.

"A fine company," the archdruid mused, watching the turrets grow larger and more detailed. Boats bobbed in the wharf as they crested the hill.

"His majesty sent some of his finest to collect you, your holiness. Wouldn't want the prince's wedding cursed with a missing holy man," one of the guards chatted.

He shifted. "Has the prince been troubled in the past with ill fortune?"

The soldier sighed. His horse was busy nibbling at the high grass, so he pulled on the reins to bring the horse's head up again. "Aye, your holiness. The prince has refused the hands of ladies from far and wide. The king was sure he would never marry." He swallowed. "Until now."

Archdruid Cian nodded. He had dealt with stubborn princes before. No doubt the beauty of the landscape had jaded the prince's opinion of what was acceptable. The castle grew before them, the walls bristling with guards heralding welcome. He pressed his fingers to his lips, which the guards returned. Stable boys rushed to meet them.

Archdruid Cian placed his hand on the shoulder of a stable boy with a freckled face. "Take good care of Phillipina. She is getting on in her years. Be gentle."

The boy nodded, bowing his head low to both the archdruid and the horse. With a soft click he led the mount into the stable. The archdruid allowed the flow of humanity to lead him into the castle, where King Dominic greeted him with open arms. Banners of white and gold were hung in the Great Hall, the table laden with food and drink. Candles with gold runes burned in salute. Archdruid Cian rested his hand on King Dominic's shoulder.

"Thank you for the welcome, majesty." He released his hand and walked toward the table. "Thank you for remembering the roasted plums, my favourite." He popped one into his mouth and nodded with pleasure.

"Forgive us for this simple and lonely reception. All are preoccupied with the wedding plans, even my son." King Dominic offered Archdruid Cian a seat.

"It is to be expected. The same with the ladies?" the archdruid asked as he brought more foodstuffs to his plate.

King Dominic seated himself across from the archdruid. "Yes, the princesses have been swept up in the details of flowers and finery. Unfortunately, my nephew is in need of the peace of your counseling. I fear he will cause a scene from the stress."

The archdruid sipped the wine. "He is a young boy. His rash heart shall soon be tamed by the fine golden bridle of marriage. We must leave the youth to their fussing and flitting about. Your presence is welcome enough."

The king smiled and shook his head. "I thank thee."

****

Peter studied a map of King Dominic's territories when a knock at the door jarred his thoughts. He grimaced and turned toward the door. "Enter."

A foot soldier walked into the room, his feet unshod. His uniform reeked of sweat. Peter wrinkled his nose, but stretched out his hand in welcome. "I trust you found my answer?" Peter gestured toward a chair, but the soldier held up his hand in polite refusal.

"Thank you, sire, but my horse needs tending. Here is the letter. I am sure you will find the information you seek in its contents." The soldier saluted Peter, and then rushed back out the door.

Peter stared at the dusty folded parchment. He opened it —there was no wax seal —and took in the neat scrawl.

My Lord Peter of Paradine,

My men have scoured the surrounding coastal territories down to the quaint villages. Not a soul have heard of this enchantress, Lady Asrai, you speak of. Neither has any man been able to point to a kingdom by the name of Sulu. Some of the maidens in Ostollo have spiced the minds of my men with appalling rumours of the Lady Asrai, but I am certain these are simply the jealous defamations of those that his majesty, Prince Cormack, had rejected.

The seafaring men have spoken of similar sorceresses. Sea hags perhaps. This also may just be more fanciful yarn, but I caution my lord to watch this lady. Such a woman may be after more other-worldly things, and not the titles which come with the hand of his majesty. I humbly ask that you, sire, look upon this letter with the effort of myself and my men, rather than the fruitless answer.

May your highness live forever. This letter written by my own hand,

Lord Gar of San Bai

Peter crumpled the paper. He made to tear the letter, but then smoothed it again. No, he must not destroy this evidence against Cormack's sorceress whore. If his uncle were to believe him, Peter would need proof.

****

The garrisoned foot soldiers were given the task of erecting the wooden platform where the spoken vows would take place. Nephara leaned in the window, watching the pavilion take shape. Rainclouds loomed overhead, egging the workers on to finish their task. The Archdruid Cian was out on the lawn, also watching the bustling activity. When heavy rain forced the workers to drop their tools and rush inside for shelter, she saw the archdruid make a strange gesture with his hands before heading back inside. She wrinkled her nose, then looked up at the structure again. The left side of the platform had part of the banner stand built, but the right was unfinished. It resembled the gallows. Nephara raised her eyebrows, and pulled away from the window. She decided instead to see how the preparations for the banquet were getting on.

The kitchens were a bustle of crashing pots and pans. Several boars would be roasted in honour of the king and his blessing of the union; Asrai saw to it that several kinds of fish would be served at the banquet as well. Nephara did not care for Paradine's simple food, nor Asrai's strange obsession with fruits of the sea, which meant there needed to be proper foods of elegance, like toucan and sponge cake. Her hovering presence began to annoy the cooks and scullery maids. Pamela brought Nephara to her side.

"Dear, I know these days are consuming you. Please, let the kitchen alone and focus on other tasks for now."

Princess Nephara bristled at the head cooks' familiarity. Even so, she allowed Pamela to steer her into the sewing room. "Embroidery usually soothes the nerves of ladies such as yourself." Pamela pressed Nephara into the room and greeted the maids. "Good morning."

"Good morning," they murmured, glancing up from their sewing.

"Lady Nephara is feeling restless and would like to join you." Pamela waited, ensuring that Nephara would take a seat and not run to harangue another group of servants. The princess seated herself close to an elderly maid whose shaking hands stitched a beautiful scene of a deer in the forest on a length of silk.

"We are pleased to have you, m'lady," the women murmured again. They bowed their heads, pausing their needles only for a moment.

The elderly maid next to Nephara handed over a length of material and a needle, already threaded. Nephara had never sewn while living in Caraway. It was a task for servants and merchants. She was far too busy with her studies in court life, music, dance, and combat. At first, Nephara pricked her finger. She cursed the tiny silver needle.

The elderly maid took Nephara's hand, ignoring how the princess stiffened at the contact. "My dear, do not fight the needle. Each stitch is a tiny thought. Concentrate. Hurrying will slow your hands and make them clumsy."

Nephara allowed her sloppy stitches to be picked out. A fresh thread was knotted onto her needle. She soon discovered the soothing rhythm. The women chatted, their embroidery growing at a steady pace, revealing lace, simple hems, and scenes created by heavy stitching. A bride was not allowed to sew her own wedding dress, but Nephara was able to aid in creating the canopy that would cover the platform.

****

The gardeners swarmed the gardens, preparing the best blossoms for the celebration. Nephara had insisted on large red and yellow astrantia and dahlias. Asrai had not yet chosen her flowers. She rode Nonna toward the gardens. The head gardener waited for her near the late queen's bench.

"Ah! Good afternoon, princess." He stood and bowed his head. "A fine day to gaze upon beautiful things."

He helped Asrai slip down from Nonna. The gardener took Nonna's bridle to lead, while Asrai leaned against the old mare for support. Her legs were still weak and her steps faltered. Her ankles wobbled from the effort. Their progress was slow, but neither Nonna nor the gardener seemed to mind. "Tell me, princess. What are your favourite colours?"

Though Asrai was quite proud of her crimson scales, Nephara had already made it clear that she would be wearing the bold colour. Her next choice brought a smile to her lips. "Blue, like the sea."

The gardener grinned. "It does not surprise me that his majesty would be taken with a lass who loves the sea as much as he."

They wound through the garden path. The air seemed to shimmer with the buzzing of insects. A golden honey bee landed on Asrai's skirts, resting on the cool fabric. She let it be, unperturbed. The gardener noticed, and said nothing.

Asrai pointed to a patch of flowers that reminded her of the feathery plume corals that she adored and had often decorated her sleeping area with. "What is this flower?"

"That is astilbe, or false goat's beard." He plucked a sprig and handed it to Asrai. "In the language of flowers, it means 'I will be waiting for you,' or 'I shall remember you always.' They say that those of the White Veil use astilbe to help restore the memories and minds of mad people."

The sprig was made up of feathery branches of tiny white blossoms. She inhaled the delicate smell. She had nothing to compare it to from her life underwater. "Would you like this flower for your bouquet, princess?" The gardener broke Asrai from her reverie.

She nodded. "Yes, I would enjoy them." Asrai tilted her head. "Dear gardener, who are these 'White Veil' everyone speaks of?"

"All of Paradine and many of our allies believe in the Truth of Poseidon and the deities. But the White Veil is a collective that works on a higher plane, and some are able to commune with the deities themselves."

Asrai raised her eyebrows. She wondered how much of this belief was based in truth. They walked onward. When they passed one of the junior gardeners, the head gardener gave instructions on collecting astilbe for the ceremony. Asrai continued to sniff the sprig in her hand, pleased that the task had been far less difficult than she had anticipated.

"Your highness, might I suggest blue asters?" He stopped Nonna near a patch of blue flowers. Asrai peered down at the little round flowers. Their petals were pointed, like shards. Their soft yellow centers were like glimmers of gold sunlight winking in the sea.

"They are the flower of love and patience, princess," the gardener explained, picking one and handing it to her. "Those of the White Veil burn the petals to ward off evil serpents, protecting us from such poisonous creatures."

She touched the soft petals. The scent was a whisper, and Asrai drank it in. "These will do. Both of them."

When they reached the center of the garden, Asrai's feet were bleeding. She refused to wear shoes, even soft slippers, as Asrai found it easier to balance with her feet connecting directly to the ground. The gardener gasped when he saw the blood upon the cobblestone path.

"My lady!" He scooped her up and sat her upon the lip of the fountain. "Your feet!"

Asrai fought her body. Her chest and back trembled as she held back the heaving gulps her lungs screamed for. Her hands were sweating as she set her face to be that of a placid princess out for an afternoon stroll. "It is all right. I am still becoming accustomed to walking."

The gardener shook his head and pulled a handkerchief from his trouser pocket. "Please, let me help you." Asrai allowed him to dab his handkerchief in the fountain, then wipe the blood from her feet with the cool, wet fabric. Relief washed over her.

"I see you, princess," the gardener whispered as he cleaned her blistering feet. "I truly see you."

Her heart jolted at his words. She swallowed the surge of panic. "See what, dear gardener?"

He washed the handkerchief in the fountain, and then wrung it out. Asrai's blood stained the simple white fabric. "I have seen people such as you. The people of the Unseelie, and the people of the Vale. As a gardener, you see these things. But you are also different, so unfamiliar with earth and fauna."

Asrai's eyes were wide in alarm as he spoke. No one else was there to hear. She stared at him, all arguments fleeing her mind. The gardener locked eyes with her. "Fear not, princess. I am glad for it. T'is a blessing. And I know these blessings have their rules. I shall say not a word."

Chapter Twenty-Three

Asrai could feel eyes on her. The gardener seemed unperturbed. The wind ruffled her curls, bringing with it the scent of danger. Asrai flinched as she looked up, locking eyes with Peter. The gardener noticed her discomfiture, and turned his head. He leapt to his feet. "Your highness! How may I assist you?"

Peter waved his hand. "I must speak with the *Lady* Asrai. You are dismissed."

The gardener's face fell when he heard the acid on Peter's tongue. He fidgeted with his soiled handkerchief, then took Asrai's hand. "I have some repotting to do, princess. Please call upon me for anything you might need."

He turned to Peter, fixing a stern look upon the young prince, then excused himself to a nearby flowerbed behind a row of box hedges. Peter turned his gaze to Asrai once the gardener was out of sight. He approached the fountain. She stiffened as a smile crept up his face. The magick spiked at her alarm. Her eyes brightened as she cocooned herself in a layer of magick.

"Well, you are quite alone today. A pity," Peter purred as he leaned against the fountain. The magick set a barrier between them. His brow furrowed as he tried to move closer. He fidgeted his shoulders and drew back.

Asrai straightened, further pushing the magick outward, making him edge away from her. "I am not alone. The kind gardener is attending me today."

Peter laughed. The coldness cut through Asrai. She stifled a shiver. "Not a proper escort for a *princess*, now is he?" Peter's eyes flicked down her body, then back up her face. "Though you're not a proper lady either."

"My ways may not be as *gaudy* as the Princess of Caraway, but my sailor prince finds me to be a most suitable bride." Asrai hardened the magick, edging him further still. Her eyes were bright blue, her chest quaking as she held the magick despite the pain in her feet.

"How dare you slander my bride!" Peter growled. He leaned over Asrai, though the magick kept him at bay. "You have enchanted my cousin and bamboozled my foolish uncle! But I see through your charade!"

Panic flooded Asrai as Peter reached for his belt. She screamed, sending a pulse of magick at Peter, knocking him off his feet. The head gardener came running, putting himself between Asrai and the now scrambling Peter. "I knew it!" he bellowed. "You *are* a sorceress!"

The gardener clicked his tongue, and Nonna trotted up to them. "Come my dear, I think it's time for you to head back inside."

"No!" Peter pulled his dagger from his belt. "You will not aid this foul *creature*! I forbid it!"

The gardener scrambled to help Asrai mount Nonna. "Your highness! You are not well, please, the princess means you no harm!"

"No harm!" Peter threw his head back and laughed, the dagger flashing little flecks of light as it twisted in his hand. "No, no harm directly, but she will bring this kingdom ruin! She seeks to make a puppet of my cousin and rule us all!"

The gardener gave Asrai a final push, getting her up onto the horse. He turned to face Peter. "Please, your highness, you are not in your right mind. The princess is the dear love of the crown prince! She is not a threat to—!"

The head gardener's screams startled Nonna, sending her galloping toward the castle. Asrai whipped her head back and saw the gardener fall, bright red blossoming from his shoulder. She freed one of her hands from the horse's mane, whipping out her comb.

Undo the harm done unto him I trust. Harm that has been done, undo unto him that is true!

The spell was cast, but Nonna was too fast for her to see if the gardener lived. Peter stared after her, rooted to the spot. A deep sadness overwhelmed Asrai. She whispered a prayer to Poseidon as Nonna brought her to the gates, hoping her frazzled words to the guards were not too late.

****

A feast was being prepared for the evening of revelry in the Great Hall. The sun was low, pouring gold and orange onto the horizon. Cormack steered *Anita* to the docks. The sailors cheered and greeted him as he moored his boat. His grim stare dissolved their joy. The sailors whispered and grumbled with worry. Their once cheerful prince had become brooding and silent. They shaped their fingers into wards, fearing that he would leave the beautiful lady standing at the altar.

His feet knew the way up the worn path, back toward the castle. What had started as a jubilant day playing on the sea became an endless expanse of water that left him staring and thinking. His thoughts soured to morose anxiety for his kingdom and his people. His hands had trembled as he steered *Anita* aimlessly round the harbour.

The sea calls to me, day and night. My heart is engulfed with warmth and love for the bride of my wildest dreams. And yet, is it all just a selfish rouse?

The castle was bathed in golden sunset, making it seem more brilliant than any treasure. Cormack stood in the kitchen garden, staring up at the West turrets. He ran his hand through his hair and slumped his shoulders.

And what would I do? Become a warlord king like Father? Have Peter breathing down my neck, questioning every decree? That is no life.

Cormack wandered through the kitchen toward the hall. Pamela's face fell when she saw his sordid scowl. She went back to preparing the boar, knowing full well to let alone.

Servants rushed up and down the halls. The castle was beginning to look like some sort of faerie court with banners and flowers draped everywhere. Cormack found a maid worrying over a large gold vase of yellow dahlias.

"Have you seen the Lady Asrai?" Cormack flinched when he startled the maid.

She bobbed a curtsy while still holding the polishing rag. "No, majesty. I have not."

Cormack sighed and found his way to the stairs. He bumped into another maid carrying a pitcher of water. He held up his hand. "Pardon, but do you know where the Lady Asrai has gone?"

The maid bobbed a curtsy while still walking. "No, your highness! My apologies!" she called over her shoulder.

He reached Asrai's apartments and knocked on the door. There was no click, but the latch was unlocked. He pushed the door open and peered inside. "Asrai? Are you in here?"

The candles had been lit, the first tears of wax dripping down. Cormack started when he heard the sloshing water. He charged the bathroom door. "Lady Asrai!"

She jumped. Asrai was seated on the washing stool next to the empty tub. In her hand was a stained linen, a bucket of soiled water at her side. Cormack felt his body go numb when he saw that Asrai's feet, and the floor, were tinged pink with blood.

"What happened?" Cormack kneeled beside her. He took one of her feet into his hands. She winced, but allowed him to examine the appendage. The skin on the bottom curled away in ribbons, revealing soft pink flesh. He looked up again, his eyes wide with horror.

"I-I have been...practicing...in the garden...." Her voice shook as her body trembled.

"Practicing? For what?"

She took a deep breath to still her voice. "For the ceremony." She took another breath. "Walking for the ceremony." Asrai clenched her fist, pushing back the tide of pain. "Walking for you."

Cormack lowered her foot. He strode to the cabinet and pulled out several small linens, then knelt at her side and began washing her feet. Asrai stared at him. His ministrations were gentle and soothing. Her face relaxed as he tended to her feet, her breathing became more even and slowed.

"My lady, my dear Asrai," he whispered as he pressed linens against her feet to clot the blood, "never hurt yourself for me. Your pain is my pain."

She pulled her comb from her hair as Cormack doctored her feet. Her eyebrows knitted together, her face pained. "Cormack, I worry for your cousin."

He looked up at her, his hands frozen. "Has something happened?"

Asrai looked away. "Peter tried to attack me in the garden." Her chest shuddered. "He wounded the gardener for protecting me."

Cormack sat back on his haunches, staring at the floor, the linen limp in his hand. His mind buzzed as he filled in the unsaid words. He looked at Asrai. "Peter drew a weapon on you?"

"Yes. He intended to kill me. He is consumed with madness. I fear there is little left of your true cousin amidst all that rage."

He dropped the linen and took her hands. "But you were not harmed?"

"I used magick to keep him from touching me, and the head gardener helped me escape on Nonna—" Her words died in her throat. "*My poor gardener*," she whispered.

Cormack squeezed her hand. "He will be given the highest of honours for keeping you safe at the risk of his own life." His voice dropped. "He *is* alive?"

Asrai nodded. "A maid sent word that the guards found him in time. He is attended by the doctor." She squeezed her comb. "I would heal him myself, but then that would make your cousin correct in his accusations."

"Not to worry. Our doctor has worked many wonders." Cormack felt the shock drain from his body. "I am glad to hear that he lives."

"Peter has been locked away again. Your father has insisted he attend the feast this evening, under guard." Asrai took a deep breath. "My sailor, it seems the only solution to all our problems is for us to proceed. Without your soul, Peter will destroy himself and all you hold dear."

Cormack flinched. *To lose my soul to live in the sea, but also to save my kingdom.* He nodded, his gaze locked on Asrai. "My kingdom must be kept safe from his madness. Even if I were to stay on land, Peter would still be a threat to my people. You are sure my soul will change him?"

Asrai straightened, her gaze fierce. "It has never been done. I cannot promise you what is unknown, but I can promise you I will use every drop in my wellspring to make it so."

"Then, we will be together in the sea," Cormack whispered. His voice choked.

She took his hands in hers, and squeezed them. "My sailor, the trials I have faced here have shown me that I cannot do this alone. I need you. Sulu needs you. Peter is a far cry from the tyrant that usurped my throne. He found my weakness with ease, and threatened my life. I will need you if I am to succeed against the usurper and take back Sulu."

Cormack's eyes widened. Asrai was such a proud creature. To hear her speak of weakness cut him deep. "If my sacrifice will not only save my kingdom, but also yours, then I will be there at your side, as a mer."

Asrai's face brightened, her hands flew up to her chest. "My dear sailor, I love you!" Then her eyes darted away, coy and warm. "Together, we shall realize your true destiny as Fredsmegler and bring peace to our kingdoms."

He looked at her and smiled. "Destiny or not, I love you, Asrai. I shall love you always."

****

The Great Hall echoed enormously as Asrai rode the gold palanquin to the table, Cormack walking at her side. King Dominic stood and saluted them as they took their seats. "Three days from now we shall join Paradine with Caraway and Sulu! Tonight, we begin the celebration!"

Everyone clapped and cheered. Asrai's eyes flashed as she glanced around the table. Peter and Nephara whispered to one another, their faces pinched. Two guards stood at attention behind their seats. The hooded ladies bristled at their presence. Five more guards leaned against the back wall, their eyes scanning the table. Nephara turned and met Asrai's gaze, and Asrai felt a chill run through her. She turned to look at the king instead.

"The Archdruid Cian has come all the way from Umber to lead us in the joining of hearts and hands!"

The archdruid stood, and more clapping followed. He bowed his head and held two fingers up. "Poseidon, we beseech you this evening to show your favour. May the waters be calm, and the wind sweet. Bless these two unions and let us join together as one people."

He held a spool of gold ribbon and a pair of gold scissors, decorated to look like an egret. He held them high, then walked to Peter and Nephara. As the archdruid approached, their faces softened into smiles, and they held out their hands. He tied the gold ribbon to Peter's left pinky finger. He pulled at the spool until a good three feet of ribbon was slack, and cut with the scissors. He tied the loose end to Nephara's right pinky finger. He held up his hands again.

"Your hands are bound, and therefore your hearts are bound. Wherever one goes, the other follows. So it shall always be from this day forth."

Peter and Nephara bowed their heads, their foreheads nearly touching, their joy at odds with the stiff guards that stood behind them. The archdruid rounded the table and repeated the ceremony with Asrai and Cormack. This time, he placed his tools on the table, and his hands upon each of their heads.

"Pray, Poseidon! Look upon our future king and queen! Bring them the deep wisdom of the mysterious sea, and the swift reasoning of the ever-changing sky!"

The archdruid picked up the scissors and thread, and sat down again. He put the tools away, then lifted his cup in salute. Everyone raised their cups, and waited.

"Tonight, we feast in your honour! Brave Poseidon! Wise Poseidon! Immortal Poseidon!" The archdruid held his arms aloft as the two serving girls stepped forward. The archdruid nodded, and they tipped the gold pitcher so that sparkling mead spilled onto the floor.

"We offer to you the ambrosia of our mortal world! We offer you our thanks and prayers. Pray, Poseidon, hear us!" When the pitcher was empty, the serving girls curtsied and trotted off toward the kitchens. The puddle of mead was left shimmering on the floor.

"Let us eat." The archdruid broke the spell, and chatter rose once more.

Asrai stared at the ribbon, turning her hand this way and that, examining the tiny bow. "This is most inconvenient," she muttered.

Cormack stifled a laugh. "Do not worry, my lady. It is only for tonight. The archdruid will cut the ribbon once supper is over."

Asrai nodded and set her hand back on the table. The ribbon held no magick, just as the ceremony had not yielded any true spells. She turned her gaze to the archdruid. For all his pomp, he seemed an ordinary human. Asrai turned her gaze back to Cormack, wondering how such a simple creature would forge the bond she required.

Chapter Twenty-Four

The first course was at odds with the fine golden platters, as the dishes were stone bowls. Burly serving men set the bowls before each of the guests. They were filled with a grain Cormack had never seen—bright yellow with flakes of red. It was mixed with chopped vegetables and cubes of meat.

One of the Caraway servants all in yellow stood. "A specialty of Caraway! This grain is rice, a hearty food that our people eat every day, whether as grain or bread, from the highest king to the lowest servant. We are all equals at the rice bowl."

Murmurs went around the table as portions were spooned onto plates. Cormack found he did not care for the dish. It tasted of perfume and too much spice. Asrai shared his lack of enthusiasm, but ate a few mouthfuls to be polite. Peter fed dainty spoonfuls to Nephara, their eyes lost in one another.

A course of Asrai's choosing followed. She had sent a message to the sailors with careful instructions on how to gather her favourite dish. Individual gold bowls were set before each guest. Mussels nestled a bed of emerald green seaweed. Hunks of coarse bread were handed out for sopping up the delicate broth.

At home in the sea, mers enjoyed eating the mussels straight from the shell, then slurping up mouthfuls of feathery seaweed. She settled for this modification with the mussels stewed in a fish bone broth and herbs from the garden. She cleared her throat and addressed the table.

"This is the food that reminds me of home." Asrai smiled at the king. "In Sulu, we give thanks for the bounty of the sea. My favourite has always been the richness of mussels mixed with the delicate seevoo seaweed."

The guests were wary of the bright green. Cormack brought the strange plant to his lips. It was salty, but not unpleasant. The mellow taste reminded him radish greens. Asrai ate her portion with care. Her face was bright with joy as she ate. When the bowls were cleared away, she took Cormack's hand and squeezed. He squeezed back.

Wooden boards were set upon the table. Thin slices of cured meats and blocks of yellow and white cheeses were arranged upon them. There were fruit preserves and boar's blood jelly as spreads. The rich, coarse bread was warm. Everyone's hands intermingled as hunks of bread were ripped and piled with meats and cheese.

"What a charming dish." Asrai murmured as she spread fruit preserves on the bread.

Cormack tilted his head. "How so, my lady?"

She took a bite and licked the corner of her mouth. "It reminds me of the friendly feasts I once attended as a child while my parents still lived. All enjoyed the feast together. There was not a grand table or furniture separating the guests."

He nodded, biting into a piece of cheese as he cast his gaze about the table. "It is a rather friendly dish, I suppose."

"Though I am still getting used to how familiar the people of Paradine seem to be." Asrai mused as she accepted a bite of cheese from Cormack. "The people of Sulu, from what I remember as a child, kept largely to themselves and their things day to day. It seems the people of Paradine are quite entwined with one another."

"The people of Paradine are a *friendly* sort of folk, aren't they?" Nephara tilted her head, addressing Asrai. "And yet, I can't help but think of how these feasts are so different from those of my home." The joy had been extinguished from her face, and she wore a cold smile instead. "I am sure you feel the same, Lady Asrai?"

Asrai nodded, unperturbed. "Yes. Sulu is a rather unique kingdom. I think of it often."

"For example, my people lounge upon cushions whilst feasting, rather than these high chairs." She gestured to her ladies that were indeed lounging on cushions behind her.

Cormack kept his gaze on his plate, spreading strawberry preserves on a hunk of bread. His actions were slow and deliberate to prevent his hands from shaking. He could feel Peter's gaze on him. He lifted his gaze, trying to appear nonchalant. When he met Peter's stare, Peter grinned, though there was no mirth in his eyes. Cormack swallowed the dull panic.

"Yes, I find the furniture to be rather unfamiliar as well." Asrai placed a slice of prosciutto on her hunk of bread. "However, my position as princess calls for the importance of adaptability. So here we are, sitting in chairs and eating bread."

Cormack turned his gaze to Asrai as she took a delicate bite of her food. Her smile was genuine, and yet, the gleam in her eyes revealed the undertone of her words. Nephara blinked at Asrai, caught off guard. Her smile soon returned, the same glint revealing the lack of innocence in her own eyes. "How right you are, my lady. How right you are."

Cormack felt his stomach twist in knots. All along Asrai had anticipated these suspicions. She had been successful at completely throwing his father off her trail and turning him into a puddle of adoration.

The servants now bent to her will and questioned none of her oddities. Asrai's eyes flashed as she smiled at him.

Of course, she planned for all of this! That night when Peter discovered her true form, her life was in danger! Since then she has been busy organizing and calculating while you have been nothing more than a moonstruck child! She nearly lost her life and you just now caught on? Fool!

He looked at Asrai again. She was sipping from her goblet of water. His heart ached as a new realization struck him. *Do you truly love me? Or am I simply a calculated move as well?*

Asrai tilted her head. "You are staring. What troubles you, my sailor prince?"

Cormack straightened, flustered that he had been so transparent with his thoughts. He plucked a piece of cheese from one of the boards. "Nothing, my lady. I am simply enamoured with you."

She raised an eyebrow, but said nothing. Cormack reached over and took her hand in his. He could feel the warmth of her skin as he squeezed. Asrai smiled and squeezed back.

"My love for you frightens me at times, my lady," Cormack whispered.

"Do not fret, my sailor." She rolled her eyes up to meet his gaze. "Soon we shall be bonded and all shall be well."

Cormack nodded, handing more morsels of food to Asrai. Nephara had withdrawn her sparring of words, and settled into whispering with Peter. More courses came and went, but Cormack hardly tasted them. He kept his gaze on Asrai, noting her delicate movements and her measured words. The ribbon tugged at his pinky, reminding him of their bond; their promise. His heart was heavy with dread as the words ran another lap around his mind.

Soon I shall be in the sea. Soon I shall leave here and never return.

The guests began to leave the table and mill about the hall, dancing or in private conversation. Asrai leaned closer to Cormack and put her hand over his. Her ring sparkled in the candlelight. Her breath tickled his ear. "Fear not, my dear sailor prince, for my love for you is as deep as the abyss. I suffer in this form because of my faith in you as my mate, and as the Peacemaker."

His thoughts softened, recalling her determination to walk for the ceremony. She squeezed his hand, and he squeezed back. *Yes, there is love there. I trust you, my Asrai.*

****

King Dominic was red in the face, merry with drink as the preparations for the wedding went bustling around him. He was so delighted that he grabbed a passing maid, her hands full of flowers for the hall arrangement, and kissed her full on the lips. "My son is to be wed! Go and be glad!" King Dominic shouted as he released her, her face now as red as his.

She bobbed a quick curtsy. "Yes, m'lord." She ran off, giggling.

Peter was following a pace behind the king, scowling at the flowers and banners tied to the walls. "Don't you think this is all a bit much, Uncle?"

King Dominic swiveled. "Mind your place. T'is a happy day!"

Peter cringed, swallowing hard. "Uncle, how are you so sure that this maiden is suitable for Cormack? He is to be king after all."

King Dominic rolled his bloodshot eyes and took a messy swig from his wine flagon. "Nonsense! I led all the best lasses through these very doors," he pointed a chubby finger at the doorway, the heavy rings sparkling in the sunlight, "and he didn't pick a single one! If Cormack picked her, she must be the most suitable lass in all the land!"

Peter clenched his teeth and crossed his arms. "I suppose so, Uncle." Peter fingered the letter in his pocket.

Cormack joined them, dressed in his formal attire. The sun glinted off the gold thread in his doublet. King Dominic hugged Cormack, flagon still in hand. "My boy! You are finally getting a lass! My boy! My boy!"

Cormack laughed, straightening his clothes. "Yes, Father. The day you have been so patiently waiting for is finally here."

King Dominic looked over Cormack's shoulder. "Where is she? I want to kiss the bride," he winked, "for luck!"

Peter rolled his eyes. "The brides are in confinement. It's bad luck to see them before the ceremony."

King Dominic nodded. "That is so! Well, I shall have to wait then, won't I? So many children! So many children!" The king ambled away, his gait unsteady, leaving Cormack and Peter alone.

Cormack turned to follow when Peter grabbed his shoulder. "And where are you off to, Cousin?" Peter's voice was low.

Cormack faced him. He could see the guards standing at attention a few paces down the hall. "I don't see how that is your concern."

Peter lowered his hand back to his side, his teeth clenched. "I fear you are playing a dangerous game. Pray Poseidon returns your senses before it is too late."

"As are you, Cousin." Cormack lifted his chin. "Pray Poseidon washes away this affliction of madness and brings peace to Paradine."

The guards shifted. Peter bristled at the sound. "If you do not rid yourself of that *sorceress*, I shall do it for you. The wedding is nearly upon us. Make your choice." Peter turned heel, the guards following a few paces after him.

****

Maids set chairs for the ceremony. High maypoles were erected around the altar, flowers braided into the ribbons hanging down from them. Cormack resisted the urge to rush up to Asrai's room. Pamela had assured him the night before that she would attend to Asrai herself and that there was nothing to fear. Cormack wrung his hands, wondering if Asrai could make it down the aisle unaided.

He found his way into the gardens. They were buzzing with gardeners manicuring the flower beds and field maids picking apples and berries for the tartes and pies. Cormack ambled down the cobblestone paths until he came upon the fountain of Poseidon. He lowered himself to the ground and leaned against the basin wall. He tilted his head back with his eyes closed.

Archdruid Cian saw Cormack in the garden. He bowed, which Cormack returned with a bob of his head. The archdruid spread his hands. "My son, soon you shall be wed and begin life with your new wife. Is there anything you would like to absolve so you may embark on your journey with a clean heart?"

Cormack fidgeted his hands. The guilt of leaving his people weighed on him. "What if I cannot fulfill my father's expectations?"

The archdruid smiled. "My son, it is reasonable to have these doubts. So long as your heart stays true to the path you were given, you can be assured that you will not fail your father."

Cormack swallowed. "Thank you." He bowed his head and the archdruid blessed him by waving his two fingers in a circle in the air. Cormack bobbed his head again. The archdruid wound his way back to the castle to consult the others.

****

Archdruid Cian walked up the stairs to the tower where Asrai was confined. He had found it odd that the bride had refused bridesmaids and only let the head cook attend to her. He was worried that she was timid and might run at the altar. When the archdruid came to the door he heard rustling noises and concerned female voices. He tapped his fingers on the wooden door. "Good morrow, Lady Asrai. I have come to speak with you."

There was a pause, and then the voices and noises reached a frenzy. He waited for a few moments before a disheveled Pamela flung the door open and bowed. "Please forgive me, your grace, the lady was not yet decent."

The archdruid nodded and strode past her. Asrai was sitting on the bed in a simple white gown, her hands folded. Her eyes seemed to glimmer as she upturned her pretty face at him. "Hello, your grace. Cormack told me that you would be coming. Thank you for presiding over our wedding."

Archdruid Cian nodded and Pamela hovered nearby, ready to start fussing over a wrinkle or a lock of hair. He smiled at the cook and then turned his attention to Asrai. "Thank you, my child. I am here to absolve you of past incursions that plague you. It is important to start your marriage with a clean heart."

Asrai looked from Pamela to the archdruid and then at her hands in her lap. He stepped a little closer and smiled. "Please, do not be nervous. There is much to worry over, but the state of your soul should not be one of them. I do not judge."

Asrai glanced at Pamela again, who had a worried look on her face. Asrai turned back to the archdruid and sighed. "I want nothing more than to be bonded with him, to fill his world and his heart with all he desires."

She dropped her chin and Pamela put a hand on her shoulder. Archdruid Cian stared at Asrai, judging to see if this were the work of theatrics, nervousness, or the guilt of something more sinister. "My dear, is there nothing that weighs on your heart? Nothing you wish to be scrubbed clean from your soul?"

Asrai shook her head. "No. You are most kind. We of Sulu have great respect for the selfless service of divine persons. Your blessing is all I need."

"Perhaps you wanted to confide in me before the ceremony? You may also see me after the wedding feast if the excitement of the wedding is overpowering you right now."

Asrai straightened. Her eyes flashed. "Poseidon knows all that is in my heart. My purpose is clear. I thank thee."

The archdruid nodded and blessed her. "Then I will take my leave." He looked back at Asrai, who was still staring at him, before closing the door and making his way back down the hall.

****

Once the archdruid exited Asrai's room, she stood and placed her hands on the stone wall next to the window. Her limbs shook as she looked at the platform and the wedding banners. Pamela took Asrai's hand and patted it. "Don't worry, dear, it's just the jitters. Once you put on your dress you will feel much better."

Asrai nodded, but could not tear herself away from the window. Another knock sounded, and Pamela let in the head seamstress. Behind her streamed a trail of fabric and lesser seamstresses. Asrai turned and caught herself before she was snared in their groping hands.

"I thought my gown was finished." Asrai swiveled her head, trying to keep up with the women adding ribbons and lace to the dress that had been shoved over her head.

The seamstress removed a few needles from her mouth and pinned a row of lace around the midsection of the skirt. "It was, m'lady. However, his majesty requested that the dress be made even more grand. We are making a few last-minute adjustments. I'm sure my lady doesn't mind."

Asrai very much wanted to say that she *did* mind, but there was little she could do about it. Her gaze fell back onto the window as threads were pushed back and forth around her knees and waist like bows over a gigantic fiddle. She caught a glimpse of Cormack standing on the platform, surveying a couple of servants arranging flowers. Her heart leapt into her throat.

Pamela grabbed Asrai's arm. "Careful, ladies, she's going to swoon!"

Asrai folded into Pamela's arms, her ribs straining against the corset bones as she tried to breathe. The seamstresses went on with their work, not missing a stitch, as Pamela righted Asrai. "I'll fetch you a cool rag." She hurried to the bathroom and returned with a soaked square of linen.

The water droplets dripped down Asrai's face and she sighed. All at once the room had become too small and her dress too hot. Her heart jumped again and Pamela laughed. "A blushing bride." Pamela joked and the seamstresses gave a small laugh. "You are a lucky girl, my lady. A lucky girl to marry for love."

Asrai shook her head. "I am not used to such feelings. Everything is so overwhelming, Pamela."

She patted Asrai's hand. "Not to worry, dear. That's just how love is. Too big to hold onto sometimes."

Asrai smiled and touched Pamela's hand. "Thank you."

Before Asrai could say more she felt a sharp pain in her calf. She cried out, and Pamela pushed the offending seamstress off Asrai. "Out!" Pamela yelled. "Out!"

The seamstresses curtsied and left the room with hushed voices. Pamela closed the door after them. Asrai examined the leg. The wound was small, but bleeding. Asrai held the linen Pamela had used against the pinprick. Pamela lifted folds of the dress, inspecting the seamstresses' work.

"Well, it will have to do. Thankfully they didn't add too much and there are no loose ends." Pamela let the heavy fabric drop and stroked Asrai's cheek. "No tears, dear, a pinprick is nothing."

Asrai rubbed a piece of lace between her fingers. She was growing annoyed with King Dominic's desire for greatness in everything. It would not matter for long. Soon she and Cormack would be at home in the sea, far from human exploits.

Love of the Sea

"I shall miss you, Pamela," Asrai whispered.

Pamela smiled, but her cheeks were red. "I will miss you as well, Lady Asrai, you beautiful creature. Take good care of my boy for me."

A shock ran through Asrai. "Your boy?"

"Not by birth. His mother died just as the lad took his first breath of air. She made me promise to care for him in her stead. She was a noble lady, beautiful and the apple of his majesty's eye." A sad smile broke on Pamela's lips. "Queen Amaris was my dearest friend. My Ammi. I was a tribute prize sent to Paradine as a child. Paradine does not believe in slaves, much less slave children. So, I was given to Amaris as a playmate, as she too was sent here as a child to be the betrothed of his majesty."

Asrai tilted her head. "And how did you become a servant? Forgive me, I am still ignorant to your human ways, but—"

Pamela shook her head. "His majesty was distraught after his beloved died. He disbanded most of the court. Sent them away to their estates. I had nowhere to go. I was Cormack's wet nurse, and then began working in the kitchens. I'm an honest woman, though in my heart I think of him as my own."

Asrai nodded and hugged Pamela, who at first froze at the sudden affection, then encircled Asrai with her thick arms. Pamela was warm and smelled of fresh baked bread and marinade. "You have also been a maternal figure for *me* these past moons, Pamela. Kindness such as yours is strange and wonderful to me."

Pamela gave Asrai a final squeeze before releasing her. "Let's get you out of this monstrosity of a dress and into something more comfortable. You need your rest. Tomorrow is the big day!"

Chapter Twenty-Five

The archdruid crossed the expanse of the castle, heading toward the tower where Nephara was being kept. One of the yellow-clad men opened the door. Nephara lounged on her stomach, her body cradled by a red cushion. One of her yellow-clad servant boys was kneading her back, while another braided her hair. They ceased their ministrations, allowing Nephara to stand.

"Peace, my child. I come to absolve you, so that you may start your wedded life with a clean heart and a clear mind."

Nephara bowed her head. "Thank you, your holiness, however, I've nothing to confess."

His eyebrows shot up. He cleared his throat. "My dear, do not be afraid to confide in me. I am sworn to offer love and forgiveness."

"I walked the burning coals of Truth before coming to Paradine. My heart is pure, your holiness." Her eyes gleamed as a smile crossed her face. "Though the same cannot be said for Lady Asrai."

Archdruid Cian straightened. "My child, it does not do to be jealous on your own wedding day. Joy is more beautiful when it is shared with others."

Nephara waved her hand as if swatting a fly. "I am the jewel of Caraway. Envy is not something I possess. No, the Lady Asrai is harbouring a dangerous secret. One that my betrothed is determined to expose."

The archdruid paused, he had seen alliances crumble and kings fall due to the petty envy of whispered secrets and untruths. "What proof do you have of the Lady Asrai's mischief?"

Nephara lowered her voice. "My beloved Peter confronted the Lady Asrai one evening in her chambers. He saw the lady undressed, and she was not human. There have been incidents of her using her powers to thwart my beloved from exposing her for the monster she is."

The thought of confronting a lady in her personal chambers at night made the archdruid leery of Nephara's story. He also recalled the lady taking faltering steps around her chambers when he had spoken to her. Such an accusation of sorcery was dangerous, and the archdruid did not want to raise alarm. "If this is indeed true, then her purpose must be discovered. I have my ways of divining a creature's intent. Leave the Lady Asrai to me."

Archdruid Cian blessed Nephara. She glowed with her small victory. The archdruid frowned, but said nothing. There was still had plenty of time for things to go awry. He exited the chambers, and started his way to the lesser dining hall for refreshment.

****

Peter was alone in his apartments, furiously scribbling letters when a polite knock on the door startled him. Peter whirled around to see the archdruid Cian entering the room. He flinched, then scrambled to his feet, and bowed as the archdruid made the sign of infinity.

"Be still, my child" He approached Peter. "I have come to bring you peace."

Peter drew himself up, his eyes wary as the holy man stretched out his arm. "I am quite well, your grace. However, there are urgent matters I must attend to."

The archdruid nodded. "I am sure there are many preparations for the upcoming nuptials. I am here so you may unburden your heart before your wedding day. You must enter this new season of your life with a clean heart and a clear mind."

"My father has worried you, I am sure." Peter flashed him a smile. "May I assure you that *I* am in my right mind, but I fear my cousin, the crown prince, is perhaps losing *his*."

Cian stopped, flustered by Peter's words. "And what concerns you for his majesty? Surely he is currently overjoyed with his bride."

Peter shook his head, and held out the letter from Lord Gar. "I suspect that the lady is not at all what she appears to be. In my worrying, I sent an envoy to the far reaches of our vassals to reassure my thoughts. Unfortunately, it seems that no one has heard of the Lady Asrai, or the land of Sulu where she claims to hail from. It is a worry indeed."

The archdruid accepted the letter, his trained eyes skimming the paper, then handed it back. His eyes and brow wrinkled with concern. "This is a heavy accusation, my lord. I understand that you worry both for the prince and for your kingdom. However, how can you be certain that the lady has given such offense?"

Peter picked up one of the half-finished letters in his hand. "There is no such place as Sulu! There is no such lady as the Princess Asrai!"

"Yes, yes," the archdruid held up his hand for quiet, "I understand your fears. But did it ever occur to you that the lady could be one of the fey?"

He shook his head. "She is no fey. I *saw* her tail! Like a great serpent! She is a sorceress and has enchanted my cousin!"

Cian bowed his head, alarmed by the accusation. "If the Lady Asrai is indeed such a monster, then the matter shall be discovered. Rest assured, my child, I shall take the utmost care in this. Concern yourself only with your own bride, so you may forge a bond of love."

"My mind can only be cleared once my cousin unburdens his heart." Peter scowled.

"I have already spoken with his highness the prince. His heart seems no more troubled than the typical lad. Please be sure before acting against the fair lady. I have ways of investing such things, rest assured." Cian made the sign of infinity again, then turned to leave.

Peter darted his eyes to the floor. "I thank you, your grace."

Peter clutched the letter, reading it over again, then folded it away into his pocket. He bowed as the archdruid exited the room.

****

Asrai sat in her chemise as two handmaidens braided her fiery hair. Pamela had returned to the kitchens to ensure the preparations for tomorrow's feast were in order. Her heart called to Cormack. She cursed the humans' silly rules, keeping her separated from him. Her mind plagued her with suppositions of his resolve weakening. Asrai twirled her ring around and around her finger.

"Do not fret, my lady." One of the girls placed her hand atop Asrai's to stop the fidgeting. "His majesty adores you. I'm sure he is just as anxious as you are."

The other handmaiden looped a blue ribbon into Asrai's hair. "Yes, my lady. He chose you above all others. His heart is indeed yours."

Asrai held her hands over her chest. She sighed. The sun was sinking low on the horizon, signalling the approaching hour of the feast. Asrai found that her hunger had fled, her stomach full with worry. She flinched as she saw the glint of something, like a spider's thread. Asrai's eyes darted about the room, as she had been instructed not to move her head. The glint sparkled again, and this time a sensation of tiny pin pricks began crawling up her skin.

What is this? She brushed her arms, but there was nothing there. *A strange magick? Who dares?* Her blood ran cold as she remembered the holy man. Asrai had not taken him seriously. He had been hiding his magick, and now he was reaching out to her.

No! Asrai's eyes turned ice blue, nearly clear with magick. She pushed the crawling threads away. *I shall not let you sway me!*

She focused her thoughts and pushed back. Not wanting to raise alarm with a fellow creature of the tipped world, she pushed back with a crafted reflection of herself: a demure lady with no threat or hint of magick. She built the reflection strong.

Divert! Divert your path! The pin pricks raced over the reflection, sinking in and exploring the false vision. When they receded, she sighed, and allowed her magick to fade. Her eyes darkened again.

Love of the Sea

I was foolish to underestimate him. I had heard stories of such humans that could rival our magick, but I did not believe in them. I must be careful. We only have one more day, and then we shall be home. We cannot falter, not this close.

The handmaidens were unaware of Asrai's turmoil, their deft hands weaving and plucking hair into a high coronet with waves of crimson curls flowing over her shoulders. The room was quiet, save for the bustling servants echoing in the halls. Asrai looked down at her ring. It sparkled in the dying evening light.

You shall not take him from me. Enough has been taken from me. The tides are shifting, and I shall rise above with all that I hold dear behind me.

****

The Great Hall was even more splendid than the previous evening. Day and night the servants had worked to prepare decorations for the ceremony. Birds and butterflies had found their way into the castle. They flitted upon the flowers and rested on the banners. The musicians and minstrel were playing a quiet, but lively tune as people gathered for supper.

After his meeting with Archdruid Cian in the garden, Cormack had found himself drained. The anxiety of leaving his kingdom weighed upon him, but the thrill of being one with the sea made his heart race. He had lain in the garden for the better part of the day, going round and round inside his head.

"Cormack, my boy!" The king rose, clapping his hands. "Join us! Join us! The festivities are about to start!"

The table clapped and cheered as Cormack took his seat. The musicians struck up a merry tune, and the serving girls began pouring ale and wine. Cormack avoided Peter's gaze, and focused on the food before him. A trail of servants took platters out of the hall to the separate towers for the brides.

"Playing with your boat again, Cousin?" Peter smirked as he lifted his flagon of ale to his lips.

Cormack shook his head. "No. I simply lost track of time in the garden. Tomorrow is our future. We must be prepared for it."

Peter laughed, his eyes cold. "We shall see what the future holds, won't we?"

His words chilled Cormack. Before he could formulate a response, the archdruid stood. The musicians ceased, and conversation grew quiet. He lifted his hands. "We are gathered here this eve to prepare our hearts. Tomorrow we shall celebrate the union of our youth, securing the future of Paradine. We humble people of Umber rejoice that our allies will continue to prosper and grow. With these tidings, we grow the hope that once more our lands shall be free."

Archdruid Cian drew a gilded dagger from his robe. The scabbard was decorated with ancient white runes. He presented it to Peter, handle first. "Take this, my prince, and spill your blood. Seal your fealty to the kingdom of Paradine."

Peter took the dagger, unsheathing it. He dragged the blade across his palm, allowing a slow trickle of blood to ooze. He clenched his fist over his flagon of ale, allowing a few drops to mix into his drink. The archdruid wiped it clean with a linen and presented the dagger to Cormack. "Take this, my prince, and spill your blood. Seal your fealty to the kingdom of Paradine, and take your place as our leader."

Cormack mirrored Peter's actions. His hand stung as he forced the blood to drip. He handed the dagger back to the archdruid. He locked eyes with Peter, his mouth hard and grim. "Drink from thy cups and complete the seal. Your blood bond to your people shall never be broken."

Peter watched as Cormack lifted his flagon. Both men allowed the brew to pass their lips, swallowing ale and blood. Cormack set his flagon down, the liquid severely depleted. He smirked at Peter, as if challenging him.

You think you can catch me with the oath? Not so, Cousin. No matter where I go, or what form I take, I will always have love in my heart for this land. A blood oath cannot be broken, but Cormack knew that even if he resolved to sacrifice himself to the sea that he would always be loyal to Paradine. He would make them allies with Sulu, somehow.

Peter scowled as they sat. He fidgeted with something in his pocket, his eyes darting to the king. The archdruid waved his hands, making the sign of the infinity. "In peace, my sons, in peace you shall rule this land forever more!"

Everyone clapped and cheered. King Dominic in particular thumped his boots on the floor, overjoyed that his line was at last secure. Archdruid Cian gave the old king a warm smile.Servants lowered heavy platters onto the table, and the music struck up again. The minstrel sang a cheery song of a farmer's boy and a milkmaid falling in love. Some of the generals clapped and sang along, their faces bright. Bands of linen had been brought to Cormack and Peter for their hands. The dull throbbing of the cut prodded Cormack's mind. He tamped down his anxiety and focused on the rich food.

****

Asrai sat on the bed. The candles had been lit, and the moon shone bright above the sea. It was nearly fully waxed; only one more night. She shivered in the thin robe, her hair piled upon her head. The handmaidens had rubbed her feet with a cream mixed with soothing herbs; dandelion root, lavender, and juniper. They were clean and wrapped with bands of linen.

Love of the Sea

A knock startled Asrai. She sat up, her robe falling open. "Who is there?"

No answer came. Instead, the door opened and a procession of three women dressed all in white entered, their faces hidden behind white veils. "Do not be afraid, sister." The eldest woman held her hand to Asrai. "We are of the White Veil. We are here to bless you."

Asrai flinched. The magick flashed in her eyes and she held the deflection once more. Her startled heart fluttered. The woman smiled. "There is no need for alarm. Come, we must prepare you."

The women approached the bed and helped Asrai to her feet. It was an ancient tradition for brides to be visited by the White Veil the night before their wedding. The rite was a secret, never spoken of, not even between women who had already known its mysteries.

One of the younger women slid Asrai's robe off, revealing her naked body. Her pale skin was luminous in the candlelight. "We see you for who you are. Be not afraid."

Asrai shivered, though the room was warm. She held her deflection, appearing a perfect demure bride. The elder woman pulled a solid crystal wand from her robes. Light raced through it. She waved it in an anti-clockwise circle before Asrai's chest. The deflection shattered, spiking Asrai's anxiety.

"There, now we may begin." The elder woman held the crystal up, the light flickering inside it.

The third woman opened a satchel and pulled out a waterskin. This was poured over Asrai's body. Her heart leapt as she smelled the salt and the wild; it was seawater. "Cleanse this woman with your waters of wisdom. Open for her the doors of knowledge." The elder woman struck the air with the wand. "We call upon you, Poseidon!"

The second woman patted Asrai down with a linen towel. Once she was dry, the third began drawing runes on Asrai's body with a piece of charcoal. "We are but ash between this life and next. Our souls burn bright as flames in this mortal husk, the tinder for love and hatred. Burn into this woman's skin, and therefore her heart, the burden of hatred and the enlightened power of love! We call upon you, the ancient and capricious Will o' Wisps!"

Asrai's magick dissipated as the woman drew. Though the elder woman had easily broken the spell barrier, she seemed either unaware or unconcerned with what Asrai truly was. Though, she did not relax and watched each of their movements with care.

The third woman finished drawing and put away the charcoal. She pulled out a leather purse and handed it to the second woman. Upon opening it, Asrai saw that it was filled with white rose petals. These were sprinkled over Asrai's head. "The earth gives us life, and the earth takes

183

our life. We are bound by the cycle. The wheel turns and returns. So shall you come into season and take your place as woman, wife, and mother. We call upon you, Gaia!"

The purse returned to the satchel. A white lace fan carved from animal bone was last to be retrieved. The second woman flicked it open, revealing the carved runes on the spines. "Our secrets and our thoughts are carried upon the wind. Our words float on forever, heard for centuries by the Breeze of the North. We must remember to weigh our words, and cast only goodness to the winds. We call upon you, the Anemoi!" The second woman waved the fan up and down Asrai's body. The breeze chilled her, and made her skin break out in gooseflesh.

"Mother of the Moon, we now call upon you!" The elder woman held out the crystal, pointing it at Asrai's forehead. "Bless this woman as a woman in all she is and does! Bestow upon her the mysteries of the moon!" She waved the crystal in a clockwise circle in front of Asrai's face. Then she pressed the crystal to Asrai's forehead. It felt warm. An odd sensation took hold of her. The crystal waved before each of her breasts, her stomach, and her pelvis.

"Love is the strongest bond of all." The elder woman placed the tip of the crystal against Asrai's heart. "No earthly or magickal thing may break it. Cultivate deep love in your heart, and that of your beloved's, and you shall be forever at peace. So Selene, our Mother, has taught us."

A clockwise circle was drawn in the air before Asrai again, then the sign of infinity. The elder woman put away the wand and embraced Asrai. "You are ready, my sister. Our love is with you."

Each of the women embraced her and whispered the same. They exited the chamber, saying nothing further, leaving Asrai standing alone and naked. White flower petals lay upon drops of water. The runes covered her body. She was unsure if she was supposed to leave them or wash them off. Asrai gathered up her robe and stumbled back onto the bed. Another knock sounded.

"Pardon us, my lady." One of the handmaidens bobbed a curtsy.

They carried in a bucket of warm water and a stack of fresh linens. Asrai sat on the bed, naked, as they scrubbed the ash from her body. Asrai watched as the grey marks disappeared. She wondered at them. Her body felt invigourated, her wellspring deepened. She smiled.

Humans are such surprising creatures. Their capabilities have certainly exceeded my suppositions.

Once Asrai's skin was clear, they began dressing her in the simple white gown she had worn earlier in the day. When one of the handmaidens exited into the hall, Asrai took the hand of the remaining handmaiden. "My dear, please call the footmen. I'm sure the feast has already started—"

Love of the Sea

The handmaiden patted Asrai's hand. "Yes, the feast has started. But you shall partake of your own here. A ceremony for the princes is being held in the Great Hall."

Asrai wrinkled her nose, annoyed. Her soured mood was cut short when the second handmaiden returned with a trail of servants bearing covered platters. "Your supper, my lady!"

They helped Asrai take slow and wobbling steps toward the table. Once seated, they filled her goblet with cool water and chattered on about the delicacies that had been prepared, the very same that were being enjoyed in the Great Hall. Asrai felt a strange mood take hold. She twirled her ring as a gnawing loneliness spread through her body, both sad and thrilling.

We are so close, my sailor. Her breath caught with excitement. *Soon we shall be home.*

Chapter Twenty-Six

Sunlight gilded the trees, the castle, and the constructed pavilion. Dew sparkled like tiny gems scattered over the grass and flowers. An egret flew overhead, scanning the sprawling estate. The sea was calm and smooth, brightening as the sun rose. Asrai stood at her window, her legs trembling beneath her. The smell of the sea filled her as the salty spray wafted up from the shore down below. The gulls screamed, calling her name. The low vibrations of a passing whale trembled her heart. Asrai let go of the wall and spread her arms, her eyes closed.

I am here! I hear you! I see you! Soon we shall be home! Soon we shall be one!

Asrai held onto the ledge again. A grin spread across her face. Joy had blossomed in her heart overnight, and now she was bursting. The magick coursed through her body stronger than ever. The handmaidens arrived, flanked by serving boys. The handmaidens checked Asrai's hair to ensure the braids were not mussed from sleep while the serving boys laid out Asrai's breakfast. Pamela had decided to spoil Asrai with a treat. There was still leftover seevoo seaweed and the fisherman had brought in a good haul of amberjack. She had left it cooked rare with little seasoning and only a bit of fish bone broth. Asrai was delighted.

The handmaidens helped steady her as she walked. The boys exited the room, allowing Asrai to eat. A troupe of maids entered the room once Asrai's plate was empty. They carried in the enormous gown, a sparkling veil, and an ornate jewelry box. The handmaidens helped Asrai to her feet, while one of the maids cleared the table.

The maids hovered about Asrai, pulling on her small clothes and chemise. The handmaidens held her as the corset was tightened, her feet slipping out from under her. The heavy gown was lifted by three of the maids, and Asrai was guided through. Her braids were straightened, and her curls fussed over as the stays of the dress were tightened. The maids began sewing on the sleeves. Tiny crystals and pearls glimmered on the cuffs. The bodice of the gown was embroidered with a glittering seashell outlined in more crystals, pearls, and silver thread.

A scene of seahorses, dolphins, and sea turtles came to life as they smoothed the embroidered train. The hem was trimmed in silver, catching the early morning light. Tiny crystals were woven into her braids with silver settings. A simple silver chain was clasped about her wrist. She wore no rings other than the one Cormack had given her.

The handmaidens steadied Asrai as one of the maids lifted Asrai's dress. Another maid burrowed under it and began pushing shoes onto her wounded feet. Asrai cringed. She slowed her breath, controlling the pain. *All is temporary. This too shall pass.*

****

Someone shook Cormack awake. His eyes were gummy. The offending person handed him a goblet of cool water. "My lord, we need to get you ready for the ceremony."

The bright sun flooded his room. Cormack rubbed his eyes and sat up. He drank in frenzied gulps, a balm upon his parched throat. The feast had gone on long into the night, and many flagons of ale had passed through his lips.

A pair of serving boys laid out breakfast for Cormack. He pushed himself out of bed and stumbled to the table. His mind fought to assign why he was awake as sleep tried to reestablish itself. Cormack stared at the black coarse bread and the soft white ewe's milk cheese. His mind clicked, finding the right track, and anxiety and joy overwhelmed him.

Cormack flinched, then lowered his head. "Poseidon help me."

His stomach tied itself into knots. Cormack's hand shook as he drank more water. Tonight, he would be home in the sea. Tonight, he would leave Paradine to Peter. Cormack tore off a hunk of bread and looked at the waiting groom. "How is the Lady Asrai?"

"I expect she is also preparing, your highness."

Cormack rolled his eyes at the bland answer. The simple breakfast soothed his nerves and cleared his head. His uniform had been arranged on the bed, ready for the groom. Cormack ran his hand through his hair and changed out of his nightshirt. The groom helped Cormack button the twenty-seven silver buttons on the jacket and attach all the appropriate pins to their designated places. A heavy silver chain adorned with sapphires was placed over his shoulders and across his chest. The boots were swiftly laced, encasing his calves and feet in soft black leather.

The dark blue jacket and breeches were simple, allowing the pendants to catch the eye. A silver saber was slung onto his belt. He selected the least-ornate silver rings from the presented tray of jewelry. A silver circlet engraved with the crest of Paradine nestled into his hair, crossing his forehead.

A knock sounded. Cormack straightened the cuffs of his sleeves. "Enter!"

Pamela rushed into the room. Cormack grinned and held his arms out to her. "My dear boy!" Pamela hugged him tight, his body melting into her soft bosom and arms.

Cormack hugged her back, his heart fit to burst. The groom took his leave, allowing them to be alone. Pamela released her embrace and looked Cormack over. "You look like a true prince today." She sniffled as tears welled. "Her majesty would have been so proud."

He nodded, swallowing tears of his own. "Thank you, Pamela. For everything."

Pamela shook her head, laughing as tears rolled down her cheeks. "T'warent easy! But we made it work. We did!" She scrubbed them away with her apron.

Cormack hugged her again. "I shall miss you."

Their tears mixed as they embraced fiercely. After a moment, Pamela pushed him away. She dabbed her face with her apron. "You have grown into a wonderful man. I'm so proud."

He nodded, struggling to speak. "Thank you, Pamela. I shall always love you."

Pamela squeezed his hand. "As will I. And the lady loves you fiercely!" she cheered. "I am overjoyed for you both."

He nodded, his breath caught in his throat as his heart swelled. Pamela patted him on the shoulder, her face bright with joy. They shuffled their feet and scrubbed their eyes, their faces hot and chests shuddering. At last, Cormack took a deep breath. "Until we meet again."

She nodded, unable to speak. Cormack looked away, and Pamela turned toward the door. She stood in the hall, gathering herself. The servants rushed to and fro, ignoring her. Pamela straightened and sighed. The ceremony would be starting soon. She made her way to Asrai.

****

The small chamber buzzed with maids when Pamela opened the door. Asrai heard someone enter and turned her head. The sun gilded her, sending rainbows and sparkles bouncing off her jewelry and the gem encrusted gown. The jeweler had kept his promise and made a string of the raw mermaid's tears into a necklace. There had been several leftover, and these were mounted into her tiara along with sapphires and tiny diamonds. The veil was pinned into the braids behind the tiara, letting a waterfall of sparkling gauze float above her crimson curls. Pamela's breath caught. Never had she seen anything so beautiful.

"Pamela!" Asrai laughed. "You're here!"

She walked toward Asrai, the maids scurrying out of the way. Pamela took Asrai's hand and patted it. "In all my years. You are radiant, dear. Today you are a queen."

Asrai lowered her lashes, her heart fluttering. "Thank you. For all that you have done for me, thank you."

Pamela patted her hand and nodded. "You know I would do anything for that boy." Her voice thickened. "I know you'll take good care of him."

"I promise." Asrai squeezed Pamela's hand.

Love of the Sea

The two women embraced. Joy overwhelmed Pamela as she felt Asrai's heart thunder against hers. The maids stepped away, finished with the dressing. Pamela pulled away, and the handmaidens nodded to her. "Well, let's get you to the garden." Pamela took Asrai's weight, allowing the handmaidens to retreat.

****

Asrai leaned against Pamela as she was steered down the stairs. The human legs felt like congealed jelly as she fought to maintain her balance on the steep staircase. She missed the powerful muscles of her tail, their ability to send a small shark crashing into the reef or propel her out of the water in dizzy backflips.

"Careful dear, this one is a bit slick." Pamela's arms jerked Asrai over a polished step. She held onto the wall for balance.

The shoes made walking even more difficult and uncomfortable. Asrai's feet were crammed inside them at an awful angle. Her toes throbbed, and she wondered how human women went about their business so cramped. The naked ocean would be a balm on her aches later that night. Her legs felt like they were being torn as they walked past the Great Hall and the servant quarters. The garden was on the far side of the castle from the West tower. Asrai fought to keep her breathing even.

The sunlight beamed through the archway entrance to the garden. The pavilion opened before Asrai. King Dominic waited on the landing with a bouquet. Pamela patted Asrai's hand and released her. Asrai walked to his majesty, who presented her the flowers with a flourish.

"M'lady, let me have the honour of walking you." He extended his arm to Asrai.

She took it, sliding her arm through his, careful not to scratch his sleeve with the jewels on hers. Together they began down the stone path. Pamela watched, tears running down her cheeks. Had she been more brazen, she would have demanded to walk Asrai herself, but the king had wanted the honour, and she took her place in the door's shadow instead.

The light reflected off the jewels and stark white fabric of Asrai's gown. The spectators sighed as she passed. Each seemed to be exhaling the breath they had been holding since Cormack had refused the last of the noble ladies. The line would continue. The kingdom was safe.

A sea of chairs had been set out for the spectators; diplomats of allied kingdoms, local nobles, generals of the army all glittered in the rows closest to the altar. The first to behold Asrai were the simple villagers, farmers, and sailors. All had put on their best clothes and heirloom jewels. Asrai gave them a warm smile, pleased that the people would share in the joy. The yellow and red of Caraway dotted the spectators.

Princess Nephara was already in her place at the altar. One of the men in gold had escorted her down the aisle. Her gown was the deep shade of currants, draped in gold gauze. She did not wear a veil; instead she wore the heavy crown of Caraway clustered amongst a wreath of yellow and red dahlias. The back of her dress was opened, and exposed her from the neck down to her lower back. Intricate swirling designs had been painted on her skin with red dye. Tiny droplets of garnets and amber had been sewn onto her dress, twinkling in the afternoon sun. Her lips were blood red, and her face painted with cosmetics. Tiny gold bells were sewn onto the tips of her long sleeves, tinkling as she fidgeted.

Peter stood at her side, his jacket and breeches also currant red, a gold sash draped over his left shoulder. He wore large gold rings, but no circlet or crown. His boots were a dark brown laced with red stays. His eyes met Asrai's. A chill went through her as he nodded to Nephara, then advanced down the aisle. King Dominic froze, his face reddening.

"What are you doing?" the king hissed. "You get back up there right now!"

"Uncle I must speak to you, I—" Peter fumbled with his jacket pocket.

The king's meaty fist cuffed Peter over the head. "Get up there, now!"

Peter clenched his teeth and did as he was bid. Princess Nephara shot Asrai a hot glare before turning around again. Asrai's heart thundered as they resumed walking. Fear crawled over her body.

"Don't worry, my dear. Nothing shall spoil this day," King Dominic whispered.

Asrai looked at the altar again. Cormack stood on the left side, glaring at Peter. When he felt her eyes on him, he turned and met her gaze. Cormack smiled, easing her frenzied heart. She took in his beautiful uniform. A blush rose in her cheeks. Her body felt hot, and she leaned against King Dominic for support.

A plush, golden stool had been provided at the altar next to Cormack. He helped Asrai sit and arranged her skirts. She folded her hands in her lap with the bouquet. The sweet smell of the astilbe and blue asters wafted up to her nose. The delicate scent soothed her.

Chapter Twenty-Seven

Archdruid Cian looked them over, then cleared his throat and lifted his hands. "Greetings to you all on this fine day! The sun has shown us warmth, and the wind has shown us favour with gentle weather this afternoon. We are gathered here to celebrate the glorious union of these two couples. Every union of love is glorious, but today we also celebrate the union of kingdoms."

The archdruid waved two fingers in a circle over the crowd. "We open our hearts today to share our joy and love with these four people. We will strengthen their bonds and their unions with our blessings this day."

He approached the ancient stone dais and picked up a white birch branch. "We call to the Air of the East," he turned and pointed the branch, "to send the fair and juste winds of Fate through their lives."

"We call to the Fire of the South," he turned again and pointed the branch, "to send the fire of passion, and the warmth of love to their hearts and their minds."

"We call to the Water of the West," he turned again and pointed the branch, "to send the wisdom and patience they will need to guide their lives, and the lives of their children."

"We call to the Earth of the North," he turned so that he was facing the altar again and pointed the branch, "to remind them from whence they came, and whence they shall go. To steady their steps on the path of Truth."

He set the branch on the dais and approached the altar again. "Before you today, we petition for the union of Prince Peter of Paradine, and Princess Nephara of Caraway. Do you give your blessing to them?"

The crowd cheered and raised their fists in the air. The archdruid nodded and turned to Cormack and Asrai. "Before you today, we petition for the union of Prince Cormack, the future king of Paradine, and Princess Asrai of Sulu. Do you give your blessing to them?"

Peter thrust his flat palm in the air. "No!"

Archdruid Cian stood blinking at the prince. King Dominic shot to his feet, his body shaking. Peter waved a piece of parchment clutched in his hand. "I must put a stop this despicable union!"

King Dominic tromped up the steps. "Boy, how dare you ruin this day!"

Peter thrust the parchment out to the king. "She is no lady at all! I saw with my own eyes, Uncle. She is a fraud!"

King Dominic shook, crumpling the paper in his clenched fist. "You insolent brat! Spouting such lies in the face of a lady!"

"She is no human. She is a sorceress! Her body was covered in red scales, and her legs were a fish's tail. I saw it with my own eyes!"

Asrai lifted her skirts, revealing the shoes. "My legs may not work as they should, but here they are, nonetheless."

Peter sneered at her. "Yes, now that you are cloaked in your human guise!" He turned back to the king, pleading. "Please, Uncle! You must read the letter! It is by Lord Gar's hand!"

King Dominic grabbed Peter by the scruff of his neck, like a dog, and shoved him back to his place beside Nephara. He clenched his hand, making Peter wince. The king shoved his finger in Peter's face, his voice a low growl.

"If you don't stop this I will have you hanged, kin or not!"

Peter stayed put as King Dominic ordered everyone back into their seats. The archdruid was still frozen, his hands clenched together so that the veins popped up from his wrinkled flesh.

"We will continue!" King Dominic barked. "We will not let my nephew's lunacy ruin this remarkable day!"

Archdruid Cian nodded. He cleared his throat and fumbled his hands. "Now, where was I–Oh! Oh yes! We petition for the union of Prince Cormack, the future king of Paradine, and Princess Asrai of Sulu. Do you give your blessing to them?"

The crowd gave a hearty cheer and jabbed their fists in the air. Cormack put his hand on Asrai's shoulder and squeezed. She looked up at him and smiled. Nephara stroked Peter's arm, her eyes apologetic. Peter put his arm over her shoulders, his head bowed.

"Now we ask for the blessing of the bright salamanders to ignite the fires of the heart!" The archdruid turned to the dais and used quick sticks to ignite a fire in a shallow bowl of straw and twigs. At its center was a large red stone, now glowing in the flames.

He held out his hands to the audience. "We walk thrice round the fire as we live as three—ourselves, as a unit with our beloved, and as a unit with our family. All we put into the world comes back threefold. Thus, we walk thrice."

Peter held out his hand, and Nephara took it. Their faces were pained on their first circle around, their eyes darting to Asrai and Cormack. But as they walked the second circle, their gaze locked on one another. The third circle, their smiles were warm and filled with joy. They took their places on the platform once more. Asrai watched as Peter's gaze dropped, and he sighed. Nephara's smile disappeared, and she leaned close.

Cormack offered Asrai his hand. She rose and took it, her legs shaking. They made three slow circles around the stage. Their shoes echoed on the wooden platform. Asrai's chest was shaking when Cormack helped seat her on the gold stool again. Her body trembled as she fought to maintain her composure.

Archdruid Cian held out his hands, palms up. "Do you promise to love, honour, and support your bond?"

The princes and princesses responded in unison. "I do."

Archdruid Cian turned again to the dais, and picked up an ancient stone bowl filled with seawater. He approached Peter and Nephara first.

He swirled his first finger into the water, and then signed on Peter's forehead. "I bless this man to seal this bond." He then dabbed his finger in the bowl again and touched the water to Nephara's forehead. "I bless this woman to seal this bond."

The archdruid turned and approached Cormack and Asrai. He repeated the blessing. Excitement flooded Asrai as she smelled the seawater and felt it upon her skin. *Soon we shall be home!* Her heart fluttered.

He replaced the bowl on the dais and gathered up a basket of flowers: simple white roses, a symbol of the White Veil. The musicians struck up a soft melody as the archdruid approached Cormack. "And now we dance the Dance of Hearts! For we are forever tied with the Moon and the Earth. Our hearts beat as one with the cycles."

He showered flower petals over them. Asrai stifled a shudder as she recalled the ladies from the midnight ritual. The archdruid stepped back to the dais and spread his arms.

Peter and Nephara glided toward the center of the platform. Their dance was close and slow. Nephara's sleeves jingled as she swept her arms and twirled. Their foreheads touched, their eyes lost in one another. Cormack looked down at Asrai. She nodded, her heart fluttering.

I must do this. I must seal the bond!

She rose, aided by Cormack's strong hand. They moved toward the center, giving space for Peter and Nephara. Asrai took a deep breath and arranged herself as she had seen the dancers do at previous feasts.

All is temporary.

The crowd gasped as Asrai pulled away from Cormack in a smooth spin. Her eyes were colourless, crackling with magick. She dove deep into her wellspring to keep her feet floating a hair's breadth from the wood. She tossed her elegant hair and flared her hands. Cormack was stunned, frozen at first, then fell into the dance with Asrai.

Peter's eyes widened as he watched Asrai dance, her lithe movements smooth, not at all like her halted steps down the aisle. He glared at her. Asrai ignored him, all her focus on the magick. Never before had she called upon the air for her bidding, but it came to her now, keeping her afloat so no pain came to her feet.

The musicians ended the song, and the guests clapped and cheered as the couples bowed. Asrai winced as the magick slipped away, her feet on the platform once more. Cormack led her back to the golden stool. She sighed as her body relaxed, her feet curled to the side.

Archdruid Cian smiled, bobbing his head. "And so, you have expressed your joyful feelings with the Dance of Hearts. All here can see how true and strong your love is."

He picked up the branch again. "We salute the Air of the East." He turned and pointed the branch. "We thank you."

"We salute the Fire of the South." He turned again and pointed the branch. "We thank you."

"We salute the Water of the West." He turned again and pointed the branch. "We thank you."

"We salute the Earth of the North." He turned so that he was facing the altar again and pointed the branch. "We thank you. Elements of Four, steady our steps on the path of Truth!"

He set the branch down and approached the altar. The archdruid raised his hands and smiled. "I present to you these bonded hearts! Let us celebrate this blessed day!"

Everyone cheered and scrambled to their feet. Peter and Nephara led the way back down the aisle toward the castle. A knot of guards followed. A stable boy led Nonna up to the altar. Cormack lifted Asrai into his arms and settled her onto the old mare. He took the bridle and led them down the aisle. King Dominic followed, tears in his eyes.

****

The crowd poured into the castle. Extra benches had been laid out in both the Great Hall and the lesser dining hall. The spectators gawked at the splendour. The musicians and the minstrel took their places and began to play. The Caraway dancing girls spread out on the floor and began entertaining the guests. Serving girls and boys rushed about to fill goblets and flagons. Chatter filled the hall like an invisible cloud. King Dominic waited until everyone was seated and comfortable before he stood, holding his flagon high. A hush flew unto the hall, and he spoke.

"Today we celebrate the union of my nephew and the beautiful Princess of Caraway. This union was unexpected, but a wondrous gift to our kingdom. Our alliance with Caraway is welcomed with open arms and warm hearts. We look forward to becoming good friends."

Clapping and cheers erupted. The people of Caraway banged their hands on the tables. King Dominic raised his hand for quiet again. "We also celebrate this day, the day that every king, and every father, waits for. Today my son, the future king of Paradine has wed the beautiful Princess of Sulu. He has chosen a queen at last, and now our two kingdoms can become allies and grow a secure future together."

Love of the Sea

The applause was thunderous. King Dominic shuddered as he drew a tearful breath. He smiled and waited for the clapping to subside. "We thank you all for witnessing and celebrating this day with us. Now I ask you lend your ears to our fine minstrel, Daniel Ratherford."

He took his seat and allowed the minstrel to step forward. The dancing girls sat down on one of the servant benches near the kitchens. The minstrel cleared his throat and bowed.

"Thank you, my lords and ladies, and all the wonderful people who are with us today! I have composed a song for this splendid occasion, and am delighted to share it with you."

The musicians took up the tune, and the minstrel began to sing.

"Great Paradine, named for paradise,
your sprawling lands and fertile fields,
the friendly sea and all it yields,
this kingdom be mine and yours!

Our prince wandered far aboard his ship,
His charms and gentle ways were much adored,
Princesses from far and wide sent to our lord,
But nary a one he picked!

The sea is vast and revealed at last,
The one no one could possibly predict,
A princess most perfect,
The true love, the prince's bride!
Lady Asrai! The beautiful Lady Asrai!
We chant her name and dream of her tribe!
Our joy, Paradine cannot deny!
The princess bride!

You may think this story done,
A tale that has been rung and closed,
Yet, this gave way for Peter to propose,
To the lovely Caraway princess!
From far off lands, here she did arrive,
Prince Peter saw his one chance,
And offered Nephara blessed romance,
Their union clear as day!

And now we have much more to celebrate,
The powerful fate of love,
Rejoice these bonded hearts thereof,

How lucky we, this splendour thus witnessed!"

The minstrel bowed, and clapping engulfed him. King Dominic turned to his general and threw his arm about his shoulders. "We did it, Weston, my old friend. We are finally here."

The old general nodded. "The mantle has passed. A new age shall dawn tomorrow."

****

Bawdy laughter filled the hall as platters of food flooded the tables. Twelve courses were served to all. The common folk were beside themselves. The feast progressed, and Asrai watched the moon rise from the skylights in the eves. She became more fidgety as the night wore on. Cormack waited until King Dominic was deep in the sweet clutches of drink before taking their leave.

Cormack carried Asrai out of the Great Hall. They slipped through the throngs of merry people and frazzled servants. He reached the hall that led to the stables. A stable boy was curled up on the landing with Nonna's bridle tangled in his sleeping hands. The old mare stood over him.

"Wake up, boy!" Cormack ordered as he helped Asrai onto the saddle.

The stable boy scrambled to his feet and scrubbed his face. He bowed low. "I'm sorry, m'lord! I'm sorry!"

"Take this," Cormack handed the boy an envelope with his official wax seal and a gold coin, "and give it to the king tomorrow morning."

The boy nodded and stuffed the envelope into his jacket. He pocketed the gold coin, and looked at the royal couple. "Thank you." Cormack smiled at the stable boy. "You have done well." Cormack pulled himself onto Nonna behind Asrai. He urged the horse toward the beach, away from the docks.

Chapter Twenty-Eight

The cool night air whipped their faces as Nonna galloped down to the scrubby beach grass. Cormack slowed her and led them toward the sands by the cliffs. He halted Nonna and dismounted, then slid Asrai down as well. She seated herself on the cool sand. Cormack led Nonna back to the grass. He slipped the silver circlet from his head, his fingers tracing the engravings.

You shall be safe in Peter's hands. I was never meant for this.

Cormack slipped the circlet, his silver rings, and the medals from his jacket into Nonna's saddlebags. He sighed and embraced the old mare's neck. *Thank you.* He looped her bridle back over her head. He smacked her rump, sending her galloping back to the royal stables.

Cormack returned to Asrai. He sat beside her and gazed at her moonlit form. "Now what are we to do?"

"Now we wait for Illyana." Asrai broke her gaze from the moon and turned to Cormack. "And we rid ourselves of these clothes. They will strangle you when the change takes hold."

His fingers trembled as he undid the stays of her dress. Cormack used the point of his pocket dagger to cut the sleeves from her shoulders. He helped heave the cumbersome dress over Asrai's head and threw it onto the grasses, then flicked the sleeves to join it. The air rushed from Asrai's lungs as Cormack cut the stays of her corset. She ran her hands over her skin, the imprints from the corset bones deep. Asrai ripped off the shoes and threw them onto the discarded gown. Cormack began undressing himself as Asrai tore off her chemise and small clothes.

"I'm free!" Asrai laughed, throwing her arms in the air.

Cormack smiled, gazing at her naked body. "Soon, we both shall be free."

Arai looked up and watched as Cormack tossed his clothes on the heap. He looked at Asrai. She was still wearing her crown and jewels, though the veil had been discarded. He remembered the old sailors' tales of proud mers guarding their hoards of treasure. Cormack sat beside her again, awkward with his nakedness. She ran her hand down his arm.

"Soon the sea shall call us. Be not afraid, my sailor."

Cormack shivered at her touch. He took her hand in his and kissed it. "I will face anything, so long as you are at my side."

****

King Dominic went to sip from his flagon, but it was bone dry. He looked up, scanning the table for a server, when he saw that Cormack and Asrai's seats were empty. He turned to his general. "Weston, did I miss Cormack's announcement?"

The old general shook his head. "No, majesty. Are you sure they are not tucked in a corner of the dance?"

The king shook his head. "No, no. The lady cannot walk, let alone dance properly. How she was able to perform so beautifully for the Dance of Hearts is a mystery to me!"

Alarm whispered in his mind. He recalled Peter going on about something with sorcery and 'human guise.' He pulled the crumpled parchment from where he had stuffed it in his dagger holster. He smoothed the letter, his eyes scanning the text. There was no seal, but the signature was the unmistakable swirl and flourish of Lord Gar.

Weston read over the king's shoulder. His face blanched. "Majesty! What can this mean?"

King Dominic shook his head. Anger and fear warred in his mind, lubricated by ale. He stood, and marched over to where Peter and Nephara were seated. "My boy, what is the meaning of this?" He thrust the letter under Peter's nose.

Nephara's face lit up as Peter took the parchment. He turned, facing the king. "Uncle, I tried to warn you."

"They're gone!" Nephara gasped, pointing at the empty chairs.

Peter blanched as he whirled about, his eyelids peeled back into his skull. "But I was watching them!"

King Dominic's face reddened. He had waited years for this day, and even extended patience toward his son in his desire for a love match. Now, all those years were crumbling before his eyes. His guttural bellow pierced the hall. "Guards!"

Horses' hooves drummed over the sand as the tide came in. Peter and Nephara headed the search party, King Dominic close behind. The cool evening air and the frightening letter had the wedding party sobered. The guards were assembled, the festivities long forgotten.

****

An eerie song pierced the air, sending Cormack into a fit of shivers. The waves came closer, and Asrai's chest heaved with excitement. "She is here! The sea hag is here!"

Cormack's shudders gave way to a sharp groan. Asrai turned, taking his hand in hers. The shaking became more violent, his face contorted with pain. The screams seemed to die in his throat as he clenched his teeth. Asrai watched, unable to help as blue-and-black scales began pushing through his skin. Cormack thrashed as his legs began fusing together. His mouth opened at last, releasing piercing screams as the scales and bones began to fuse, creating his armoured plating.

The wind changed, bringing the scent of horses and fear. Asrai bristled. She pushed herself toward Cormack. Her body trembled as her scales pushed their way through her own skin. She took his shaking hand. "All is temporary, my love," Asrai gasped. Her heart thundered as the words rushed from her lips.

He nodded, unable to speak. He held her hand tight. Sand sprayed as his lower half flailed, the bones sealing into a tail. His feet widened, as if they were melting, until they became the delicate cerulean membranes of his fins. The water began lapping at the edges of Cormack's tail. His fins curled away from the strange sensation.

Asrai felt fear strike her heart cold as the pounding of hooves on sand whispered in her ears. She could hear the frantic cries of a search party. She curled her body against Cormack, willing the change to quicken. Cormack's sternum was widening and thickening. The scales on his chest fused together and became plating, much like that on Asrai's shoulders. His neck split open as if a dagger had slashed his throat to create gills on the sides. They opened to the chilly night air and quickly closed again.

The voices came closer. Asrai could smell the heavy scent of lathered horses. Peter's whoops ignited terror in her mind. She bared her fangs and screamed. "Illyana! Deliver us!"

The song became clearer, the lyrics soothing. Cormack's body began to relax as the music washed over him.

> *"Come my children of the sea*
> *Here I build the waves for thee*
> *Feel the foam and smell the spray*
> *Take your first breath beneath the waves!*
>
> *More frightened now than ever been*
> *Man no more, no land, no kin*
> *Seek the treasures of the deep*
> *Learn our song and what wonders sleep*
> *beneath the waves,*
> *Your soul now shall flee!"*

Asrai felt Cormack's hand go limp as a small orb of light rose from his chest. The sea hag began a chanting wail, colder than any banshee scream. Asrai bowed her head. She lifted her free hand, raising it high above her head. Her scales glimmered in the moonlight as the magick took hold.

Go forth. Go swiftly. Serve your true purpose.

The orb halted its slow ascent. Red light surrounded the orb, then brightened to gold. It flickered for a moment. The sea hag's song became a high-pitched shriek. Asrai closed her fist, then flung her hand open again. The orb took off like a cannon shot. Asrai watched as it flew overhead, then out of sight into the darkness. She could hear confused shouting, and the sound of a startled horse.

****

Nephara gasped as she heard shrill screams pierce the air. Raquisa was already at full tilt, foaming at the mouth. She clenched the horse's mane, praying to the Anemoi for speed. As the cries grew louder, a second voice rose. A great wailing, like a banshee. The horses shied, their hooves kicking up sand as they shrieked.

"Peter!" King Dominic barked over the din. "Peter, what is happening?"

He fought Demos, trying to get the horse's head reigned in. "I don't know, Uncle!"

As quick as it had started, the wailing stopped, and Cormack's anguished voice fell silent. The horses' eyes rolled, prancing around, spooked. "Infernal beasts!" King Dominic roared, trying to regain control of his steed.

Nephara froze as she saw a golden light flying toward them. She screamed, further scaring the horses. The orb hit Peter square in the chest, disappearing into him. The force knocked him from Demos, throwing him to the sand, his body lifeless. The guards flung themselves from their horses, gathering Peter' limp frame before he was trampled to death. They threw him over one of the saddles.

"Onward!" King Dominic roared.

Tears streamed down Nephara's face, ruining her makeup. Her heart was shattering, rage filling the quickly forming void. She pulled the gold chain, freeing the panya from the back of her saddle. Nephara turned and saw Peter's body flailing as the horse jostled him against the guard. Devastation spread through her mind, removing all rational thought.

"Quinquetta! Kill!" she shrieked, her voice spurring on the great beast.

****

Asrai hurried and pulled her comb from her hair. *Be the leader you are meant to be. Kind and just. Do not reject the soul of my dear sailor. Hold on! Hold on! Poseidon, give us a sign!* Asrai's hands were trembling. The frenzied sound of horses and men were coming closer.

A splash broke her thoughts. Asrai hissed.

"No time! We must get your mate into the water!"

Asrai slipped her comb back into her hair. She helped the sea hag drag Cormack further into the surf. His head wobbled as they pulled him into the rising tide, the waves pulling them toward the sea. A piercing scream tore through the night, and Asrai's blood went cold. The panya circled overhead, a bright flame against the inky sky.

"Poseidon, protect your own!" Illyana called, holding her comb aloft.

One of the waves curled high, dragging them into deeper waters. The panya dove as the waves curled down. The defeated beast shrieked as the mers were pulled deep into the sea, its muffled cries sending Asrai into a frenzy. She clung to Cormack, her muscles screaming as she kept him from sinking. Joy surged through her heart when she felt his body tremble.

****

His eyes snapped open. Dark water surrounded him. There was no up or down. He flailed. "Cormack! Cormack! Stop!"

Asrai's words reached him. Her voice was different underwater — or was it the words that were different? Cormack's mind whirred as he tried to orient himself. He kicked his legs, but found those muscles changed. He looked at himself and saw the deep blue-and-black tail where his legs had once been. He screamed.

Asrai's arms wrapped around him. "Shhh. Be still, my sailor prince."

Memories surged in Cormack's mind. Their moonlit ride to the shore. The pain of the change, his body contorting and reforming. And something else. Something was missing.

"There now." Asrai released him.

Cormack pumped his tail as Asrai was doing. The water pushed and pulled, but he soon found the rhythm.

"Do you know who you are?" The sea hag swam closer to them. Her eyes glinted.

"Yes." Cormack ran his hand through his hair. "I am Cormack, crown prince of Paradine."

The sea hag pulled out her jeweled comb. "Were."

She swished her comb, calling up the water mirror. Peter was sitting on the beach, his wedding clothes covered in sand on his left side, his eyes wild. Nephara had her arms around him, her body shaking as she wept. One of the guards found Asrai's discarded gown. King Dominic's face crumbled, and tears slipped down his cheeks.

"Was it done?" Asrai's eyes raked over the water mirror. "Was it successful?"

The sea hag shook her head. "The soul was implanted. Beyond that, I do not know."

Cormack stared at the water mirror, his eyes locked on his father. He had done it. He had left Paradine behind, and now he was in the sea with Asrai. His mind whirred as he watched his father's torment. Tears should have been pricking his eyes, guilt and sorrow should have clenched his heart. He felt hollow, as if he had been wiped clean. Sadness plucked at the corners of his mind, but not the deep grief that shakes one's bones. Cormack reached out to the water mirror. It shimmered at his touch.

"In any case, we have more important matters to face." The sea hag swirled her comb into the mirror, dispelling it.

Cormack's hands balled into fists, anger taking over. "But my kingdom! My people! What of them?"

The sea hag's eyes flashed. "You made your choice."

The remark cut him deep. He shook his head. "Yes. I did."

Asrai nudged him. "We will make sure your people are safe. But now, we must finally make *my* people safe."

The sea hag led them into deeper waters. Cormack found it a challenge to follow their smooth twists and turns through the craggy rocks and sprawling reefs. His tail was clumsy, still exploring the different fins and movements. Asrai slowed her pace, allowing Cormack to catch up.

"This is all so strange." Cormack could not look at Asrai, focusing instead on relearning how to swim.

Asrai nodded. Her sleek fins fluttered with ease. "You will find your way."

Cormack was exhausted when they reached the caves, hidden in a shelf of rock. The abyss yawned below the sheer drop.

"It is good to be home." Asrai sighed as they entered one of the larger caves.

The walls had been carved into shelves to hold a variety of odd things; seashells, old glass bottles, coils of rope. Rocks had been hewn into furniture of sorts, and sea plants growing upon them made them soft. Sea creatures Cormack did not recognize were trapped in fishing floats, acting as candlelight.

"Let us rest now." Asrai tugged on his hand. "There is much to explain tomorrow."

Exhaustion took over the strange absence of feelings, leaving Cormack struggling to keep his eyes open. He followed Asrai deeper into the cave. Other passageways opened, revealing more spaces. Asrai led him to her chambers. More creatures in floats lit the room. On the shelves, he recognized the spyglass and pocket dagger he had lost while sailing aboard *Anita*. A thick carpet of sea plants covered a large section of the sandy floor. Asrai curled up on this and gestured to Cormack. "Here, my sailor."

The sea plants tickled his scales as he folded himself onto the floor. He faced Asrai, pressing his forehead against hers. "I am truly a mer now?" His voice sounded strange to him, low and muffled in the water.

Asrai nodded. "Yes. The change is complete. This is who you are. Sleep well, my dear sailor prince."

Love of the Sea

He wrapped his arms around Asrai. Their tails entwined. The empty relief of slumber overtook Cormack, blotting out his father's anguished face.

Chapter Twenty-Nine

Cormack felt something brushing against his body. He fidgeted, but the sensation did not go away. He opened his eyes and ran his hand through his hair. His body felt strange and light. Cormack sat up. He was in some sort of cave. The previous night rushed back to him, and panic flooded Cormack's mind.

What have I done? He stared at his hands. The thin membranes between his fingers shimmered. *I have abandoned my kingdom! I have destroyed all hope for Father!*

Fear gnawed at Cormack, but he found that true guilt eluded him, and he could not cry. His emotions were not as hot and sharp as they once were. He curled his tail, as if he were hugging his old knees. The scales on his arms slid against the plating on his tail. He looked down at Asrai's sleeping form.

The gentle water played with her hair, like a soft breeze. Her crimson scales shimmered, the gold sheen winking as her chest rose and fell. He felt a strange buzzing in the back of his mind as he stared at her. Asrai's eyes clenched in her sleep, and her body twitched. Cormack placed his hand on her shoulder.

"Asrai, wake up. We are in the sea." His voice was gentle as he nudged her sleeping form.

She flinched away from him, grumbling. Cormack shook her a little harder. "Asrai, wake up. It's me, Cormack."

Asrai jolted awake and her head darted about, her eyes wide. He put his arms around her and felt her heart race against him chest. "It's all right, you are home again."

Her body relaxed in his embrace as she gathered herself. It was comforting to feel her against him, and grounded his thoughts. *We are in the sea. I actually went through with it. Paradine is at Peter's mercy.*

Asrai slowed her trembling breath and embraced Cormack. "I'm so glad! We are finally home!"

When they released one another, Asrai looked down at her wrist and her eyes sparkled upon seeing the silver bracelet. She touched her throat and her head, and found the necklace and tiara still there. She looked at Cormack and pointed to his head.

"Where is your circlet?" She began unclasping the jewelry and placing it on her stone shelves.

Love of the Sea

Cormack watched her arrange her new treasures. "It was not mine to take. Many before me have worn it. I sent it back with Nonna."

Asrai's face puckered with concern. "It is your crown. I doubt that boy can resist keeping such a treasure for himself."

"I know in my heart that the circlet is in the treasury, where it belongs." Cormack shook his head. "It represents Paradine and that those who wear it *are* Paradine. It is the same for you. You *are* Sulu. As queen, you will not belong to me, or even yourself, but to your people. The circlet is a reminder of that."

Asrai's eyes widened as she absorbed Cormack's words. "Yes. I am Sulu. The fate of the kingdom rests with me. I suppose your circlet is similar to the great trident, although that is a magickal artifact, whereas yours is simply treasure."

Cormack watched as she fiddled with her things, deep in thought. She turned back to Cormack. "I'm sure you're feeling a bit peckish now." She took his hand. "Shall we go out and find our meal?"

Cormack allowed her to lead him through the network of caves. He had played at fishing with the sailors in the past, but he had never truly fended for himself. They swam over the abyss. Cormack shivered as he looked into the darkness. Asrai kept a firm grip on his hand until they reached an expanse of reef. There were many schools of fish floating this way and that. Sea plants waved with the current, and creatures scuttled about in the sand.

Asrai flexed her hands. Claws shot from hidden folds under her fingernails. Cormack flinched as she darted into the center of a school. The fish fled in all directions. Some bumped into Cormack as they tried to escape. Asrai returned to his side with three fish speared between her clawed hands.

She offered him one. Cormack flexed his hands as Asrai had, and claws shot out. He speared the fish and took it from her. The dead eyes looked at him. Cormack glanced at Asrai. She stuck the fish, head first, into her mouth. She crunched, beheading the fish. She spit out the head and it floated to the sand. She began ripping chunks of flesh from the body.

Cormack looked at his fish again. Before, such a meal would have turned his stomach. Now he found that it was not as gruesome as it seemed. The boney head clicked against his teeth before he spit it out. The taste lingered, and he was quick to begin eating large bites.

Asrai showed Cormack how to dart after fish and spear them with his claws. He managed to catch one on his own, but Asrai kept them supplied with fresh food throughout the lesson. Something darted near the edge of the reef, and Asrai halted their game.

"What is it?" Cormack only saw coral and fish.

"Someone is here." Her voice was a low growl.

A large yellow mer darted from the reef and charged them. Cormack felt the low buzzing again, and a strange anger crept over him. His scales bristled as the yellow mer advanced. Asrai hissed, her scales puffed like knives. Before he closed the distance between them, the yellow mer darted in a figure eight, waving his arms so that the sunlight that filtered through the water flashed off his scales.

Cormack felt his mind go numb. Something primal took over and he darted away from Asrai. He charged the mer just as Asrai had taught him to do with the schools of fish. Cormack flipped his body, and the momentum sent his tail slamming right into the yellow mer's chest. The mer flew across the reef. He threw out his arms and pumped his tail to stop himself. Asrai stared at Cormack as he hissed at the mer. The yellow mer conceded, and swam back to the far side of the reef. Cormack returned to Asrai, confused about what exactly he had done.

"Are you all right?" Asrai took his hand in both of hers.

Cormack nodded. "That was strange! Who was that?"

Asrai shook her head. "I don't know. Strange mers pass by here on occasion."

"Why was he trying to attack you?" Cormack put his arm around Asrai.

She laughed at him. "He was trying to *mate* with me!"

Cormack flinched, and the strange anger welled up again. "What?"

Asrai waved her hand through the water. "The warm tides are passing through this area, which signals the quickening of the mating season."

The strange buzzing in Cormack's mind was becoming more intense by tiny fractions. He understood. "I see." He knew he should have felt embarrassed, but somehow that feeling eluded him. All he felt was uncertainty.

She took his hand again. "We should return to the cave. I still have much to explain to you. Out here it will be distracting."

****

The sea hag was perched on one of the stone seats when Cormack and Asrai returned. She pulled out her jeweled comb as they sat on the sandy floor. "Your bond has not yet been sealed." The sea hag played with her comb. "You know your magick won't be strong enough without the bond."

Asrai nodded. "Yes, but he is troubled by the loss of his kingdom. We are safe now. Show us what has become of Paradine."

"Very well." The sea hag flicked her comb in a circle, opening the water mirror again.

Love of the Sea

Peter was in the map room with King Dominic and his generals. The letter Cormack had left was open before them. Cormack felt a pang of regret as he watched his father mourn. Peter seemed to also be mourning, rather than angry and raging. Cormack hoped it meant that his soul had been successfully placed in Peter.

The sea hag pointed with her comb. "What is this?"

"I left my family a letter." Cormack could not tear his eyes away from his distraught father. "I explained that I was leaving to join Asrai in Sulu."

The sea hag rounded on him. "You told humans about our kingdom?!"

He shrank away from her. "No! They have no idea! They think Asrai is from a far off human kingdom called Sulu."

The sea hag made a low hiss and settled back onto her seat. Cormack watched the water mirror again. Weston comforted the king while Peter said something to them. They could not hear anything, but Cormack could see that they were trying to formulate some sort of plan.

"This accomplishes nothing." The sea hag swirled her comb, breaking the water mirror. "There is still much to discuss."

Asrai put her hand on Cormack's shoulder. "This will become easier."

He nodded. The deep sadness still eluded him. He turned back to the sea hag. She leaned forward, her comb between her hands. "Asrai is the proud daughter of Tuande, our once brave king. His queen, Seelacante, was killed by sharks when Asrai was a child. Shortly thereafter, Tuande was assassinated by a cowardly usurper. I was the royal advisor and closest to the family. That night, I took Asrai out of Sulu to protect her from the usurper. Otherwise he would have plotted to kill her to extinguish the line."

Cormack took Asrai's hand and squeezed it. She smiled and squeezed back. The sea hag slipped her comb back into her hair. "We have lived here many moons. Asrai has been trained in combat and ancient magicks so that one day she can reclaim her throne and justly rule Sulu. But these studies are not enough. We as mers are all connected to the mysterious deep. When we make a bond with another mer, our well of magick increases. That is why Asrai found you. She chose you to be her life mate."

Asrai leaned her head against Cormack's shoulder. He drew his arm around her, feeling her weight press against him. The buzzing in the back of his mind throbbed now. He fidgeted.

"I can feel that your bond is already growing strong. But in order to share one another's wellspring, you must also be physically bonded. Once the bond is complete, we will be able to begin our journey back to Sulu."

Lauren A. R. Masterson

****

Asrai nudged Cormack, leading him back out toward the reef. The yellow mer was nowhere to be found. Cormack felt an unfamiliar excitement taking hold in his mind and heart. She swam under him, dragging the membranes of her tail up his body toward his chest. She then flicked it, making his chest sting, before she giggled and darted into the reef. Cormack stared after her. Then his mind clicked and he joined her game. He darted about the reefs, trying to find her. When he spotted her hair floating behind a large brain coral, she darted away again, laughing. His darting about and searching soon became more elabourate as the excitement took over his mind. He liked the way the sun flashed off his dark scales, and how his quick movements created low pulses through the water.

Asrai shot from the reef, twirling her body. The gold sheen of her scales flashed. The thrill slammed into Cormack's chest like a fist. He grinned and darted after her, zig-zagging ever closer and creating small thudding booms with the powerful slams of his tail. The buzzing in Cormack's mind became overwhelming, and he bull-rushed Asrai. She allowed her body to go limp as his arms ensnared her. He ran his fangs over the smaller scales at the base of her neck. She shivered and brushed the fins of her tail against his.

Cormack felt his body was moving on its own. He had no idea as to the mechanics of a mer, but his body seemed to. Spines in his tail hooked into Asrai, digging into the armoured scales of her tail. Rather than hurting her, this seemed to excite her more. Cormack pressed his body into hers, and he felt the scales in the center of the spines begin to fold aside. The same happened on Asrai's tail, and at long last, he felt himself penetrate her.

Their thrashing kept them suspended above the reef. The spines kept them connected, but allowed room for leverage. Cormack sunk his fangs into the thick plating of scales on Asrai's shoulder. She threw her head back and emitting a high-pitched keening. As a man, hearing that shrill wailing had been frightening. Now as a mer, it made his blood hot. He licked the smaller scales on her neck, and bit her again.

His claws were sunk deep into the scales on her hips. Asrai's claws were sunk into the rough scales of his back. The rhythm was ancient and familiar. Cormack prodded and nipped at Asrai, eliciting different shrieks and clicks. Asrai then sunk her fangs into his shoulder, her body convulsing against his. Cormack became overwhelmed by the sensations, and the blinding explosion of pleasure blotted out the world around him.

The spines released Asrai, and Cormack felt himself pulling away. Asrai opened her eyes and kissed him, her arms behind his neck and her tail wound round his. The scales slid back into place, and Cormack slowed his breathing, his gills fluttering open and closed. Asrai's hair swirled about her like a red cloud. Before Cormack could find the mental capacity to speak, Asrai's eyes flashed and she dragged her claws up the scales of his tail. She then darted off into the reef, restarting the delicious game. Cormack's mind woke from the frenzy when the water began to turn orange from the filtered sunset. The reflections off his scales and Asrai's were dazzling. She gleamed brighter than any ruby he had ever seen.

They had coupled several times, and Cormack began to feel exhaustion creep into his body as rational thought took hold. Asrai nipped at him, and the way she flicked her tail was appealing. Cormack grinned and pretended to turn his back on her. She became annoyed and rushed him, slamming her body into his back. Asrai slid her body over his until she was against him again. She nipped at him again, pouting.

He sunk his claws into her back and coupled with her one last time. Asrai was insatiable, but accepted defeat when he allowed his body to sink down to a large bed of table coral. Asrai traced lazy circles on Cormack's scales as she lay beside him.

"You truly are a mer, my sailor." A mischievous glimmer flashed in her eyes.

Cormack nodded. His mind was coming down from the rampant primal need, and he began processing the decision he had made. He sat up and kissed the crown of her hair. "Yes. I am, aren't I?"

Asrai led them to another section of the reef. Cormack followed Asrai's lead and captured more fish. She discovered a small patch of brown seaweed that looked like rounded tree branches. She snipped some of them with her claws and ate them. Cormack did the same and found the flavour reminded him of root vegetables.

The water was darkening when Asrai led them back to the caves. The excitement had drained, leaving Cormack exhausted. The sea hag was not in the main cave when they returned. Asrai led Cormack back through the passage into her chambers. She took out her comb and ran it through her hair. Cormack sprawled on the patch of sea plants. His body became heavy with sleep.

"It will be difficult to leave this place behind," Asrai murmured as she combed her hair.

He fought to keep his eyes open. "And you just returned."

Asrai shook her head. "I have spent more moons of my life here than in Sulu. It will be strange."

"Mmm...." Cormack mumbled.

She slipped the comb back into her hair and stretched out on the bed of sea plants. Asrai rested her head on the smooth plating on Cormack's chest, her arm thrown over him. Her tail leaned against his. Cormack embraced her, his eyes closed.

Chapter Thirty

Cormack was jostled from his sleep when he heard strange clanking sounds. He sat up. Asrai selected treasures off her shelf and placed some of them in a small bag. "Good morning, my sailor." Asrai continued sorting through her belongings.

The muscles in his tail were sore, but he woke feeling refreshed. The buzzing still nagged the back of his mind, but he was able to push it away. "Are we leaving for Sulu?" Cormack yawned and stretched.

Asrai closed the bag. It was made of kelp she had woven together with a small clasp made of an old bent spoon. "Yes." She brushed against him as she headed toward the passage. "Aren't you coming?"

Cormack pushed himself off the bed and followed Asrai. The sea hag was waiting in the main cave. She had a bag similar to Asrai's, but her clasp was from a jewelry box.

"Are we ready?" The sea hag examined them.

Asrai nodded. "Yes. I only took a few things."

The sea hag darted out of the cave. Asrai and Cormack followed. She took out her jeweled comb and waved it before the entrance. The rock grew, until a solid wall blocked the cave. She slipped her comb back into her hair and led them over the reef.

They caught fish for their first meal before leaving the territory. The reef gave way to an expanse of sands and sea grasses. Asrai handed the sea hag her comb while they were swimming. The sea hag took out her own and touched it to Asrai's. The gold glowed bright, and runes began to appear on the handle. The gold split, revealing a ruby pushing its way to the surface.

The sea hag gasped when tiny emeralds blossomed along the spine. She jerked her head. "This is extraordinary magick." She traced her finger over the emeralds. "This is more than bonding."

Asrai gasped as the sea hag returned her comb. The new gems were a signal that Asrai's magick had increased. She traced her finger over the ruby. She shook her head. "I'm not certain what caused this. Perhaps because of the circumstances of our bond?"

The sea hag shook her head. "There is more to this." Her eyes glinted as Asrai slid the comb into her hair. "We will need to study this later."

****

The sands became rocky as they swam. Large white spidery bones grew out of the ground. Cormack reached down and touched one. It was like stone.

"That is dead coral." The sea hag picked up a pronged piece. "This is the outskirts of Sulu's main reef. The devastation was sudden and widespread. The kingdom has suffered greatly in our absence."

Asrai stopped swimming. Her scales shimmered, agitated. Cormack darted his eyes to Asrai, then shifted his gaze back to the sea hag and the graveyard.

"When the usurper took the throne, it came at a price." The sea hag dropped the coral. It sank like a stone. "Poseidon saw the Truth and punished Garradi."

Cormack swam closer to Asrai. She brushed her fingers against his chest plating, but she did not look at him. "Can it be fixed? Can Asrai use her new magick to fix it?" Cormack took Asrai's hand.

The sea hag tilted her head. "It will take powerful magick to heal the wrongs that have been done. The first step is Asrai taking back the throne, and winning redemption for her family."

Cormack nodded. He squeezed Asrai's hand. Her eyes flashed. "One step at a time, my sailor." Her face was strained. "I must win my people back before I can feed them."

The sun began dipping low when the ocean floor dropped off, revealing structures that looked like dwellings. The sea hag led them to the sands. "We'll need to find shelter for the night. We will approach Sulu tomorrow."

The water was cooler, and Cormack shivered. The sea hag took out her comb and drew a circle in the sand. Her comb glowed, and the sand fell away, revealing a large hole. Asrai and Cormack followed her down the dark passage. She lit the way with her glowing comb. Asrai took out her own comb and swirled it in the water. It glowed and pushed the rock walls outward until a large cave opened. Asrai swirled her comb over the sands, and a carpet of soft sea plants sprung up. The sea hag conjured more glass floats, filled with glowing sea creatures.

The sea hag pointed her comb at Cormack. "For Asrai to be successful, we must awaken your wellspring. Then the magick between you can be shared."

He shook his head. "I would not know where to start."

The sea hag rummaged around her bag. "Every mer needs an object they can channel the magick through."

Asrai sat down on the bed of plants. The sea hag presented Cormack with a small dagger. The metal gleamed in the strange light of the cave. The sea hag held out her comb. "Hold the object and close your eyes. Concentrate on the feeling you have when your mind begins to wander."

Cormack felt silly, holding the dagger with his eyes closed. He began to wonder about his father and Peter. He hoped that Paradine was not rebelling. Cormack's hand began to feel warm. He opened his eyes and saw the dagger glowing.

"Very good!" Asrai smiled.

The sea hag nodded. "Yes. That feeling you just had is the key that unlocks the wellspring. Now, hold onto that feeling and think of something you want to do. I want you to focus and make that patch of sea grass grow bigger."

Cormack pointed the dagger at the sea grass. Grow! Grow! The grass remained unchanged. Cormack looked at the sea hag. She shook her head.

"You can't just command something. You have to feel it."

Cormack nodded and pointed the dagger again. He imagined the sea grass growing bigger, taller, lusher. The dagger glowed and the sea grass seemed to move. He imagined the sea grass growing long and waving in the water, like Asrai's hair.

"Enough." The sea hag broke through Cormack's thoughts.

He lowered his arm and saw that the patch of sea grass had grown twice as tall, the fronds waving. He grinned. "I did it! By Poseidon's wave, I did magick!"

The sea hag smiled. "Indeed, you did. Now you must learn to hide your object. I want you to focus and imagine the dagger slipping into the armour on your arm, like a sheath."

Cormack nodded. He held the dagger near the armoured scales on his arm. He swiped the dagger downward, imagining it slipping into the armour and disappearing. It took him a few tries, but he was able to slip the dagger into his armour the way Asrai slipped her comb into her hair.

"You will need to practice. The bond allows you to tap not only into your own wellspring, but also that of your mate's." The sea hag tapped the hilt of his dagger. "Asrai will need to use every bit of strength she has to defeat the usurper and take her rightful place as queen of Sulu. That could also mean draining your strength as well. You must be prepared."

Cormack flexed his claws. "Can I not fight in her stead? In Paradine, I was skilled in fighting. The risk is so great—"

The sea hag shook her head. "Asrai has been training for this battle for many moons. The mers of Sulu will not honor a cowardly queen who hides behind the might of others. She must fight Garradi herself."

"We all have our place, my sailor. It is my destiny." Asrai stroked Cormack's arm.

The sea hag nodded. "Now then, I think it is time for rest."

Love of the Sea

Asrai stayed up with Cormack, helping him practice the simple magic, their hushed voices excited as he slipped the dagger in and out of his armour.

****

Cormack followed Asrai and the sea hag out of the cave. The reef was barren, so they scoured the sands for small crabs and clams. Asrai's body trembled as she hunted. Cormack swam near her and swept his fins over her tail.

"I am not sure I am ready for this." Asrai shied away from him.

The sea hag's eyes flashed, but Cormack took Asrai's hand. "You were there for me when I doubted my desire for the sea. This is your home. You are ready to return and take it."

Asrai nodded. She squeezed Cormack's hand. "You are right, my sailor. I am a descendant of Poseidon, and I cannot allow this usurper to defile the throne any longer!"

Cormack felt his heart swell with pride at her vicious words. He traced a lazy claw over her shoulder plating. "You will make a tremendous queen."

Asrai flushed, then her face melted into a grin. "Yes. It is my destiny. I shall make my father proud."

The sea hag pulled her comb from her hair. She pointed it at Cormack. "We must prepare to enter the kingdom today. That means we must be at our full strength." A smile broke her lips. "I know you have been practicing." Cormack suppressed a laugh, and Asrai swished her tail.

"Present your dagger." The sea hag held out her hand.

He slid the dagger from his plating. He felt an odd sense of possessive jealousy as he settled the hilt into her waiting palm. The sea hag slid her hand down the dagger until her claws were holding the naked blade. She touched her comb to the hilt until the dagger glowed and runes raced along the blade. The hilt began to grow, creating a curved hand guard that resembled a spiny whelk. Two tiny sapphires bloomed between the spines. A large emerald grew from the butt of the hilt. The sea hag frowned as the glow dimmed.

"This is most unusual." The sea hag muttered as she handed Cormack the dagger. "Mers do not typically receive emeralds, as they are indicators of Earth magick, and to see both of you have them...perhaps this is the unique bond. But we cannot be certain of that."

Asrai lifted her hand, as if about to speak, then closed her mouth and swam after the sea hag. Cormack raised his eyebrows at Asrai's hesitation. He swam close behind. The dead reef was eerie in its still silence. He flicked his tail to dispel his unease. If the sea hag or Asrai were perturbed, they did not show it.

He swam closer to Asrai, his eyes trying to meet hers, but her gaze was fixed straight ahead. The water grew colder, and the tide seemed to press in on him. Slag jutted out of the sands beyond the dead reef. Green patches of sea grass grew around the base. A few fish braved to dart about. Asrai shuddered. She slowed, her gaze on the rocks.

"We must press on." The sea hag's voice was gentle, but firm.

Cormack raked his eyes over the rocks. Antler seaweed and small coral formations grew from one side. A clump of seaweed drifted from one section of coral to another. It was then that Cormack noticed the jewel-like eyes: sea horses.

He flinched. *Is this where Asrai's mother was ambushed by sharks?* He hurried back to Asrai's side. Her scales bristled, but she said nothing.

Colouring began to appear in patches as they swam over the reef. Small fish darted about, their scales gleaming. A large crab waved its claws at them from its perch in a basket sponge. Asrai flitted into the reef and speared one of the small fish. Cormack followed her, chasing down a large parrotfish. They had been swimming for hours, and their meager breakfast of shellfish was long gone. The sea hag joined them, snaring colourful fish in her claws. Cormack felt a change in the water. He jerked away from his pursuit and saw a pair of mers swimming on the other side of the reef.

"They are of Sulu," the sea hag whispered.

The trio watched as the unfamiliar mers swam toward Sulu. The dark outlines of dwellings and the glimmering spires of the castle came into view at the edge of the reef. Asrai's eyes were hungry with longing as she stared at the looming castle.

"Stop!" The sea hag flicked her comb as Asrai took off.

A water pulse hit Asrai off guard. She whirled about. "But we are here!"

The sea hag waggled her comb at Asrai. "Yes. And we mustn't go charging in. We need the support of your people first. Conserve your energy. Draum will come soon enough."

Asrai conceded and speared another fish. Cormack turned to the sea hag. "Who is Draum? I thought the usurper was Garradi."

The sea hag crunched a small crab. "Draum is the battle Asrai has been training for. It is a fight to the death. The victor becomes ruler of Sulu." She snatched another crab. "It is a challenge rarely summoned. Once called, there is no turning back."

Cormack stared at Asrai. He watched as she flicked out her golden claws, stabbing fish, her fangs gleaming as she rent the scales and flesh. He knew he should have felt cold horror, knowing she would do the same to Garradi, but he found that all he felt was anxious anticipation.

Love of the Sea

The sea hag played with her claws. "You seem surprised. It is known to me that you humans kill one another for the same reason. Kings slaying kings."

He nodded. His father had overthrown and slain kings. Others had tried to do the same. Cormack looked at his hands. He played with his claws. "I came to the sea to escape the wars of kings."

The sea hag laughed. The shrill note sent shivers through Cormack. Her eyes flashed. "You are a fool to think you can escape such basic instincts."

Cormack's scales flashed blue. "I see that now."

"It will take time to undo the damage Garradi has done." Her eyes flashed as she captured Asrai's gaze. "The first step is securing the trust of Sulu." She swam toward Sulu again, Asrai already ahead of them. "We must learn from our mistakes. Only then can we mend the future."

He followed them, his scales shimmering as he swam. Cormack looked at Asrai. He recalled the joy he had felt hearing her song; the delicious agony of waiting for the jeweler to make her ring. He smiled. "It is no mistake. But I shall learn all the same."

Mers gave them curious looks as they swam into the village. Cormack stayed close to Asrai's side. The buzzing nagged him again, his mind remembering their run-in with the yellow mer at the reef. Asrai seemed to like Cormack's closeness, and allowed her body to brush against his every now and again.

The water warmed as the sun sparkled high above. The light filtered down through the waves, shining upon the mers as they flitted about. Asrai shivered as they neared the marketplace. The sea hag swam at her right, and Cormack swam at her left, just behind her waist. The mers slowed their activity and clicked at their approach. Cormack found that it resembled the little marketplaces the farmers and villagers built to trade goods with one another and tempt travelling merchants. Those stands were built with canvas stretched over wooden frames. These were a ramshackle of shells, giant sea creature bones, sections of shipwreck, seaweed, and other various found objects. They were decorated with shells, sea glass, and some even had jewels.

The trio stopped near the centre of the market. Asrai spread her hands before the curious mers. Already, a small crowd had followed them, and now a rainbow of mers surrounded their party. Asrai's eyes flashed. "I am Asrai, daughter of the warrior king, Tuande, and the great sea hag, Seelacante. I have returned home to you."

A ripple went through the marketplace. The mers clicked, and low pulses thudded through the water. Then the mers fled the market, their scales flashing a warning. Asrai's shoulders slumped as she watched them go. Cormack could feel anxiety building in his chest. He longed to put his arms around Asrai, to comfort her, but he was unsure if it would be welcomed.

     The sea hag touched Asrai's hand. "It is only the first step."

Chapter Thirty-One

Asrai led them further into the market. There were still some mers about, sitting at stone slabs or structures constructed out of shipwreck debris. Her heart felt the warm, unmistakable feeling of 'home,' but she could not find familiarity in her surroundings. Asrai tamped down her growing feelings of self-doubt. She had been young when the sea hag had whisked her away to the outskirts. It was as if she were swimming through a dream, and she was unsure of what was truly remembered, and what was her mind grasping at blurry constructs of flawed memory. They stopped at a stone slab where a pair of mers tied large spiny crabs with rope made from spindly seaweed. A youth perched nearby, braiding more rope.

"The tide is gentle this day." One of the mers, a lavender coloured female, clicked and nodded her head before returning to work.

Asrai nodded, relief spreading through her. "A gentle tide that brings good tidings this day. May Poseidon keep you."

The lavender mer paused her work once more, and looked at Asrai. "You are of Sulu? How have I not seen you before?"

"I *am* Sulu. I am Asrai, daughter of Tuande and Seelacante. It has been many moons since I have seen my people, and then I was but a child. I wish to hold each of you in my thoughts." Asrai nodded her head and clicked.

The large orange mer stopped working and squared up to Asrai. "We of Sulu do not tolerate pretenders."

Asrai took her comb from her hair, and presented it to the orange mer. "I am no pretender. I fled Sulu many moons ago as a child so that I might return one day and restore my lineage. Illyana has protected me and instilled me with the power and wisdom of Poseidon. I am here to right the wrongs of the usurper."

"You carry the gold comb of nobility, but how can we be sure you are our long-grieved princess?" A low frequency pulsed from the orange mer, a challenge.

The sea hag pulled out her comb, held it out for the orange mer to see, then touched it to Asrai's comb. The pair glowed. The water shimmered, then the water mirror revealed a large rune, the symbol of Tuande's rein.

"It truly is you!" The orange mer clicked, bowing his head. "We are honoured by your presence, your brilliance."

"I am known as Damla, your brilliance." The lavender mer thrummed, joy pulsing through the water.

"And I am Oldrik, life mate of Damla." The large orange mer unsheathed his dagger from his wrist plating and flashed the blade. He then sheathed it. "We contribute to Sulu by hunting for crab, and I can turn my hand at stone smithing."

Damla nodded. "Yes. It is hard work. The dead reefs force us to hunt further and further from our borders, but we are proud to bring nourishment to Sulu." She gestured to the youth. "This is our child, Dara. They are a young ambiguous, but already quite skilled with the hunt as well as tide magick."

Asrai nodded. "You are well met. A beautiful family." She twirled her comb, the jewels winking. "May I bless your child?"

Damla flicked her tail fins, her eyes wide. "We would be honoured!"

Oldrik flicked his fingers at the youth. Dara set aside the seaweed ropes and approached. They held their head down, but their deep russet scales shimmered, betraying their excitement.

Asrai smiled and touched her comb to Dara's head. "Your magick is strong. Have you yet chosen your item?"

The youth nodded. From the whirled plating on their arm they took out what was once a fountain pen. Magick had lengthened the pen, and reshaped the nib to be more like a tiny barb. The end was curved to allow a better grip.

"I found it in the caves." Dara held the pen to Asrai.

She inspected the pen, a smile curling her lips. "A lovely object indeed. Your magick has already influenced it quite a bit." Dara nodded. They looked right into Asrai's eyes, unafraid.

"Poseidon sees you," Asrai whispered. She touched her comb to the pen. Both glowed, runes racing across the objects. A tiny diamond sprouted on the lever originally used to fill the pen with ink. Dara's eyes widened. Asrai slipped her comb back into her hair.

"Thank you," Dara whispered. They turned and showed the pen to their parents.

"Your wellspring is growing so fast!" Oldrik bent to inspect the pen.

"Yes, quite extraordinary." Asrai smiled. "I'm glad to see my people flourishing despite the struggles set before them."

Damla raised her hand and clicked at Asrai. "Thank you, your brilliance! Our family thanks you for your blessing!"

****

Asrai moved on, coaxing Cormack to follow. The mers in the neighbouring shop had seen Asrai give blessings, and were eager to share

218

their skills and showcase their magick. The mers began to cluster about her. One of them, a seafoam green mer, swam forward and presented their chosen item: the remains of a farming scythe.

"Your brilliance, I would be honored by your blessing." They held the snapped scythe out to Asrai.

She twirled her comb. "A most unusual object."

The mer bowed their head. "Yes, your brilliance. I found it after a storm."

Asrai touched her comb to the scythe. The two objects glowed, then a small diamond and a sapphire the size of a coin blossomed on the jagged blade. The mer squealed with delight when Asrai withdrew.

"Thank you, your brilliance! Praise Poseidon!"

One of the mers flashed their scales, their arms crossed. "You may be a powerful sea hag, but that does not mean you are truly our fallen princess. She disappeared many moons ago. How are we to know you are she?"

Asrai clicked, trying to soothe the bristling mer. "I know not the tolls Sulu has suffered from the usurper's rule. But lend me your voices, and I shall mend the great hurts so that Sulu can flourish once more."

They glared at Asrai, keeping their distance. "You claim such things, but even a powerful sea hag cannot regrow the dead reefs all on their own."

Cormack watched as the mer swam off, the group parting to allow them passage. The mers shook their heads, and pressed their items toward Asrai, their voices insistent. "Please, your brilliance." A red mer, graying with age pushed a youth forward. "Our lineage has run dry. The wellspring is locked to them, as Sulu has no sea hag or enchanter to open the way."

Asrai bent down toward the youth. It was a young, pink mer. Her hair was cropped to her ears. She held out what was once a hairbrush. All the bristles were gone, and in their place large whelk shells had grown, like porcelain spikes. Asrai touched her comb to the chosen item, and a single diamond grew on the handle.

"I mourn for you," Asrai whispered. "To live so many years without awakening the wellspring, without widening the flow when your abilities have grown. Surely, this has further stunted Sulu."

Cormack pulled out his dagger and examined the emerald that winked on the hilt. His gaze scanned the excited mers, showing one another the new gems on their items. A young mer with radiant celadon scales swam up to Cormack. "An emerald?" he whispered, his eyes wide as he scanned the dagger. "How did you develop such a rare quality?"

"I'm not sure." Cormack shrugged. "I just recently received it."

Lauren A. R. Masterson

The mer nodded. He slid a dagger from the armouring on his arm. It had small sapphires dotting the hilt, and a large jet on the butt of the handle. "Earth magick is rare for mers, even rarer than honing the abyss."

Cormack pointed at the mer's dagger. "You mean that black gem?"

"Yes! It's because I can do this!" He spread his arms, and suddenly, great swirling lines of light pulsed just under his skin. "I can luminesce like the jellyfish of the abyss!"

His eyebrows escaped into his hairline as he watched the mer. "That's amazing!"

The mer lowered his arms, and the light faded from his skin. "What about you? What are your skills?"

Cormack froze. *Asrai has created those water mirrors, but if I say that, he'll ask me to do it. I don't know how to do anything!* He fidgeted the dagger in his hand, words tumbling from his lips. "Well, you see, I'm a warrior. I fight battles."

The mer cocked his head, narrowing his eyes. "Oh, I see."

The sea hag hovered nearby, allowing Asrai to move about her people undisturbed. Cormack slipped away and prodded the sea hag. "Illyana, why don't you speak for Asrai? Surely, you can vouch for her identity? Help put the others at ease?"

She smiled at Cormack, then shook her head. "Your unwavering support for her is a blessing. However, this part of the journey is one she must do on her own. Her people must trust her on her own merit. I would only turn her into a figurehead."

Cormack looked again at Asrai. Some of the mers were wary, floating several yards away, their scales flashing. Asrai remained friendly and serene; he realized that she appeared regal, as if she had always been queen. The mers that clustered about her seemed eager to share and believe, but something still held them back.

"Asrai is not the first Sulu has seen." The sea hag broke Cormack's thoughts. "Past rulers have fallen, and Sulu fell prey to pretenders seizing the throne. In the end, the sea knows its own, but the damage is done and the true heir made to rebuild. So it is with Asrai."

****

Asrai broke away from the marketplace, allowing the mers to go about their business. She led them to a sprawling structure that resembled a bungalow of sorts. The rock walls were low with large windows. Seagrass and coral covered large portions of the walls, making the exterior colourful and bright. Asrai went inside, and Cormack followed. They were met by a lavender mer.

"Good afternoon." She clicked and swept her hand. "Our invalids will rejoice to have company this day."

220

Asrai nodded and darted down one of the halls. Cormack followed and found the space opened into a lounge carpeted in lush sea grasses and sturdy sponges. Among them were mers here and there. They raised their hands and clicked, then touched their foreheads and lips. Cormack was overwhelmed by their joyful greetings.

He clicked back at them, unsure of where to put himself. Asrai swam to one of the mers and took his hand. Cormack realized the mer was missing a chunk of his bicep. A snarl of scars ran down the length of the arm. He looked further still, and saw the mer's fins were mangled into feathery ribbons.

"My brave warriors of Sulu," Asrai thrummed, "I have returned. I, Asrai of Tuande and Seelacante wish to bring you from the abyss of neglect and raise you up to warmer tides."

The wounded mer squeezed Asrai's hand. "Is it true? Have you come here to become our brilliant queen?"

Another mer swam up to them, clicking, his scales flashing. "It has been many moons since the gentle tide of the mighty Tuande. We have languished, forgotten, under the fist of Garradi. Why would you return now?"

Asrai turned to the mer, and bowed her head. "I was but a child. Garradi would have seen me slain, forever ending my great legacy to Poseidon. I come before you now, grown as a warrior with the great skills of a hag."

The mer with the mangled arm nodded. "A pretender would not seek the lowest of Sulu. They would be courting the proud and the strong. She is Sulu!"

Asrai lifted her comb high above her head. "Poseidon sees you." Asrai raised her voice, "As do I! I see you!"

The mers cheered, beating their fists against their armoured plating. Cormack scanned the room again and noticed that all the mers were injured from what looked to be shark attack wounds. Large scars and missing limbs decorated the mers like garish blood runes. He swam closer to a deep viridian mer whose left hand and arm were gnarled, two of the fingers missing and tortile scars twirling around the wrist and up the arm.

The mer touched their hand to their forehead and lips. "Áinle, we are honoured to meet you."

"Áinle?" Cormack turned to Asrai, his head tilted.

She nodded, her hands entwined with a yellow mer's, his midsection deeply scarred. "It is your title. You are my life mate, the champion of Sulu."

He turned back to the viridian mer. "But I have done nothing to earn such a title."

221

The mer smiled and patted Cormack's hand in both of theirs. "We see what lives in your heart. You have sacrificed much."

Panic blazed down Cormack's spine. He swallowed. "Y-you...you do?"

"We know not your tale, Áinle, but the heart knows when another has suffered a loss." The mer released Cormack's hands. Their smile pierced through him, softening his anxiety.

Asrai clicked, raising her hand. She brought it down in a swift swipe, beating her shoulder armour. "You shall ne'er be forgotten! All of Sulu are loved! All of Sulu are drops in the great wellspring! Together we find purpose under Poseidon's wave!"

The mers bellowed and cheered. Asrai's scales shimmered, the excitement plain on her face. Cormack found his chest fit to burst with their shared joy. The invalid mers also shimmered, their renewed hope palpable.

Asrai darted back out of the building. Cormack followed. Golden light filtered into the water. Asrai flirted about. Her fins flicked as she emitted clicks. Cormack watched her as she spun and played. He had never seen such a jubilant display. The water seemed to glow as he joined her. Their exuberance flared, sending a low frequency of water pulses rolling from their sport. Their scales flashed as they twirled faster. As the excitement spiraled down, Cormack felt his gills fluttering, his blood rushing through him. Asrai laughed, her gills flickering in an effort to keep up.

"We are home, my sailor." Asrai embraced Cormack.

His arms tightened around her, their plating scraping. He could feel her body shuddering as she fought to slow her breath. "Thank you." Cormack nuzzled her, emitting a low frequency. "Thank you for sharing this with me."

The sea hag sent a water pulse at them, jarring them from their joy. "Do not celebrate yet. You are not yet queen."

They drew apart. Cormack felt the excitement ripped away. Asrai's face was lined with worry. She flicked her tail, and looked up at the sea hag. "I will be queen."

The sea hag nodded. "Yes. You have done well this day. However, we must rest. Tomorrow you shall go out again and help change the tide."

Chapter Thirty-Two

Mers were finishing their tasks for the day, the marketplace nearly empty. The water was fiery with a blazing sunset. The sea hag slid her comb from her hair, and the magick created a new warren in the sand near the dead reef. Cormack wondered at how the two were able to create a living space from nothing.

"Asrai, if your magick can create all this," he gestured to the glowing floats, "then how are your people suffering? Can they not simply regrow the reef?"

She fiddled with her comb. "No, my sailor. It is rare for mers to possess this deep of a wellspring. We are known as hags for our great prowess. All mers have a wellspring, but most can only perform simple tasks. Creation is difficult and draining."

Cormack slid the dagger from his armoured plating. "Then why waste your magick on creating this place? Won't you need all your strength to fight Garradi?"

Asrai settled onto the plush carpet of sea grass she had created from the sandy floor. She slid her comb back into her hair. "That is why I am a hag. This is a simple feat, especially with the help of another great hag like Illyana. I inherited great power from my mother, Seelacante. She was the greatest hag of her time. And now I shall follow her tide."

"Then why did you need me?" He slid his dagger back into his armour. "Surely I don't possess great magick? I have never known magick in all my life."

She slid her arm up Cormack's side, pulling him into an embrace. "There is an ancient prophesy of one known as Fredsmegler the Peacemaker, a human who relinquishes their ego and unites humans and mers in peace. My heart believes that is you, my dear sailor."

Cormack pulled away, staring down at Asrai. "Yes, you spoke of this before, but I believed it to be just a story."

Asrai shook her head. "All tales are based in Truth. And you have shed your human soul and become my Áinle, just as it was foretold. Now, our bond grows tenfold and nourishes the old magick of the abyss."

"I did not sacrifice my kingdom for some grand prophesy. I simply fell in love with you. I was selfish, and wanted to stay with you, no matter the cost." Cormack felt a strange excitement creeping up his spine. It was mingled with fear at daring to believe something so incredible and impossible.

She drew him into a strong embrace once more. She thrummed, soothing his frantic thoughts. "The sea cares for its own. Poseidon saw you as his own, and now you are here. There is still much to be discovered, my dear sailor. No need to unravel our own tale all at once."

Cormack allowed the lull of the sea grass under him to soothe his nerves. She was right; there were more urgent matters at hand, and they needed their strength for the days to come. He began to drift off as Asrai's heartbeat thrummed against him. As his limbs relaxed, his mind perked up with a sudden, curious thought. "Why doesn't Illyana have a mate?"

Asrai's eyes popped open. Then she smiled and yawned. "That, my dear sailor prince, is a tale for another day."

The morning brought a cold tide, making Cormack shiver. He woke, having to orient himself to life as a mer once more. It was becoming less shocking each day, but his mind still nagged at his lost humanity. Asrai ushered him into the reef, where the sea hag was already making breakfast out of an unfortunate flounder. Cormack found a few small crabs hiding under a large sponge, while Asrai chased a parrotfish. Their meager breakfast pitted Cormack's stomach, adding to the growing knot of anxiety.

The sea hag led them toward Sulu once more. As they approached the market, they found that the mers were gone. The cold tide stirred, making Cormack shiver. He turned to Asrai. "Where is everyone?"

Asrai's scales bristled. She pulled out her comb. "I don't know."

The sea hag pulled out her comb, leading them into the market. Cormack pulled out his dagger, and realized he had no idea how to fight with magick. He tried to take a stance, but realized that his tail made his form all wrong. He settled for following Asrai, his skin prickling at the quiet.

A mer shot from one of the small structures, and the sea hag threw out her arm to block Asrai. Two more mers sped toward them, small hand tridents poised for attack. The sea hag flicked her comb, sending strong water pulses. Two of the mers dodged the attack, but the third was thrown off balance. Asrai twirled away from the sea hag, and sent an attack of her own at the remaining mers. They dodged her attacks and then halted before the trio.

"His greatness, Garradi, has heard of intruders in Sulu!" One of the mers glared at Asrai. "We are to bring you to Garradi for judgement!"

Asrai drew herself up. "I will be the one to pass judgement."

"You are not of Sulu," he growled at Asrai. "Where do you hail from?"

Asrai hissed. "Tell Garradi that the heir has returned."

He blinked at her, shock stretching his face. "How dare you speak the king's name!"

"He is no king!" Asrai bellowed in the mer's face. "I am Asrai, daughter of Tuande and Seelacante!"

The mer shook his head. "That family is dead. Leave now, pretender!"

Asrai growled, baring her fangs. "I, Asrai, challenge Garradi to Draum!"

The mer gaped, then smiled, his fangs gleaming. "Garradi will see you dispatched to the abyss."

They were led through the market toward the castle, a large mass of rock and strange materials Cormack did not recognize. The towers spiraled upward like whelk shells. A guard was posted near the entrance. The mer saluted the guard with his fingers to his forehead, then to his lips. The guard returned the gesture. "Who are these mers? They are not of Sulu."

The mer grinned. "This pretender has challenged Garradi to Draum."

The guard shook his head, flustered. "Is this true?"

Asrai brushed aside the mer, squaring herself up to the guard. "Draum has been called!"

The guard froze. He darted his eyes over Asrai's face, then took his conch shell from his hip strap and blew the summons. The water became cold and still. Cormack shivered as he felt a strange dread seep into his mind. He looked around and saw mers peeking out from the various structures, their eyes wide.

A group of armed mers poured out of the stone archway. Each had a trident in their right hand, and a conch at their hip—all different, as each was picked and hand-crafted by its owner. The guard addressed the soldiers. "This mer has challenged the great king to Draum!"

The soldiers shot Asrai a heated glare. She drew herself up and flashed the scales on her forearms. They bared their fangs at her and hissed. The guard blew his conch again, and the soldiers joined him.

"The king has been challenged to Draum! The king has been challenged to Draum!" the soldiers chanted in unison. The villager mers joined in, punching their fists against the plated scales on their chests or shoulders. The frenzy of beating tails churned the water.

A low bellow silenced them. A guard in one of the spiraling towers leaned out the window, blowing a ram's horn. The low trumpeting sent shivers through each mer. When it stopped, a mer approached from the stone archway. Asrai bared her fangs.

Garradi was not a large or flashy mer, as some rulers were. His body was slender and his scales were yellow and white. His skin was darker, as his tribe had migrated from more tropical waters. His back sported a bright yellow, spiny dorsal fin, fully open and flashing a warning to all.

"Who dares summon Draum?" He swept his gaze over the crowd. He paled when his eyes landed on Asrai's fiery face and exposed fangs.

"I am here to take what is mine!" Asrai screamed, beating her fist against her shoulder plating.

Garradi's face crumpled into a grimace. "Draum de Tuath-e!"

"Draum de Tuath-e!" Asrai shouted the challenge back.

The soldiers took their tridents in both hands and held them horizontal over their bowed heads, conceding to the duel. The sea hag pulled Cormack away from Asrai, and thus a circle was made. Asrai hissed as Garradi took his place in the circle. He flashed his scales at her.

"Finally, I will have the chance to wipe out your fetid bloodline!" Garradi taunted. "Foul Sulu no more!"

Asrai beat her tail. "You killed the great Tuande by cloaked scale! Never would you have defeated him in Draum! You are a coward!"

Garradi charged Asrai, his scales flashing. Asrai dodged him, and swiped his tail with her claws as he passed. He used his dorsal fin to halt his momentum. Asrai pulled out her already-glowing comb. She waved it in a zig-zag, sending a pulse straight for Garradi. The water crashed into his body, jolting him. She charged, fangs barred. Garradi pulled a hand-trident from the armour on his forearm and sent the sands flying upward.

Asrai screamed as she was blinded. Cormack flinched. The sea hag put her hand on his shoulder and shook her head. "No one must interfere. This is Draum."

Cormack clenched his fists as he watched Garradi slam Asrai, sending her crashing into the ocean floor. The thud resonated through the water, making the mers wince. Asrai pushed herself up. Garradi slammed his tail, but Asrai rolled and dodged before the impact could hit her. She twirled her comb and hissed at him.

Garradi was hit with another water pulse. This one sent him sprawling. Asrai charged, darting to flash her scales, her whole body a burning flame. She slammed Garradi down to the ocean floor. Sand erupted from the impact. Garradi whipped his hand-trident and a water pulse caught Asrai by surprise. She spun, struggling to right herself. Garradi beat his tail hard, pushing himself upward.

The mers gasped as Garradi charged Asrai and struck her with his hand-trident. Asrai blocked the attack by lowering her shoulder; the trident clanked against her armour, rather than sinking into her flesh. She bared her fangs and drove them into his neck, strangling his gills. Garradi screamed and hissed as she tore the vulnerable flesh, blood racing into the water.

Asrai flipped and slammed her tail into his side, sending Garradi crashing into the sandy floor again. A cloud of blood trailed after him. Asrai charged down. Her fist connected with the soft flesh just below his chest armour. Blood floated from his mouth; his eyes rolled into the back of his head.

The mers were silent, their eyes on Garradi. Apart from the sway of water moving his hair and fin membranes, he did not move. One of the soldiers approached. She pressed her hand to Garradi's gills and felt no movement. She raised her conch and blew a closing signal.

"Finite du Draum!" She held her trident high and shouted. "Finite du Draum!"

The soldiers blew their conches and took up the chant. The mers joined in, filling in the circle and approaching Asrai. Cormack beat his tail to join her, but the sea hag stopped him again. "It is over. Let them celebrate."

The mers flashed their scales and shrieked clicks of joy. Asrai glowed, her face lit with pride. She reached out to all of them. The soldiers and the guards saluted Asrai, raising their tridents high and beating their tails. They began chanting.

"Our daughter has come home! The great warrior Tuande lives again! The wise hag Seelacante lives again!"

The water changed, becoming warmer and brighter. Cormack could feel the excitement flood him. He flashed his scales and charged Asrai. The mers flinched as he collided with her, embracing her tightly, his tail winding round hers. He pressed his forehead against hers, low clicks escaping his throat.

"I am so proud of you." Cormack's whisper was low and husky.

"This is our home," she whispered back. "We are finally home."

****

The soldiers led them into the castle. Mers pulled down statues of Garradi with ropes. Others smashed seashells carved with runes depicting his name. Asrai darted about the receiving hall, her foggy memories becoming clearer as she saw the high walls and carved ceilings.

A giant clamshell had been carved into a great throne, a soft bed of sea grass planted inside. The stone wall behind the throne was carved with runes and depictions of ancient rulers. Jewels and precious metals had been set in the walls to decorate different parts of the pictographs. Asrai took her seat on the throne. One of the guards pulled down the whalebone trident strapped to the wall high above her. The soldier handed Asrai the trident, their head bowed. The soldiers bowed their heads, as did the mers in the receiving hall.

Asrai straightened. She held the trident aloft and emitted a low frequency that sent a pulse through the water. "I am Asrai of Sulu!

Daughter of Tuande and Seelacante! Descendant of Poseidon! Sulu is restored!"

The mers struck their chests and beat their tails. Asrai pumped the trident again, then handed it back to the guard to put away. "Posei-don grants us a queen!" the mers chanted. "Posei-don grants us a queen!"

The sea hag's eyes shimmered as she watched the ceremony unfold. Pride overflowed her heart. "Well done, my child," she whispered.

"A feast shall be spread in your honour, my queen." One of the mers approached the throne. "What is your first decree for our great kingdom of Sulu?"

Asrai nodded, joy spiking her heart. "I wish all to celebrate with me. Their beloved daughter is home and she wishes to share with all."

The mer smiled and bowed their head. "Yes, my queen." They darted off, their purple scales flashing.

Asrai sank into the throne, grinning at the ceiling. Cormack approached her. Asrai's eyes flashed. "My home is restored! My ancestors rejoice!"

He grinned. "Your joy is my joy, my dear lady."

****

Mers flooded the castle that evening as Asrai's feast began. There were no tables or chairs, as mers felt more comfortable seated on rocks or soft beds of sea plants. The Great Dining Hall was filled with a rainbow of mers lounging and swimming.

Kelp nets hung from the ceiling and walls, and large stone basins dotted the floor. These were filled with fish, crab, mussels, and other various foodstuffs. Yards of sugar kelp draped over iron rods embedded in the walls. The mers flitted about, tasting the different foods and socializing. Asrai enjoyed a purse of seevoo seaweed that had been brought as a present from one of the mer families. She sucked up handfuls of the emerald green plant, and watched as scales flashed about the space.

Cormack tried to figure out how to eat a large spiny crab. A group of nearby mers watched his confusion and whispered to one another. Asrai put down her purse of food and took the crab. She snapped off one of the legs, then sliced the shell open with her claw, revealing the meat. She plucked the morsel and held it to him.

"Delicious!" Cormack exclaimed with his mouth full. He began dismantling the crab with ease.

One of the mers approached Asrai. She had bright green scales that shimmered like sea grass. She bowed her head, then darted her eyes to Cormack. "My queen, is this your life-mate, the Áinle?"

Asrai nodded. "Yes. This is Cormack of Paradine."

"Paradine?" The mer furrowed her brow. "I have not heard of that kingdom."

Love of the Sea

Cormack stopped eating, alarm ringing in his ears. Asrai tipped her head. "I met him while in exile. We fell in love, and he vowed to return me to Sulu."

The mer nodded and swam to another knot of mers, her demeanour stiff. Cormack turned to Asrai, knots of anxiety clenching his stomach. She looked at him, her gaze placid. "Fear not, my prince," she whispered. "I am queen."

Another mer approached, a darker green than the first. Their hair had a blue sheen that played tricks on the eyes. "My queen," they beat their shoulder plating with their fist, "I am honoured to be in your presence. Your return brings hope to us. Sulu has suffered in your absence."

Asrai nodded. She flicked her hand. "This is my home. I spent many moons preparing for this day. I can only imagine the atrocities that occurred under such a pretender."

The mer bowed their head. "We thank Poseidon for your return. It is a new day."

They swam away. Cormack stared after the mer. He fidgeted his hands.

They seem reluctant to speak of Garradi's rule. Was he truly such a tyrant?

A group of mers formed a circle in the center of the hall. They joined hands, their scales shimmering. The room quieted. Cormack watched as the mers began to move in unison, slow at first. Their bodies were swaying, and their tails were sweeping. Their voices rang clear, the singing no longer like a banshee's eerie cry, but clear like deep humming cellos.

> *"Our daughter has returned,*
> *Come home, the tides have turned,*
> *Smash the shackles, raise us up!*
>
> *At your feast as equals we drink and we sup,*
> *Long the moon has shone clear*
> *Poseidon draws the mighty waves near*
> *The path was set, the seasons long*
> *Come back home, daughter where you belong!*
>
> *Gone are days of empty hope*
> *The tides of change spill from the false king's throat!*
> *We are free! Our queen has come!*
> *Prosperous we shall be, the sadness undone!*

Lauren A. R. Masterson

They raised their hands, all still linked together. Their swaying made them appear as a blossom blooming in the breeze. Asrai raised her palm and emitted clicks. The other mers followed suit, and Cormack copied them. He smiled as he realized it was applause.

"Thank you for the gift of your voices." Asrai quieted the hall once more. "We are one again. Sulu shall grow wild and beautiful with me. I have many things to teach you, and many things to learn from you."

The mers held their fists in the air, saluting their new queen. Cormack was unsure of what to do. He raised his fist in the air as well, which Asrai promptly ensnared. "Áinle is eager to learn of Sulu and rule by my side. He too has much to teach us." She held her hand high, entwined with his. "A new tide has swept Sulu clean. Let us grow anew and bring forth new life!"

The mers cheered and clicked. Asrai lowered hers and Cormack's hands. "I am queen, my sailor," she whispered. Her scales shimmered.

Cormack felt his mind buzzing again. The water felt warmer, and Asrai's closeness made his scales bristle. He looked down and saw his scales were shimmering, the blue running through the black. Asrai smiled, showcasing her fangs. Cormack twitched with excitement. "Later," she whispered. Her eyes flashed.

Chapter Thirty-Three

Asrai wove the tiara into her hair as she sat in the sea hag's old bedchambers. The diamonds and tears sparkled in her nest of curls. The sea hag snapped her comb, sending a small pulse of water at Asrai. "Are you paying any attention to what I have been saying?"

Asrai glowered. "I know my past! You've told me over and over—"

"Not the beginning." The sea hag held Asrai's gaze. "The reason Garradi stole your throne. It is time you know." The water became colder as Asrai settled onto a smooth, bare stone. Asrai shivered.

"Your mother was of the same tribe as Garradi." The sea hag slipped her comb back into her hair. "They came from Kichi, the warm waters that boil in the South." Asrai flinched. The idea of sharing blood with the usurper made her mind haze with rage.

"A great storm had smashed their reef, and there was not enough food to go around. Their tribe needed to disperse and allow the reefs to regrow. A small clan came here to Sulu. Tuande was a mighty warrior king, but also welcoming. He knew that Sulu was a great kingdom, and wanted mers from all across the oceans to understand and enjoy its greatness."

Asrai trembled. Knowing her father had welcomed this traitor with open arms made her reimagine her battle with such ferocity that her scales glimmered. The sea hag took out her comb again. She swirled it in a slow circle. "Be still, my child. You must listen."

The water around Asrai became warm and soothing. Her rage dripped away. The sea hag twiddled her comb and continued. "Your father took notice of one particular mer: your mother. Her exotic beauty enticed him. And so, he set out to claim her."

Asrai curled up on the rock. Her parents had never shared their first encounters with Asrai. She smiled at the sea hag. "This is not a happy story, my child." The sea hag shook her head. "For you see, your mother was in love with another member of her own clan."

It was not uncommon for mers to claim mates from already established pairs, if the mate is willingly won. Asrai shrugged. "My mother and father were loving mates. Old lovers belong to the past."

The sea hag held her comb tight. "Your father was king. Your mother could not refuse any more than a mer could refuse you now. Your mother was torn from her love. It was either that, or the banishment of her clan."

Asrai bristled. No! Her father was a just leader; he would never use his power so selfishly. She flashed her eyes. "You are wrong! My mother loved my father!"

"Yes, she grew to love him. Even more so when you were born. Your father showered your mother with treasures and trinkets. He wrote her songs and poetry. But that was the price he paid for breaking her heart." The sea hag met Asrai's gaze. Her eyes flashed. She held her spell of calm over Asrai, like a loose net hovering above a rabid animal.

"Garradi never forgave your father. When your mother was killed, he saw it as part of your father's betrayal. He killed your father and vowed to kill you as well, that last evidence of your father's evil deeds."

Asrai felt a yawning void of despair open in her heart. Losing her parents had been the devastation that had turned her life into exile and lonely study. She had seen her new purpose as redemption for her lineage. Now her heart ached and her mind was numb, her victory hollow.

"The usurper needed to be removed." The sea hag maintained the net of calm, though Asrai did not bother to fight it. "He had refused to take a mate, vowing that your mother was his only mate. Sulu would have fallen into chaos without a secure lineage. Restoring you to the throne with a life mate was the only way to save our kingdom from war."

The words hung in the water, buzzing about Asrai's head. Her mind replayed Draum over and over. She imagined Cormack being taken away from her, to be loved by another. Though her heart did not flare in a fiery rage due to the spell, she still felt the agony and the searing jealousy.

"And my father? He is a tyrant then? I am the offspring of a great shame?"

The sea hag shook her head. Her face softened. "No, my child. You are the daughter of two great mers, one a warrior, and one a hag such as myself. Now it is up to you to rule as Asrai. As yourself."

****

Cormack retreated further down the hall. Asrai's horrified face burned into his mind. His chest was tight and warm. He was reminded again of the princesses who had been sent to court him. How many were torn from lovers and sent off to marry in the name of a kingdom's security? Guilt boiled in his stomach. He had sought the sea to escape, and yet the nightmare of broken love followed him even here.

I was a fool to think the sea was as calm and perfect as a sunny summer day. I was sailing on its surface, merely playing. The sailors had always said the sea is a cruel mistress, and I refused to take heed.

Cormack settled on a rock carpeted in seagrass. He played with his dagger, sheathing and unsheathing it. The day whirred through his mind on a loop. Asrai had gone from exile to queen in an instant. Her brutality was swift, her anger raw. Cormack ran his fingers over the runes carved into the dagger hilt.

I have never known a need for vengeance. I have never felt such anger. His mind shied away from the memory of his petty jealousy. *My worries have been nothing. My cares, insignificant. I have never known the true loneliness as she has.*

His thoughts were cut as Asrai darted into the room. Cormack sheathed his dagger and sat up straight. She halted with such a fierce jerk that it sent a water pulse into the stone wall.

Cormack fidgeted his hands, unsure of how to help. Asrai slid her claws in and out of her fingers. Her fangs were bared, her eyes wild. Gold and crimson flashed a warning, rippling through her scales like dragon fire.

"Asrai, are you—"

"No!" she snapped, rounding on him. Magick crackled through her hair. "Do not pretend! You know my pain! I can feel you, always!"

He darted his eyes away, chastised. "You knew I was listening?"

Asrai shivered. "Yes. The wellspring connects us. We shall always know where the other is. Feel what the other feels."

Cormack ran his hand through his hair. The dull burning in his chest flared. *So that's what that is.* "I'm sorry."

"Do not pity me!" Asrai bellowed, sending a shock of water pulsing toward Cormack.

He threw himself to the sandy floor to avoid her tantrum. The water smacked into the stone walls.

"I *don't* pity you." Cormack straightened and inched toward her. "I cannot describe what I feel. But I do know that there is no sense in drowning in your past."

Asrai hissed as he neared. Cormack ignored her defensive front. "As the sea hag said, you are you. Today I saw an entire kingdom rejoice at your return. Your connection to Garradi means nothing to them."

She bristled as he reached his hand out to her. Asrai bared her fangs again. "I was born of broken love and suffering! I should not be!"

Cormack took her arm. She wrenched it away and hissed at him again. He took her arm again, his grip firm. "Don't ever say that." His voice was low. "Do not ever wish yourself away."

Asrai started at Cormack's sudden aggression. He pulled her into his arms. His scales vibrated as he emitted a low frequency. It went right through Asrai, breaking her anger.

"I chose you just as much as you chose me," he growled. "Never forget that."

Asrai wound her arms around him, her anger dissipating. She hummed a low frequency as well, joining her voice with his. They stayed still for a moment, the water around them growing warm again. Cormack pulled away so he could look at her face. Asrai looked up at him, her gaze gentle and curious once more.

"So long as you are at my side, I shall bear it," Asrai whispered.

He nodded and kissed her forehead. "You have already done so much for your people. They know you shall be a magnificent queen. And I know it as well."

Asrai made soft clicks. She nuzzled Cormack's neck.

"You flatter me." Asrai's voice trailed off into a low hum.

Cormack nipped at her collarbone, his scales glittering. She flinched, her chest and shoulders shivering. He bit again, harder this time. "And though I can only have you all to myself in small moments such as these," he dug his claws into the scales on her back, "it is so worth it to be life mate to such a queen."

Water pulses thudded against the stone walls as they fought and chased one another in a frenzy of mating. Their scales shone bright like living jewels. Cormack dug deep into their shared wellspring; he found Asrai's hurt, her fury, and deeper yet, her loneliness. He squeezed each one of these rooted pains, his heart thundering to break them.

Asrai found there was no up or down, only the overwhelming surge of joy and the panicky need for more. Cormack answered her throaty growls and playful clicks with love spun even sweeter with magick. She could feel him invading her wellspring, and she opened further, allowing him deeper into her heart.

It was then that she felt her wellspring growing and spilling forth. She dug into Cormack's wellspring and found the doubt, the guilt, and the desperate desire to please his queen. Her heart shuddered to see his Truths laid bare. It was then that she knew.

My dearest sailor, my Áinle. You are my champion, the gentle hero that Sulu needs. We are truly healed, at last.

****

Cormack sat up and rubbed his eyes. Asrai was seated near one of the large open windows. Her hair floated about, her scales shimmering in the early morning light. "Good morning, my sailor," Asrai murmured, her gaze fixed out the window.

He stretched and moved toward her. "You're up early."

Asrai shivered as Cormack draped his arms about her shoulders. She dropped her gaze and smiled. "Yes, I could not sleep." She tilted her head back.

Cormack furrowed his brow. "Oh? Are you feeling unwell?"

"I am with child." She squeezed his hand.

Cormack felt a rush of joy surge through his chest. Shivers washed over him as Asrai's words echoed in his mind. "You-you are with child?"

Love of the Sea

Asrai giggled. She twirled and embraced him. "Yes, my dear sailor!"

"I am to be a father!" he bellowed as he embraced Asrai tight. "I'm a father!" They laughed and flirted with one another.

"You must not say a word about it." Asrai's voice lowered. "I must tell the council first so they may begin the plans."

Cormack's smile dropped. "Plans?"

Asrai nodded. She took both his hands in hers. "Fear not, my sailor. I am queen. And you are my Áinle. There is much to be done to inform the people of our joy, as well as prepare for the new life."

He squeezed her hands. "I understand. I shall stand by you through all."

She hugged him. His chest plating scratched the delicate scales and flesh on her chest; it heightened her excitement. "You are truly strange, my sailor. And I love you for it."

He held her close, a low thrum emitting from his throat. Their tails swished. Asrai dropped one of her hands to her stomach. "Knowing that this child shall be born of love mends the past," she whispered. "We have come full circle, and I have all that my mother desired."

Cormack kissed the crown of Asrai's hair. He could feel her happiness, along with the aching pain. "I am here. No one can take me away from you. I would die first."

Asrai joined his low frequency. The water pulsed around them as they became enthralled in the wellspring of their magick and emotions. At long last, Asrai pulled away. "Ready?"

He grinned. "Absolutely."

****

The guards greeted them. Asrai took her place on the throne. She emitted a low frequency that cut through the room. Cormack flinched, then gathered his wits and sat beside her. He realized it was a call of summons as the sea hag and a handful of mers entered the room. Stones had been magicked, seating the council in a crescent. Cormack fidgeted on his stone seat to the left of Asrai's throne. The sea hag sat in the place of honour, on the stone closest to Asrai's right.

"I have met my people once more. I looked into the many eyes of Sulu." Asrai shifted in her throne, her gaze piercing. "There are those who have suffered under the rule of the usurper. They cry out for care. No mer shall languish under my rule. No triumph or injury shall be forgotten!"

The council bowed their heads. The sea hag was first to look up again.

"The invalids have been last in thought. Today, they shall be first." Asrai twirled her comb. "I know Sulu is struggling to feed itself, and that we have little to spare. I implore the council to leave no coral undiscovered, and find what workers we can to assist those in such great need."

The council murmured. An older maroon coloured mer swished his tail. "You truly are the brilliant light of Sulu." He tilted his head. "However, as you said, there is not much to be spared."

Asrai let her eyes scan the hall. "I see that much work was spared for the atrocities the usurper built. I do not ask my people to battle the tide. I only ask them to swim together, as one."

The maroon mer nodded, his eyes finding the cracks and gouges in the stonework. "Yes, and Sulu suffered greatly for his selfishness. We are heartened by your desire for generosity, but we must also be vigilant to the greater needs of Sulu."

Asrai banged her fist on her plating. "Are they not Sulu? Am I not Sulu? All are Sulu, and Sulu is all!"

The council flinched. The maroon mer dropped his eyes to the sandy floor. Asrai flared her fins, but lowered her voice. "What in my home can be spared?"

The maroon mer looked up again. He tilted his head. "There are mers who currently serve you who may be able to leave the household for a time."

"See to it then." Asrai flicked her comb. "They do Sulu a great service. See to it they are honoured."

The council clicked in approval. Asrai allowed a smile to curl her lips. Cormack let the water rush from his lips. It was then he realized the loosening knot of anxiety in his chest was more than his own. He looked at Asrai, pride swelling in his heart.

Chapter Thirty-Four

"In addition to my first order, I have also called you all here for a joyous announcement." Asrai swept her gaze over the mers. "I am with child."

The room exploded with cheers and clicks. Cormack grinned, his fangs gleaming as his scales flashed. Asrai waited for the excitement to subside before continuing. "This child shall be a powerful mer, sharing the lineage of both Sulu and the warrior tide of Paradine. This new life will also expand our wellspring, bringing us closer to repairing the damage done to our kingdom."

Asrai's scales shimmered as she shifted in her throne. "I want the people of Sulu to know of this child's greatness. I want to instill the same thrill in their hearts, that our joy may be one."

The sea hag straightened. "Every mer shall delight in your joy, my dear. May we have your word to begin preparations for the formal announcement and first blessing?"

Asrai lifted her hand and emitted a few clicks. "You may begin. However, I do not want a feast planned. Instead, I would like a simple communal meal shared for the second blessing, as the reef is not yet restored. It is hard for my people to be joyous if they feast one day, and starve the next." The council clicked in approval.

She held her hand up. "You are dismissed."

Cormack stretched and swam at Asrai's side toward the small dining grotto. The council dispersed, but the sea hag followed the couple. "This is joyous news, my child," she murmured. A low frequency hummed through her.

They seated themselves in the grotto. One of the serving mers brought out bowls of brown antler seaweed and a spool of sugar kelp. A second mer approached with a net filled with glossy sardines. "Your brilliance." The mers bowed their heads. "Our scouts found a large school of sardines during the night. Sulu is currently enjoying them."

Asrai nodded, plucking a few from the net. They wriggled between her hands. She speared them with her claws one at a time. Cormack also took a few sardines. He followed Asrai's lead, and ate them whole. Their oily flavour was pleasing. He grasped a handful of brown antler seaweed as the net was passed to the sea hag.

The serving mers exited, allowing Asrai peace. The sea hag flicked her eyes about, then smiled at Asrai. "I shall perform a blessing to

Poseidon in your honour." She swallowed a few bites of seaweed. "Long have I waited for this glorious day."

Asrai smiled as she helped herself to more antler seaweed. She played with her claws. "Poseidon be praised. I have been blessed with every treasure."

The sea hag's eyes flashed. "Do not underestimate your sacrifices, my child. You spent far too many moons in darkness."

"It is a new tide. We must swim ever forward with it." Asrai speared a few more sardines.

Cormack felt a hot flare of pain in his chest. He swallowed. Asrai's past still plagued her. He took another handful of seaweed and mulled a few platitudes in his mind, but none seemed sufficient. His heart ached, wanting to soothe her great hurt. A low thrum escaped his throat. Asrai turned. She smiled and took his hand in hers. He could feel the small joy growing in her heart.

The maroon mer approached them. He touched his hand to his lips and clicked. "Forgive me for interrupting, but we are ready for the announcement, your brilliance."

"Yes, we are ready." Asrai squeezed Cormack's hand. "May our joy be one with Sulu."

They followed the maroon mer to the great balcony that was positioned high above the main square. The sand glittered with the rainbow of mers. They cheered when Asrai leaned over the railing. Clicks and the beating of armour plating filled the water. Cormack grinned, his throat thrumming with joy.

Asrai held up her hand, silencing the mers. Her voice rang out, a low frequency carrying it. "My people! Poseidon has answered our prayers. Sulu shall live on! My people! Join me in celebration, for I am with child!"

The wall of noise struck Cormack with such force that it took his breath away. The rainbow shimmered as scales glittered with magick and joy. Little fizzes of light bounced through the water as the mers celebrated.

"Take my hand." Asrai grinned at Cormack. "The celebration has begun!"

He did as he was bid. Asrai led him off the balcony. They dove toward the surging crowd. Asrai cried a joyful note as she headed straight for the center. Cormack joined her, his body in control. Soon the mers were all singing the same high note, the sound connecting them. Hands and arms encircled them as Asrai and Cormack entered the center of the crowd. The mers joined together, as they had at the banquet, their arms entwining like a giant blossom. The water was warm, and balls of light and magick still rocketed about. Asrai touched her forehead to Cormack's. Their hearts beat as one. His chest felt hot as he felt their wellspring filling.

Love of the Sea

The sea hag floated above them, her jeweled comb brandished high. "Vi er ett! Sammen er vi Sulu!"

Asrai picked up the chant, and soon the water was filled with the joyous words, "We are one! Together we are Sulu!" Cormack had never felt more alive, more connected. Low frequencies burst from him as his emotions overwhelmed him. He finally belonged. The sea hag swirled her comb, sending radiant aurora borealis surging through the water. The mers grew quiet as they watched the flickering colours.

Cormack put his arms around Asrai. "I would like for us all to be a family, together," he whispered, his fangs tickling her ear.

Asrai smirked and flinched away from him. "But we are together, my sailor. We are finally one with Sulu."

He shook his head, the warmth still radiating through him, making him bold. "I would like to join Sulu and Paradine. I may have abandoned my throne, but I can never abandon my family."

She nuzzled his neck. "In time, my sailor. There is much to be done here. In time, they will know us again."

****

The water was bathed in fiery orange light as the sun set. The sea hag swirled her comb again, fading the aurora borealis. The mers began to disperse, back to their homes. Asrai led Cormack back into the palace. A large stone table had been set before the throne. Small stone seats were clustered on the outer ring. Asrai took her place on the throne, Cormack at her side. The council trailed in, taking their seats. Serving mers appeared, bearing a giant coelacanth.

Cormack wondered at the strange fish. It looked more like a sea monster than something the fishermen would bring up in their nets. It was heaved onto the stone table. One of the serving mers handed Asrai a large, curved knife, the handle decorated with woven seaweed and abalone shell.

"May Poseidon grant me the strength and wisdom of the abyss as I carry my child to fruition!" Asrai held the knife aloft, then plunged it into the carcass. She dragged it along the belly, innards spilling out onto the table.

She handed the knife back. "As a mother, I shall become servant to my child. As queen of Sulu, I shall become servant to the future of my kingdom."

Cormack watched as Asrai cut hunks of flesh with her claws. She handed the first cuts to the serving mers. They bowed their heads and held the food in their hands, waiting. Asrai then cut portions for the council and the sea hag, who also waited. Finally, she handed Cormack a cut of flesh and held her own portion before her.

"Together we shall feast on this ancient being. Together we are bonded to serve this child, to serve the future!"

Asrai took the first bite, gobbling up her portion of food. The council and serving mers followed suit. Cormack took a bite. He found the flavour to be strange, but not unpleasing. Once the first round was completed, the serving mers began butchering the fish with small knives and sharing them with the small group. Soon the table was covered with fishbones and scales. Bowls of seaweed were brought out, and the mers lounged, their bellies full.

Cormack picked at the seaweed. He wondered at how quickly his body had adjusted to life in the sea. He did not miss boar and potatoes, and found his belly craved the freshness of seaweed and the sweetness of crabs. A pang went through him as he remembered Pamela's oat cakes. He sighed.

"Let us retire, Áinle. Tomorrow's festivities will require sharp minds and strength." Asrai touched Cormack's hand.

He nodded, squeezing her hand. "As you wish."

The council and serving mers dispersed to their own sections of the palace. Asrai led Cormack back to their quarters. The water grew dark, and luminescent creatures gave off an eerie glow in the gloom.

"Do not be troubled, my sailor." Asrai embraced him. "Once the official ceremonies are over, I shall see about creating an alliance with Paradine. But for now, let your worries escape you. This is a time of great joy."

Cormack pressed his forehead against Asrai's. He snuck a kiss from her lips, then a low thrum escaped his throat. "Your joy is my joy."

****

The morning broke through Cormack's strange dreams. The water was warm as the sun filtered through the waves above. Asrai was still asleep, curled beside him. Cormack pulled her against him. "Good morrow, my Lady Asrai," he whispered into her ear.

Asrai stirred. She hugged his arms against her. Their scales scraped against each other. "My dear sailor."

Cormack lowered one of his hands, ghosting his fingers over her belly, still flat and taut. She shivered. "Do not tempt me." She fidgeted away from him. "There is a hunt today. We will need all our strength."

He released her, stretching. "A hunt?"

Asrai rose and stretched her arms high above her head. "Yes. Today we shall join the best hunters to create a feast for Sulu."

Cormack's eyes darted from Asrai's face to her stomach. "But you are with child! Should you risk such strenuous activities?"

She laughed. "Are humans truly so fragile that the world must stop when their bellies are filled? No, my dear Áinle. To quicken the life inside me I must hunt, I must cast magick, I must do all that I intend for my child to do once they are borne from me."

Love of the Sea

His eyes scanned Asrai's body one more. Her powerful frame seemed unfazed by her new maternal status. He felt the excitement rising in him again.

"Come, Áinle. We have much to do." Asrai flitted into the hall.

Cormack followed, his mind still whirring. They were met not by the council, but a group of fierce mers holding various weapons and nets.

"Join us, your brilliance!" one of the mers cheered upon seeing Asrai enter.

She thrust her fist in the air. "Today I join you, mighty hunters of Sulu!"

Cormack was handed a long driftwood spear and a sharpened piece of iron. Asrai was given the same knife she had used to carve the coelacanth. The party led them out into the main square, then out into the wilds of the reef.

****

The hunting party swam East toward deeper waters. The leading mer held their hooked spear aloft, signaling them to halt. Cormack's eyes adjusted to the shimmering gloom. In the depths were large shadows. Unfamiliar clicks twirled toward them.

Asrai swam to the leading mer. She took out her comb. Low frequencies emitted from her, traveling down into the depths. The clicks changed to the same low frequency. Asrai slipped her comb back into her hair, and nodded to the leading mer. They tilted their heads to the hunting party, then began swimming further East, away from the shadows.

Cormack approached, his hands fidgeting. "What were those things?"

"A family of porpoises." Asrai smiled, as if remembering something. "They already claimed the area for hunting today. We shall find somewhere else."

He wondered at the idea of asking other creatures for permission. The fishing vessels of Paradine simply went where they would, forcing dolphins and larger fish out of the way. The hunting party stopped again, this time at a sloping rock shelf. A small reef was growing from the outcroppings. Colourful fish darted about.

Hunger rumbled through Cormack's stomach as a small school of parrot fish flash through the reef like balls of turquoise. He started when Asrai led the hunting party toward the murky sands below. Movement caught Cormack's eye. A few spiny crabs strolled over the sand, disturbing a school of flounder. The lead mer emitted a shrieking click, and the hunting party rushed forth.

Asrai speared several flounder, urging Cormack to keep up. The mers chased down the fleeing flat fish, their strange bodies trying to swim sideways across the sand. The nets soon filled with the writhing fish, and a few of the crabs were hooked onto a fishing belt.

The hunting party rejoiced at the lucky find, but Cormack felt a shudder rip away his joy. The water changed. Large shadows raced toward the group. They did not click and cheer like the porpoises had. The mers screamed as Cormack charged right at a trio of ridgeback sharks. He sunk the spear into the eye of the lead shark. His claws dug into the shark's side, raking the flesh and spilling blood.

"Áinle! Fall back! Fall back!" one of the hunting mers shrieked.

Asrai was held back by two of the hunting mers. They brandished their spears, protecting their queen. "Cormack!" Asrai shrieked, trying to escape the mers. "Cormack! Don't leave me!"

His blood boiled with Asrai's fear. The blood in the water caused the sharks to frenzy and attack their fellow. Cormack wrenched the spear from the carcass and made a wide loop around the scene. His tail beat hard as he charged again.

"Áinle!" the lead mer bellowed, charging at the outlying shark.

Together, they slaughtered the sharks. Three of the hunting mers followed Cormack's lead, raking claws and tridents down the sharks' sides. He stabbed the belly of one of the great beasts, spilling entrails. Cormack's low calls boomed across the abyss. Asrai shivered. The mers held their position, tight, shielding Asrai.

Cormack collected himself, reason pushing aside the primal instincts. His gills fluttered as he took in the scene. The water clouded with blood. His eyes darted over the mers, counting for casualties. The lead mer whooped, twirling their spear. Cormack joined in, his voice rising in triumph. The mers relaxed and gathered the shark carcasses. Asrai slammed into Cormack, her body shaking. He held her tight with his free arm. She hummed a low frequency. Their wellspring shook as her fear rolled into relief and joy.

"Áinle, slayer of sharks! Áinle, slayer of sharks!" the mers chanted.

Cormack grinned, releasing Asrai. She looked at him, her face filled with awe. It crumpled and she punched him in his chest armour. "Don't you ever leave me!" Her fierce voice belied her excitement. "Don't you ever leave me!"

"Never," he trilled. "Nothing can take me from you."

Chapter Thirty-Five

The hunting party led them back to the castle. The mers rejoiced at their return, and cheered when they saw the nets straining with the fresh catch. The hunting mers shared the story of the sharks as they swam toward the castle, the knot of followers growing into a large crowd. News reached the council, and they waited outside.

"Áinle!" The maroon mer spread his arms wide. "Áinle, our great slayer of sharks! We welcome you home!"

The green mer of the council raised her hands high, her fangs flashing as she smiled. "Asrai! Asrai, our brilliant queen! We welcome you home!"

"Sulu shall feast well! Our people will rejoice!" The lead hunter gestured to the straining nets.

Asrai led the way into the receiving hall. The maroon mer magicked the stone table as Asrai took her place on the throne. Cormack hesitated, watching as the hunters dumped the prizes on the table. One of the hunting mers touched his forehead, then his lips. "Áinle, we are moved by your courage. Even our bravest warriors balk at the mighty shark. Your love for our beloved queen is legendary."

The other mers touched their foreheads and lips as well. Cormack fidgeted his hands. The three ridgeback sharks were still bleeding, their bodies rendered to fleshy carnage. His eyes darted about the mers. "I have been trained in combat since my youth. It seemed only natural to protect my lady and her people." Cormack played with his claws.

The emerald mer flinched at his words. "The warriors of Sulu train from youth as well. However, charging at not even a single shark, but a group of sharks…it is simply unheard of!"

One of the hunters put his hand on Cormack's shoulder. "Áinle's bravery swept a fierce tide in our hearts! It was all we could do not to rush to his side and assist his attack."

Cormack could feel the warmth of Asrai's pride growing in his chest, mixing with his sheepish thoughts. He looked up and saw her radiant smile. Her scales shimmered when she caught his gaze. "Our Áinle is truly a champion, as are all warriors of Paradine." Asrai widened her smile, showcasing her fangs. "They are to be our great allies, our friends in tide."

The mers cheered, clicks and shrieks echoing in the hall. "Paradine, our friends in tide! Paradine, our friends in tide!"

Cormack felt his own pride growing. His heart ached for the sounds of the combat drills in the courtyard, and even his father's map room. He cheered along with the mers, his eyes on Asrai as she nodded to him. The spoils of the hunt were divided under Asrai's orders. She sent large portions to the invalids, as she feared they were only receiving inferior seaweed and scraps. The bulk of the share was to be sent to the villagers, so all could go home to a satisfying meal. Asrai only kept a small portion for herself and the royal staff.

"We are all Sulu. My position as queen does not entitle me to feast while my people go hungry. All shall eat. All are equal."

A small party of scouts returned with fresh antler seaweed and sugar kelp. Asrai kept the bulk of this, as it was crucial to the growth of her unborn child. Cormack entwined his tail around hers as they ate in the dining grotto. His claws flicked over her belly every now and again. "Thank you for acknowledging Paradine today," Cormack whispered. "My people will be proud to be allies of Sulu."

Asrai swallowed her mouthful of kelp. "Our alliance must be a secret. The other human kingdoms must never know."

"But what of the prophesy you spoke of? Of Fredsmegler?" He darted his eyes over Asrai's face.

She shook her head. "Though I know it to be true in my heart, the danger is too great. I am sorry, my sailor."

Cormack flinched, then realized the peril that could creep over their kingdoms at the knowledge of a merfolk ally. "Yes, I understand."

"Remember, this is your home now. We honour your kin, but Sulu shall always have priority." She took his hand and placed it over her stomach again. "You are of Sulu now."

He softened, his face stretching into a smile. "Yes. I am truly a mer now."

****

Daily life in Sulu had eased into a secure lull. Cormack was eager to learn and followed Asrai on her excursions out into Sulu. Together, they spoke with the mers, addressing problems large and small. Asrai continued to open and expand the wellsprings of her people through their chosen items. Cormack was often addressed as "Shark Slayer" alongside his official title as Áinle, and all misgivings about his strange naiveté was wiped away.

The undercurrent of anxiety from hunting further afield for food mounted the pressure for Asrai. The recovery of the reefs remained stunted, even with the surge in magick to the deep wellspring of Sulu. Their efforts were still not enough. Drastic action was required, and she knew where she could find a deeper source of magick to quell their desperation. Asrai's comb glowed as she swirled it. The water in their sleeping chambers shimmered, taking on a more solid appearance until Cormack was staring into Peter's bedchambers. The sun filtered through the arrowslit windows, shining slices of light over the floor. Peter sat, his chin resting in his hand, his elbow on the table. His other hand curled around a flagon.

The comb glowed brighter, and Asrai tested the mirror with her fingers. The water did not ripple. She nodded to Cormack. He approached the water mirror, a knot of anxiety tightening around the ball of excitement in his stomach.

"Good morrow, Peter."

His cousin's head jerked, his eyes wide. He flinched when he saw the water mirror. "Peter, it's me, Cormack. Your cousin."

Cormack pulled Asrai closer so Peter could see her. "Asrai and I wanted to reassure you. We hoped enough time had passed."

"Sorcery!" Peter managed to gasp. His body shook as his eyes darted about the vision.

"It's all right." Cormack held up his hand. "We can hear and see you, but we cannot touch you or come through. It's like a window."

Peter looked around at the edges of the water mirror. His eyes narrowed. "Such feats are only accomplished by the most talented of the White Veil. I knew she was not human! She bewitched you!"

"Yes and no." Cormack ran his hand through his hair.

Asrai kept her face smooth and impassive, but her heart wilted as she watched Cormack struggle. "Asrai granted me my greatest wish," Cormack continued. "I am one with the sea. I am one with Asrai and the sea."

Peter sneered. "I knew you were a childish fool, but to abandon your kingdom for such frivolity!"

Cormack shook his head. "Not so, Cousin. I would never abandon my home. I saw to it that the kingdom had the ruler they deserved. We both know that certainly was not I."

The words sent shivers racing through Peter. He gasped at the water mirror. "You-you planned this?"

"Yes, well, as best as I could. You have always had a head for strategy and economy." He grinned. "I was just a silly prince with a boat."

Peter's face softened and darted his eyes away. "At the very least, it is good to know you live."

"Please, Cousin, I come to you with an offer of peace." Cormack's voice shook. "Asrai and I would like to make ourselves known again. We wish our kingdoms to be allies."

"What?" Peter's mind whirred. "Kingdom? What on earth are you talking about?"

Cormack laughed. "Not on earth, under the sea. Asrai's home, the kingdom of Sulu. She is queen, and I am still kin of Paradine. I hope our two homes can work together."

Peter stared at the water mirror, mouth agape. His eyes darted about over Cormack's face and torso. He scrubbed his face with his hand. "That's it...I have finally gone mad...." he muttered. "I'm seeing visions and have finally gone mad...."

Cormack sensed Peter's change in mood. His voice became firm. "If you doubt me, or any of this, call upon Pamela. She will know this is true."

"The head cook?"

Asrai stabbed her comb at the water mirror, her eyes bright with magick. "Bring us Pamela! Now!"

Peter found he could not help but obey. "Poseidon help me," he muttered as he exited into the hall.

****

He followed the hall until he found the servants' staircase. It was dark and cramped. He wondered at how Cormack would gallivant up and down it at all hours. He soon reached the kitchen, the heat bearing down upon him. The servants froze, wide-eyed when they saw Peter enter. A serving girl dropped her scrubbing brush. It fell into her bucket and splashed soapy water all over her apron and dress. Another serving girl snapped to attention and bobbed a curtsy.

"Yer majesty, what c'n we do you fer?"

Peter swiveled his gaze, locating Pamela's hulking frame. He spoke with far more confidence than he felt. "I require the head cook, immediately."

Pamela froze. She pulled her great wooden spoon from the stew she had been stirring and turned 'round to face Peter. "Yes, your majesty?"

He nodded, and turned, indicating she follow. "I require your expertise."

The servants stared as Pamela slipped her spoon into a tin cup. She wiped her hands on her apron and bobbed her head. "As you wish, sire."

She followed him back up the servants' staircase. As soon as their footsteps became faint, the kitchen was abuzz with whispering, their faces pale as they worried Peter had been afflicted with the same madness that had stolen their dear crown prince.

****

Pamela puffed up the stairs. Peter ignored her discomfort. When they reached his bedchambers, Pamela flinched. "Your majesty, I don't think—?"

"I assure you, my intentions are diplomatic. Nothing more." Peter escorted Pamela inside. She gasped when she saw the water mirror. She felt her body flood with a sharp excitement that clenched her heart.

"Pamela!" Cormack shouted. His eyes glittered.

"Poseidon's wave!" Pamela croaked as she stepped toward the vision. "Cormack, is it truly you?"

He nodded. "Yes, Asrai and I are here."

Asrai fidgeted with her glowing comb. "It's a simple spell, really."

Pamela sat down in one of the chairs. She gaped at the water mirror. It shimmered quite close to her face. "Where have you been? Everyone thinks you were stolen away, or worse."

Asrai had instructed Pamela on the wedding day to play the fool. If it was found that she knew of and aided in their escape, she would have been executed. She needed no play-acting, her relief and excitement genuine.

Peter approached the water mirror again. He looked at Pamela. "Then, this is real? This is truly my cousin?"

Pamela nodded. A fat tear rolled down her ruddy cheek. She scrubbed it away. "Aye."

"Don't worry, we are quite real." Cormack laughed. "Alive and well. Asrai has found her kingdom once more. And we are bonded." He looked down at Asrai, and she up at him. They touched foreheads for a moment, a low humming emanating from them.

"I knew your love was true." Pamela's voice was thick. "It does my heart good to know you are happy at last."

Peter waved his hand. "Yes, well, this certainly did not do Uncle any good."

Cormack jerked his head. "Something has happened to Father?"

Pamela darted her eyes away. Peter sighed, crossed his arms, and regarded the floor.

"King Dominic is dead. Poseidon keep his soul."

****

The water rushed from Cormack's gills. He gripped Asrai's shoulder for support. Asrai felt Cormack's pain deep in her chest. She cast her eyes down and took a shuddering breath. His pain mixed with hers. While she had felt the king was a foolish human, she had known his kindness to be true. Her grip on her comb tightened.

"Uncle could not bear it when you disappeared," Peter whispered. "His heart simply broke."

Cormack's mind whirred. He found his tongue thick and his throat tight. Words escaped his grasp, and a numbness crept over him. Asrai took Cormack's hand in hers. "We are devastated by this news."

Peter snapped his head up. "Do not speak, vile sorceress! This is all your doing!"

Pamela jerked to attention. "Now see here! His majesty, Poseidon keep his soul, was an old man! We were all preparing for his great departure!"

"Do not speak out of turn!" Peter bellowed.

"Enough!" Cormack's voice was low, his eyes crackling with magick and fury.

Peter glared at the water mirror. "If you think to return and take the crown, you are mistaken." His voice was hard and poisonous. "I shall not allow your selfishness to harm the kingdom any further!"

Cormack felt his anger loosen. "I never wanted the crown to begin with. Asrai and I are happy in Sulu."

"Then for what purpose do you return? Other than to haunt me?" Peter fidgeted, the urge to pace overwhelming; a habit he had picked up since Cormack had disappeared.

"We bring you peace, Cousin." Cormack lifted his hand. "It would be my greatest joy for our kingdoms to be allies."

Peter scoffed. "And what could Sulu possibly offer us?"

"Safety." He ran his fins over Asrai's tail while keeping his gaze on Peter. "Sulu can keep squalls and storms out of the harbour, as well as sink any enemy ships that dare too close to our watery borders."

Reason began to take hold. Peter nodded. "That would be a welcome change. Paradine has been plagued by misfortune. It seems Poseidon punishes us with squalls for your misdeed."

Cormack recalled the change of tide during Draum and when Asrai had learned her true origins. He frowned. "So it seems."

"And what would Sulu expect in return?" Peter rubbed his hands, his old calculating icy grin slipping back into place.

"Apples!" Asrai's voice was firm.

Cormack flinched. He looked at Asrai. *I knew she liked apples, but in exchange for a thing so great?* "Paradine is a wealthy kingdom with many vassals." Cormack flicked his fins against her tail. "Apples are what you wish for most?"

She held her gaze firm. "The same apples that we supped upon together, Áinle."

Cormack looked back at Peter and nodded. "Apples. The Lady Asrai demands ruby apples."

Peter raised an eyebrow. "Safety in exchange for apples...well, we shall draw up the treaty." He smirked.

Asrai held her comb high, the glow pulsing with her excitement. "We shall meet you in at the sandy shores, far from the docks. And be sure to bring Pamela."

"Of course." Peter sighed, a touch of sarcasm creeping into his voice.

"We shall meet you in three days' time." Cormack hardened his gaze. "And speak not of Sulu as its true nature. No one must know."

Peter held up his hand. "I swear an oath that none shall know of the mers." While great fame would come with Paradine allying with such a fantastical kingdom, it would attract enemies to their already rich borders.

Asrai nodded, satisfied. She turned her gaze to Pamela and softened. "We miss you and your company. It will be a joy to embrace you on the shore."

Pamela nodded. "Aye. I hope to hear much about your beautiful kingdom."

"Yes, there will be much to tell." Cormack grinned. "Farewell."

Asrai swirled her comb, dissipating the water mirror.

Cormack rounded on Asrai. "Apples? Why apples?"

She blinked at him. "And what would you have proposed, my sailor?"

"Anything!" He waved his hands. "Paradine has weapons, jewels, gold, almost anything you can imagine!"

Asrai petted her swollen stomach. "There are more important things. Like securing food for our kingdom."

"You're going to feed our people apples?" Cormack raised an eyebrow.

She looked up at him again, a cross pout puckering her lips. "No. Poseidon killed the reef as punishment for Garradi's cowardice. It will take strong magick to restore it and invite the fish back."

Cormack cocked his head. "And apples will fix the reef?"

Asrai shook her head. "You humans are so disconnected. I felt my wellspring grow when I ate those apples you offered me. I have heard of such fruits and herbs that contain earthen magick. The apples must be one of those sources."

"The mers will become more powerful if they eat them?" Cormack ran his hand through his hair. "But I thought mers loved treasure. Why stop at apples?"

She flicked her eyes up at him. "I don't trust your cousin. If we asked for riches he will expect a great deal. Besides, if he does ask more of us we can up the price."

Cormack shivered at her smirk. He shrugged. "As you wish."

Chapter Thirty-Six

The council fidgeted as Asrai scanned the room. She twirled her comb. Her voice filled with confidence that escaped her heart. "We are presented with a boon this day. We shall write a treaty of trade, and strike an alliance with the homeland of my dear Áinle, the kingdom of Paradine."

The sea hag's eyes flashed, her face stony. Asrai flicked her gaze at the sea hag, then spoke to the room. "This alliance shall grant us access to a resource filled with unusual magick. It is my hope that this will be the key to restoring our great reef."

The council murmured to one another. Asrai tapped her comb in her palm. The sea hag sent Asrai another withering glare. Asrai straightened. The emerald coloured mer stood from their seat and approached Asrai. They clicked, then touched their fingers to their forehead. "We trust the wise and brilliant judgment of our beloved queen. However, we know little of the people of Paradine."

The maroon mer nodded. "With respect, your brilliance, we understand that the kin of Áinle are great warriors. However, it is worrisome that we are aligning with their kingdom with little knowledge of their customs."

Asrai pointed her comb at them. "You mistrust my Áinle and his people? You mistrust my judgement?" All eyes of the council widened, save for those of the sea hag. They were quick to shake their heads and protest.

The emerald mer spoke again. "The fear of the usurper is fresh in our minds. It is not easy for us to see calmer waters ahead when we have weathered such a storm."

Cormack shivered as a grin curled the sea hag's lips. She turned her gaze upon him. "Áinle can speak for his own people. He is best suited to put our minds at ease."

Asrai turned to Cormack. Her gaze was hard, the turmoil of emotions swirling in her heart spilled into his. She tilted her head. "Tell us of Paradine, my dear Áinle."

Cormack straightened and approached the council. Their faces turned to him. He fidgeted his hands. "I can assure you there is no plot against Sulu." He turned to Asrai. "I came here because of the love I bear for Asrai. She is everything to me," he turned back to the council, "so much so that I was willing to leave my claim as king behind."

Love of the Sea

Excited clicks and rumbles exploded from the council. Scales shimmered and a frenzy of hands gesticulated as Cormack felt the hot stab of Asrai's fear strike his heart. He knew better than to look back at her. The sea hag's mouth was a hard line, her eyes boring into him.

"Yes, it is true," he continued. "I chose to leave so I could be with my love. I have never held dreams of power. I have no desire for the heavy weight of a crown. I want only to live with Asrai, and here with all of you."

The maroon mer rose again. "This is most concerning!"

Cormack nodded and held out his hand. "I understand your fears all too well." The old guilt flared hot in his chest again. "I was afraid to leave Paradine; afraid to leave my people. They are strong and good-natured. Oft I would go out among them and share their stories, their burdens. But my father was a warlord, hungry for power, seeking to take. I wanted no part in this."

Fear flared in his chest again. He knew Asrai was fighting the tremble in her hands and her heart. He continued. "But I chose to leave Paradine in far more capable hands. Peter, my kin, is king now that my father has passed on. Poseidon keep him."

Whispers and fervent glances wove through the council. Cormack fought the tide of unease. "Peter is my kin. He is a great warrior, and a just ruler. His queen, Nephara, joined us from a far-off tribe, and she too seeks the good in Paradine." He measured his words with care, sure to use terms that hid the true nature of his home. The sea hag's glittering gaze was upon him, though not as fierce as before.

Asrai flicked her comb. "Áinle speaks the truth. I have met his kin. They are strong warriors, true to Poseidon's wave. They are also true of heart and of honest mind. They welcomed me with great feasting and revelry. We were bonded before the entire kingdom, and all rejoiced."

The emerald mer fidgeted. "My queen, these new developments are a shock to the council. Such events are unfamiliar and worrisome. You speak of the strength of Paradine. How are we to be assured they will not see Sulu as theirs for the taking?"

The council had calmed their whispers, but their glances and low clicks revealed their unease. Cormack spoke once more. "Paradine is a true ally. They protect their borders, and the borders of those they call friends. My people do not break oaths. They do not subvert their alliances."

The sea hag rose, causing a ripple of tension to cascade over Cormack and Asrai. She touched her fingers to her forehead, then to her lips. "I acted as the royal advisor in times past." She emitted a low click, which the council parroted. "Since then I have devoted myself to the safety of our queen, and the necessary training and planning for her glorious return."

Her eyes flashed as she glanced at Cormack. She flicked her tail, turning about to address the council. "Finding a suitable life mate was crucial to returning to Sulu. Our exile forced us to look to other tribes. Asrai went to Paradine, alone, to win the heart and hand of her Áinle. If Paradine were to hold such treacherous intent, they would have done so then, never allowing our brilliant queen to return home without ransom." Gentle clicks rose from the council. Some nodded to the sea hag.

Cormack felt a flare of fear strike in his chest. He darted his eyes and saw Asrai take a deep breath, her gaze firm. "This alliance is more than a benefit to Sulu. It is our destiny. The prophesy foretold of mers and humans once again becoming one people. This alliance will do exactly that."

Outrage burst from the council. Excited clicks and water pulses bounced through the room. The sea hag stared at Asrai in horror. Cormack could feel the warring emotions inside Asrai. He longed to shield her from their rage, but her stony demeanor kept him at bay.

"It was foretold that Fredsmegler, the Peacemaker, would shed his immortal human soul to live as a mer and unite our peoples." She swept her hand over Cormack. "The Peacemaker lives as our dear Áinle."

The council froze, staring at Cormack. The sea hag's jaw shook as she clenched her teeth. Fear ignited in his chest. *Asrai! You are sending me to my death! What madness is this?*

Asrai continued. "Paradine is a human kingdom, and our Áinle was a human prince. I used my wellspring to walk among these humans, and they accepted my love for Cormack. Through this powerful love I was able to perform what no mer has ever done – I ripped the soul from Áinle's breast, and implanted it into his cousin, the current ruler of Paradine. The prophesy shall be complete and Sulu will flourish!"

Cormack was spellbound as the council, one by one, bowed their heads and thrummed a low frequency. The sea hag raised her hands, adding her voice to the music. "The prophesy foretold of our dear Áinle! Through the alliance with Paradine Sulu's reefs shall live once more! The curse is broken!"

The mers straightened up, the silence returning. The sea hag spoke again. "I trust the judgement of our queen, and the intentions of Áinle. What say you?"

The maroon mer touched his fingers to his forehead, then his lips. "Poseidon has smiled upon Sulu and granted the return of our brilliant queen. To know Sulu will know the vibrance of the ancient wellspring once more through the vibrant reefs is a joy unimaginable! We put our trust in your hands." The maroon mer sat again. The mers murmured and nodded.

Love of the Sea

Asrai straightened and tapped her comb against her tail. "I am pleased we are swimming together with the tide. The summit will be held in two days' time. May Poseidon keep us."

Cormack let the water rush from his gills as the council departed. The sweet release of Asrai's anxiety rolled through him as well. The sea hag remained on her perch. "The prophesy may be true, but you must be cautious." Her voice was low. "I shall remain here as guide to the council in your stead."

Asrai slipped her comb back into her hair. "Thank you, Illyana, for all your guidance."

****

The sun was low as the sea hag led them to an outcropping of stones. Cormack stabbed at a crab that skittered across the rock shelf. Asrai scanned the area. There were no mers about. She furled and unfurled her fins. "We are indeed making an alliance with Paradine." She pulled her comb out of her hair and twirled it. "In exchange for protecting their water borders and their ships, they will give us an extraordinary commodity known as 'apples'."

The sea hag flexed her claws. "And why do we want these 'apples'? What value do they possess?"

Asrai stroked her comb. "I believe they are the cause behind the emeralds on our items. They possess deep Earth magick and are believed to house a variety of qualities. This earth magick is the key to uniting our people according to the prophesy."

"And what makes you so sure of this?" The sea hag speared an unfortunate crab in her claws.

Cormack slid his dagger from his plating. The emerald sparkled as he turned the hilt this way and that. He recalled the way Asrai's eyes had lit up when they ate apples together; how her scales had shimmered. *Could that be why she was so insistent on apples? Are they truly magick?*

"I ate several apples while in Paradine. They are a food, nourishing and sweet. They will help feed Sulu in this time of need." Asrai combed her fiery locks. "But, as I said, these apples also contain Earth magick that increased my wellspring by dramatic measure. I believe that we can harness this magick to regrow the great reef."

The sea hag took out her own comb and toyed with it. "If these apples are a magickal resource, why would the humans be willing to share them so easily?"

Cormack sheathed his dagger again. "Because they are unaware of the magick. They even feed their pets and beasts of burden apples as common feed."

The sea hag raised her eyebrows. "The apples do not affect the humans? I knew they were dull to magick, but—" She trailed off. Cormack slid his dagger in and out of his plating.

"There are those who are not so blind." Asrai flicked her comb. "Some have regained their connection and house powerful Earth magick."

"And how would you know of this?" The sea hag's eyes flashed. "We must be cautious."

Asrai nodded. "I encountered such creatures. Some knew me, some did not. A benevolent group call themselves 'The White Veil.' They came to me the night before we were bonded. They knew me, but did not seek to reveal me to the others. They blessed me."

The sea hag's eyebrows rose. "And what of them? Surely this 'White Veil' would protect such a resource?"

Cormack tamped down his questions. He had no idea the White Veil had visited the castle. He shuddered. "As I said, this resource is abundant. Apples are fed to animals as cheap feed. There are acres of land devoted solely to growing them."

The sea hag flexed her claws. "If you are sure. As I said, I trust your judgement, Asrai. We cannot afford for our people to be noticed by the humans."

"We have informed Peter to keep the party small and trustworthy. We are in safe hands."

Asrai frowned. She turned to Cormack. "I would like to amend the receiving party."

He tilted his head. "Who else would need to be present? Pamela will be there."

Asrai turned her gaze to the sea hag. "There is another human I put my trust in. One that saw my Truth and kept it to himself."

Cormack's eyes widened, as did the sea hag's. Asrai paid no heed and continued. "The keeper of the apples, the head gardener." She smiled. "He told me he oft sees things borne of magick, and that he saw the same in me. His heart is kind. He wishes only to tend to his plants and trees. We can trust him."

The sea hag wrinkled her nose. "And why would this 'keeper of apples' be so willing to part with his treasure?"

Asrai shook her head. "He is the one who first spoke of apples as being magick. He would be best suited to secure the shipment and ensure we are not cheated."

The sea hag twirled her comb. "An honest human. A rarity, indeed."

"This may be our one chance to save the reef." Asrai locked eyes with the sea hag. "Any other magickal resource would have to be taken by force. Then we are no better than the usurper; a parasite."

The sea hag nodded, her reluctance burning bright in her gaze. "It seems so. Your success is everything. Should this fail, the council may lose trust, and that I cannot fix."

Asrai touched her fingers to her lips, then held out her hand to the sea hag, which she took. "I trust you Illyana. May Poseidon keep you and Sulu in my absence."

They embraced. The sea hag softened, a low thrum emitting from her. "May Poseidon keep you, my precious child."

****

The guards bristled as the current became choppy. Cormack felt the familiarity wash over him. He shivered at the memory of their wedding night on the beach. His bones ached as his mind replayed the painful transformation. He balled his hand into a fist, his other hand tight on his dagger. They fought the tide as they neared the shore. The waves pushed them back. Asrai began to fatigue. Cormack felt something sapping his energy. He turned and saw Asrai's eyes bright with magick. Suddenly, the tide shifted; a great wave thrust them forward. The sandy beach scraped Cormack's scales. Cormack straightened, his tail curled under to prop up his body. Asrai and the guards did the same. The warm air hit their skin, and the sound of the surf beat their ears.

A red and gold pavilion had been erected a few yards from the water. Cormack could see the glint of the guards' halberds. Peter rose from his lawn chair and offered his hand to Nephara. Two valets trotted ahead of them, carrying a small wooden platform. They placed it on the sand at the water's edge. Peter led Nephara to the broad, flat platform. Their shoes clicked on the wood.

One of the guards followed them. He stood on the sand next to the platform and lifted his halberd. "Presenting his majesty, King Peter of Paradine! And his consort, Queen Nephara!"

Asrai held her gaze steady. She held back her smile as Peter and Nephara flinched at the sound of the conch. One of the mer guards beat his chest plating. "Presenting our majestic queen, Asrai, descendant of Poseidon! And her life mate, Áinle Cormack!"

Peter nodded. "Right then. Here you are, truly alive and *real.*"

Cormack tilted his head. "And here you are, a king."

Peter turned and waved his hand. The minister stepped forward, bearing a lap writer and his rucksack.

"We discussed a treaty, dear Cousin." Peter flicked his hand. The minister pulled a large scroll bearing red-and-gold ribbon from the rucksack. "I had the formalities written in advance. Please read them over."

The minister stepped into the water and held the scroll out for the mers to read. Cormack struggled with the technical writing. He had slacked off during his lessons on diplomacy, and cursed himself for his slothful will.

Asrai nodded. "We understand and agree."

Peter clasped his hands as the minister returned to the sand. "Wonderful! Are there any changes required, or can we move forward?"

"We cannot move forward until Pamela is present." Asrai raised her chin a fraction, her gaze hard.

"Of course." Peter fought the urge to roll his eyes. He waved his hand to one of the guards.

The guard trotted off, then reappeared with Pamela astride Nonna. The old nag found her way over the sands with ease. The guard led, holding the bridle, Pamela's hands buried in the horse's mane. Cormack and Asrai's eyes brightened upon seeing their beloved friend. Peter sighed and waited as the guard helped Pamela dismount.

"Your majesty." Pamela bowed to Peter. Her voice and body shook with restrained joy.

"Good." Asrai nodded to Pamela. Her eyes flashed. "She shall bear witness to the signing. But first, we would like to amend the treaty."

Peter started. His gaze darkened. "Yes?"

Asrai waved her hand. "We would like the head gardener to be present upon the delivery of our goods."

"Yes, of course." Peter let his breath escape in a controlled rush. He motioned to one of the guards.

The guard took off, up onto the grassy area toward the pavilion. A waiting squire alighted one of the horses and rode back to the castle. Cormack kept his gaze fixed on Peter, but confusion writhed in his chest. The minister added the amendment. He held it up to both parties once more for their approval. He presented the quill to Peter and held the scroll over the lap writer. Peter signed, then passed it to Nephara. She flicked the quill across the page. Her eyes glittering as she handed the treaty back to the minister.

Asrai clenched her jaw as the minister waded into the surf. He held the lap writer high so Asrai could sign without the parchment becoming wet. She drew her name with all the royal runes. Nephara glared at Asrai as Asrai handed the quill to Cormack. He signed on the space indicated by the minister's careful script. He signed with his new title as Áinle, which he found he rather liked. The minister returned to shore and sprinkled sand on the ink to help it dry. He rolled it and tied the scroll with the affixed ribbons, then handed it to Peter.

"We welcome you once more, Cousin." Peter spread his arms. "Paradine embraces Sulu!" Peter and Nephara began to clap, and the guards joined in. Cormack gave a hearty cheer as Asrai led the mers in human applause.

Asrai pulled her comb from her hair. "We of Sulu are delighted to at last be kin with Paradine, the land of our beloved Áinle, my life mate, Cormack." She held her comb high. It glinted in the bright sunshine. "We grant this reef our protection and our love!"

Her comb glowed brighter. The waves became choppy. Cormack and the guards steeled themselves as the tide sucked out further. A great wave built near the edge of the harbour. It raced toward shore. Peter's face blanched as he beheld the tower of water speeding toward them. Nephara's eyes grew wide. Pamela began crossing herself, her face gaunt. Before they could scream, Asrai flicked her comb. The wave crashed down upon itself in the center of the harbour. The tide returned, the water calm once more.

Asrai lowered her arm and nodded. Her gaze locked on Peter. "You may rest assured that the watery borders of your kingdom shall be safe."

"That was truly incredible, your highness." Peter bowed his head. "Here is your bounty, as promised."

One of the guards rushed down the shoreline toward a boat that was anchored near the shallows. He thrust his halberd in the air three times. A sailor aboard waved a blue flag. The guard returned to Peter's side and bowed. "The head gardener is aboard the boat. They await your orders, majesties."

"Very good." Peter tilted his hand toward the boat. "The crew is ready to follow you and drop the crates wherever you like. We had them weighted so they would not float."

Asrai bowed her head. "We thank you. My people shall feast and savour this delicacy of Paradine."

Nephara took a step. She flicked her eyes at Peter, then at the mers. "Now that the formalities are out of the way, Paradine would like to present Sulu with a picnic. We would like to celebrate our new bond as allies."

"Our journey was long, and we are in need of refreshment." Asrai smiled for the first time at Peter. "We would be delighted."

Peter snapped his fingers, and there was a flurry of activity. The guards summoned the servants that had been waiting behind the grassy hills. Low chairs were brought to the water's edge, along with more wooden platforms. The serving girls swarmed, bearing goblets and pitchers. Kitchen servers brought large baskets of foodstuffs and plates.

As the confusion unfolded, Asrai softened. She smiled at Pamela. "My dear friend, it is wonderful to see you!" She held her hand out.

Pamela choked back a sob, then splashed into the water. "My dears! It is a blessing!"

She flung her arms around Asrai first. Her soft body engulfed the mer. Asrai embraced her back, careful of her armoured plating. When they drew away, Pamela traced her hand down Asrai's cheek. "You are even more beautiful as yourself."

Cormack embraced Pamela, his scales and plating catching on the fabric of her homespun dress. He squeezed her hands when he pulled away. "Pamela, I have wonderful news. I am to be a father!"

She gasped, snapping her shocked gaze on the swell of Asrai's stomach. "You are with child! Poseidon keep you! A child!"

Asrai beamed. Nephara laid a hand on her own belly, which was just beginning to poke out beneath her breasts. Cormack grinned as Pamela continued to fawn over Asrai. He turned his gaze to Peter. Nephara flicked her eyes at her husband, and he placed his arm about her shoulders.

"It seems we have much to celebrate." Cormack nodded to Peter.

"Indeed, Cousin." Peter let his own grin take over. "Uncle would have been proud."

Pamela swallowed Cormack into a tight embrace. "Poseidon bless his soul, yes! His majesty would have been a proud Poppa this day!"

Cormack laughed and hugged Pamela back. "It is good to see you. Thank you for being here."

She drew away and swatted at him. "You think these silly guards could keep me away? Huh! I would be here, summoned or not!"

A feast was spread with cold cuts of boar, whole roasted squab, soft ewes' milk cheese, dark coarse bread, honeyed figs, and oat cakes. Everyone settled. Pamela sat on the sands a pace away from Peter and Nephara. Only the guards remained standing, keeping their post.

Cormack turned his gaze to the castle. It gleamed in the afternoon light. A seagull cried overhead. He took a deep breath, drawing the salty air deep into his lungs. He turned and met eyes with Peter. There were lines on his cousin's face now, but he wore them well. Peter looked at Nephara. His hand petted her belly, his eyes warm. Cormack saw a familiar light in Peter's eyes; kindness and gentle patience. Peter ran his hand through his hair and grinned, his smile easy. That was when Cormack knew he would never have to worry about Peter again.

The End

Author Note

"Start at the beginning, and when you come to the end, stop."
–Mad Hatter from Alice's Adventures in Wonderland

Life is short, and few are remembered. It has always been a challenge that my talents and aspirations are not seen as viable by the greater society. This imbalance motivates me to continue creating, and to prove that my work matters. In that quest, I have become "Alice" - more than just a little girl stuck in Wonderland, but a state of being in a constant search for the extraordinary.

In this search, I have fragmented myself and have several white rabbits to chase. My writing is the strongest thrill, due to the massive page count for novels I can create at the sacrifice of sanity and sleep. Or how jolted I feel when I write my poems. My pen flies over the page *needing* the words, almost shouting them as I write. And when the poem is completed I read it over and over, full of joy at the sound the words make, the taste of the colors and the scent of each sound. Due to my synesthesia, but I find myself almost tempted at times to lick a good poem.

But at the same time this rabbit drives me to madness with the high expectations I have made for myself. I have been writing on a professional level since I was about twelve years old. Since then I graduated from Columbia College of Chicago with a degree in Fiction Writing.

During my college days, I began working as a freelance model. After graduation, this became my full-time profession. I toured nationally, met scores of creative people like myself, and had many adventures. Experiencing different perspectives helped my creative spirit evolve, and therefore, my writing. After retiring from modeling, I went through a time of great emptiness, as I was going through a divorce, and felt devoid of my creative spirit.

From that void, I found a new community of love and support, and began exploring my writing and my art again. Since then, I have become a regular in the local Chicago writing communities and have become more powerful than ever with my craft. I have learned many great lessons about working as a writer, and getting my stories out to the public.

Love of the Sea

My life has always been full of challenges, restrictions, and people telling me "no." But ultimately, I keep pushing forward, and sometimes I persevere. Life is short, and I want to be sure that life is worth living. I want to be remembered for all that I accomplished, and leave this world with no regrets.

www.ingramcontent.com/pod-product-compliance
Lightning Source LLC
Chambersburg PA
CBHW020823260626
47169CB00003B/806